Crucible of Fate

Crucible of Fate

Andy Johnson

Crucible of Fate

Spiderwize
3rd Floor
207 Regent Street
London
W1B 3HH

www.spiderwize.com

ISBN: 978-1-908128-41-6

This book is dedicated to all those who took part in Eisenhower's 'Great Crusade'.

It is also for Derek Johnson, Harry Oldfield, Dave Common and Ken Mower; for showing me the way.

And of course, for Mum; my biggest fan.

Contents

Acknowledgements

The author would like to thank Dave Hebden, Tim Shellcock, Andrew Dixon, Darren Pyper, Dale Heaton, Adam Heaton, Dave Wilson, Andy Etherington, Mick Lycett and Gary Hancock, all from the 2nd Battalion East Yorkshire Regiment Re-enactment Group for their assistance with research and in producing the cover photographs.

My thanks also go to James and Rachel Holmes for 'lending' me a piece of Normandy for a day. I would also like to thank Mr Roy Robotham, who landed on Gold Beach on D-Day, for sharing his memories with me.

The cover photographs are Copyright Andy Johnson/Shaun Johnson/2nd Battalion East Yorkshire Regiment Re-enactment Group.

All maps are the author's own.

Foreword

I f you were born in the last fifteen to twenty years or so, you could be forgiven for thinking that the D-Day landings consisted simply of the British glider-borne assault on the Orne River/Caen Canal Bridges, the US Airborne drops, and the US assault landings against Omaha Beach. This of course reflects the surge in books, films and TV series that have appeared since the late 1990s that have, on the whole, tended to focus on these particular aspects of the D-Day operation.

The vast majority of these various works have been extensively researched and in the case of the film and TV shows, expertly produced, and are a welcome addition to the historical record. The downside however, is that if you are nowhere near old enough to remember the classic war film *The Longest Day,* or don't really go in for reference books, then you might easily miss the fact that the D-Day operation was unimaginably vast in both scale and scope; so vast in fact that nothing of comparable size and intricacy was ever attempted prior to it, or has been attempted since.

There are so many tales that could be told about this, the most famous day in military history, and there is an endless supply of books on the subject for any interested party. In writing this, the third of my novels set in the Second World War, I have steered away from trying to tell the whole story. Instead, I have taken just one small part of the great event and tried to do it justice. Even so, there is a part of me that feels the book could have been twice the size, even without broadening its scope. Such is the scale of the task when writing a novel about D-Day.

I have, as with *Seelowe Nord* and *Thunder in May,* mixed historical 'fact' with a fair amount of fiction and dramatisation, and that has included 'playing' with certain timings. The majority of units and battles described within this novel were real enough, as were some of the more prominent, senior ranking characters. A handful of units and several of the battles, along with some of the words that I have placed in the mouths of famous figures, are figments of my imagination. The ferocity, horror and stress of battle are not however. If anything, I have understated these things. When you read the accounts of those who fought in that momentous battle, it is quite clear that some of the things they witnessed are quite simply indescribable.

Once again, I emphasise that this book is not an historical work. It is, like my others, an adventure story of men at war, set against a well known historical backdrop. Once upon a time however, real men did the deeds about which I have written. None of them had any choice about their involvement. Fate put them at that particular time and place. That they accepted their fate and did their duty is immensely humbling to those of us who still enjoy freedom and democracy, and when you walk the beaches and battlefields of Normandy, you cannot fail to appreciate the extraordinary events that played out there, one damp June day in 1944.

Lest we forget...

Andy Johnson
March 2012

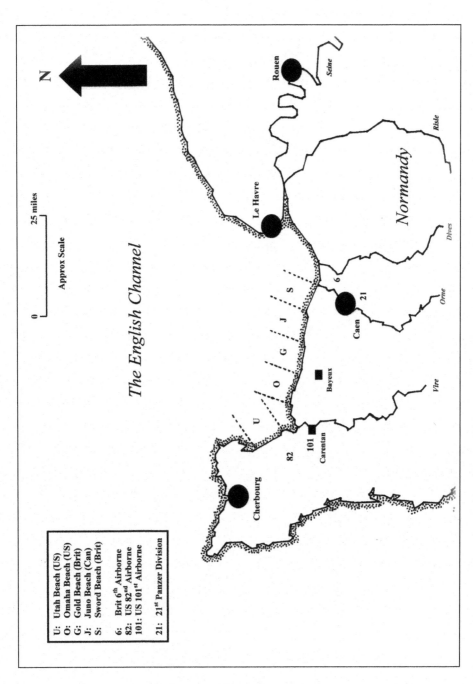

Primary Battle-space

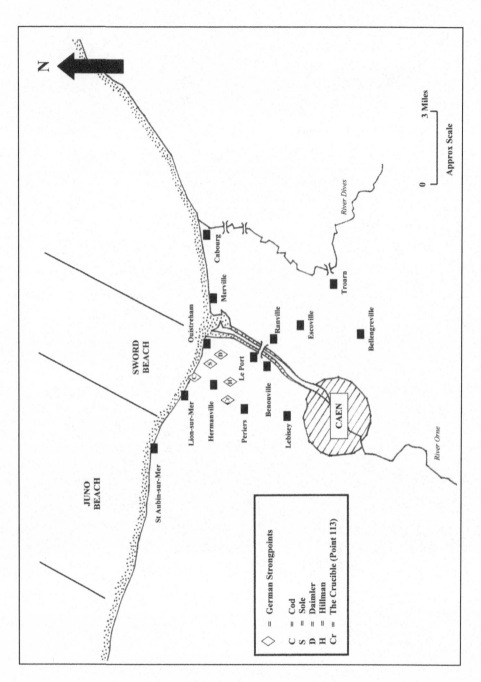

Sword Beach and Environs

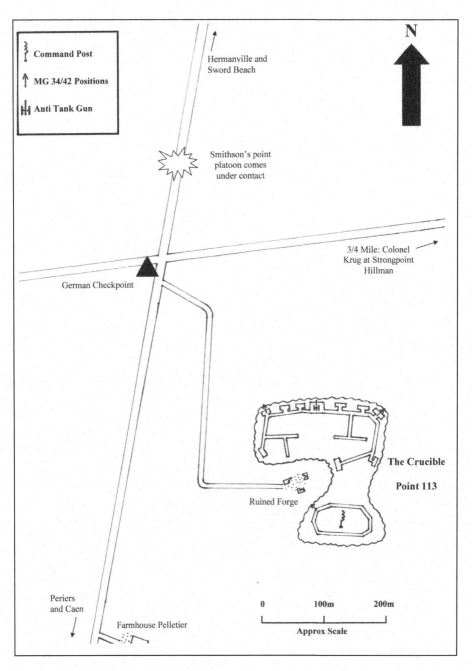

The Crucible – Point 113

PART ONE
ANTICIPATION

D – 1
MONDAY 5TH JUNE

POINT 113 – NEAR CAEN IN NORMANDY, FRANCE
MONDAY 5TH JUNE 1944 – 0230 HOURS

The pounding was rhythmic, mesmerising, and terrible. Not for the first time of late, Sergeant Major Roland Gritz, the commander of what was generally referred to as a 'Strongpoint Company', gazed towards the distant red glow somewhere in the direction of Le Havre, and thanked his lucky stars that he had been sent here to this nondescript wood to take charge of the tiny, disparate force of waifs and strays who were known throughout the regiment as 'The Cripples'.

This position was the latest of many to be established along the coastline of France, in an attempt to give depth to Hitler's much-vaunted 'Atlantic Wall'. Unlike most of the other defensive positions however, this particular site was something of an after-thought. Its existence had resulted from a tour of the divisional area by General Marcks, the commander of 84th Army Corps, and the man responsible for the defence of Normandy.

During that tour, which had taken the Corps and Divisional Commanders from one concrete fortress to another, the eagle-eyed General Marcks had spotted the small wooded knoll that over-looked a minor crossroads, just north of the ancient city of Caen. Within minutes, it had been established that the modest topographical feature also happened to be situated in a blind spot between two of the larger strong-points that had been developed around heavy artillery batteries. Marcks had issued an immediate order. The gap was to be plugged; the wood occupied and the area mapped out for defence in order to cover the flanks of the bigger positions, whilst also blocking one of the smaller back roads into Caen.

Carrying out the order had been easier said than done for the division's staff. Already stretched thinly, with every man working at full tilt on the endless lines of fortifications and obstacles along the beaches, the division was struggling to find the resources needed to fulfil the Corps Commander's wishes. But then, arriving on a troop train from a brief spell of sick leave in Germany, Roland Gritz, hero of the Eastern Front and winner of the Knight's Cross, had appeared within the division's ranks and solved the problem.

Like many men in the 716th Coastal Defence Division, Gritz had been posted into this particular formation due to a physical inability to partake in high tempo operations on the Eastern Front; in his case due to a torn cruciate ligament in his left leg that often caused his upper and lower legs to pop out of joint at the knee. That injury had been caused during a vicious and bloody hand to hand struggle in a trench-line somewhere in the endless wastes of Russia. Although his hard pressed force had eventually defeated the huge Russian attack, with Gritz signalled out as being worthy of the Third Reich's highest honour, the senior non commissioned officer had been left with a bad limp and a frustrating inability to march for long distances, or for any distance at all across rough terrain. Thus, he had been packed off, complete with leather knee brace, to help boost the garrisons of the Atlantic coast.

And that made Gritz, to some extent, the answer to the Divisional Commander's prayers. Within a day of his arrival, Gritz had been whisked in front of a dozen senior officers, one after the other, before being put in front of the Divisional Commander himself. Fifteen minutes after his first meeting with the general, Gritz was on his way again, escorted by a staff captain from the headquarters, with firm instructions to cobble together a 'company-sized force' and establish an 'impregnable' defensive position on Point 113, north of Caen. Point 113...Not an auspicious name.

Now however, Gritz was beginning to think that he had dropped lucky. For two weeks since his arrival in Normandy, he had watched the nightly bombing raids that had taken place with monotonous and terrifying regularity across this part of France. The bigger, more obviously sited gun batteries that were dotted along the coastline had all been targets, as had the railways and bridges, and anything else of obvious military utility. But here on Point 113, where Gritz and his hastily assembled force of sick, lame, lazy and conscripted had gone about the task of fortifying their small hill, all had remained quiet. No bombs, and none of the terrible low level strafing or rocket attacks from the enemy 'Jabos'; the deadly little fighter-bombers.

You could call it luck, but Gritz preferred to make his own luck. He knew how omnipotent the Allied air forces had become. Out east, the Luftwaffe still had some degree of control over the skies, but here in Western Europe it was a different matter. Germany itself was being pounded constantly. American bombers came by day, and then the Tommies came again in the night, dropping ton upon ton of deadly high explosive and incendiaries. Passing through the bigger towns and cities of Germany, Gritz had seen for himself the scale of the destruction. Once thriving towns had become derelict, haunted ruins; devoid of life and function. Factories were laid low, railways and stations torn up and made unusable.

And even when you got away from the bombing raids in Germany, still there was no escape from Allied air power. Twice, en route to Normandy, Gritz had been forced to evacuate his troop train as it was pounced on by Jabos. He had never felt so helpless in his life, and only now was he beginning to understand what the Tommies and the French must have endured back in those heady, victory filled days of 1940, when the Luftwaffe reigned supreme and nothing could stand in the way of the German Army.

The days of not worrying about what was above your head had long gone. Aircraft had changed the dynamic of war forever; and over France these days, the only aircraft to be seen were of the enemy variety. To that end, Gritz's first instructions to his rough and ready force had been a set of stringent rules on camouflage and concealment from aircraft, or from civilian observers on the ground who could well be feeding information to the resistance movement. As he gazed now on the distant vision of hell to the north-east, he reminded himself once more on how vital those rules were. If their position was given away, then it would only be a matter of time before the Tommy air force came calling. And then... Well, then it would be a bloody day.

"Poor bastards."

The comment from someone nearby shook Gritz from his reverie. He glanced to his left and stared at the dark outline of Sergeant Gunther, one of his two platoon commanders.

"Glad it's not us on the receiving end of that lot." Gunther elaborated grumpily as he stared towards the distant flash of explosions in the far distance.

Gritz rumbled his approval.

"Me too, Gunther." He agreed. "But it *could* be us; quite easily. It only takes one man in the company to compromise this position; get seen by a local civilian or spotted by one of the enemy recce planes... Then it'll be our turn."

He saw the pale blob of the sergeant's face turn towards him, and Gritz stared back at the veteran through the gloom.

"So get yourself around the position, Gunther, and make sure that none of our steely eyed warriors are having a crafty cigarette or cooking outside their shelters. Strict noise and light discipline needs to be enforced at all times, otherwise we'll pay for it with our lives."

Gunther gave a small grunt of laughter at Gritz's facetious description of their little company, yet even so, acknowledged the seriousness of the situation.

"I will that, Sergeant Major; don't you worry. I'll cut the balls off any little scrote I catch breaking the rules, and then send them home to his mother so she can use them as a pair of ear-rings."

And with that, the sergeant shuffled off along the trench-line to begin his rounds of the positions at the forward edge of the wood. Having watched the man's dark figure disappear into the gloom, Gritz walked slowly back towards his command post. It was a grand term that, 'command post'. His headquarters was, in effect, a biggish dugout with a couple of sleeping bays and enough room for the duty telephone orderly to man the two land-lines that had been laid from Point 113 to neighbouring positions; one being the Regimental Headquarters along the ridge, a kilometre or so to the east, and the other to the small check-point at the crossroads that had been established as a 'cover' for the real position up here in the wood.

Even those telephone lines had been subject to Gritz's obsessive rules about keeping the position secret. Both lines had been laid at night, dug into the earth beneath the natural linear features created by the thick Normandy hedgerows. The line to Regimental Headquarters, or Resistance Nest 17 as it was also known, had even been diverted about a hundred metres so that it could pass through a culvert under the road, rather than lie exposed on the cobbles where even a blind man could spot it.

Arriving at the entrance to his command post, Gritz leaned in close to the double thickness ground-sheet that served as a door and blackout curtain.

"Kole? It's me; Gritz. I'm coming in; cover the light."

A moment later, a quiet voice came from within.

"Okay, Sergeant Major; you can come in."

Gritz pulled back the weighted curtain and ducked inside the dug-out, then turned and quickly pulled the ground-sheets back into place; his fingers deftly checking around the doorway to ensure he had achieved a lightproof seal.

"Okay, Kole; she's fastened up again." He said once he was sure the curtain was properly closed.

Instantly, a feint yet comforting glow filled the dug-out, illuminating the subterranean command post. Gritz blinked a couple of times as his eyes adjusted, and he immediately noted Corporal Kole sitting on the ammunition crate in the corner, right next to the field telephone and the small, flickering candle.

"All well?" Gritz asked the corporal.

Kole, a veteran of the Eastern Front like Gritz, nodded back at his commander.

"Quiet as a mouse, Sergeant Major; on the telephone at least."

Gritz instinctively flung his gaze towards the cot-bed at the very back of the dug out, where the second of his two telephone orderlies lay curled up under a blanket.

"Has Kellerman been shouting about the Ruski's again?" Gritz asked.

Kole nodded sadly.

"It was quite a bad one, tonight. I had to cover his mouth and then wake him up. Poor bastard's not far from losing his wits completely."

Gritz mused on the comment as he shuffled across to his own bed and began removing his helmet and equipment.

"Yes… well, I suppose we're all getting close to that, aren't we? Can't say my memories of Russia are particularly pleasant either."

Kellerman was a private soldier who had been undergoing punishment in the Divisional Detention Centre for several minor infringements of military discipline when Gritz had sprung him to help boost up his fledgling force's numbers. Within less than forty eight hours, Gritz had realised why the young soldier had fallen foul of the Army's rules. The man was completely shell-shocked; battle-happy. Some would say deranged; others would call him a coward.

The man would suffer panic attacks for no apparent reason, or else appear lost in thought for long periods. And of course, at night he would call out in terror during his sleep as he relived horrors from the Russian campaign. Gritz clamped his teeth together as he considered the poor soldier's state of mind. He understood what it was like. Gritz might be a holder of the Knight's Cross, and still a determined enough fighter, but he too had his own demons to wrestle with from time to time. Kellerman was no coward. He'd just had too much of Russia; just as Gritz had.

"Huh, Russia!" Kole grunted from across the dug-out. "Fucking shit country that is. God knows why the Fuhrer wants the place."

Gritz smiled. Of all people, Kole had good reason to hate Russia. He had lost no less than four toes, a finger and part of an ear to frostbite in that terrible frozen wasteland. Having said that, Kole had been lucky in a way, because his unit had been part of the ill-fated Sixth Army; the one that had been cut off, starved, and then captured at Stalingrad. At least Kole was better off here than in some Russian prisoner of war camp.

"Speaking of which, how's the weather outside, Sir?"

Gritz considered the query for a moment.

"Pretty shit actually." He replied. "Very windy, and the rain's started up again. I reckon we're in for a storm. Hard to believe it's the middle of summer. Still, it's not keeping the Tommies away. They're pounding the shit out of Le Havre by the looks of it."

Kole shook his head slowly.

"How do they know where they're dropping their bombs? Wouldn't have thought they could see a thing with all the cloud and rain and what have you?"

Gritz let out a sigh as he dropped his trousers and released the straps of his knee-brace.

"It's called science, Kole. There's nothing like a good war to get the scientists scratching their heads and coming up with all kinds of new gadgets. Look at the panzer; the Tommies invented the thing in the last war to try and break the stalemate. Look how it's changed the way we kill each other. The same goes for aircraft. I don't think the weather will help us much anymore."

Once more, the dour Kole grunted his comment on the situation.

"Mother nature is a fucking bitch." He cursed without any real vehemence.

"She is indeed." Gritz allowed as he swung himself onto his own cot, massaging the wasted muscles around his kneecap as he did so. "But we're under cover, so I don't really care. I just need some sleep."

He adjusted his position and pulled his greatcoat across his torso until it was tucked under his chin, then glanced over at the corporal by the telephone.

"Kole, if I start shouting out in my sleep, wake me up too…"

THE CONFERENCE ROOM, SOUTHWICK HOUSE, NEAR PORTSMOUTH
MONDAY 5TH JUNE 1944 – 0425 HOURS

The conference had been going for ten minutes and, already, the only point on the agenda had been heard. There hadn't been much need for preamble. After all, this collection of senior officers and lower ranking subject matter experts had been meeting like this, twice a day, for nearly a week now, all to discuss one thing; the weather. At the back of the room, sitting just behind General Bernard Law Montgomery, Major Jamie Haldane gazed around the room at the serious, anxious looking faces. Not that *everyone* looked anxious of course. Ramsay, the Royal Navy Admiral in charge of the seaborne forces appeared his usual calm self, and despite the early hour, Montgomery,

Haldane's own boss, was bright eyed, alert and full of his usual brash confidence.

The air force men looked much more pensive however, and the American, Eisenhower, overall commander of the imminent operation, looked strained. Hardly surprising given the enormity of the burden he was shouldering. At the far end of the big conference table, standing by their maps and charts, were the weathermen. A small army of them it seemed, commanded by Group Captain Stagg of the RAF, who now stood like a dour vicar officiating at a funeral. Stagg had just finished speaking. He had given his frank assessment of the weather, in that understandable yet infuriatingly impartial manner peculiar to meteorologists.

The weather had frustrated this immense operation once already. Hundreds of thousands of men, ships, planes and vehicles sat ready; yet as ever, Mother Nature was playing God with them all. But now there was a glimmer of hope; a small one mind you, but a glimmer all the same. A 'slightly calmer period' was how it had been described. For twenty four hours, or maybe thirty six; from about midnight today and running right through tomorrow… the Sixth of June.

Eisenhower was turning that information over in his mind. His clear, bright eyes darted around the room, from one face to another, trying to judge what his senior commanders were thinking whilst struggling to reach a conclusion in his own mind. Haldane could only imagine the terrible weight of responsibility now weighing upon the personable American general. After a few moments of silence that seemed to stretch into hours, Eisenhower stopped stroking the side of his chin and glanced towards the Commander of 21st Army Group.

"Monty? What do you think?"

Montgomery's reply was instant, categorical, and succinct.

"I say *go*."

The sharp reply rang through the otherwise silent conference room like the peel of a bell, and Haldane noted with grim amusement how some of the other junior staff officers around the room jumped at the sound of Montgomery's voice. Eisenhower looked directly at Montgomery for a couple of moments, holding the smaller man's gaze and perhaps judging the commitment behind that bold statement. Montgomery gazed back at him calmly, his pinched, wily features set with purpose and determination.

Apparently happy that Montgomery had spoken his true mind, Eisenhower flicked his gaze along the table, this time settling his eyes on Ramsay.

"Bertie?"

Ramsay nodded slowly as he gathered his thoughts.

"The conditions aren't perfect… But there again, they rarely are in the English Channel. There might be a few issues we have to work around but on the whole I'm pretty confident we can deliver the invasion force onto the French coast. We can accept these conditions and I don't think we'll get a better chance than this, so… I say we may as well get on with it and go."

Haldane thought he saw a small flicker of a smile play at the corner of Eisenhower's mouth. The American general simply nodded his acknowledgement to the British admiral and switched his gaze to Air Chief Marshal Leigh-Mallory, commanding the Allied air forces allocated to the operation.

"Trafford? What do you think?"

Leigh-Mallory took a deep breath and played with the pencil between his fingers as he glanced up at the weather charts, before sweeping the whole room with his eyes in a quick, fluid movement. He looked at Eisenhower momentarily, then down at his notes, then back up at the American.

"There *will be* some difficulties. We must understand that. The cloud may affect the accuracy of our bombing. And that same cloud, along with the winds, could result in quite a few of our paratroopers missing their drop-zones and spread them over a wide area. But I suppose we're going to have to take risks, no matter what. So yes… I think we can probably do it."

Eisenhower nodded thoughtfully before glancing toward Arthur Tedder, another RAF Air Chief Marshal, who had been appointed as the American's deputy. Tedder gave the slightest, barely perceptible nod of his head. That was all Eisenhower needed. He allowed the sad smile that had been hovering at the corners of his mouth to spread across his face suddenly and gave a huge sigh as he released the tension from his body. He looked down the length of the conference room, his eyes sparkling.

"Okay." He said. "Well… let's go."

THE BRIEFING ROOM, RAF DOWNHAM MARKET, NORFOLK
MONDAY 5TH JUNE 1944 – 0730 HOURS

"Excuse me, Flight Lieutenant? Flight Lieutenant Hargreaves, Sir? Excuse me?"

Raymond Hargreaves, a pilot in 635 Squadron, one of the elite Pathfinder units from the Royal Air Force's No.8 Group, stopped dead in his tracks at the doorway to the briefing room as he heard the female voice calling after him. Turning back to face down the corridor, he stepped out of the way of several other aircrew and spotted a somewhat agitated young WAAF hurrying towards him. He recognised the woman instantly. It was Corporal Wilkinson, the girl who worked in the Sergeants' Mess kitchen.

As pre-occupied as he was, Hargreaves held on for the WAAF to catch him up and spread his most charming smile across his features for her. She might have the strongest Geordie accent he had ever heard, but by God the girl was pretty.

"Corporal Wilkinson, good morning. Yes? What can I do for you?"

"I'm sorry to bother you, Sir? But I was just wondering, is Flight Sergeant McWilliams on ops today? Because he came through for bacon and eggs this morning, Sir, and he came through yesterday too; only I know you don't normally go out two nights on the trot…"

She left the accusation hanging in the air for a moment as Hargreaves tried to stifle a bark of laughter.

"And we can't just keep giving 'em out to everyone, Sir. Bacon and eggs are only for those on ops. The Master Cook will go mad if he finds out, Sir."

With an effort, Hargreaves managed to keep his face relatively straight.

"Absolutely… Well, I think Flight Sergeant McWilliams might have been a bit confused about what he was doing yesterday, although he *is* definitely flying today. We're just going in for briefing now. I'll have a word with him."

The petit young WAAF gave Hargreaves a pleading look.

"Would you, Sir? Only it's not the first time…"

"I'll get it sorted, Corporal Wilkinson, don't you worry." Hargreaves promised. "And what's more, I'll get him to take you out for lunch when we get back in order to make it up to you."

Suddenly, a look of shock took hold of the woman's features.

"Flight Sergeant McWilliams? Take me out for lunch? With respect, Sir, I'd rather do a week in the pan-wash."

And with that waspish comment, Wilkinson turned on her heel and stamped off back towards the Sergeants' Mess.

Chuckling away to himself, Hargreaves joined the press of men flooding into the briefing room. As he entered the huge hall, he searched for the row of chairs where his own crew would be seated together, as was customary. He spied them immediately and made his way across. They were all there, ready to go; Murphy the navigator already noting down information from the large display board that sat to one side of the main map. As Hargreaves took his seat beside him, he threw a smile at the rest of the crew.

"Morning chaps." He said cheerfully, noting as he did so that McWilliams, his rear gunner, was already wearing his Taylor-Suit, the padded overalls that they would usually wear for ops.

"What's the matter, Mac? Worried you might miss take off?"

McWilliams, looking tired, gave him a sullen look, but it was Flight Sergeant Murphy who piped up.

"The ruddy minger slept in the bloody thing last night! He'll be breeding maggots before long!"

"Ha, bloody, Ha, Murphy." McWilliams retorted in his harsh cockney accent. "It's bloody freezing in that hut they've got us in. And I can't afford to catch my death of cold; not when I've got you lot to look after. Lynch-pin of the whole crew I am."

Murphy almost choked with laughter.

"I'm telling you." McWilliams continued. "It's a skilled job being rear-gunner. I've kept you lot alive so far haven't I?"

Murphy placed his pencil down and waggled the digits of both hands at his fellow Flight Sergeant.

"The only thing rear-gunners need is big thumbs…"

McWilliams looked set to respond, but Hargreaves interrupted the exchange.

"Never mind that now, *children*; Mac, you've got something more important to worry about."

The gunner regarded his pilot with suspicion.

"You've upset Corporal Wilkinson from the Sergeants' Mess Kitchen."

"Me? How?" Spluttered McWilliams.

"Because you've been going through for bacon and eggs when you're not on ops, haven't you, you naughty rear gunner you? She's very cross with you."

The guilty look on the gunner's face said it all.

"When you've got a responsible job like me you need to keep your strength up." He moaned.

Hargreaves gave the flight sergeant a disapproving stare.

"Really? Well, as soon as you get back from this op you can go and apologise to the girl and take her out for some lunch as compensation."

McWilliams suddenly jerked upright, a look of alarm on his face.

"What? You're not serious, Skipper? Me? Take her out? She's a bloody Geordie! How am I supposed to understand a word she's saying with an accent like that!"

Hargreaves made a pretence of being stern.

"I don't care, Mac, but take her out you will, or else buy her a ruddy great bunch of flowers; *and* you can stop taking extra portions of bacon and eggs to boot."

The sound of a loud, business like voice calling the room to order interrupted the discussion.

"Alright gentlemen, settle down… quiet please. Let's get on with business, shall we?"

The squadron operations officer was standing on the stage at the front of the room, a snooker cue held in one hand, ready for use as a pointer.

"Slightly different op for us this evening, chaps…" The officer went on. "Shorter trip than normal for you, but some complicated routes and some interesting targets. It's important that we get this one right, because in addition to the main force behind you, there will be a follow up operation at dawn tomorrow by a force of Typhoons from 2nd Tactical Air Force."

Instantly, every man in the room sat up straighter, suddenly alert. This was far from normal.

"So, on with the briefing." The ops officer continued. "No long haul to the Fatherland tonight gentlemen. Instead, we're packing you off on a little jaunt to France."

Hargreaves looked sideways at his crew. They all looked back at him. An unspoken realisation passed through all of them. An op over France? Not a regular occurrence, yet not completely unknown over these last few months. And followed up in the morning by fighter-bombers? The ops officer didn't pause long enough for anybody to interrupt.

"Okay Met', let's have the weather first, please?"

POINT 113 – NEAR CAEN, NORMANDY, FRANCE
MONDAY 5TH JUNE 1944 – 1045 HOURS

"Let me just get this straight? Neither of you have anything wrong with your legs or feet or hips at all? Not even a blister?"

Gritz studied the youngest two soldiers in the trio with a doubtful look. For their part, they stared back at him in obvious bemusement.

"No, Sergeant Major." They chorused back obediently after just a heartbeat.

Gritz cocked his head and regarded them with an impatient look.

"And you've got no other ailments at all? Weak lungs? Bad eyesight? False teeth?"

He raised an enquiring eyebrow as his tone drifted towards sarcasm, but the two soldiers shook their heads and repeated their assurance that they were fully fit.

Forced to accept that he was speaking to a pair of medically fit soldiers, Gritz shook his head in mock wonder.

"In that case, lads, I don't know how you ended up here. I'm surprised that two fine specimens like you didn't end up with 12th SS Panzer down the road."

Gritz caught the smallest flicker of alarm, or was it distaste, in the eyes of the two youngsters. Not Nazis then.

"You see, lads, about ninety five percent of us here are crocked; long term sick and permanently downgraded. Lower limb injuries mainly; including me. I got my cruciate ligaments torn in half by some big hairy Ruski out east. Got my left leg strapped up like a nun's chastity belt; but my knee keeps popping out all the same. So, they've sent you to a company full of has-beens. They call us 'The Cripples' up at Regimental Headquarters."

The two young men just stared back at him with wide, innocent eyes.

He turned his attention to the third man; a small, lean, weather-beaten looking individual who was probably in his early twenties but had the eyes of a cynical fifty year old.

"But you *are* on a sick chit, you say?"

The man, who wore a wound badge and an infantry assault badge, nodded back.

"Yes, Sir. Got covered in phosphorous just outside Kharkov. Burnt half my calf and thigh muscle away. Got legs like a sparrow now."

Gritz nodded in acknowledgement, imagining the pain the man must have suffered from the burning phosphorous.

"Well, thankfully you won't have much walking or running to do. You look like you've got a bit of experience so I'm going to put you with First Platoon over on the forward left of the main wood. They've got our only MG42 on that corner and I could do with a third crew member who knows his way around a machine gun. Sergeant Gunther is in charge down there; I'll get someone to take you over in a while."

The veteran accepted the news without comment.

"As for you two…" Gritz looked back at the two fit men. "You're a bit of a commodity. So you'll be staying up here on the knoll with Corporal Stadler's platoon. I call it a platoon; it's actually a large squad of eleven men; the only ones besides you two who can run more than a few metres. They act as the reserve platoon; ready for counter-attack if required. I'll get Stadler to take you through everything shortly…"

Gritz paused as he saw Kole's head poke out from behind the improvised door of his command post. The soldier blinked several times in rapid succession as his eyes adjusted to the daylight.

"Kole? Are you after me?" Gritz asked.

The corporal squinted in Gritz's direction.

"Yes, Sir. The checkpoint has just rung through. We've got visitors. Two car loads of senior officers with motorcycle escorts."

Gritz frowned.

"Senior officers? How senior exactly?"

Before Kole could answer, Private Kellerman's head appeared beside him.

"Sergeant Major; the phone just rang again. It was Colonel Krug over at the Regimental Headquarters position. He says we should expect a visit from the Divisional and Corps Commanders. Apparently they left his position a few minutes ago."

Gritz digested the information for a moment then, making the connection, stiffened suddenly.

"Shit!"

Instantly, he was rapping out a string of orders.

"Kole, tell the checkpoint to hold them there and get the cars pulled in against the hedgerows. I'll go down to meet them and walk them back up. You three…" He pointed at the trio of new arrivals. "Get along the trench to the large dugout and find Corporal Stadler. Wait with him until I get these generals seen to."

Gritz went to turn away but checked himself.

"Wait. Tell Corporal Stadler that we've got at least two general's visiting the position. Tell him to get his arse round and make sure everyone's warned off."

With that, Gritz hurried off towards the makeshift ladder at the end of the trench. He was just placing his foot on the first rung when Kole's urgent voice sounded behind him.

"Sergeant Major; the checkpoint crew say the cars are coming up the track to us."

"What?" Gritz spluttered as he turned back towards the telephone orderly. "No vehicles up here on the position; that's the fucking rule!"

Kole shrugged and made a sheepish face.

"Two generals and their staff, Sir? I reckon they make their own rules…"

Gritz swore a foul oath and shot a look down the trench to where the three new arrivals were about to poke their heads inside Stadler's dugout.

"You three! Cancel my last. Get over here; sharpish!"

The sergeant major threw a dark look at Kole.

"Leave Kellerman on the phone." He ordered. "Grab those three new boys and get the spare cam-nets from the store; then get your arses down into the saddle by the ruins."

Without waiting for any kind of acknowledgement, Gritz hauled himself out of the trench and began working his way down from the wooded knoll on which his command post was situated, towards the small saddle of land between that feature and the larger wooded rise where his main fighting platoons were positioned.

"Bollocks, bollocks, bollocks!" The sergeant major cursed as he descended the steep slope as fast as he dare, knowing that one badly placed foot would see his knee come out of joint and result in him taking an unceremonious dive through the sodden undergrowth.

As he struggled down into the saddle, Gritz considered the implications; not of the visit by the senior officers, but of the possibility that their vehicles would be spotted up here in the wood and that, consequently, somebody would deduce that there was a significant German force dug in here. In his mind's eye, he saw the heavy, concentrated bombing of the night before towards Le Havre. He really didn't want to experience that kind of bombing here on his own position.

"Aagh, fuck!"

Gritz swore out loud as his knee almost went and a sharp jab of pain went through his left leg. Reaching out quickly, he grabbed a nearby branch and steadied himself, hopping on his right leg for a moment until the pain subsided. Taking a deep breath and gritting his teeth, Gritz continued downslope until he emerged into the treeless depression where the tumbledown ruins of several small buildings were situated at the terminus of a narrow, muddy track. Word had it that the ruins had once been a small blacksmith's forge and Gritz had been careful to leave the ruins undisturbed. A local peasant would quickly notice if the large, grey stones suddenly disappeared, and so the sergeant major had forbidden his men to make use of the stone blocks in their bunkers and dugouts.

A roar of engines brought Gritz back to the present. He gazed down the long, curved track to see the first staff car emerging from around the bend. It had been raining for almost twenty four hours and the ground was saturated. As the car ground its way up the steady slope, the wheels threw up great clods of mud and water as it bumped over the ruts and through the puddles. Gritz spotted the officers in the rear seat of the vehicle and the gold braid on red collar-boards betrayed the rank of at least one of them. A second vehicle hove into view behind the first. At least they hadn't brought all the motorcycles up with them, Gritz thought sourly.

He held up his free hand and waved the first car to a halt and gestured to the driver that he should pull in against the hedgerow, before the track gave way to open grass land and mud in the immediate vicinity of the ruins. The driver did as ordered and the car behind followed suit. Within moments, the drivers were out of the vehicles, yanking open the rear doors and saluting. The generals dismounted.

Gritz didn't get that excited about generals any more. He'd seen enough of them in his time. Since his first campaign in Poland, through the 1940 offensive and then through several years in Russia, the sergeant major had come across just about every type of general you could imagine. The jovial ones who had once been field grade officers and knew how to come down to the same level as their men; the arrogant ones, who'd spent their lives doing staff jobs and to who the common soldier was just an expendable cog in the wheel. He'd met the brave ones and the inspirational ones, the cowards and the weak ones, the clever ones and those who were thicker than a concrete gun emplacement.

So now Gritz watched with curiosity as the little collection of officers came towards him, automatically falling into their accepted places, with the two generals at the front, flanked by their aides-de-camp who trailed a few paces behind. The two generals walked slowly towards him, negotiating the puddles and thicker mud. One of them Gritz recognised instantly; the man who had given him this command in the first place, Major General Wilhelm Richter. The other man, a full general, had a walking stick and a pronounced limp. Gritz saluted.

"Good morning gentlemen." He snapped formally. "Point 113 is ready for your inspection."

The party of officers stopped a few paces short of him and stared back. One of them; the one with the stick who was wearing spectacles, returned Gritz's salute.

"Good morning, Sergeant Major." Replied General of Artillery Erich Marcks as he stared at Gritz with shrewd eyes. "I can only assume by the Knight's Cross around your neck that you are the Divisional Commander's secret weapon? He's just been telling me all about you."

Next to Marcks, Richter gave a small chuckle.

"Sergeant Major Gritz, General." The veteran introduced himself formally. "Commanding the defence company here."

Marcks nodded in acknowledgement then jerked his head back down the slope.

"I was surprised to find only a checkpoint. I expected to find a defensive position."

Gritz responded immediately.

"The checkpoint is just a bluff, General; designed to keep the locals from sniffing about up here in the wood. The less that people know about what we have up here, the better. Our main position is up here in the trees. I will give you a tour, Sir, if I may."

"Aah…" Marcks smiled. "A sensible precaution."

Just at that point, the whole group was distracted by four men emerging from the trees behind Gritz. The sergeant major turned and saw Kole and the three new boys stumbling into the position of attention, their arms laden with folded camouflage nets.

"Get them over the cars." Gritz snapped as soon as he laid eyes on the group. "Quick as you can. I don't want anything visible."

Looking slightly intimidated by the group of officers, Gritz's men shuffled hurriedly past and began to spread the camouflage nets across the two stationary cars. As they did so, the officers looked on with interest, and Gritz noticed Marcks raise one eyebrow.

"You seem very keen not be discovered by the locals." The Corps Commander observed as he looked back at Gritz.

Gritz nodded briefly.

"It is a concern, General, but it's not my biggest fear. It's the Tommy planes that worry me the most. I don't want a shit-load of bombs being dropped on my head any time in the near future."

The use of the foul language wasn't normally what you'd expect in a discussion between a general and a non-commissioned officer and, for just a moment, there was no response from any of the officers; but then Marcks gave a series of energetic nods.

"Indeed you do not. Indeed... So... where is this defensive position of yours?"

Gritz first indicated the large wooded feature behind him.

"This is our main fighting position up in the trees here, General." He swung his arm back towards the smaller knoll on which his command post was located. "We have a depth position on this smaller hillock here. I use it for rear protection and as a command post. It's also where I keep my fit men together in one place, so I can use them as a small counter-attack force."

Marcks stepped forward a couple of paces to stand beside Gritz. He stared up towards the smaller of the two woods and wrinkled his brow.

"Fit men?"

Gritz allowed a wry smile to cross his face

"Yes, General. There are only a few men in the company who do not have serious injuries to their lower limbs, including me. I'm afraid we're all a bit knackered. I'm led to believe that our nick-name amongst the other units is 'The Cripples'."

Marcks gave a bark of laughter.

"Really? Well, perhaps I should come and command you personally then?"

Gritz gave the general a blank look.

"I lost my leg in Russia, you know? So now I hobble around like an old man."

Gritz pretended surprise although it was pretty obvious the general was seriously disabled.

"Come on then." Marcks smiled back at the sergeant major. "Let's go for a limp around your position, shall we?"

So they did.

As they hobbled up the hill and then dropped down into the network of trenches on the main position, Gritz rattled off the details to his Corps and Divisional Commanders. Fifty four men including Gritz and the three new men who had just arrived was the total strength of the company. He had three machine guns; one of the new MG42s, the other pair being the older MG34 variants. Their only anti-tank weapon, other than several Panzerfausts, was an old French 47mm gun that had been delivered only yesterday. He had situated the gun at the front edge of the wood, directly between his two forward platoons, where it could sweep the open ground below. Even so, he only had twenty six rounds of ammunition for the gun.

Gritz led the party of officers through the position, and, much to his satisfaction, he found that his men were actually complying with his detailed instructions on defensive routine to a surprising degree. The trenches were tidy, with no unnecessary equipment on display, and the men on sentry duty were properly dressed and well briefed. Range cards were in position, spare ammunition covered, and the improvised revetments created the impression of a well-organised, properly administered position. They paused briefly, halfway along one of the communication trenches, so that Marcks could stare at a pair of soldiers who were busy with shovels in the middle of the wood.

"Latrine duty?" He guessed.

"Not quite, Sir." Gritz shook his head. "That's the old cart track through the middle of the wood. We had to wheel the anti-tank gun in through there when it arrived. Problem is, the tree canopy isn't too thick overhead and the wheels left deep ruts in the track. I've got those two men covering the tracks and spreading some foliage over them. It's only a matter of time before the Tommies send another recce aircraft over."

Marcks regarded the sergeant major with a contemplative expression.

"You really *are* paranoid about the Tommy air force, aren't you?"

"Yes, Sir." Gritz replied, holding the general's gaze.

Again, Marck's head dipped in that curt nod.

"Then you are a wise man, Sergeant Major."

The tour continued. They looked at everything, and Gritz fed the generals endless bits of detail and answered their questions exhaustively. It was obvious to the senior officers that the right man had been given the job of plugging this particular gap in the defensive network north of Caen. They ended their tour at the newly dug gun pit, where the barrel of the 47mm gun, draped in a camouflage net, pointed menacingly across the gently sloping meadows and towards the distant sea. Marcks stood there for a while, taking in the view; not with an aesthetic eye, but with they eye of a master tactician.

"Good spot." He quipped. "You've maximised your arcs of fire here. You can cover the cross roads and all the approaches to this part of the ridge. Well done."

Gritz tried not to blush under the praise.

"Thank you, Sir."

Marcks remained silent, staring intently out towards the coastline. Suddenly, he turned and looked directly at Gritz.

"You know, many people... most people in fact... they think it's going to be the Pas-de-Calais. They are convinced that the Allies will cross there, at the shortest point. I disagree; as all my divisional commanders are aware. This coastline here, in Normandy, is perfect for a landing. That river there..." He gestured vaguely towards the mouth of the River Orne where it emerged into the English Channel next to the town of Ouistreham, several miles distant. "And the Caen Canal. They allow access several miles inland to the city of Caen. And Caen is the perfect pivot point for swinging a force off the coast and into the guts of France. Not to mention those beaches. Look at them... They're perfect."

The general gazed back out across the landscape for a second, before reaching out a gloved hand to his ADC. The captain instantly handed the general a map. Marcks took the map and studied it quickly, murmuring to himself as he did so.

"Point 113... Point 113... Aah, here we are; two wooded knolls with a building in the dead ground. It says 'Forge' on the map..."

He looked up at Gritz again.

"That will be the ruins where we left the cars?"

"That's right, Sir." Gritz confirmed.

Marcks pulled a thoughtful face and gazed out over the fields once more.

"If I'm right…" He began. "And if the High Command *are* wrong; and if the Allies *do* land here, in Normandy… Well, make no mistake, this bit of ground you have here, Gritz; this will be the key terrain. If they come here then they need Caen. They need the river, the canal, their bridges, our airfields, and they need that city. So this…" Marcks turned to look at Gritz again and jabbed his walking stick into the parapet of the gun pit. "This is where the greatest question of all will be decided. The battles fought over these fields will decide whether Germany wins or loses this war. This place…" Marcks said, fixing Gritz with a serious look. "This place will become the crucible of fate."

Everybody stared at the general in silence. The Divisional Commander, the ADCs, Gritz, the gunners; they just stood there, a sense of foreboding creeping into their minds as they remained transfixed on the hawkish looking general with the walking stick. It was Marcks who broke the spell.

"What are we calling this place?" He demanded, looking back at his map. "Has it been given a Resistance Nest number yet? Or a code-name?"

The Divisional Commander cleared his throat.

"Not yet, Sir. We're just calling it Point 113 at the moment."

Marcks gave the slightest shake of his head.

"It needs a name or a number; for security purposes."

Richter looked meaningfully at his ADC, who scribbled the requirement down in his notebook. Gritz however, interrupted.

"You've already given it a code-name, General."

All eyes switched to the sergeant major. Before anyone could speak he went on.

"You've said it yourself. Why don't you just call it *The Crucible?*"

Marcks stared back at Gritz for several moments, his sharp features unreadable. Then, like a chink of sunlight, the general's face cracked into a broad grin.

"The Crucible? Yes… I like that." He pointed his stick at his own ADC. "Make a note and have it passed to all subordinate headquarters. With immediate effect, Point 113 is to be marked as *The Crucible.*"

More scribbling. Gritz hid a smile of satisfaction. Marcks took a deep breath and looked up at the grey sky, screwing his face up against the incessant drizzle.

"The invasion can't be too far off, but the High Command thinks the Allies won't come just yet because of the weather."

Gritz pulled a face and shrugged.

"The weather never bothered the Ruskis, General." He commented.

Marcks regarded him with another owl-like stare.

"No... it didn't, did it?"

Another brief pause, and then...

"I think differently. What is it I said at last week's conference?"

This time, Marcks was looking at the Divisional Commander. Richter stirred and made a cautious answer.

"You said that you knew the way the English think. You said that they would go to church one more time on the Sunday and then come the next day... Today."

Marcks nodded.

"Yes, that's exactly what I said."

One of the ADCs ventured a smile and interjected in a jovial tone.

"It's your birthday tomorrow, General. Thanks to the weather, it doesn't look as though the Allies will be spoiling your party after all."

Marcks gave the young captain a sideways glance.

"Give them time Hoffman... Give them time."

HOLDING CAMP, 13TH BATTALION THE PARACHUTE REGIMENT – SOMEWHERE IN SOUTHERN ENGLAND MONDAY 5TH JUNE 1944 – 1320 HOURS

The weather was shit. There was no other way of describing it. Rain, wind, and then a bit more rain. It had been like that for two days now, and Corporal Jack Dawes was bored stiff. The former Grenadier Guardsman lay on his camp-bed, his gaudy, camouflage Denison Smock draped over him like a blanket, and stared disconsolately around the barely waterproof tent. The damp interior of the small canvass shelter was heavy with the fug of cigarette smoke and the flimsy khaki structure shuddered with each new gust of wind.

Dawes had been waiting a long time to have another go at Jerry. Ever since his battalion had endured the foot blistering and desperate fighting withdrawal from the River Dyle to Dunkirk back in 1940, the corporal had been harbouring thoughts of revenge. His parent battalion, the 3rd Grenadiers, had suffered terrible casualties during that campaign, and his own company, No.4 Company had been hammered during the defence of the River Escaut, losing more than forty percent of its strength in one day. So, yes, Jack Dawes wanted payback. And he'd waited a long time for it.

Desperate to get back into action, Dawes had volunteered for 'special duties' on his return to England from Dunkirk. He'd had no idea what those special duties would be until he'd been granted his wish, and thus he had found himself to be a member of the newly established Parachute Regiment.

Already made an acting Lance Corporal by his own battalion after Dunkirk, Dawes had excelled within his new environment, immersing himself in the new tactics and new equipment of this elite force. He had done so well that when that force was expanded to divisional size he had been promoted to full Corporal and posted to the 13th Battalion of the Parachute Regiment, as part of an experienced cadre of old soldiers. But despite the promotion and the intensive training, action still evaded him.

That was due to change, at last. The invasion was imminent. Everyone knew it; even the Germans. It was just a case of exactly where it would fall; and *when*. The knowledge that the great confrontation was almost upon them made the waiting even more frustrating for Dawes. Like all driven men, he was impatient for action. He'd trained enough now, and memorised the terrain features and code names and plans until he could recite the whole damned lot in his sleep. It was time to get on with the job.

And this time it would be different he told himself. This time it was the Allies who had the air superiority. It was the Allies who had all the tanks, and the artillery, and every other means of destruction that one could wish for. The Americans had joined the British and Commonwealth Forces, who were already supplemented by the units of Polish and French exiles who had stayed on in Britain to help fight on against the Nazi war machine. And the Yanks of course, had everything. They seemed to produce things out of thin air. Stories abounded about their wealth of equipment and their preponderance of luxury ration items. Yes, Britain now had a pretty powerful backer in this scrap, and the Germans were going to learn all about it soon enough.

Dawes glanced up at the sets of equipment that hung from the internal frame of the tent. The strange camouflage smocks of the airborne forces that still seemed a little odd to the old soldiers; the strange pot helmets covered with scrim-net, the maroon berets with their silver winged badges; the new version of the Lee-Enfield with its nasty little pig-sticker bayonet; the Sten Guns and PIATs and all the other new bits of kit that had been introduced were hanging there, or else piled neatly beneath them on a wooden pallet. Yes... a different army they were, and a different result they would be demanding this time around.

His thoughts were interrupted as Private Hodges struggled up off his bed and walked across to the flap of the tent door. Stretching his back and shoulders off as he moved, Hodges stopped by the door and squinted through the closed flap.

"Do you know what?" The young man said. "I think it's easing off a bit..."

He was met by a torrent of good natured abuse.

"Oh, fuck off you daft Scouse git!" Came the groan from another member of Dawes' section.

"You've said that about a dozen times already since scoff." Complained another.

Dawes shook his head at the much maligned paratrooper.

"Hodgie, lad; stop watching the bloody weather, will you? It's like waiting for a kettle to boil. We'll know when it's time because they'll bloody well tell us."

The dark haired Liverpudlian glanced down at his section commander with serious eyes.

"Honest Corp', I'm telling you. It's definitely easing up a bit."

The voices sounded from around the tent again.

"In that case make yourself useful and go over the cookhouse; see if you can scrounge a brew out of the tight bastards."

Hodges shook his own head now, looking aggrieved; but dutifully walked across to where the section had piled its mugs and mess tins.

He'd barely leaned over to grab the nearest handful of mugs when the sound of raised voices stopped him dead in his tracks. He looked back over his shoulder towards the tent door. Around the tent, without speaking, his comrades pushed themselves up onto their elbows; their faces etched with anticipation. Even Dawes pushed himself up into a sitting position.

The voice was getting louder and every man in the tent could recognise it. There was no mistaking the harsh snap of their platoon sergeant.

"Two Section! Get off your scratchers!"

The direct reference to their own section sent a bolt of urgency through the men in the tent as if they had just been struck by lightning.

"Corporal Dawes?"

The head of Sergeant Haywood appeared through the door flap.

"Sarnt." Dawes confirmed, jumping to his feet.

The sergeant spotted Dawes and rattled off a string of orders without pause.

"Get your lads stood-to in full kit. We're moving out in a couple of hours; for good. Make sure you've got everything with you. Pay parade and back-loading of personal effects at 1400 hours; kit-check and grenade priming at 1430 hours. Ready to move by 1530 hours. Any questions?"

Dawes stood there blinking for a moment, his heart suddenly beating like a trip hammer.

"Is this it then, Sergeant?" Is all he could manage to blurt.

Haywood gave him a devilish smile.

"What do *you* fucking think, Jack?"

HIDE LOCATION, 21ST PANZER DIVISION – NEAR CAEN, NORMANDY
MONDAY 5TH JUNE 1944 – 1415 HOURS

"Just a little more…"

Staff Sergeant Max Weimer shouted the instructions to the driver over the growl of the tank's powerful engine. The sickly smell of exhaust fumes permeated the air as the young soldier eased the big Panzer IV backwards ever so slightly. At the rear of the tank, the gunner and loader were leaning backwards, straining on the rope that was attached to the track. The co-driver, squatting by the running gear of the big armoured vehicle, looked up at Weimer suddenly.

"Neutral left, just a gnat's knacker…"

Weimer passed on the order to the driver, who responded immediately.

"Hold!" The co-driver shouted suddenly.

Weimer slapped his hand down on the hull of the vehicle in front of the driver and repeated the command.

Within moments, the co-driver was reaching for the track-pin by his feet. Weimer reminded the driver not to move a muscle then went across to help with the job of replacing the pin into the track.

Track-bashing was one of the least popular pass-times of the Panzer Corps, but on this occasion, it was absolutely necessary. The division was chronically short of just about every item of equipment you could mention, so when several new track links had come his way, Weimer wasn't going to waste any time in changing them for the worst of the worn out track pads on his battered vehicle. Despite the rain that dripped relentlessly from the tree canopy, through the camouflage nets and onto their heads, he and his crew set about the final stage of linking the track back together.

"Ready when you are, Staff Sergeant." Hartmann, the co-driver shouted over his shoulder.

Hefting the large sledgehammer, the tank commander positioned himself directly behind Hartman, gauged the angle, and swung with all his might. There was a dull, metallic 'thunk' as hammer and pin connected.

"That's it, she's going in." Hartmann encouraged him.

Thunk.

A second swing pushed the pin even further and Hartmann stepped aside. With a clear swing now, Weimer slammed the heavy sledge into the pin twice more, driving it fully home. He took a deep breath, rested the sledge and nodded at Hartmann.

"Alright, that should do it. Get the rope off and run the track backwards and forwards a couple of times; make sure it's secure."

He laid the sledge hammer on the trampled foliage of their hide and walked off to one side whilst his crew went about clearing up the detritus of the track-bashing session. As he did so, Corporal Bauer wandered over from beneath his own camouflage net.

"Crap afternoon for track-bashing, eh, Staff Sergeant?"

Weimer glanced at the corporal and accepted the offer of a mug of steaming, black coffee.

"Certainly is. So much for summer. Still, I'd rather be doing it in the rain in France, than in the snow in Russia."

"I'm with you on that one." Bauer agreed. "And I supposed it helps stave off the boredom."

Weimer gave a wry smile.

"I'd enjoy the boredom while you can, Bauer. Once the Tommies and their American friends turn up, you'll be busy enough."

Bauer regarded his platoon commander inquisitively.

"You think they'll be here soon?

Weimer hesitated only slightly before he nodded his head.

"Oh yes, Bauer. They'll be here soon enough. It can't be long now."

Bauer looked up at the rain sodden tree canopy and grimaced.

"Don't think I'd like to be bobbing about on the ocean in this weather…" He murmured.   ·

Weimer grinned at his old comrade and clapped him on the shoulder.

"I wouldn't worry about it just yet. I think we've got a few more nights of decent sleep ahead of us. Even the Tommies aren't stupid enough to start a battle in this weather…"

LANDING SHIP INFANTRY EMPIRE BATTLEAXE, PORTSMOUTH, ENGLAND
MONDAY 5TH JUNE 1944 – 1500 HOURS

Sergeant Les Downey of the 2nd Battalion East Yorkshire Regiment flicked his cigarette end over the side of the 7,000 ton troopship and stared bleakly at the murky water far below. He was bored. Bored and agitated. Having last seen action in 1940, Downey had spent the last three years training, training and training some more. At first, when he had joined his reformed battalion in the October of 1940, he had been celebrated as a bit of a hero; a man who had seen some serious fighting, and, to be truthful, that was very much how he had felt. Fresh from the vicious fighting around Holme-on-Spalding Moor during the failed German invasion, he had developed a feeling of invulnerability, along with a new found desire to excel as a soldier; inspired as he had been by the example of a sergeant from the Coldstream Guards, with whom he had shared his adventures.

Downey had thrown himself into the business of learning the new methods of war, becoming familiar with the ever improving weaponry in the battalion's arsenal, and passing on his experience and advice to the young conscripts who were rapidly filling the unit's ranks. But whilst he and his men were training, other units were going off to fight the enemy; in North Africa or in the Far East. And far from sitting on their laurels and licking their wounds, the Germans had thrown themselves into Russia in the summer of 1941, thereby obtaining yet more valuable frontline experience. Meanwhile, Downey and his men had gone from one battle school to the next, from one major training scheme to another, and now he was impatient for action. Or was he?

A wolf-whistle made him look up from the water. To his left, leaning over the ship's rail like himself, a whole bunch of young lads from his company were waving and shouting at two members of the Women's Royal Naval Service who were walking along the side of the dock. He glanced down at the two women in their smartly tailored navy blue uniforms. The blonde and the brunette blushed visibly and exchanged embarrassed comments with each other, before the blonde, feeling slightly more confident than her companion, gave a small wave and a dazzling smile up at the ship. The crowd of young infanteers at the rail responded with a delighted cheer and whistled some more. The two women, blushing an even deeper red, hurried on past.

Downey couldn't help but smile at the antics of his men. A few years ago, he had been just the same; young, reasonably care free, and enjoying himself enormously by chatting up the WAAFs at the airfield in Driffield where his company had been responsible for security. Now however, he was older, wiser, and in no doubt at all about the reality of what was about to face him. They had been given their orders a couple of days ago whilst sealed in their assembly camp. Invasion. A landing in France; sometime soon. The long anticipated return to the continent where they could fight the Germans face to face once more.

They needed just two more pieces of information. Exactly where they would be landing... and when. He had the map of their assault beach firmly imprinted in his mind, but all the names on that map were code-names; Cod, Sole, Daimler, Poland, the list went on. But he would dearly love to know exactly where it was on the French coast. Perhaps it would be Dunkirk? Now that would be ironic. As for when… Well, it had to be sometime soon. They were fully kitted out and fully bombed up. It was imminent. They had made to leave harbour the previous evening but then turned back and anchored again within two hours. A false start? Testing the ships engines? Downey didn't know. The only thing he did know was that very shortly, he and his men would be in battle, and the chances were that it was going to be bloody.

The soldiers to his left began to laugh as one of their number explained in somewhat lurid detail what he would like to do to the pretty blonde WRNS girl were he given the chance to get ashore. Downey looked towards the group again and studied their young faces. Not much chance of that, big lad, he reflected. The next bit of land you're going to be setting foot on will be bristling with enemy bunkers and machine-guns.

They were good lads these. Good, hard working, down to earth lads from the farms and the villages of East Yorkshire. The reality was that if they found themselves in a bedroom with a willing lass, they wouldn't know where on earth to start. Most of them had probably never even kissed a girl, let alone sleep with one. And as for battle. Well, that would be their first time too. Yes, they'd been trained for it. Yes they were equipped with everything the modern infantryman could want. But the first time in battle is the same for everyone. Excitement, nerves, fear, chaos, confusion, anger, exhaustion…

"Alright you lot; get yourselves below, sharpish!"

The sound of the Company Sergeant Major's voice snapped Downey out of his private thoughts. The sergeant turned to see the short, stocky warrant officer striding along the deck, chivvying the various groups of soldiers along and directing them to the steps down into the hold. Downey stood up straight and adjusted his battle dress as the nearest group of soldiers pulled reluctantly away from the ship's rail and headed for the stairs.

"Quickly now; the Company Commander is briefing everyone in ten minutes."

Downey took a couple of paces towards the warrant officer and gave him a searching look.

"Something up, Sir?"

The Company Sergeant Major came up level with Downey and leaned in close.

"Certainly is, Les. The Company Commander has got some news for us all. He's got a sealed envelope in his hand. I saw him open it a couple of minutes ago and now he wants to speak to the whole company together. I've spotted 'C' Company doing the same thing too."

"D'you think…" Downey began.

"It's on." The Company Sergeant Major murmured quietly, fixing the sergeant with a serious expression. "Tomorrow morning; definitely. D-Day…"

FARMHOUSE PELLETIER, 300 METRES FROM POINT 113 – NORMANDY
MONDAY 5TH JUNE 1944 – 1610 HOURS

Fifteen year old Maurice Pelletier sat at the kitchen table and watched the rain splatter against the small window. The dull, grey sky outside allowed only a puny amount of light to intrude into the building's interior. Fortunately, his mother had been baking and the room was warm, the big iron oven throwing out just as much heat as the open fire that fed it. It was a warm and comfortable place to be after cycling back from school in such terrible weather. What had happened to the summer, he wondered?

Despite the mug of hot milk that the youngster cradled between his hands, and the delicious smell of freshly baked bread that permeated the air throughout the rambling farmhouse, Maurice Pelletier was feeling a little less then settled. Not only would he be expected to help his father milk their herd that evening, he was busy thinking about Chantal Lisseur. Chantal Lisseur was a goddess. Petit, with luxurious brown hair, plump lips that were always set in a provocative pout, and possessed of a smile that could melt an iceberg, Mademoiselle Lisseur was the answer to every teenage boy's dream. The only problem was; Chantal Lisseur was six years older than Maurice. And of course, she was also his school teacher.

Unlike most young people in the Normandy area, Maurice had stayed on in education after the age of fourteen at the request of his school headmaster who believed the young man to be 'exceptionally bright'. Maurice's father hadn't been convinced initially, believing that Maurice should just leave school and learn how to do a proper job, like work a dairy farm. In the Pelletier household however, there was a strong female influence, and faced with a relentless onslaught from his wife, Monsieur Pelletier had been forced to admit that their son had a talent for learning that was not usual for their family and it would indeed be a shame to waste such talent. Thus, the young Maurice had been enrolled in the grammar school in Caen where he was duly educated in a range of subjects from advanced mathematics, through geometry and science, to classical literature. Monsieur Pelletier secretly wondered how a knowledge of classical literature would ever help his son to run a farm, but his wife was enormously proud of their clever son and that made for a quiet life, so on the whole, the dour farmer was happy enough to let things run their natural course.

Maurice was still sitting at the table, wrestling with the disturbing yet exciting thoughts of Mademoiselle Lisseur, when the kitchen door banged open allowing a cold, damp gust of air to rush through the room. Turning, Maurice saw the hulking outline of his father stamp through the door, droplets of rain water dripping from his cap. The sodden farmer slammed the door shut and stood there for a moment, shaking himself dry.

"Damned weather." He grunted without any real conviction. "Hard to believe this is the start of June."

Madam Pelletier glanced over at her husband from where she was setting down a steaming loaf, fresh from the oven, and smiled.

"Get your things off, my love, and hang them up by the door. Then come and have a warm by the stove. There's freshly warmed milk here, look. Come and warm yourself."

Monsieur Pelletier gave another grunt; this one slightly more amiable. He was the kind of man who tended to communicate by grunting; his precise moods and meanings identified by the variance of pitch and volume, and sometimes reinforced with a frown or shrug as the fancy took him.

The big man shambled across to the stove, grabbing a kitchen towel as he went. He stopped by the oven and wiped the thick cloth across his weather beaten features.

"Once the milking is done tonight, we'll put the herd in the bottom field." He said to nobody in particular. "They'll have to graze that field for a while now. We can't put them back in the top field. They'll start disappearing if we leave them up there."

Madam Pelletier gave her husband a questioning look as she passed him a mug of the hot milk.

"Why ever would they disappear from the top field?"

The farmer threw the towel onto the table next to Maurice and accepted the proffered mug gratefully.

"Because the damned Boche are in the wood above the old forge." He said phlegmatically before raising the mug to his lips and taking a long draught.

At the table, Maurice set his own mug down with a surprisingly loud thump and looked up at his father with wide eyes.

"The Boche? In our wood?" He gasped.

"Whatever are they doing up there?" Madam Pelletier frowned. "I thought they had just put a checkpoint on the Hermanville Road? Do you think they are sheltering in the trees because of the weather? You know... when they're off duty sort of thing?"

Monsieur Pelletier lowered the mug and smacked his lips in satisfaction before giving his head a shake.

"That's what I thought it might be at first. Those Boche on the checkpoint have been keeping me away from the ridge all week. At first I thought they were just being a bunch of typical Boche swine, but this morning I saw two cars go up there. They were up there for more than an hour, and when they came down, I saw who was in those cars."

At this, the farmer set his mug on the table switched his gaze from his wife to his son, then back again.

"I'm no expert on soldiers of any kind, but I know what a general looks like when I see one. And this morning, I didn't see just one; I saw two. At least two..."

Maurice was staring at his father now, his young, academic brain working fast.

"But why would two German generals be up in our woods?"

Monsieur Pelletier shrugged.

"Well, I don't think they were having a picnic. In fact, I'm sure they weren't. I've been hearing the odd noise from up there over the last few days. The sound of wood being chopped and the like. And there's the vehicle movement we've heard over the last few nights too."

At this, the farmer gave his wife a look as if asking her to confirm that he hadn't been dreaming it all. Madam Pelletier nodded her head slowly.

"Yes, now you come to mention it, the Boche vehicles have been coming past here quite a lot these last few nights. I thought it was just the checkpoint..."

As the woman's voice tailed off, her husband sat down on one of the sturdy kitchen chairs and let out a long sigh.

"Well, I reckon I know what they're up to. I reckon the bastards are building some kind of command post up there. If you think about it, you can see the entire coast from up there; from Hermanville right the way across to Ouistreham and beyond to Le Havre. I think the Boche have realised that and they're moving in as our neighbours."

With that, Monsieur Pelletier began removing his boots. As he bent low, his wife and son exchanged worried looks.

Still bent forwards as he fiddled with his laces, the farmer continued with his monologue.

"If that's the case, then we'll need to keep our eyes on things. Those Boche swine will probably steal a cow a night if they get the chance; thieving bastards that they are. The eggs too; the Boche like their eggs. We'll need to keep the coop well shut up on a night time."

He sat up straight again and looked straight at Maurice.

"And you and your friends need to keep away from the place, my lad. I don't want you upsetting them. Monsieur Benoit told me that the Boche have got some boys locked up in the jail in Caen; some of them just your age. They'd been having a nosey at what the Boche were up to, in the way that young boys do; always wanting to know the ins and outs of everything. Anyway, the Boche said they were spying and locked them all up. They may end up being shot."

At that, Monsieur Pelletier went back to the struggle with his boots. Madam Pelletier, looking a little unsettled, went back to her place at the kitchen workbench. Maurice was forcing himself to remain calm, despite the urge to jump up and just dash out of the door. As he drained the last of the milk in his mug, he knew he had to see Chantal again before tomorrow. She would be interested in this information, he was sure. That was one of the other things that was so exciting about Mademoiselle Lisseur. She was in *'The Resistance'*.

She'd never told him outright, of course; you couldn't expect that. But she had, very early on during his time at the grammar school, got intoxicatingly close to him as they discussed a particular piece of work, and intimated that she was very interested in what was going on in the coastal areas. Most people were not allowed near the coast; only those with farming or other useful work that demanded their presence in the 'defended zone'. She would be *'very grateful'* she had told him, for any news he could pass on to her. Looking into her big brown eyes at such a short distance, whilst drinking in the scent of the woman's perfume, had almost been enough to make the young man burst. Of course he would keep her informed. It would be his pleasure; the least he could do for her.

Maurice pushed his chair back and stood.

"I have to go out for an hour." He said. "I'll be back in time for supper and to help with the milking."

Madam Pelletier looked round from her work, one eyebrow raised.

"Going out? In this weather? Where to?"

"Oh… I'm having a bit of trouble with one of the classical texts we're studying at the moment. Mademoiselle Lisseur has said she will go through it with me some more. We have a test tomorrow, so tonight is my last chance. I said I'd go over for an hour this evening."

Maurice was already reaching for his coat.

"It's a long way to go, Maurice. She lives in Lebisey doesn't she? You're almost back in Caen. Why didn't you just stop on after school?"

Maurice was at the door now, desperate to avoid a cross-examination.

"Oh… she couldn't do it then; there was a meeting… the school governors I think."

He was halfway out of the door.

"Well, make sure you're back in time to help your father. Supper is at nine thirty."

He was closing the door as his mother's voice came after him.

"And remember there's a curfew…"

The door slammed shut and Maurice was gone.

For a while there was silence in the kitchen, and Monsieur Pelletier stretched out his feet and warmed them against the fire. After a few moments, his wife spoke.

"Well, I suppose we should be grateful that Maurice is taking his studies so seriously. That school is expensive after all. And Madam Lisseur is a very dedicated teacher…"

A series of grunts that passed for laughter came from near the fire place and the farmer's wife looked round at her husband.

"What is it?"

Monsieur Pelletier smiled knowingly at his wife.

"You're right; Mademoiselle Lisseur is *very* dedicated to her students."

She caught the tone in her husband's voice and frowned.

"What do you mean?"

"Let's just say…" Monsieur Pelletier replied, a licentious grin starting to spread across his face. "Mademoiselle Lisseur is very young and very pretty, and I suspect that our son's interests probably lie more in her looks than her teaching ability."

For a moment, Madam Pelletier just stared at her husband in bemused silence, but then, with a look of realisation, she blushed deeply and pretended outrage.

"Emile!"

LANDING CRAFT INFANTRY 998 – NEWHAVEN, ENGLAND MONDAY 5TH JUNE 1944 – 1950 HOURS

Major Dickie Smithson, commanding 'A' Company of the 1st Battalion Hambledon and Moorlanders knew where they were going. He'd known for nearly a week. The awful thing was, he hadn't been able to tell anyone, because that would have been a breach of security.

The officers of the battalion had been taken into a guarded hut with blacked out windows on arrival at their assembly camp, which itself had been sealed shut and placed under armed guard. Over the course of three hours, a group of intelligence officers and members of the brigade staff had briefed them on the mission for their battalion on D-Day. An amazingly detailed scale model had covered more than a third of the room, and the wall behind it had been covered in high definition air photographs of the coastline and its hinterland.

There had been no *real* names used of course; just code-names for places and beaches, and they hadn't even been told which country's coastline they were going to invade. But Dickie Smithson had holidayed in France with his parents several times before the war and he had immediately recognised the large section of terrain on the model with its distinctive river estuary and the large city that sat inland from their landing beach with its ancient cathedral.

They were to land just to the west of the river estuary in the second wave, on 'Queen White Sector' of a beach called 'Sword'. They would be preceded by the 8th Infantry Brigade; men from the East Yorkshires, South Lancashires and the Suffolks. Those battalions would overwhelm the beach defences and then destroy the large enemy strongpoints; all of them with strange code-names like Cod, Sole, Daimler, Morris and Hillman. Smithson's battalion would come ashore just a couple of hours later, and then make a mad rush for the 3rd Infantry Division's main objective for the day; the large cathedral city some 6 miles inland.

It was a bold plan, and a plan involving a seemingly endless list of units and regiments, ships and aircraft. The enormity of the operation was not lost on the officers of the Hambledon and Moorlanders, and, as it always did when he was in contemplative mood, Smithson's shoulder had begun to throb; right where he carried the scar from the German bullet that had smashed into his collar bone back in 1940.

As he had sat there, taking in all the information, Smithson had been able to picture much of the terrain in his mind. The wide flat beaches; the gently rising land as one progressed inland. In particular, he was able to visualise the stunningly beautiful medieval cathedral city with its narrow cobbled streets and old world charm, and of course, that huge and impressive edifice of the cathedral itself.

"The Brigade's objective for the day is the city itself, and that is code-named *Poland*."

That was what the intelligence officer had said, back in the hut. Smithson of course had already worked out that 'Poland' was actually the city of Caen... in Normandy. Carrying that knowledge about for almost a week had been an excruciating burden for the young major, but now the frustration of being the only person in the know was almost over. They were gathered together in the hold of the ship; the Second in Command of their battalion standing before them. The Commanding Officer was on the other ship with 'B' and 'D' companies; probably doing the very same thing at this very same moment.

"Gentlemen." The Second in Command, Major 'Bunty' Brown, announced in a voice filled with gravity. "I can now inform you of our destination. Our invasion area is in Normandy... in France. Our objective for the day, 'Poland', is actually the historic city of Caen. This time tomorrow, if all goes according to plan, we shall be wandering its streets. D-Day is on. It's tomorrow; at dawn. The ship will be slipping anchor in the next ten minutes."

Smithson's shoulder began to throb. This was it. After three and a half years, Smithson was going back into battle. This time, he promised himself, it would be a different outcome. At the same time, somewhere in the back of his head, a little voice kept reminding him of the realities of war.

"*If* all goes to plan..." The voice was saying. "*If...*"

THE COTTAGE OF MADEMOISELLE LISSEUR – LEBISEY, NORMANDY
MONDAY 5TH JUNE 1944 – 2000 HOURS

"Are you sure?"

Chantal Lisseur stared at the young boy across her parlour. Well, she classed him as a young boy, but the reality was that Maurice Pelletier was growing up fast, his sturdy frame and rugged looks just what you would expect from a farmer's son. If she were honest, she had used his adolescence to her own advantage; easily reeling him in as a willing informant. And his obvious infatuation with her, although dangerous, would never-the-less ensure loyalty. Actually, if she were a little younger, and he a little older, she might even have been tempted to indulge that infatuation a little further.

"Yes, Mademoiselle; definitely. There has been a checkpoint by the crossroads below the wood for some days now, and the Boche have told my father to keep his distance. At first he thought it was just a bit of the usual German arrogance, but today he found out why. There are more Boche in that wood than we first realised; and they were visited by not one, but two

German generals this morning. They were up there for more than an hour. There is no doubt that the ridge is being used as a command post. It is the perfect place to cover the land down to the coast. And there have been truck loads of German troops arriving there at night."

His information came tumbling out, complete with a few additional points of dramatic detail that he had conjured up in his own mind in order to ensure that the smoulderingly beautiful Chantal Lisseur would take him seriously.

Now, the young brunette was standing before him, arms folded below her bosom, her dark, intelligent eyes sparkling by the light of the small lamp as she stared back at Maurice, turning his revelations over in her mind.

"That makes sense." She said curtly. "The Germans have accelerated their programme of constructing fortifications just recently. Not just the concrete bunkers either. They have been driving wooden stakes into all the open fields round about. People say it is to stop English aircraft from landing."

"Yes." Maurice agreed excitedly. "They have done it just north of our farm; in the fields beyond the wood where the command post has been established."

Chantal accepted the information in silence, nodding her head thoughtfully, until a sudden knock on the door made both of them jump.

Chantal walked briskly to the window and peeked out from behind the thick curtains, her eyes alert for danger. After just a couple of moments of squinting into the fading light, her face relaxed slightly. She flicked her gaze to Maurice as she put the curtains back in place.

"Stay here, Maurice, while I answer the door."

Puzzled, he watched her go. His gut reaction was to follow her, make sure she was alright; be there to protect her. The pupil-teacher relationship must have been the more dominant feeling however because instead of following Chantal, Maurice did as he was told and remained in the parlour. He heard the front door open then shut again. The sound of a man's voice, and Chantal's too; both conversing in hushed yet urgent tones. At one point, he thought he heard Chantal give a little gasp of surprise; or was it a sob? For just a moment, he considered going through into the hallway to see if she was okay, but as he tossed the idea round his mind, Maurice heard the door open again, the sound of a brisk farewell from the male voice, and then the sound of the door closing again.

Moments later, Chantal reappeared in the parlour. Her eyes were as big and dark and serious as ever, but her skin had changed colour markedly. She was ashen.

"Mademoiselle..." Maurice stuttered, a feeling of unease settling in his stomach. "Are you alright?"

For a moment, Chantal just stared at the young man. Eventually, after taking a large gulp of air, she replied.

"You must go home, Maurice; straight away."

"But… Are you…"

"Go home, Maurice. Go back to your family as quickly as you can."

She stepped in close to him and grasped his upper arms with her hands, staring into his face with eyes that were now welling with emotion.

"You are a good boy, Maurice…" She said earnestly, "to bring me such valuable information."

'Boy', he thought. She called me a *boy*.

"You are brave too. A good, brave Frenchman." She hurried on, still staring into his eyes. "But now I have things to do that cannot wait, and you must go back to your parents. Get home as quickly as you can and do not go out again tonight. Do you have a cellar?"

Maurice blinked in surprise at the unexpected question.

"Yes, but why…"

"Sleep in there tonight. Tell your parents. You must all sleep in the cellar tonight. And stay there until the firing has stopped…"

"Firing?" Maurice blurted. "What firing?"

Chantal put a long, elegant finger to the boy's lips.

"I have said too much already. Do not ask me anything else; for your own sake."

She smiled suddenly, and leaned forward and up, placing a gentle kiss on the young man's cheek.

"Please? Do as I say, Maurice. Go home and stay there; in your cellar. Stay there until you are sure it is safe to come out. You will understand what I mean very soon."

She stood to one side and placed a hand in the small of his back.

"Go home now, and be careful."

She ushered him gently towards the hallway.

"Go." She whispered in a voice filling with emotion. "Go…"

'OBJECTIVE COD', SWORD BEACH - LA BRECHE D'HERMANVILLE, NORMANDY MONDAY 5TH JUNE 1944 – 2100 HOURS

Private Walther Lehman would not have recognised his garrison location by the name 'Cod', nor the stretch of coastline adjacent to it as 'Sword Beach'. As far as he, and the rest of the German Army was concerned, this was just another strongpoint among many dotted along the coast of France. Situated amongst rows of former holiday villas near a place called Le Breche, this particular garrison location had been designated 'Resistance Nest 20' and, to be honest, there were much worse places you could be; like Russia for instance. Just the thought made him shiver. Like many of his comrades in the company who manned this strongpoint, Lehman was an ethnic German from the Danzig province and he had always known that the Russians were not people you wanted to get on the wrong side of. The full-blooded Poles were bad enough, but Russians... No thank you.

For that reason alone, Lehman had no real objection to his posting. Having accepted that he had no choice but to do war service, he could think of few better places to be standing guard. The coastline here was beautiful, although admittedly, these last couple of days had been rather wet and windy; unusual for the time of year. But in general, the Normandy coast was relatively peaceful and unspoilt. Even the growing rows of beach defences and the concrete anti-tank wall couldn't spoil the serenity of the place on a good day.

Not everyone thought so of course. Amongst the ranks of his company, indeed the whole battalion, were reluctant conscripts from the 'liberated' provinces such as Poland, the Ukraine, Czechoslovakia and the like. They had been pressed into service by a German military growing desperate for manpower, and having been given little alternative, they now went about their duties with little enthusiasm. For the regular German NCOs and officers, it was a constant battle to keep those individuals on their toes. Still, that wasn't Lehman's problem. He did as he was told, enjoyed his days off by cycling into Caen to enjoy a bit of culture, and passed his days away writing letters home; when he wasn't laying mines or building obstacles of course.

Now, Lehman was looking forward to a bit of fresh air and relative solitude. He had drawn wall duty. He had a four hour stint of patrolling the anti-tank wall, which ran along the sea front, along the very edge of the dunes. His section was some three hundred metres in length; right along the frontage of the company position. The luckier men had drawn stints inside the fortified villas that were the hub of the strongpoint. High up in third floor rooms or attics, those men would stand watch from within heavily sandbagged bunkers, relatively warm and most definitely dry.

Lehman shrugged away any jealous thoughts. No matter. What was a bit of rain? He would be back under his blankets again by 0100 hours. Things could be much worse. He fastened the last button on his greatcoat and grabbed his rifle from the corner of the room, just as Corporal Fuchs walked in.

"You ready, Lehman?"

"Yes, Corporal." The eighteen year old replied, slinging his weapon over his shoulder.

"Good man. Don't forget to take the flare pistol off Gruber when you relieve him, will you?"

"No, Corporal."

"I'll bring you some coffee out in a couple of hours, son. The weather's still pretty shit. Looks like we might get a bit more rain."

Lehman smiled back at his NCO.

"No matter, Corporal."

And with that, Lehman left the room and began climbing the cellar stairs towards the hallway of their platoon house. As he went, the young soldier began whistling softly to himself. There were plenty of things that made Lehman a reasonably contented soldier, in addition to the lack of fighting and relative safety of his posting. And tomorrow, Lehman would be enjoying one of them. It was his day off.

RAF DOWNHAM MARKET – NORFOLK, ENGLAND
MONDAY 5TH JUNE 1944 – 2255 HOURS

The airframe of the Lancaster juddered ever so gently as the four powerful Merlin engines hummed contentedly away. Looking out of the cockpit, Hargreaves could see very little, which was pretty normal. They'd had engines running for a little over five minutes now. This was the bit that everyone hated. Waiting. Briefed up, bombed up, and keyed up, the Lancaster and its crew were ready to go. All they needed was the signal that the mission was on.

Behind the scenes, the Met' chaps would be wringing their hands over the flying conditions. The brass hats might even be making last minute decisions that could see the mission scrubbed. Either way, Hargreaves always detested these final few minutes before take off. This was the time when your fears came to haunt you. All kinds of unwelcome thoughts could just pop into your head, completely unannounced. Like everyone, he just wanted to get on with it, do his job, then come back and forget all about it until next time.

As he was reflecting on this, trying to stay calm, and trying desperately not to remember the sight of a burning Lancaster plummeting right past them on their last op, Hargreaves saw the green lamp suddenly flash into life from the window of the control tower. He clicked on the intercom.

"Okay, boys; we're on. Everyone good… Bombs?"

"Yes Skip'." Came the bomb aimer's reply.

"Nav?

"Skip'."

"Spanners?"

"Skip'." The flight engineer replied.

"Mid-upper?"

"Skip'." The dorsal turret gunner acknowledged.

"Guns rear?"

No reply.

"Guns rear?"

Silence.

"Mac', did you get that?"

Again, there was no reply from McWilliams in the rear gun-turret.

"Nav'? Can you pop down and give Mac a poke, please?"

"Skip'." Acknowledged Murphy.

Inside the long fuselage of the aircraft, the navigator cursed silently and unplugged his head set from the junction box, before starting the difficult process of negotiating his way along the inside of the huge bomber. After a minute or so, he reached the rear of the aircraft and slid open the balsa wood door that covered the rear gun-turret. As Murphy opened the shutter, he caught a brief glimpse of McWilliams slumped in his harness. The image only lasted for a brief moment however, because the gunner suddenly sat bolt upright and began fiddling, rather ostentatiously, with his traverse switches.

"Wake up, Mac', for God's sake! There is a war on, you know?"

"Eh? What?"

McWilliams looked round innocently.

"What you on about?"

"Didn't you hear the Skipper checking in? We're about to go."

"Er, no… Hold on…"

The gunner began fiddling with the junction box for his intercom; or at least pretending to.

"Hello… Skipper? Can you hear me? It's Mac'…"

Up in the cockpit, Hargreaves smiled and shook his head.

"Hello Mac'. Are you hearing us all okay now?"

"Yes Skip'. Just had a bit of bother with the intercom but I'm hearing you fine now."

Again, Hargreaves smiled.

"Righto, well, we're off now. Beginning the taxi onto the runway. Everyone stay sharp. Next stop France; let's make this a good one."

THE CAEN CANAL BRIDGE, NEAR BENOUVILLE, NORMANDY
MONDAY 5TH JUNE 1944 – 2350 HOURS

Private Manfred Krause came to a halt in the middle of the cobbled road and glanced up at the dark night sky where the clouds were gradually beginning to break up. They weren't breaking up completely of course. Great dirty blobs still clogged the air above, so that only the occasional star managed to wink at him from the vast expanse of space. He grimaced sourly. There was danger up there beyond the ragged cloud-base. Somewhere high up, beyond his field of vision, he could hear the distant drone of aircraft. Enemy aircraft.

And Krause knew what enemy aircraft sounded like. A young boy from Essen in the industrial heartland of Germany, he had spent the last three years cowering in an air raid shelter on many occasions as that terrible drone had filled the night. And that monotonous drone brought only one thing in its wake; bombs.

He felt his heart pounding inside his chest, the terrible memories of those destructive onslaughts from above still fresh in his youthful mind. He shivered, and told himself it was because of the unusually chill night and earlier rain. He stood there for long moments, staring blankly up at the sky, until the drone began to fade. As the noise of engines drifted south-eastwards, the eighteen year old began to relax slightly. He was surprised to realise that he was holding his breath, so he let it out in a great sigh, which, he noted with some shame, was full of relief.

"Someone else's turn tonight…" He whispered to himself.

Lowering his gaze once more, he glanced sideways at the dark silhouette of the Café Gondree, which sat hard by the approach to the canal bridge. It would be hours until the place would be open, and Krause's stomach groaned at the thought of the delicious coffee and pastry that one could purchase there. The proprietors were not the friendliest bunch in the world, but they were French of course, so what could you expect? They were at least civil to their military neighbours in a coldly formal way, and their menu was first class. That was enough for Krause. All he wanted to do was keep as far away from the war as possible, and if the Fuhrer wanted him to hang around by some bridge in a remote part of France, drinking coffee and sampling the local delicacies, then that was fine. And of course he longed for a letter from his family. The poor souls were still stuck in Essen, having to endure the nightly bombing raids, whilst also worrying about their eldest son, Manfred's brother Georg, who was somewhere on the Russian front.

Somewhere in the distance, the sound of anti-aircraft fire began to thunder in the night. The enemy bombers had been spotted on their way to the target. Krause peered across the canal and through the blur of trees and scrub on the far bank and saw the dim red light that had begun to illuminate the distant horizon. He shrugged suddenly, deciding it was no use worrying if some other poor bastard was in for a packet. All was nice and quiet here by his little bridge in Normandy. He had just over an hour left on duty, and the war was far, far away…

LANCASTER F2-Z, 635 (PATHFINDER) SQUADRON – OVER OUISTREHAM, NORMANDY
MONDAY 5TH JUNE 1944 – 2355 HOURS

By their usual standards, this was a short and relatively simple operation. No lengthy flight across the North Sea, followed by running the gauntlet of flak across Belgium and Northern Germany, before then trying to avoid hordes of night-fighters on the return leg. This time it was pretty short and sweet. Fly due south-west to Southampton, turn south for France, cut the French coast at Le Havre, then follow the river as it meandered south and east until the newly erected engineer bridges were spotted. Then, it was simply a matter of marking the target by boxing it off on both banks, before turning east, then north, and running for home, leaving the main force to do their deadly work.

It was standard stuff for Hargreaves and his crew. They were an experienced bunch who had already done a complete tour of ops, before being selected to join the elite Pathfinder Force so that they could do another tour all over again. Some thought that was tempting fate; going to Pathfinders for a second tour of ops; but for Hargreaves and his men it was just something that needed to be done. They weren't going to win the war sitting in a training squadron.

Despite the relative simplicity of their task, Hargreaves and his crew knew that there was something a little different about this op. They'd hit targets in France before of course, especially of late, and despite terrible protests from Arthur Harris, the man who ran Bomber Command. But this one was different. They were being followed up by a main force of over fifty aircraft, all of which were to deposit their payloads inside the relatively small target box that the Pathfinder crews were to mark out with their incendiaries;

the ultimate aim being to either destroy the two new engineer bridges over the River Seine or else turn the approaches to those bridges into a moonscape that would be impassable to vehicles for days afterwards.

And then, at first light, an entire wing of Typhoons would descend on the target area in a third wave to make absolutely certain of the bridges themselves. To Hargreaves, this seemed to be the most clinical operation that had yet come their way; completely different to the massed carpet bombing of German industrial targets that was their bread and butter. It felt odd. The top brass were definitely up to something; that was for sure.

"Greens Skip'."

The bomb-aimer's voice cut in on Hargreaves' thoughts and he searched the darkness ahead at the prompt.

Sure enough, there they were, maybe ten miles distant. Unmistakable through the broken cloud, the green coloured target indicator incendiary bombs were lighting up the target area for all to see.

"Confirm that Skip'." The navigator cut in. "Three minutes to target."

"Hello Deputy One, this is Whitebait; my greens are on target, both sides of the bridges. Let's have your whole load five hundred plus. Deputy Two, drop yours five hundred minus as discussed. Watch out for a bit of light flak on the way in."

The Master Bomber's voice came into Hargreaves ears via the RT, confirming that the plan for dropping was unchanged.

Hargreaves didn't reply; the strict protocol being that nobody but the Master Bomber came on the air unless it was an absolute emergency. Instead, Hargreaves switched to the Lancaster's intercom. "Starting the run-in. Over to you bombs."

The bomb-aimer responded immediately.

"Roger Skip', left, left."

Hargreaves tweaked the controls and the Lancaster eased to port gently.

"Steady." Came the bomber-aimers voice. Then, "Open bomb-doors."

Hargreaves held the plane steady as he operated the lever for the bomb doors. The 'greens' were filling his field of vision now, lighting the target quite clearly; the river was a little over to their starboard. Their aircraft was responsible for marking the northern half of the target area. Another crew would mark the southern half. Two more Pathfinder aircraft would then stay on station with the Master Bomber whilst the main force pounded the target, ready to intervene in case of 'bomb creep'.

"Bomb doors open." A crew member in the belly of the aircraft confirmed.

The flak began. Heavy calibre, but not much of it. A small orange ball filled the night sky well over to their starboard momentarily, causing the heavy bomber to shudder a little. A few moments later, another explosion detonated to their port, somewhat closer, and the bomber rattled even more.

"Left, left, Skip'." The bomb-aimer's voice sounded over the intercom, quite calm.

"Steady."

A pause of several heartbeats, and it looked as though the green target indicators would soon be out of sight under the starboard wing.

"Right, Skip'"

Again, Hargreaves tweaked the controls with a light touch.

"Steady... On." The bomb-aimer's voice had developed a slight urgency now.

Another pause which seemed to go on for ever. Another explosion rocked the aircraft, but Hargreaves held it steady.

"Markers gone, Skip'" The bomb-aimers voice snapped with satisfaction.

Hargreaves held the plane on a steady course for a moment, allowing them to get beyond the target, before closing the bomb doors and executing a wide turn to port. He could hear the pounding of flak, and light filled the cockpit every few moments, but the explosions were well behind them now. As the heavy bomber came round in its graceful sweep, Hargreaves strained to look over at the target.

"How's it looking?" He asked over the intercom.

"Spot on, Skipper, by the looks of him." Came McWilliams' voice from the rear gun-turret.

As the bomber levelled out again, Hargreaves got a perfect view of the target area, and he grunted in satisfaction. The entire target was now sparkling with dozens of twinkling green lights on both sides of the river.

"Well done, Bombs, that was a cracking drop; absolutely wizard."

As Hargreaves congratulated his bomb-aimer, the voice of the Master Bomber crackled over the air-waves once more; this time his instructions intended for the three Lancaster and Halifax squadrons of the main force.

"All callsigns main, this is Whitebait; bomb on the greens, bomb on the greens."

A feeling of grim accomplishment settled on Hargreaves and his crew. Once again, the die was cast. Far below, dozens of green flares would be burning fiercely all across the target area, defying every effort of the Germans to extinguish them. And shortly, hundreds of tons of deadly high explosive would rain down on top of those marker flares, turning this designated patch of France into a living hell. This was the way of the bomber war. Harsh, business-like, uncompromising. Total war.

"Okay chaps; good work so far. Stay sharp on the way home. Nav', course please?"

PART TWO
ALARM

'THE CRUCIBLE' – NEAR CAEN, NORMANDY, FRANCE
TUESDAY 6TH JUNE 1944 – 0010 HOURS

G ritz had promised himself an early night. He'd spent the best part of
two weeks turning this rather shabby, non-descript wooded ridge into a
small fortress, and today's inspection by no less a person than the Corps
Commander had been a great success. Not only had General Marcks been
extremely impressed by the work that Gritz had done thus far, he had
promised the sergeant major additional stores and resources. Barbed
concertina wire would be forthcoming to supplement the single strand stuff
they'd been forced to use initially. Mines too, would come in due course;
both anti-tank and anti-personnel varieties. And of course, despite the
General's dire predictions about the enemy's intentions, the weather had
remain awful throughout the day, with wind and driving rain saturating the
lush green landscape of Normandy.

If ever there was a night on which to get a good sleep, tonight was the
one. Gritz had duly climbed into his cot at 2300 hours and had quickly settled
into a comfortable slumber, well wrapped up in a blanket and his greatcoat.

His cosy repose was interrupted suddenly, just after midnight.

"What the fuck is that?" The sergeant major demanded groggily as he sat
bolt upright at the sound of the enormous explosions.

He stared around the dim confines of the dug-out as he tried to clear his
sleep fuddled mind. The earth was shaking with feint tremors, and the noise
of the bombing sounded worryingly close.

Across the dug-out, Corporal Kole was staring up at the roof of their
subterranean shelter with concern as small specs of soil trickled through the
supporting wooden beams and planks. The telephone orderly looked across at
his commander.

"Sounds close, that does." He stated the obvious. "Heavy too."

A sudden streak of alarm shot through Gritz's mind. The cars! Someone
had seen the staff cars on the position that morning and realised that there
was something going on up here in the wood on Point 113. In one swift

movement, Gritz was out of bed and scrabbling for his boots. He was in them in seconds. As he stood and grabbed for his helmet and equipment, Gritz realised that he had omitted to fit his knee brace. No time now, he decided. Do it later.

"Ring the checkpoint." He ordered Kole. "Ask them what's going on. I'm going outside for a quick look."

With that, Gritz snatched up his machine pistol and hurried outside. Emerging from the dug-out and into the darkness outside, Gritz was surprised to find that he could actually see quite well. A strange ambient light seemed to glow through the trees, making it easy to pick out the line of the trench. He glanced to his right and saw some figures crowding together at the far end of the trench, close to the reserve squad's shelter. Quickly, he hurried towards them and pushed his way through to the far end of the trench.

"What's going on?" He demanded sharply, his mind still reeling to catch up with the sudden awakening.

Nobody replied at first. They were all too busy staring in awe at the sight that presented itself. In a heartbeat; Gritz understood why.

"They must have a thousand bombers up there somewhere…" One of the soldiers gasped to nobody in particular.

Gritz suspected that the young man wasn't far off the truth there, because as he looked out through the trees, the entire horizon to the east and south-east seemed to be on fire.

There were bright flashes and heart thumping detonations just a few miles to the north-east towards Ouistreham. Well beyond that, perhaps twenty kilometres away, Le Havre was getting a pounding again for a second night running. Even further east, somewhere that must be on the horizon, or even over it, was getting hammered too; the night sky flashing orange and yellow. But it was the scene just a couple of miles to the south that caught their main attention.

Lebisey ridge stretched out from left to right as they gazed southwards, whilst beyond the stark feature, the sky seemed to be playing host to some kind of amazing thunder and lightning storm. What was left of the thinning, scudding clouds was illuminated by the garish lights; orange, red, yellow and green, that filled the immediate horizon to the south. The explosions that were causing that sickly glow resounded with mind numbing sharpness in the night, whilst the ground beneath the rapt audience shuddered slightly with each fresh detonation.

"They're hitting Caen." Someone said bleakly.

"It's the bridges." Someone else suggested. "Or the station. That's what they're after."

At last, Gritz managed to shake himself out of his trance.

"It doesn't matter what they're after." He snapped irritably. "The point is the Tommies are up there looking for targets."

The old soldier jabbed his finger upwards.

"And if they spot us sitting here then we'll be the next ones getting a piece of that." This time he jerked his thumb towards Caen.

"So make sure you stay sharp tonight. No smoking. No fires. No cooking. Nothing at all that will give us away. Otherwise... it will be the last mistake any of us makes."

THE CAEN CANAL BRIDGE, NEAR BENOUVILLE, NORMANDY
TUESDAY 6TH JUNE 1944 – 0020 HOURS

Krause didn't like it. He didn't like it one bit. He'd thought the Tommy bombers were going somewhere else. Some of them had, but then more had come. Lots more. He stood there now, right where the bridge met the west bank of the Caen Canal, staring southwards along the waterway towards the ancient city, watching with a mixture of fascination and horror as the terrible noise of exploding bombs filled the night and incendiaries cast their sickly glow across the not too distant horizon.

This was the first time he'd been out and about during a raid. Even back home in Germany, when the bombs had come much closer, he had been well underground at the time. Standing here on the cobbles in the middle of the French countryside however, he felt a whole lot more vulnerable; for the bombing wasn't restricted to Caen. Behind him, up towards Ouistreham and Riva Bella, another raid was in progress, and he could hear the sound of distant explosions from a half a dozen separate directions, even though he couldn't see the flashes. It seemed to Krause that tonight, the Tommies had decided to flatten Normandy instead of Germany. No. he didn't like it one little bit. Especially as he still had over half an hour left on duty before he could go and hide in his bunker. That said, he doubted he'd sleep tonight. Not with all this going on.

He glanced down at his watch, and as he did so, a shadow of some kind seemed to pass over his upper field of vision. Startled, he looked up into the night sky with a sudden rush of fear. The terrible feeling stayed with him for a moment, but then faded just as quickly. Nothing there. He was just getting jumpy. He adjusted the rifle on his shoulder and took a deep breath. The war was coming too close for comfort and it was making Krause nervous. He needed to calm down. Just half an hour, he thought. Forty minutes at the most and you can get into cover and forget all about the war.

Crash!

Even above the background noise of the bombing, the sudden, unmistakable sound of something heavy hitting the ground on the far bank made Krause jump and physically cry out in alarm.

"What in the name of..." He swore into the night, gawping stupidly across the bridge and into the gloom.

His mind began to race. What the hell had just made that racket? A plane? Yes, of course! That would be it. An enemy bomber; shot down as it took part in the raid. It must have crash landed. Thank God it landed over the other side. A whole range of emotions flooded through Krause in rapid succession; from shock to fear, turning to curiosity and then to a hopeful sense of relief, all in just a few seconds. But then the fear returned. If it was an enemy bomber that had been shot down, then where were the flames? Shouldn't it be on fire or something?

He could hear voices. Concerned voices. Wary voices. German voices. He recognised them instantly. It was Romer and Sauer; friends of his. Both of them conscripts and both the same age as Krause; they were on duty over on the east bank of the canal.

"Helmut?" Krause shouted. "Erwin? What's going on? What was that bang?"

No answer.

"Hey lads; what the fuck was that noise?"

He heard his two friends gabbling to each other. They were talking in excited, nervous tones now, ignoring Krause's enquiry but debating something between themselves. He managed to pick out a word. *Glider*.

"Glider?" Krause repeated the word to himself.

The sound of running came to him; lots of feet in hobnailed boots, clattering on tarmac. Krause felt a terrible sense of dread descend on him and he began to slide the rifle off his shoulder. He heard Romer and Sauer again, shouting now, their voices getting closer. What were they shouting?

"Tommies!"

The realisation made Krause go light-headed. In an instant, all the energy seemed to drain from his body, his limbs feeling like lead weights of a sudden. A flare suddenly popped into life from the far end of the bridge and shot upwards through the spars of the metal structure. Flares, especially red flares, meant only one thing. Trouble.

As the flare hit a metal spar and began bouncing crazily from one to the other, Krause somehow managed to fumble his rifle into position so that he could make it ready. With trembling hands, his eyes still staring into the gloom across the bridge, he unlocked the bolt of his rifle, drew it fully to the rear, then slammed it forward and locked it again, forcing a live round into the chamber. The shouting had stopped now and all Krause could hear was the clatter of booted feet on tarmac. He was just about to shout for Romer and Sauer again when the world suddenly exploded in a blinding flash. Even though the grenade had exploded inside the pill-box at the other end of the bridge, the bright flash seemed to fill Krause's entire field of vision and he staggered back a couple of paces in shock.

"What the fuck?"

The night erupted with small arms fire. The sound of rifles and sub machine guns echoed between the nearby buildings and the first tracer rounds began flying in all directions. Krause stared in terror at the chaotic scene that had suddenly presented itself before him. He could see indistinct figures darting around at the far end of the bridge and there was shouting now in a language he didn't understand. Krause felt that he should do something like fire his weapon, but he didn't know who he was supposed to fire at. As a compromise, the terrified young sentry raised the rifle into his shoulder and aimed vaguely over the heads of the shadowy figures at the far end of the bridge and fired rather pointlessly into the air above them. For some reason it made him feel a little better.

Then the scene changed. Another explosion sounded; this one more muffled, as if it had gone off underground, and with a sickening rush of understanding, Krause realised that it was a grenade detonating inside one of the dug-outs where his comrades were sleeping. At the same time, those illusive figures at the far side of the bridge suddenly took on sharper, more distinctive form. They advanced towards him now, in a loose mass, their helmets adorned with camouflage netting and scrim, their faces blackened; strange looking weapons held at the ready as they raced towards the lone German sentry. Krause felt his bowels loosen.

It was just after midnight on the Sixth of June 1944... and the British were back in France.

LANCASTER F2-Z, 635 (PATHFINDER) SQUADRON – OVER THE ENGLISH CHANNEL
TUESDAY 6TH JUNE 1944 – 0025 HOURS

This was reckoning up to be one of their easiest, yet strangest jobs so far. They'd had a good run into the target and visibility had been fine, with much of the cloud being broken. They hadn't been required to stay over the target with the Master Bomber and so were able to make an early run back to England. And that run should be a relatively short one all being well. By Hargreaves' reckoning, they had cut the French coast somewhere near Dieppe.

It was hard to tell precisely, as the cloud was thicker over this section of the coast, but the desultory searching fire that reached up through the cloud far off to their starboard suggested they were passing reasonably close to a major flak concentration. That flak had now petered out and Hargreaves was just beginning to hope that the remainder of the sortie would be pretty uneventful. His greatest worry in fact, was that they might collide with another aircraft.

They had been warned at the briefing that there were a number of sizeable raids taking place over the same part of France that night, and as Hargreaves' Lancaster was at the head of a long, continuous stream, there was a chance that he might encounter a significant amount of friendly aircraft coming towards him on the return leg. They had taken as wide a dog-leg as was safe before turning back for England, but even so, the night sky could be a busy place these days. The days of a couple of dozen bombers making token raids over Berlin at the start of the war were long gone. When Bomber Command mounted an operation now, it measured its air power in hundreds; at least when it was operating against strategic rather than tactical targets anyway.

He clicked on the intercom and spoke.

"Nav', give her a quick burst, will you please?"

There was no need for any more conversation. They were a well drilled crew and Hargreaves knew that down inside the aircraft's fuselage, Murphy the navigator would be warming up the H2S Radar Set and giving their flight-path a quick sweep, just to confirm their course. It wouldn't stay on for long; that would be foolish. The Germans could detect the aircraft radar with their own counter-measures and the last thing Hargreaves and his crew wanted was a Jerry night-fighter being guided onto their tail.

After a short while, Murphy's voice came into the pilot's ear piece.

"Mid Channel, Skip'. Looks like we'll cut the English coast near Brighton."

Hargreaves absorbed the information gratefully.

"Thanks Nav'. Anything of note on the screen?"

There was a slight pause before the navigator replied.

"Yes Skip'. The screen's full of ships."

Hargreaves felt a strange squirm of excitement inside his stomach.

"Ships?"

"Yes Skip'. Thousands of 'em. The whole of the Channel is chock-a-block."

Silence. Nobody spoke. Nobody commented. They were far too professional a crew for that, even though the enormity of what they had just discovered during the radar sweep threatened to overwhelm the emotions of every man on board. Hargreaves felt a rising sense of exultation that he desperately tried to hide from his crew when he eventually spoke once more.

"Righto, Nav'. Switch her off. Let me have a course once we cut the coast. Stay sharp everyone…"

THE CAEN CANAL BRIDGE, NEAR BENOUVILLE, NORMANDY
TUESDAY 6TH JUNE 1944 – 0030 HOURS

"Leave him! Get off the bridge! Shoot anything that moves and grenade anything that looks like a bunker!"

Corporal Arthur Green of D Company, the 2nd Battalion Oxford and Buckinghamshire Light Infantry roared at the two men who had paused by the prostrate body of Lieutenant Brotheridge. The officer had gone sprawling to the floor after the last burst of gunfire.

If he'd stopped to think about it, Green would have been amazed that they'd made it this far. Their mission had been unbelievably bold; some had said suicidal. Their job had been to land their entire company right next to the bridges over the Caen Canal and Orne River using gliders, overwhelm the garrison before they knew what was happening, remove any demolition charges then hold the bridges at all costs until relieved by friendly troops. It all sounded so simple, yet many of the men in the company had expected to be massacred, even before the gliders had hit the ground.

Unbelievably, they appeared to have achieved complete surprise. Moreover, the pilot of their glider had managed to bring them to a stop within spitting distance of the canal bridge. It couldn't have been a more accurate landing and, even better, it seemed that the only Germans who had been awake were a few stunned and sleepy sentries. From that point, everything had happened so fast that Green hadn't had the time to think about it. The pill-box by the approach to the bridge had been destroyed with grenades. Other dug-outs and trenches had received the same treatment, and then been sprayed with small arms fire. Green's section, with Mr Brotheridge at their head, had rushed across the bridge itself.

There had been a single sentry standing in the middle of the road as they raced across the canal bridge. He'd let off maybe two or three hasty, ill-aimed shots at them before running for his life into the shadows of the village beyond. By now though, the enemy garrison was coming to life, and just as Green and his men reached the far bank, a clatter of sub machine gun fire and rifle shots erupted from both sides of the road, tearing into the British glider troops. Lieutenant Brotheridge had gone down heavily and was lying motionless, whilst another man was leaning against the superstructure of the bridge's walkway clutching his side. It was one of those moments when everything hung in the balance. They were over the bridge, but if momentum wasn't maintained and they were stopped here, the enemy would be able to drive them back easily, and the attack would fail.

"Let's go! Get into the bastards!" Green screamed aloud as he led his men off the bridge and into the darkness where the muzzle flashes of enemy soldiers lit up the night every few seconds.

He came off the metalled road and onto the soft grass of the verge. Somewhere just ahead, something dark and bulky sat in the middle of the meadow; squat and menacing. He ran towards it just as the occupants of the sandbagged position opened fire. The crack of bullets sounded close by Green's left ear, but he kept running; straight for the position. As he went, he raised his Sten Gun to chest height and let off a short burst. The skeletal little sub machine gun rattled in his hands as the 9mm bullets spat towards the enemy, and above the racket, he heard a British voice shout out a warning.

"Grenade!"

Instinctively, Green dropped to his knees and curled up into a ball. Just a moment later, he felt the ground tremble beneath him, registered the bright flash, and then the shock wave and noise of the blast washed over him. Glancing up he saw, even in the darkness, the thick cloud of dirty smoke wreathing the enemy position where a No.36 grenade had landed either close to it, or directly on it. There was the thud of booted feet to his left and he saw one of his men spring up from the ground nearby and lurch forward towards the temporarily suppressed enemy bunker. *Good lad*, Green thought.

He launched himself upwards and onwards, hard on the heels of the private soldier.

"You go left!" Green shouted after him. "I'll go right!"

Whether the man heard or not wasn't easy to tell, yet regardless, the man did what was needed and swung around to the left of the sandbagged redoubt. He got there a couple of seconds before Green and the British soldier's Lee-Enfield barked loudly. Green heard the soldier working the bolt of the rifle and then fire again. There came the sound of terrified cries from within the bunker, but Green was there now, skirting around to the right hand side. He didn't waste time. He threw himself against the sandbag wall and poked the muzzle of his Sten Gun over the lip of the parapet and operated the trigger.

The weapon jerked into life with a metallic clatter and a dull thud, thud, thud. As he emptied the remaining rounds in the magazine, Green swept the sub machine gun left to right and back again, allowing the bullets to search into every corner of the bunker.

"I'm going in!"

The other soldier was shouting across to Green, warning him to be careful where he was shooting.

"Magazine!" Green yelled back, signalling to the soldier that he was clear to enter the enemy position.

The British private ran through the L-shaped entry point, his rifle pointing at the ground, and he quickly ferreted through the small redoubt, checking for any surviving enemy. No shots sounded, but after a couple of moments, as Green rammed another magazine into the side of his weapon, he heard the soldier make a comment under his breath.

"Fuck me! What a bloody mess!"

Green cocked the Sten Gun.

"Back in! Is it clear?"

"All clear!" The private shouted back. "They're all as dead as fuck!"

Green took a deep breath.

"Stay in there and keep your eyes peeled for depth positions."

The corporal turned and looked back towards the bridge. Tracer rounds streaked back and forth in all directions but, reassuringly, he could see two more of his men coming across the grass to join him. Beyond them, more than a dozen more figures in the baggy parachute smocks unique to the British airborne forces were pounding off the bridge and onto the near bank to join them. Then he noticed several more of their men crouching by the Café at the far side of the road. That meant there must be at least one other glider that had made it, as well as their own.

"Christ almighty!" He took another great gulp of breath. "We've gone and bloody done it!"

HEADQUARTERS 125TH PANZER GRENADIER REGIMENT – BELLENGREVILLE, NEAR CAEN, NORMANDY TUESDAY 6TH JUNE 1944 – 0035 HOURS

Major Hans von Luck, the new commander of the 125th Panzer Grenadiers, stubbed out his cigarette and glanced up at the ceiling of the old cottage at the sound of another wave of bombers passing overhead. The bombing had been going on for over forty minutes now, although thankfully the Tommies seemed to be going for some of the bigger strategic targets in the area. The dispersed billets of his grenadiers in the dozen or so villages east of the River Orne and west of the River Dives were conveniently unassuming, and so his men should be safe enough, leaving aside stray bombs of course.

That said, Fifth Company were out on a night training exercise and were not back in yet, and von Luck was concerned that they might get caught by a random bomb overshooting its target. He worried about that only slightly, but then told himself that the likelihood of that happening was about the same as being struck by lightning whilst out walking in a thunderstorm. He was sure they would be fine. Besides, they needed the training, and the background noise of bombing in nearby Caen would give the greener troops in the company just a little taste of what a real battle sounded like.

He dismissed Fifth Company from his thoughts and returned to the dull yet important task of looking through the combat power returns from each of his units. The regiment, like the rest of its parent division, the 21st Panzer, was just a shadow of its former self. The original division had been surrendered to the Allies when North Africa fell and this replacement was a hastily thrown together and under equipped substitute. There were *some* veterans in it, and by and large the morale of the troops seemed as good as any these days, but von Luck knew only too well how long it took to train armoured troops up to a high standard, even when you had all the equipment you needed... And the 21st Panzer Division didn't have half of what it needed.

Still, the poor weather had made the possibility of an Allied invasion a remote chance on this wet, windy, June evening, and thus it gave von Luck a chance to give some of his men a run-out in darkness so they could practice their infantry skills and minor tactics. God only knew, training time was in as short supply as equipment. Most of the days of late had been spent hammering anti-glider posts into the local fields, or as the troops had begun to refer to the work, 'planting Rommel's asparagus'. He decided that once he had checked on the equipment state of his regiment he would get to work on preparing some more field exercises for his men. He would have to *find* the time to train them. *If*, or rather *when* the Allies came, there would be no time for last minute practice. Battles tended to appear out of nowhere, and the enemy never gave you time to sort your act out. If you weren't ready, you were dead.

The Regimental Commander's thoughts were interrupted by the roar of yet more aircraft; this time passing very low overhead. Ensuring that the lamp was turned off first, von Luck rose from his seat and walked across to the window. He drew aside the heavy black-out curtain and peered into the dark night. Why are those aircraft flying so low, he wondered? Is it the weather? Are they having problems with the cloud-base?

The major was still wondering this when he registered the scene outside. His quarters were on the edge of the village with a clear view north-west, through to north-east, and von Luck blinked in surprise at what he now saw in the darkness. Hanging in the night sky across a broad frontage were flares. Some of them were parachute flares, the kind dropped by aircraft, but he saw at least one signal flare arc across the dark canvass of night, and that was followed by the unmistakable bright snake of tracer. As his soldier's sixth sense began to tingle, the telephone rang, making him start.

Quickly, he turned and crossed the room to where the telephone sat on a small table. He grabbed the handset and answered brusquely.

"Major von Luck."

The voice of his adjutant, Lieutenant Liebeskind, sounded in the ear-piece; serious in tone and with an edge of urgency.

"Major, something is going on."

"Going on? *What* is going on?"

"Paratroopers, Sir." The adjutant replied bluntly. "They're dropping all over the place; we've had reports from several locations. Gliders have landed too. And there are reports of fire-fights breaking out in the area around Escoville."

The major's mind immediately kicked into gear.

"Have you had a situation report from the Second Battalion? Is the Fifth Company back in yet? They're wandering around out there with blank ammunition. How much of this is fact and how much is guess-work?"

Liebeskind had the information to hand.

"The reports have come from the Second Battalion, Sir. Several of their outposts have been attacked and one of the gliders crashed near to their headquarters. They are assembling for a clearance of Troarn, which seems to be the centre of activity at the moment."

Quickly, von Luck brought the map of the local area up in his mind's eye. Troarn... where a bridge crossed the River Dives... That fact alone was enough to make these reports alarming.

"Right, Liebeskind; ring the Second Battalion and tell them to conduct a wide clearance of their battalion area immediately and attack any enemy within boundaries. I want Troarn secured as soon as possible, including the bridge. Tell them I want prisoners, and get them sent to our command post straight away. Oh, and tell the Second Battalion to find out where the Fifth Company are and get them pulled back in. We don't want those poor bastards stuck in the middle of a battle with blank ammunition!"

"Yes, Major." The adjutant responded.

"I'm on my way to the command post." von Luck continued. "I'll be there in a couple of minutes."

He slammed the telephone down and looked across the darkened room to where the curtain still hung to one side of the window. Outside, the flares continued to fall, and another line of tracer wove its way across the dark panorama in the far distance.

"Shit." Von Luck murmured to himself. "It's begun."

THE MAIN STREET OF LE PORT – CLOSE TO THE CAEN CANAL BRIDGE
TUESDAY 6TH OF JUNE 1944 – 0040 HOURS

"Halt! Halt! Who the fuck's that?"

With a mix of relief and fear, Krause stumbled to an abrupt stop and held his arms wide as the fierce voice challenged him in German.

"Don't shoot!" He babbled, gulping for breath after his mad dash from the bridge. "I'm German! Don't shoot! I'm Krause... from the bridge... I was on sentry..."

"Don't move!" The voice from the shadows in the alleyway snapped. "And keep your arms out wide!"

Krause did as he was told and stood there, his chest heaving, as first one, then another two dark figures emerged from cover and came towards him cautiously. Even in the pitch black of the alley, Krause could see they all had weapons of some kind pointing right at him.

"Please don't shoot?" The young private murmured.

"Shut up!" The voice snapped again.

Moments later, a fierce looking face came close to Krause's, the owner prodding the young soldier's belly with the muzzle of a machine-pistol, as if to warn him not to try anything stupid. Krause stared back at the man and noted with some relief that he was wearing a German helmet. Come to think of it, Krause thought the man looked familiar. Behind the suspicious owner of the MP40, the other two shadowy figures had their rifles pointing menacingly in Krause's direction.

"Who did you say you were?" The man with the MP40 demanded.

"Krause... Private Krause... from the bridge."

The man with the machine-pistol grunted; a strange noise, and one that gave no clue as to whether he believed Krause or not.

"Two platoon boy, then?"

"Yes!" Krause assured the man quickly. "Yes, I'm from Two Platoon; the bridge garrison."

There was a long moment of silence as the man continued to study Krause through the gloom.

"What the fuck's going on at the bridge then?" He demanded at last.

Krause let it all out. In no particular order, he blurted out the story of the strange bang, the sound of his fellow sentries shouting about gliders, the explosion that had rocked the pill-box, and then about the stream of dark-faced, grim looking Tommies who had charged across the bridge at him. So relieved was Krause to be among friendly troops, that he had no qualms about explaining how he had run from those terrifying men after firing just a few random shots.

The man with the MP40 weighed up the young soldier's words for a moment, before twisting around to look at his companions. As he did so, Krause noticed the man had a corporal's badge of rank on the sleeve of his greatcoat.

"The Lieutenant was right then." The corporal said to the other two. "It is a commando raid."

He turned back to Krause and removed the muzzle of his weapon from the young man's belly.

"Put your arms down lad."

Krause did exactly as he was told, glad to have someone giving him orders at last.

"I'm Corporal Lang from First Platoon. The Lieutenant's getting the rest of the platoon together and contacting the Battalion Commander to arrange support. My squad are going down to the bridge to see what's going on. You're in my squad now and you can come with us."

Krause immediately felt his stomach knot up again.

"Back there, Corporal? But there are Tommies everywhere! Loads of them!"

Lang's face remained impassive.

"Good. Well at least we're going to the right place to kill a few then."

IN A STIRLING BOMBER – SOMEWHERE OVER NORMANDY
TUESDAY 6TH OF JUNE 1944 – 0045 HOURS

Dawes was not enjoying the experience of the run-in to his first battle since Dunkirk. The Stirling bomber, which was tonight carrying men instead of high-explosive, was being thrown about mercilessly by the shock waves of the explosions from the numerous anti aircraft guns that lined the Normandy coast. All he wanted to do now was jump. He wanted to be out, down, and on the ground, somewhere in the dark with his Sten Gun in his hand. At least then he would feel like he was in control of his own destiny. Up here, he was just a sitting duck; a heavily laden one, stuck inside a huge ungainly aircraft that any minute now must surely be hit, and erupt in a ball of flame.

"Two minutes! Stand-by!"

The voice of the aircraft's loadmaster sounded above the roar of the four powerful engines and the dull crump of explosions. The aircraft door was open now and the air came whistling into the fuselage, adding to the deafening cacophony of war. As Dawes stood there, hanging onto the aircraft's frame to steady himself, the RAF loadmaster came struggling along the line of paratroopers, double checking the static lines of their rip-cords as he went.

"One minute!"

The aircraft shook as another explosion rent the night air nearby.

"I wish I hadn't volunteered for this now." The man in front of him shouted over his shoulder at Dawes..

"Too bloody late for that now, big lad!" Dawes answered and gave the soldier a reassuring pat on the arm.

The truth was, as much as Dawes wanted to be out of the plane, he too was starting to wonder what was awaiting them on the ground. Now that the moment of truth had arrived, the prospect of the impending battle seemed suddenly unattractive.

But it was too late to worry indeed, because just as those thoughts were starting to go through Dawes' mind, the loadmaster called out another warning.

"Stand-by, stand-by…"

"Shit." Dawes cursed under his breath.

"Go! Go! Go!"

The loadmaster screamed out the order to jump and there was a sudden, inexorable pressure on Dawes' back as the men behind him leaned forward in anticipation. The extra weight gave momentum to the forward pressure of every man in the queue and suddenly, like a runaway train, the paratroopers were staggering forwards with their burdens towards the door of the aircraft.

Even if a man wanted to change his mind now, there was no going back. The force of those pushing from behind was too much and one after another, each soldier was pushed out of the door, disappearing into the aircraft's slipstream immediately. Just to make sure, the air dispatcher stood by the doorway pushing the men sideways out of the aircraft in order to avoid a sudden pile up by the exit. Dawes was stumbling forwards now, his heart hammering; the black hole of the door looming ever closer. Suddenly, the man in front of him disappeared sideways out of the aircraft and Dawes found himself stepping onto the precipice of a nightmare scene. He vaguely noted fires and explosions and flares and tracer rounds, all of which illuminated momentarily the ground below like a vision of hell. Then the dispatcher was shoving him in the shoulder and he was tumbling out into nothingness.

"Fuck..."

As always, there were those first few moments of sheer terror, where one felt as if they were dropping like a stone; plummeting to earth with no means of slowing down. Then, suddenly, came the gut-wrenching jerk as the parachute deployed and the deadly freefall was arrested by the hundreds of cubic feet of invisible, yet highly buoyant air that filled the parachute silk and allowed a man to drift gently down to the ground in a more controlled fashion; and one that wouldn't normally kill him outright. And as ever, Dawes found that he was gasping for breath like a drowning man; his breaths coming in huge, rapid sobs.

He quickly went through the checks; following the drill to make sure his parachute had deployed properly. All okay with the canvas. Next he needed to release his leg bag containing his weapon. Quickly, he fumbled for the release strap, his fingers working urgently. If he landed with the leg bag still strapped to him he would probably break a leg, or even a hip. The oft-practiced routine seemed so much more difficult this time, but within a few moments he had released the strap and he felt the bag drop. As it reached the end of its strap, his whole body jerked in the harness momentarily. All done. That was the complicated bit sorted. He looked up and scanned around to get his bearings. He was higher than he thought he should be, although he could see the pale blobs of other parachutes spread out in the distance.

Something roared menacingly not too far away and Dawes twisted round in his harness to see what it was... and froze. To his horror, he found himself looking straight into the cockpit of an approaching aircraft. He had no idea what kind of aircraft it was and he didn't really care. All he could see were the four big propellers, two on each wing, spinning at unbelievable speed as the monstrous machine loomed out of the dark like some prehistoric monster coming to snap him in its jaws. He had no more than a split second of time in which he realised he was going to die, before the aircraft was on top of him. He cried out in terror as the huge aircraft filled his vision and the sound of its engines penetrated right to the very depths of his soul. He screwed his eyes up and emitted a terrible, childlike wail of anguish as the noise of those deadly propellers washed over him. He felt a sudden displacement of surprisingly warm air around him, and his parachute canvas seemed to buck and swirl for a moment or two, and then as soon as it had come, the noise disappeared.

For a moment, Dawes kept his eyes screwed shut as he hung there, sobbing openly. After a few more seconds, he registered the distant sounds of gunfire and explosions, and the realisation that he wasn't dead washed over him. He opened his eyes, terrified that he might see another aircraft coming for him. Instead, all he could see was dark night sky, the occasional white smear of another parachute, and dozens of tiny pin-pricks of light on the ground where fires blazed, or guns flashed angrily. Amazed that he wasn't dead, the corporal let out a groan of utter relief and drank in the sights around him.

As quickly as he had welcomed the sense of relief, he once more had to dismiss it when he saw that the ground was approaching rapidly. It was hard to judge in the dark, but he reckoned he must be at two hundred feet or less. He instinctively brought his body into the correct position for landing and stared intently at the solid black ground beneath him. He noticed the top of a tree loom up to his right and realised he was about to touch down. There was a light thud, which Dawes understood must be his leg bag hitting the ground, and he braced himself for impact.

"Uurgh!"

He hit the ground hard; so hard that he bent double and smashed his chin off his knees as he rolled over, biting his lip in the process. As he rolled over, winded, he felt the salty taste of blood in his mouth. His body rolled against something soft, yet bulky and he came to a stop, his canopy collapsing gently on top of him.

For long moments, Dawes just lay there, flat on his back in the deep furrow of a ploughed field, taking the time to catch his breath and compose himself. His muscles were twitching all over his body, and he felt like he needed to shit. In fact he was terrified that he would do so there and then, and so made a great effort to clench his buttocks tightly until the sensation eased. The touch of the parachute silk on his face was soft and reassuring, and he felt as though he could lay there all night, and just let the world pass him by. The sound of small arms fire sounded somewhere in the far distance; at least a mile away. It was enough to bring his mind back into sharp focus.

With a sudden urgent burst of energy, Dawes sat up and scrabbled around to pull the parachute off his face. He got there after something of a struggle and used his clasp knife to cut himself free. He would remove the harness itself later, when he had a moment. He needed to get clear of the parachute first and arm himself. He was no use at all without a weapon. Struggling to his feet, Dawes stepped away from the parachute silk and hauled on the strap that hung down from his harness. The leg bag duly emerged from beneath the parachute, and the corporal quickly unclipped the whole apparatus before opening the canvas valise of the bag itself. Inside, just as he'd left it, was his Sten Gun and two Gammon Bombs, along with an additional bandolier of 9mm ammunition. Working quickly, Dawes assembled the Sten Gun and fitted a magazine, then stowed the Gammon Bombs into his equipment and slung the bandolier over his head and shoulders.

"Who's that?"

The sudden query made Dawes jump with renewed alarm. Clumsily, he swung around, falling sideways as he did so, and attempted to get his Sten Gun into a decent fire position.

"Who is it?" The voice came again.

Dawes stared upwards and caught the silhouette of a lone figure, half standing, half crouching, just a few yards away. The accent was an unusual one; Brummy. A man from the Birmingham area.

"It's Corporal Dawes, from 'C' Company."

The Brummy voice turned suspicious.

"I'm in 'C' Company and I don't know any Corporal Dawes."

Dawes felt a flicker of irritation.

"Well my name is Dawes alright, and the last time I checked, I was in 'C' Company, 13 Para. Who the fuck are you?"

"13 Para?" The Brummy voice queried, sounding confused. "What the fuck are you doing here? This is supposed to be a 9 Para DZ."

"What do you think I'm doing here? Some fucking RAF bloke pushed me out of a plane with another twenty blokes. Now, *who* the fuck are you?"

There was the slightest hesitation before the voice replied.

"Private Ron Gilbert, 'C' Company, 9 Para. I can't find anyone from my stick."

The man's voice had lost its cautious and slightly aggressive tone now, and had developed a note of helplessness.

Dawes pushed himself up into a kneeling position as the Brummy soldier took a couple of steps closer and dropped to one knee in front of the NCO.

"Well, that doesn't surprise me." Dawes grunted as he struggled up. "It looks to me like the drop has gone to rat shit. My stick got dropped high and I nearly got chewed up by one of our own bloody planes!"

He leaned towards the other man and made out his blackened face. The man's eyes seemed to be bulging out of their sockets in the darkness.

"Are you alright?"

"I'm not injured Corp' if that's what you mean?"

"You got a weapon?"

Private Gilbert held up his hand and showed the corporal his Lee Enfield.

"Got my rifle and a few grenades; two bandoliers of ammo as well."

Dawes took a deep breath.

"Right then, Gilbert lad, let's go see if we can find anyone else. Then we'd better go and find out where the fuck we are. We've got a battle to get to…"

THE MAIN STREET OF LE PORT – CLOSE TO THE CAEN CANAL BRIDGE
TUESDAY 6TH OF JUNE 1944 – 0050 HOURS

The area around the end of the village and the approaches to the bridge were eerily quiet; if one allowed for the constant background noise of bombing and anti-aircraft fire that seemed to be going on across the whole of the region. Other than that however, there was little sign of the sudden, terrible and very short battle that had taken place a little further down the road less than half an hour before.

Up in front, Corporal Lang came to a halt and held up his hand as a signal for the rest of his men to do likewise. There were a total of ten of them, including Krause, who now stood in a half crouch, just a metre or two behind Lang. He flexed his fingers nervously around the stock of his rifle and peered at the dim outline of Lang, as the non commissioned officer scanned the darkness beyond the last house in the village. After a moment or two, the corporal turned towards Krause and beckoned him closer. Obediently, the young soldier shuffled up beside his new commander.

"Are you sure they actually came over the bridge?" Lang whispered in Krause's ear. "It's looking very quiet over there now."

Krause strained his eyes into the night to try and pick out any detail he could. The bridge was obvious enough, its box-like girder superstructure standing stark and black against the backdrop of a night sky lit by flares and distant flame. To the right of the bridge, the dim shapes of the houses in Benouville could be seen, similarly highlighted by the bombing in Caen beyond. Other than that, the area seemed to be empty.

"Positive, Corporal." Krause replied. "There must have been ten of them at least. They came running right across the bridge at me, firing their guns. They all had black faces."

The corporal absorbed the information silently, continuing to search the darkness ahead. At last, he spoke.

"Well, if they're still there, they'll have gone to ground maybe. There again, maybe they've landed in the wrong place and moved off? There target could be somewhere else?"

Krause listened as Lang went through the possible options, but made no comment, feeling neither experienced nor brave enough to voice an opinion. In truth, he didn't have a clue what was going on. It was all so very confusing; not what he'd imagined a battle to be like. The corporal didn't seem overly flustered however. He was obviously used to this kind of thing; an old hand.

The sound of urgent whispers and the shuffling of feet made Lang and Krause turn together and look back towards the rest of the squad, where they were strung out in single file against the row of houses. The figure of one of their comrades loomed up behind them from the cover of a nearby alleyway.

"Corporal Lang? Corporal Lang?" The man was hissing, a nervous edge to his voice.

"What is it?" The corporal demanded.

"There's somebody behind this house!" The soldier whispered back.

Immediately, Krause's pulse began to pick up.

"Are you sure?" Lang asked, his own voice developing an edge of its own.

"Positive; we can hear people talking and moving around. No mistake. There's at least two of them."

Lang was silent for a moment, assessing this latest piece of information. In that brief moment of quiet, they heard the English voice shouting. It wasn't that close by; probably a good hundred metres away or more, back towards the bridge, yet unmistakable all the same. Immediately, Lang looked directly at Krause.

"Did you hear that?"

"Yes." Krause replied through cracked lips, his voice barely audible.

"The bastards are still here!" Lang stated the obvious.

The corporal made his decision.

"Krause, you stay here and keep your eyes peeled down this road and across the open ground. Shout out if anything comes our way. I'll take a couple of lads round the back and find out who the fuck is hiding there."

Without further ado, Lang pushed past Krause and grabbed the other young soldier by his sleeve.

"Come on; show me where you heard these voices."

The corporal and the other man disappeared back into the shadows cast by the row of cottages.

Turning back to stare across the field towards the bridge, Krause felt suddenly alone again. What if those black-faced soldiers suddenly appeared once more, right in front of him? What should he do once he'd shouted out a warning? Run again? Shoot? Surrender maybe? He heard another distant shout from the direction of the bridge; once again in English. The sound of the voice made his blood run cold. Suddenly he wished he was back home. At least the bombing was something that could be hidden from to a certain degree. But this? British commandos chasing after you in the darkness? This was terrifying.

Krause was snapped out of his thoughts by the sudden shout of alarm from somewhere behind him. He whipped his head round as the first voice was joined by another, and his blood ran cold when he realised that the two voices were distinctly different. One was fairly familiar; that of Corporal Lang, shouting a challenge in German. The other voice was unintelligible, other than that it was most definitely English. And then the firing began.

Krause physically flinched as the crash of small arms fire suddenly erupted from around the side of the house. Flashes of light created moments of fleeting illumination by the entrance to the nearby alleyway, so that Krause could see disjointed images of the other squad members racing in several directions, nervous faces shouting God knew what above the cacophony of gunfire. The young private soldier pushed himself upright, although his legs suddenly felt as if they wouldn't support him. He looked back towards the bridge and saw nothing. He looked down this side of the house and saw nothing. He flicked off the safety catch of his rifle and took a few tentative steps back towards the mouth of the alley where several other men were peering down it, their weapons at the ready.

Suddenly, a press of men burst out of the alley, spreading left and right, a look of shock on their faces. They were all German, and Corporal Lang was among them.

"Get some fire down!" He was screaming at nobody in particular. "Spray that fucking alleyway!"

Immediately, several members of the squad began to discharge their weapons at unseen targets somewhere towards the rear of the building.

"Krause?"

Krause saw the corporal whirl around, looking for him amongst the sudden chaos.

"Watch that front corner! There's a whole load of fucking Tommies round the back!"

"Wha…"

Krause never had time to finish the sentence.

He had vaguely registered the bang above his head as a set of window shutters were forced open, yet thought nothing of it. He had also recognised the unmistakable sound of shattering glass, right above him, yet was still surprised when shards of the broken window began tinkling onto his helmet and the cobbles around him. His main focus of surprise was the small spherical object that dropped from above in the wake of the glass shower, and landed with a heavy thud on the cobbles just a couple of metres away, right between himself and Corporal Lang.

The private stared stupidly at the tiny dark object on the cobbles as the world around him was filled with shouting and gunfire. Amazingly, he heard one recognisable word amongst the racket of voices and gunfire, which cut through his dislocation to ring the alarm bell inside his mind with dread urgency.

"Grenade!"

SOMEWHERE IN NORMANDY
TUESDAY 6TH JUNE 1944 – 0055 HOURS

"So where the fuck are we, then?"

The question, delivered by the Lance Corporal named Harvey, was the same one that was on the lips of every man in that tight little circle.

There were twelve of them. Dawes and Gilbert, having gathered their own equipment, had staggered across the rough plough of the field in which they had landed, looking for some kind of landmark or a sign of friendly troops. In a short space of time, they had gathered together this little collection of men, although no officers had been amongst the gaggle of paratroopers. Thus, Dawes and Lance Corporal Harvey who, like Gilbert, was also from 9 Para, had found themselves in charge of a mixed bunch of paratroopers from different battalions and different companies, all of whom had different missions, and none of whom knew where on earth they had been dropped.

"We'll have to go and find out." Dawes replied, forcing his mind to think logically, and putting to the back of it the terrifying memory of his parachute jump. "We must be somewhere to the east of the high ground where the brigade is supposed to be digging in. Just looking around, you can see where the ground slopes away. I'd like to bet that's dropping away into the Dives valley. So, what we need to do is head uphill, and try to find a road. The high ground will give us a better view and a road will help us to fix a precise point on the map. We'll stick together until we know where we are. After that... Well, we'll just have to call it when we know more. Everyone happy enough?"

There was a murmur of assent.

"Okay, shake out into single file. Don't bunch up too closely, but don't lose sight of the bloke in front either. Harv', you bring up the rear. And just a reminder; don't start shooting at anything unless I tell you. We've all been given jobs to do. We need to find our own units as quickly as possible and get on with our own missions. Let's not start our own private war."

Nodding their understanding, the highly trained paratroopers shook out into formation.

As Dawes took the lead and began plodding slowly uphill, he reflected on the state of his own little force. Even if they did get into a scrap, they couldn't do that much good. Between them they mustered three Sten Guns and nine rifles, two dozen No.36 Grenades and a dozen smoke grenades, along with eight Gammon Bombs, although they were actually of little use without the plastic explosive that came separately in the heavy weapons containers. On top of all this, Dawes wasn't a hundred percent confident they would all be able to find their proper units in time to take part in the pre-planned operations anyway.

He checked himself mentally. Don't start giving up yet, Jack lad. You remember this from 1940. Battle is never a straight forward business. Always lots of noise, lots of confusion; lots of things happening that aren't supposed to happen. Stick with it, stay focussed.

He became exceptionally focussed when he found the dead soldier. The man was a paratrooper, like them; still rigged up in his harness, and curled up alongside a thick wooden post that had been driven into the ground so that it stood the height of a man. Dawes inspected the man's body quickly and saw no sign of bullet wounds or trauma, and surmised that the poor bugger had broken his neck on landing. Perhaps he'd slammed into this ruddy great post? The corporal frowned at the post for a moment, wondering why on earth it had been placed here in such a random spot, but then suddenly realised that he must be looking at one of the anti-glider posts that the intelligence boys had warned of.

With a sigh of resignation, Dawes called his men forward and they quickly stripped the dead soldier of everything useful, before shaking out and moving off once more. They hadn't got very far, maybe three hundred yards, when another great white blob in the darkness betrayed the presence of another parachute. This time however, their discovery was much more welcome.

A drop-canister; one of those cylindrical metal containers in which the heavier weapons and additional stores were dropped. Now that was more like it. Quickly, Dawes closed up his ad hoc force once more and placed them out in a wide circle around the container to give all-round defence, whilst he and Harvey broke into the green metal pod.

"Please tell me it hasn't just got a bloody fold-away bike in it?" Harvey murmured as they popped the catches and threw the lid open.

It didn't. Rather more usefully, the container boasted a PIAT, or Projector Infantry Anti Tank to give the weapon its full designation. The PIAT was a fairly weighty, yet man portable anti-tank weapon that gave the infantry platoon its own bite against armoured vehicles. The only downside was that you had to wait for the said vehicle to get within a hundred yards before you had a chance of hitting the thing at all, but beggars can't be choosers, and so Dawes was delighted to come across the bulky piece of weaponry. Even more usefully, the container also held a pair of bombs for the projector, and even better, a dozen sticks of high explosive for use with Gammon Bombs. On top of all that, they also found another five bandoliers of .303 inch ammunition. At last, something seemed to be going Dawes' way tonight.

The corporal was busy distributing the latest additions to his group's armoury when the sound of the vehicle came to him above the rumble of distant explosions. Instinctively he froze.

"Car!" Gilbert commented unnecessarily, as he slung the PIAT across his shoulder.

"Down!" Hissed Dawes, waving his arm franticly at the men who had closed in to collect ammunition from the container.

The little group of paratroopers threw themselves to the ground, weapons at the ready, faces pressed into the soil, hardly daring to look up. Moments later, the dark blob of a car came into view on the horizon not a hundred yards away.

"Shit!" Dawes heard someone comment.

As the corporal followed the outline of the vehicle, he saw that it was driving with hooded lights on, and the feint beam of yellowish light semi-illuminated the way ahead. In that light, Dawes spotted the hedgerow which ran across his field of view, and moments later, the car was hidden behind it. The noise of the vehicle grew even louder and it was clear that the car was on a metalled surface and not moving across country, its driver pushing it along with some speed. The group of paratroopers watched with disbelief as the car came right past them, barely fifty yards away.

"Bloody hell!" Dawes cursed quietly to himself. "We're right next to a bloody road!"

The sound of the car's engine changed suddenly, and Dawes recognised the tone of the engine shifting gear. There was a brief, final, flash of the headlamps on the vehicle before it turned a corner and began speeding away from the paratroopers down some other, unseen road. And in that final flash of light, as minimal as it had been, Dawes had spotted something that made his heart leap with hope. A road sign.

As the hum of the vehicle receded and was finally swallowed up in the background noise of bombing, Dawes leapt to his feet and hissed through the darkness.

"Harv'? Harv?"

The lance corporal appeared out of the darkness.

"Ruddy hell, Jack; that was a bit close! We're right next to a bloody road, mate!"

"I know." Replied Dawes excitedly. "And guess what? There's a junction over there with a sign on it."

Harvey frowned through the darkness.

"You what? Surely the Jerries aren't daft enough to leave the bloody road signs up for us?"

Dawes shrugged.

"We'll soon find out."

Leaving their men to finish off stowing their new weapons and ammunition, the two NCOs doubled forward to the hedgerow and approached the junction carefully. It took them a few moments to find a gap in the thick foliage, but they found one nevertheless and carefully slid over the dry-stone wall that reinforced the bushes. There they found a road alright. A pretty wide road at that, with a Y-shaped junction that allowed a slightly narrower road to branch off at an angle. For long moments, the two men sat there and scanned the area.

Everything was quiet, although from this vantage point they found that they suddenly had a surprisingly good view for miles around. They were on the top of a wide flat ridge of some kind. Far off in the distance they could see fires. Lots of fires. Some were small, whilst others appeared to be raging infernos that turned the night sky a warm orange and red colour. One such blaze appeared to be in the centre of a built up area, not very far away from their current position. And there, right next to the junction, they found the road sign.

In moments, they were standing by it, reading the words that had been carved into the wooden boards and highlighted with white paint. One of the boards bore the name *Caen* and next to it was a number four, suggesting a distance to that place of four kilometres. Another board pointed in the opposite direction and carried the legend *Troarn 7*, while the third board pointed off towards the smaller road and was inscribed *Ranville 5*.

"You've got to be kidding me?" Harvey breathed in disbelief. "They really have left the bloody signs up! Do you think it might be a trick though?"

Dawes sucked his teeth.

"Only one way to find out. We need to check the map."

The corporal went for the map that was stuffed into his smock, and as he did so, Harvey pointed into the darkness.

"What's that over there? Looks like a wood, maybe?"

Dawes followed the indication and used his peripheral vision to try and pick out some detail. Sure enough, not too far away, perhaps three hundred yards at the most, a wide dark scar ran across the gloomy landscape.

"Yes mate. Definitely trees. Not sure if it's a wood or a tree line though. And there's a village beyond it. Not to mention a bigger place beyond; the one that's on fire."

Together, the two men lay flat on the grass verge and peered at the map using Dawes's torch, which they shielded with their hands. After just a quick inspection, everything suddenly made sense.

"Bollocks." Harvey cursed.

Dawes looked up at him.

"What's the matter?"

Harvey looked grim.

"We're fucking miles off our DZ. Our battalion was supposed to drop well to the north of here. Our objective is right on the coast. It's got to be a good seven miles from here, easily."

Dawes looked at his watch.

"That's a lot of ground to cover at night. You'd be lucky to make it before dawn; if you make it all."

Harvey nodded silently, his face grim.

Dawes offered him an option.

"You could stay with us? We're a little off course too, but not as much as you and young Gilbert. Our RV is just north of Ranville. You see this little road junction on the south edge of Ranville village? That's where my company is meant to be digging in. We're forming a blocking position to stop any enemy counter-attack towards the bridges on the River Orne. If we've read this map right, then it's about three and a half miles up that road to where our boys should be."

Harvey didn't answer. He just stared at the map, licking his lips, deep in thought.

"We should head for Ranville first, I reckon. I know it's not what you came to do," Dawes continued, "but at least you'll achieve something if you come with us. If we make it to Ranville in good time, you could still strike north if you think it's worth it. You can make a judgement yourself when we get there."

Harvey wrestled with the dilemma for another moment or two before letting out a sigh of resignation.

"You're right. We may as well try and achieve something useful tonight, even if it's not what we set out to do. Now I wish there *had* been a fold-away bike in that bloody container."

He looked up at Dawes and nodded his head solemnly.

"Come on then; Ranville it is…"

COMMAND POST 125TH PANZER GRENADIER REGIMENT – BELLENGREVILLE, NEAR CAEN, NORMANDY TUESDAY 6TH JUNE 1944 – 0055 HOURS

"Hello there. No need to worry. No harm is going to come to you. We're all soldiers of honour here. Sit yourself down and rest. I imagine you've had a rough night so far."

Von Luck was speaking in his best English, perfected during his visits to that country before the war, and he smiled at the British prisoner as if he were a long lost friend. Von Luck indicated a nearby stool and pulled up a chair for himself, just a metre or two away. Slowly, suspiciously, the British prisoner settled himself on the stool, casting furtive glances at the other

Germans in the room. He said nothing; just sat down, keeping his posture upright, alert, wary.

The commander of the 125th Panzer Grenadiers offered the man a cigarette, which he accepted, again with some caution. As they went through the ritual of lighting up, von Luck studied the man carefully. Certain things were obvious to the veteran German commander straight away. Firstly, the man was obviously a paratrooper, for his uniform was unlike anything von Luck had seen amongst British units back in 1940, or since in the North African theatre. Although the Tommy wore the same strange web equipment that the British Army favoured, with ammunition pouches sitting high up on the front of the body, the man also wore a baggy, camouflage pattern smock, not dissimilar to the kind originally worn by the Waffen SS and now in wide use across the Wehrmacht.

In addition, he was wearing a rimless helmet, different to standard British pattern and covered with a camouflage net and strips of coloured hessian cloth. In truth, he was dressed very much like a German paratrooper would be. There were two other interesting features about the man. He was an officer, as indicated by the three cloth diamonds on his epaulettes, and he was also a medical man; for he wore a white arm-band emblazoned with a red cross on his left sleeve.

"Sorry, I should introduce myself." Von Luck smiled, leaning back and blowing a thin stream of cigarette smoke upwards. "My name is Major Hans von Luck; I'm the local commander here. And you are?"

The British officer stirred slightly, cast a final, wary gaze at the German military policeman standing at one side of the room, then spoke. His voice was precise, clipped, and guarded. The man stated his name, rank, number and religion, then went silent.

Von Luck nodded.

"Pleased to meet you; although, I am sorry it is in such unfortunate circumstances. I spent some time in England, you see? Before the war. I have some good friends there. I only hope they come through this madness alive and well."

He saw the flicker of interest in the prisoner's eyes.

"So, you're in the Parachute Regiment then?"

Just as quickly, the man's eyes changed again; alert for the trap.

Von Luck went on. He went on for some minutes. Eventually, he managed to get the prisoner to say something other than his name, rank and number. It was just a few pleasantries at first, but after a while, with liberal amounts of good natured banter being offered by the German commander, the prisoner let his guard slip. Von Luck registered the passing comment about the man's parent unit; the 6th Airborne Division. That was bad. A full division of elite paratroopers meant that this was more than just a large scale commando raid.

And then, von Luck played his hand; just at the point where he thought both he and the prisoner had reached a position of mutual empathy.

"Well, it's been nice meeting you." Von Luck smiled as he stood and crushed out his cigarette end. "I'm afraid I must be off. It is my unfortunate duty to drive my regiment up the road to the coast and counter-attack your comrades. I fear some good men may have to die before the new dawn breaks."

The British prisoner looked up at von Luck and offered a somewhat sad smile.

"If you are a wise man, Major, you will tell your regiment to lay its arms down and surrender; or else drive like hell back to Berlin as fast as it can. If you knew what was coming ashore behind us, you would realise that you can't possibly win."

The comment shot through von Luck like a bolt of electricity, but he forced himself to maintain his benign countenance.

"Thank you for your concern, Captain." He replied, smiling down at the officer. "But I fear we all have our duties to perform this day."

He saluted the British officer, who rose to his feet in acknowledgement.

"Take care, Captain. And do not worry; you will be treated properly. You have my word."

And with that, von Luck left the small room and walked quickly through the passageway of the house until he emerged into the larger room where the staff of his headquarters were busy processing reports and issuing orders.

As von Luck breezed into the room, Liebeskind looked up from his desk.

"It's an invasion." Von Luck snapped without preamble. "Get me Divisional Headquarters on the phone now."

Without query, the regiment's adjutant did as instructed, and seconds later, he was talking to someone at the other end of the phone.

"Hello? Messmer, it's Liebeskind here from the 125th. I've got the Regimental Commander here; he needs to speak to you."

The staff officer passed the telephone to von Luck.

"Messmer, good evening; or should that be good morning?" Von Luck began, keeping his voice even. "Is the Divisional Commander available to talk?"

Messmer's reply was apologetic.

"No, Sir. I'm afraid he's still in Paris visiting the equipment depot. We've telephoned him to say that something is going on and he's on his way back. He won't be here for several hours though."

Von Luck accepted the information with a grunt.

"I see. Listen; we've got Tommy paratroopers dropping all over our area. My Second Battalion is busy clearing their own area of responsibility and taking prisoners. I believe this is just the precursor to a much bigger operation; namely, an invasion. I need permission to launch a full counter-attack with my entire regiment towards the coast. We must act quickly whilst the enemy is still trying to organise himself."

There was a moment of hesitation from the duty officer at Divisional Headquarters. When he spoke, he sounded unsure of himself.

"I will ring Corps Headquarters again, Major, but I've literally just put the phone down to them. They refuse to give the order for a concentrated attack until we know what is going on."

Von Luck forced his temper down and continued speaking in a reasonable voice.

"I already know what's going on. The British are dropping paratroopers in depth of the coast to disrupt our reserves. They're about to invade, Messmer. Are Corps Headquarters aware of that?"

Again, Messmer hesitated before speaking.

"Corps Headquarters are aware of the reports of paratroopers being dropped, but they have been told by Army Headquarters that it is just a diversion. There are reports that the parachutists are just straw dummies…"

The Divisional Staff officer's voice tailed off. At that point, von Luck glanced up as the British prisoner was escorted along the passage of the large house and ushered towards the door.

"Straw dummies?" He murmured into the telephone, keeping his voice level. "Well, you can tell Corps and Army Headquarters that I have one of them in front of me here. It's six feet tall, has a blonde moustache and speaks with a distinctive English accent. He's a pretty impressive dummy all round if you ask me! And so are the ones fighting with my Second Battalion in Troarn."

"Err…" Messmer mumbled with discomfort at the other end of the line.

Von Luck felt for him. He understood that this wasn't Messmer's fault. He was just the duty officer and he had no power to start over-ruling higher formation directives. Even so, the situation was infuriating. They had to move quickly before the Tommies were allowed to consolidate.

"Messmer, I need you to ring Corps and Army back. Tell them both what I've told you. Our first prisoner has already indicated that there will be follow up troops coming behind these paratroopers. It has to be an invasion and therefore we must move with speed before the enemy can establish himself. Do you understand that?"

"Yes, Major." The officer assured him. "I understand. I'll ring them immediately. In the meantime they have instructed us to establish defensive positions to beat off any commando raids."

Von Luck grunted again.

"Yes, well, we're already doing that. Get back to me as quickly as you can with any news."

The major placed the handset of the telephone back down on the receiver. He resisted the urge to slam it down. There was no point demonstrating his frustration in front of the staff. It would only rattle them. He needed them to stay calm; stay focussed. And they would only do that if he set that example.

"We are still awaiting authority to attack." He said calmly. "In the meantime, we must remain stood-to and beat off any assault by these parachute troops. Tell the Second Battalion to send us a situation report as soon as they know more about what's going…"

Von Luck's instructions to Liebeskind were interrupted by the ringing of the telephone. Instantly, the adjutant reached across and snatched the handset up.

"125th. Liebeskind speaking."

Von Luck lit up another cigarette as he waited for the adjutant to finish the call. After a few moments of listening to the voice at the other end of the line, Liebeskind leaned away from the handset slightly and murmured to his commander.

"It's the Fifth Company; they're holed up in some cellars in Troarn. They withdrew there when they heard all the fighting. All they've got is blank ammo."

Von Luck nodded acknowledgement.

"Tell them to lay low and hang on; the rest of their battalion will be with them shortly. They're in the process of fighting through the town now in order to clear it."

Liebeskind nodded and repeated the instructions down the telephone. Moments later, he placed the handset back down.

"I'll ring the Second Battalion and let them know."

"Do that; and ask them for a situation report."

As Liebeskind went about his business, Von Luck wandered across to the map table; taking his time, making a show of being relaxed. He pretended not to notice the assistant adjutant and signallers watching him; trying to gauge their commander's nerve. Pausing at the table, he stared down at the map, mentally superimposing the events of the night onto it. What on earth were the Tommies trying to do? An invasion for sure; but where? Was this just a diversion of some kind?

"Major?"

Von Luck turned as Liebeskind called out to him.

"The Second Battalion is almost in full control of Troarn. They're having to proceed with caution as there are small groups of enemy paratroopers all over the place. They've got some more prisoners too…"

"I want them brought here immediately." Von Luck interrupted.

The adjutant nodded his head in acknowledgement.

"I'll tell them, Sir; but there's been another development."

"What?"

"They've come across a couple of enemy gliders, Sir; and a Tommy field-car stuffed with enemy troops has been seen driving around the area."

"Okay." Von Luck nodded.

He turned back to the map and looked down at it. Out there, somewhere in the night, were hundreds, if not thousands of enemy parachutists. And his own men, constrained by strict orders from above, had no choice but to sit and wait to see what the enemy were going to do next. It wasn't good. It wasn't good at all.

THE MAIN STREET OF LE PORT – CLOSE TO THE CAEN CANAL BRIDGE
TUESDAY 6TH OF JUNE 1944 – 0100 HOURS

"Stop firing! Stop firing!"

Green roared the instructions at the top of his voice in order to be heard above the angry bark and clatter of small arms fire.

"Stop!" He yelled again, and this time the noise of gunfire dwindled away and a strange silence descended on the house.

The enemy had stopped firing several minutes ago, having withdrawn hastily back down the road, and across it, into some cottages at the far end of the street, dragging their wounded with them. On the narrow cobbled road below, three dark objects lay sprawled on the ground. Dead Germans.

"Watch and shoot!" Green ordered from his position in the top floor of the cottage.

"Don't waste your ammo. We've got a long night ahead and we'll need every round."

He turned away from the window and snapped an instruction to the soldier who'd followed him into the upstairs room.

"Stay here. Keep that road covered. Those Jerries have gone into the third house down on the other side of the street. I'll send someone else up."

With that, Green left the room and clattered down the narrow stairs and emerged into the small room below that seemed unfeasibly packed with people. In the darkness, amongst a gaggle of soldiers, Green registered the pale coloured night shirts of the cottage's owners; a middle aged couple by the looks, with their two young children held tightly against them. The two adults were both jabbering endlessly in French, and Green didn't understand a word of it. For that matter, he couldn't even tell if they sounded frightened, angry, or even happy; though he doubted it was the latter.

"Does anyone speak French at all?" Green shouted above the racket.

"You must be joking." Someone replied in English.

"Ain't got a bloody clue what they're on about..." Said another.

"Don't ask me..." Came a third voice.

One of the soldiers turned to face Green as he spoke and, despite the gloom, the corporal saw that the man was holding a Bren Gun.

"You; get that gun up into the bedroom and cover the main street. The bloke up there will show you which house the Jerries are in."

The gunner pushed past Green and began stamping up the stairs. Meanwhile, the corporal grabbed another one of the soldiers by the shoulder and snapped out an order.

"And you; see if this place has got a cellar or a pantry and get these bloody civvies in it and out of the way. Try and explain to them that there's probably going to be a lot of shooting and they need to keep out of the way."

"Me?" The soldier asked, his eyes bulging in the darkness. "But I don't speak..."

"Just do it!" Green yelled, pushing him towards the family.

"The rest of you, get shaken out. I want someone covering every side of the building."

He began grabbing individuals and pushing them physically into firing positions, sending two men back outside to cover the rear garden and the meadow between the row of houses and the canal. Finally, he grabbed hold of one soldier and pointed him back towards the bridge.

"Right, get back across there to the bridge and find an officer. Tell them we've secured this end of the village, but tell them we've got about a dozen Jerries at least further down the road. There might be more. Tell them we're a bit thin on the ground so we could do with another section at least... Oh, and a PIAT if there's one spare. Understand?"

"Yes, Corp'."

"Good lad. Go."

He watched the soldier double off into the darkness. Turning, he noted with some small satisfaction that the French family had been successfully persuaded to closet themselves under the stairs, the soldier detailed off to arrange it busily attempting to converse with them in his own form of French. That basically involved the soldier shouting at the civilians in English whilst affecting a most ridiculous French accent. Whatever, it seemed to be working.

A sudden crash of gunfire from upstairs thundered through the house, making the two young children cry. Green was at the bottom of the stairs in an instant.

"What's going on?"

No reply; just another deafening burst of fire from the Bren Gun and the patter of spent cartridge cases bouncing on the floor boards. Swearing a silent oath, Green clambered back up the stairs. He could hear more gunfire now; the men in the garden blasting away with their rifles, and the same from the others positioned in the downstairs rooms.

"What's going on?" He demanded again as he burst into the upstairs bedroom.

He was answered by the sudden thud of bullets smashing into the wall just off to his left.

"Fucking hell!" Swore the corporal, ducking away to the far side of the room.

By the window, the two private soldiers were crouching down, either side of the shattered frame, and the Bren Gunner turned to shout a warning.

"Keep your head down Corp', there's more Jerries coming along the main street. Looks like we've stirred up a right hornets nest!"

Green cursed silently.

"How many more of the fuckers?" He shouted across the room as a single bullet cracked through the air and again hit the wall inside the room.

"Hard to tell..." The gunner replied. "Half a dozen at least; and they've got a machine gun with them too."

Green calculated the odds in his mind. Things were starting to tip in the enemy's favour. They had started to recover from their initial surprise and now they were starting to mass for a counter attack. To the best of Green's knowledge, only two gliders had reached the bridge, and so there were few men spare to support him up here in this exposed position. At the same time, he needed to hold this end of the village where it met the junction, otherwise the position at the bridge would become precarious. If only he had another section with him, or even the whole platoon, they could start to establish a proper perimeter.

The shout of alarm that now came from somewhere outside brought an even deeper sense of consternation to the corporal.

"Jerries coming from the rear! Watch the back of the houses; there's a whole load of the bastards sneaking along the back lane!"

"Shit!" Green swore.

He shouted across the room.

"Get that gun back in action! Hold that lot off in the street! I'm going out back to deal with the other fuckers!"

With that, Green slid across the floor boards, through the doorway, and across the landing onto the stairs. As he began tumbling down the stairs again, his mind was working overtime. He was going out back to where a third group of Germans were infiltrating along the rear of the village alright, but what the hell he was actually going to do about them he really had no idea.

THE GROCERY STORE - MAIN STREET OF LE PORT, CLOSE TO THE CAEN CANAL BRIDGE TUESDAY 6TH OF JUNE 1944 – 0100 HOURS

"Inside! Get in! Quickly!"

Corporal Lang was roaring the orders at the top of his voice. At the front of the group, the two men who had just blasted round after round into the door-lock, raised their booted feet and began kicking at the shop door, simultaneously battering it with their weapons. With a strange tearing sound, the door suddenly gave and broke away from the frame, flapping inwards.

None of this was particularly clear to Krause, who was too busy screaming hysterically as Lang and another soldier dragged him by his equipment braces along the cobbled street. Only two things managed to reach Krause's brain with any real clarity. One was Lang's ceaseless, booming voice, delivering a constant stream of desperate orders, liberally enhanced by a wide selection of expletives. The other was pain.

The grenade blast had thrown Krause across the cobbled street as if he were a rag doll being flung aside by a child. It had taken a few moments for the shock of the sudden blast to lift from Krause's mind, and when it did, he was suddenly aware that his ears hurt like hell, and so did his legs. Instinctively, the young soldier had reached down to check that his legs were still attached to his body. They were. However, his hands had come away from his legs dripping with some kind of liquid and in the darkness he'd pulled his hands closer to his face so that he could see what it was. He hadn't needed to look. He'd detected the unmistakable odour while his hands were still thirty centimetres away from his face. Blood. And that's when he had started screaming uncontrollably.

"Come on!" Lang was bawling above the sound of the high velocity bullets that cracked above the group of German soldiers and thudded into the stone fronted buildings beyond them. "Get this fucker inside! Pull!"

As Krause was hauled roughly through the doorway of the grocer's shop, he vaguely registered that 'this fucker' was him.

The world suddenly turned darker as Krause was dragged into the building and deposited like a sack of potatoes into a corner.

"Alright Krause, button it!" Lang was shouting at him. "We'll sort you out in a moment."

Then turning back towards the other shadowy figures in the room, the corporal issued another string of orders.

"Jurgens; get upstairs and put some fucking fire down on that house! Heyden, Litmann, knock out that fucking shop window and start firing back!"

The sound of boots thudding on floorboards and glass shattering under the impact of rifle butts filled the darkened room. Krause noted with some surprise that he was still screaming.

At that point, Lang turned and kicked him in the arm.

"Krause! I said shut the fuck up!"

Krause stopped screaming.

"We'll fix you up in a minute; now keep your trap shut for fuck's sake! I can't hear myself think!"

Krause remained silent; suddenly ashamed of his behaviour as he watched, or rather listened, to his comrades going about the business of fighting back against the enemy soldiers who had ambushed them out in the street. He lay there panting like an excited dog, wondering how bad his legs were, and hoping that he hadn't already lost too much blood. It was the sound of his name being spoken that snapped him out of his dark thoughts.

"Stahl, take a look at Krause. Get him bandaged up, will you? Oh, and take all his ammo off him."

Moments later, a shadow appeared out of the gloom and a pale face loomed close to Krause's, staring intently at the wounded soldier.

"Krause? You still alive?"

The voice didn't sound especially concerned about what the answer to the question might be.

"Yes…" Krause replied in a small voice, only just managing to avoid the reply becoming a whimper. "It's my legs…"

Almost instantly, a hooded torch came on, the partially shielded beam pointing down at Krause's legs. The sudden light made Krause squint, and before he had the chance to think about looking at the state of his own legs, the light went out again.

"Well, that's a pretty thorough peppering you've got there, matey." The voice of the unknown Samaritan chuckled. "Got yourself a handful of shrapnel in both legs by the looks…"

"Is it that bad?" Krause asked, his voice almost becoming a wail.

"No, not really…" Came the nonchalant voice once more. "Seen more blood at a whorehouse punch-up, to be honest. Nothing's hit your arteries so you aint going to drop dead on me… Not just yet anyway."

Krause winced and emitted a sharp cry as a firm hand clamped a shell dressing onto his upper right leg and began to wrap a bandage around it, securing the pad in place.

"Still…" The first-aider continued, "I don't reckon you'll be doing any dancing for a couple of days young fellah. Can you feel your feet?"

"Er… Yes. Yes, I think so."

"Good. That means you aint totally fucked. Might be a bit of muscle damage though. We'll get you to the medics come daylight. Just as soon as we've sorted these bloody Tommies out."

As Krause sat there, digesting the prognosis of his appointed saviour, something metallic and heavy suddenly landed on his stomach, followed by several other equally heavy objects. With a start, Krause realised they were machine-pistol magazines and a couple of cardboard boxes containing 9mm ammunition.

"There you are Krause, lad…" Came the harsh, authoritative voice of Corporal Lang from somewhere above him. "Make yourself useful while you're laid there and get those fucking magazines filled."

THE MAIN STREET OF LE PORT – CLOSE TO THE CAEN CANAL BRIDGE
TUESDAY 6TH OF JUNE 1944 – 0125 HOURS

"Looks like they've backed off."

The wounded soldier next to Green peered into the darkness beyond the garden wall, straining to see if any of the Germans were still lingering in the lane at the rear of the row of houses. It was hard to tell. With the bushes and trees that bordered the lane being in full leaf, an enemy soldier could easily conceal himself within the shadows. Having said that, during the course of the intense fire-fight in which Green and his two companions had just been engaged, it had become apparent that the enemy were either less numerous than they appeared, or else simply reluctant to rush across the open ground at the British paratroopers ensconced behind the sturdy stone wall.

Just as well, because Green's small section was hanging onto its toe hold in the village by the skin of its teeth. At the same time that the Germans had approached from the rear, another group of them had advanced down the village main street. In addition to that, the first Jerries they'd encountered were holed up in a building across the road and making a real nuisance of themselves. If the enemy realised just how few British soldiers they were facing, they would come charging down the road at them with all guns blazing. Green realised that essential truth and wondered how long he could remain here without support.

He glanced at the two men next to him.

"Yeah, I reckon they've fucked off for now. Keep your eyes peeled though, in case they come back for another crack. And get that ear bandaged up while you've got chance."

The wounded soldier grinned at his corporal in the darkness.

"Not sure I want to take my helmet off Corp', just in case my bloody head falls apart."

Green offered a small grunt.

"It looks a lot worse than it is, Watson; that's why you're still smiling. Now then, remember what I said; stay sharp. I'm going inside to see what's going on in the main street. I'll be back shortly."

With that, the section commander pushed himself to his feet and, moving at a low crouch, doubled back across to the rear door of the cottage. He entered the building, calling out as he did so.

"Lads! It's only me! We've seen 'em off at the rear for now."

He came to the doorway of a room that looked out onto the main street.

"All okay in here?"

A calm voice answered him from the shadows by the shattered window.

"Alright for now Corp', I tell you what though; there's a whole load of the bastards gathering further up the street. I reckon it's only a matter of time before they come at us mob-handed."

Green took a deep breath before replying.

"Well, just keep shooting the fuckers if they do. We'll have some reinforcements soon. How are you doing for ammo?"

"Eighty odd rounds still; I'm fine for now."

"Righto."

Moving on down the passageway, Green reached the narrow stairs and once again ascended them. He went straight to the bedroom at the front of the building and looked in, keeping low. He frowned into the gloom, trying to locate the two men who he'd left here.

"You alright fellahs?" He called.

There was a brief pause before a voice answered.

"Simmo's dead. He copped one right through the 'Swede'. I've got hold of his Bren Gun though."

Again, Green took a moment to steady his voice.

"Well done mate. What are them Jerries up to?"

Green never heard the reply because there was a sudden flurry of voices from downstairs that made his heart pick up pace.

"Who's in charge here?"

The upper class tone of the voice below was unmistakable. An officer. Green tumbled down the stairs again, calling out as he went.

"I am! Up here!"

As he reached the bottom of the stairs, a figure loomed up in the passage way.

"Who's that?" The figure spoke in that well bred voice.

"Corporal Green, Sir."

"Ah, just the man." Replied the officer. "Major Howard has sent us up here to secure the junction and the southern end of the village. We heard you were up here on your own. What's the sketch?"

Quickly, succinctly, Green briefed the officer on what the tactical disposition of his own men was, and then did the same regarding the Germans. The officer, who's voice Green now recognised as Mr Fox, accepted the information silently. When Green had finished his report, Fox stood there for a while in contemplation.

"Have you got a clear shot along to the junction from upstairs, as well as down through the village?"

"Yes, Sir." Green assured him. "Clear fields of fire in both directions."

"Mmm, right…" Fox murmured. "Well, in that case, I shall leave one of my sections here with you, and Sergeant Thornton too; he's got a PIAT with him. Your task is to hold this end of the village at all costs. In addition, be prepared to cover the junction too. I'm going to take the other two sections from my platoon down there and dig-in on either side of it to cover the routes to the east and south. Does all that make sense?"

Green nodded and confirmed that he understood, a sense of relief flooding over him now that his tiny force had quadrupled in size.

His sense of relief was short lived. There was a sudden, urgent, tumult of small arms fire from within the house, and the sound of enemy bullets thudding into the building with renewed vigour added to the din. Above it all, came an urgent warning of the kind that Green had been dreading for the last hour.

"Tank!"

"Shit!" Green swore; then, shouting up the stairs. "What's going on? What's that about a fucking tank?"

"It's coming down the main road towards us! A Jerry tank!" The Bren Gunner's voice hollered back down in alarm. "A great, big, fat fucker it is too!"

Green snapped his head back to look at Lieutenant Fox through the gloom. To his surprise, the officer's teeth were shining brightly in the darkness. He was smiling.

"Looks like we got here just in time then?" He offered laconically.

With that, he turned and strode back towards the rear door of the cottage and shouted out into the night.

"Sergeant Thornton? Get yourself over here with that PIAT! I've got some business for you!"

COMMAND POST 125TH PANZER GRENADIER REGIMENT – BELLENGREVILLE, NEAR CAEN, NORMANDY TUESDAY 6TH JUNE 1944 – 0145 HOURS

Von Luck watched the latest prisoner being escorted from the building as he held the telephone handset to his ear and waited for the person he had requested to be brought to the phone.

There had been four more prisoners; all paratroopers. They were a mixture of older looking NCOs, probably veterans of North Africa or Dunkirk, and slightly younger but equally tough looking private soldiers. Von Luck had personally interviewed every one of them, employing his usual, relaxed, friendly manner. Two of the older prisoners had remained tight-lipped throughout, although they had accepted the offer of cigarettes readily enough. The other, younger soldiers, had started off by sticking to their name, rank and number routine, but like the medical officer before them, had finally let slip small details without realising it; charmed as they were by von Luck's very decent treatment.

More than ever, von Luck was convinced that the invasion was upon them. The only thing he couldn't tell for sure was the exact spot on their stretch of coast where the landing would fall. It was obvious that these highly trained paratroopers were being dropped to create some sort of flank protection and depth-disruption force for a seaborne landing, thus it was essential that von Luck got his regiment up to the coast as soon as possible, should that seaborne landing take place on his frontage. But there was the sticking point. His regiment, indeed the entire division, were under strict orders to remain in their assembly areas until given permission to attack. Those orders had come from the very highest authority, and nobody it seemed, was prepared to revoke those orders any time soon.

"Forster speaking."

Major Forster, the Divisional Chief of Staff, came on the line abruptly, making von Luck jump.

"It's me; von Luck."

"Ah… How are things at your end? It's chaos here at Division. We've got reports of all sorts coming in. Corps Headquarters has received reports of enemy troops attacking the bridges over the Orne River and I've just had several Tommy paratroopers brought in from various units in the Division. They're not saying much."

Von Luck's heart picked up a beat. The Tommies were going for the Orne bridges.

"It's similar at this end." He replied. "But I've spoken to half a dozen of our own prisoners and managed to pick up a few bits of detail. It seems they are part of a pathfinder or disruption force, dropped in advance of a seaborne force. I think they're trying some kind of flank protection manoeuvre. Just looking at the map here, it would make sense for them to secure the line of the Orne if they were going to land along the coast from the Orne Estuary through Cabourg and Deauville to the Seine Estuary."

"Mmm…" Forster's metallic voice sounded down the phone. "Or even on the western side of the Orne…"

"Yes, that's a possibility too." Von Luck agreed. "The vital thing is to advance now while we can, and attack right up to the coast. It seems to me that the enemy parachute drop has become somewhat dispersed, and therefore we need to hit the enemy hard while they are disorganised. If we move now, we can be waiting for their landing craft the moment they reach the coast."

This time there was a long pause at the other end of the phone before Major Forster replied.

"Yes, well… I think Corps Headquarters feel much the same, but they have been forbidden to move any of the armoured reserves for the time being. That means us of course. The problem is that higher formation believe this is no more than a diversion; a feint if you like, to draw us away from Calais. Apparently there has been very heavy bombing up in the Pas de Calais tonight. Many people seem to think that the landings will take place there; if they come at all."

With great effort, von Luck forced himself to remain calm.

"Even so; we must attack the enemy parachute troops with all vigour. If they are attacking bridges over the Orne, then they must be trying to secure a flank. We need to stop that from happening. We need all those bridges intact in case we are called away by higher formation. We can't just let them run amok in the night."

Again there was a pause.

"Well, the orders are quite specific. We may engage any enemy that fall within our assembly areas, but we are not authorised to close on the coast or leave those assembly areas without orders from above."

The commander of the 125th Panzer Grenadiers bit his lip in frustration. Only after a supreme effort to keep his temper did he speak.

"Ring them again, Forster. Tell them how vital it is that we move now. We're wasting time here; just wasting it."

"I will Hans; I will."

Von Luck lowered the handset and made a show of placing it back on the receiver gently, despite his natural instinct to slam it down in foul distemper. That would do nothing but harm, von Luck realised. When faced with chaos and uncertainty, men always looked to their commanders. If the commanders were rattled, then their men would be too, and that would be disastrous for morale and cohesion. Von Luck had to appear totally calm, regardless of the frictions of war. Even so, in his head, he was screaming out in frustration. The battle was joined, yet his superior headquarters had forbidden him to act in anything other than a defensive manner. This was not how a Panzer Division was supposed to fight its battles.

He settled himself on the corner of the table, lit up another cigarette and glanced across at his adjutant.

"We wait." He said quietly.

CLOSE BY HEROUVILLETTE - HALF A MILE SOUTH OF RANVILLE, NORMANDY
TUESDAY 6TH JUNE 1944 – 0240 HOURS

"This has got to be it."

Dawes whispered his belief into the ear of Lance Corporal Harvey who had come to kneel beside him in the hedge bottom.

"I've been pacing it out. I make it 1500 yards since that last junction. You can see the outline of the village just up ahead, and what looks like a ruddy great church tower."

Beside Dawes, Harvey was nodding.

"Yeah." He whispered back. "I reckon you're bang on. I paced it at about 1450, and there's no mistaking this road to our right and all those trees to the east."

Dawes felt a certain amount of relief when the only other NCO in their group confirmed his calculations regarding their current position.

"Are you supposed to be going all the way into Ranville?" Harvey asked.

Dawes shook his head.

"That wasn't the original plan. There should be a small track that meets the road just up here. It leads onto a Y-Junction above a small hamlet called Herouvillette, and my platoon was supposed to dig in on it and block the southern approaches."

Harvey accepted the information quietly. After a moment or two of studying the darkness ahead, he glanced back at Dawes.

"Looks quiet'ish at this end. Somebody's having a scrap though, and not too far away. Sounds like it's out the other side of the village to me…"

Dawes stared back towards the dark silhouette of the distant buildings. Harvey was right. Although the village itself looked quiet, there was definitely sporadic gunfire about a mile away to the north beyond this smaller settlement. In addition to that of course, the whole of Normandy seemed to be filled with the noise of dozens of small, distant battles. Lines of tracer competed with flares and bomb explosions to light up the horizon in every direction, creating a lurid and somewhat spectacular backdrop.

"Well… I reckon we take it slowly up until we reach the Y- junction." Dawes suggested. "Once we're there, we can shake out in all-round defence. Our first task is to do what we were briefed to do; that is, to block the road to Ranville. Once we've done that, we might send a couple of blokes into the village itself to see if they can find any of our own blokes."

Harvey nodded his agreement with the plan without hesitation.

"Okay, Jack; let's do it. I'll bring up the rear again."

Thus decided, the two NCOs quickly moved their tiny force on again; Dawes leading them cautiously along the hedgerow of a large meadow. Across that field, another hedgerow marked the path of the road as it ran towards the village. It was just as the small British patrol approached the corner of the field, that Dawes spotted the low stone building tucked into the side of the field. He paused briefly, using his peripheral vision and the occasional surge in ambient light to try and establish what kind of building it might be. A few moments later, the doleful low of several cattle gave up the building's secret. A cattle shed. The animals sounded uneasy; frightened. Hardly surprising giving the relentless barrage of alien noises that filled the night. Even at a distance, the noise of battle and bombing had an unsettling quality about it.

Moving cautiously on, Dawes reached the wall of the long stone building and began to skirt it. He had only turned one corner when he noticed that he had come upon the doorway to the building, from which a track ran off to his right; straight towards the road. Directly beyond the barn, perhaps two fields away at the most, lay the village. This was it. The track junction must be off to his right just a hundred yards or so. Dawes caught his breath suddenly. In an instant his senses, already at an acute pitch, were tingling with an alarm born of long experience. He could hear voices.

He cocked his ear to the wind and strained to pick up the noise once more. Nothing at first, but then… There. No mistaking. Voices talking to each other somewhere up the track. Hard to tell what language they were speaking. Another sound. A door on a car this time, slamming shut. Then the sound of stamping feet. Not the sound of someone walking. More like the sound of a cold, tired sentry stamping his feet to keep them warm.

"What is it?"

Dawes turned as Harvey slid down next to him once more.

"This is the track here, mate. It runs up to the road that way. That's where our position is meant to be… But there's somebody up there. I just heard 'em talking. They've got a car too."

Harvey cocked his own head to one side now, straining to listen in the same manner that Dawes had. They both knelt there for long seconds, holding their breath, trying to detect the slightest sound above the background rhythmic pounding of exploding bombs. Then they both heard it.

"Shit!"

Dawes and Harvey swore together, turning their eyes to look at each other simultaneously. They had both heard the same thing. A sentence rattled out in a foreign language; one that neither of them understood. There was one word in that sentence however, which was obvious enough… *'Englander'*.

"We've got Jerries on our fucking objective!" Dawes cursed.

"Only one thing to do then…" Whispered Harvey mischievously. "Let's go and start a fight, shall we?"

THE MAIN STREET OF LE PORT – CLOSE TO THE CAEN CANAL BRIDGE
TUESDAY 6TH OF JUNE 1944 – 0300 HOURS

The night was about as quiet as it could be. The Germans were still out there; of that Green was certain. For the time being however; indeed for the last hour or so, they had been very quiet, restricting their activities to just the odd shot towards the British glider troops who were now ensconced on the junction and in the first two buildings at the southern end of Le Port. It had become, Green realised, a bit of a stalemate. It was really now a case of who was able to get their act together first. Would the remainder of the British 5th Airborne Brigade land on time and in the right place, and succeed in getting to the bridges over the canal and the River Orne before the Germans realised the danger of the situation and mobilised a larger force for a proper counter attack?

It was anybody's battle, Green thought, as he stared at the still crackling flames emitting from the burning German tank; the one that Sergeant Thornton had destroyed at almost point blank range with the PIAT during the last German attack. Turning away from the window, Green glanced down at the man who crouched behind the Bren Gun. The original gunner had been killed by a single shot through the head earlier in the night. This replacement gunner had now taken a grazing wound to his upper right arm. It was only a matter of time before a German bullet scored another bulls-eye. The young soldier probably realised that too. Even so, he gave no indication that the possibility was worrying him. Like all the men in this tiny, elite force, the young lad knew his duty. They had to hold on here, regardless of the cost. The fate of thousands of men depended on them, and the fate of the invasion itself, too. There was no option. They had to hold.

"You alright Watkins, lad? How's your arm doing?"

The Bren Gunner grinned up at the corporal through the darkness, his teeth flashing white against his blackened face.

"Hurts like fuck, Corp!" He said phlegmatically. "But I'd rather have a sore arm than a hole in the head like poor old Simmo here."

"Well, just keep it down as much as you can. Those Jerries haven't gone anywhere. They're still down the street somewhere in those buildings at the other side of the road."

Green made to leave the room, but paused to give the young private one more cautionary word.

"Keep your eyes peeled all the same. The bastards will be coming for us again eventually."

With that, Green exited the room and began thumping down the stairs. As he descended the narrow wooden stairway, he realised how tired he was starting to feel. It had been a bloody long day and night so far, punctuated with intense physical activity and filled with the constant psychological strain that was the burden of any man with command responsibility. He wondered how long it would have to continue. In his heart, he knew that this was only the beginning. There was a long day ahead yet, possibly several, before he and his men were finally overtaken by the flood of advancing troops landing from the sea.

Emerging into the hallway, he turned into the main downstairs room and peered under the staircase where he saw the French family huddled together in a heap of pale coloured nightgowns and pyjamas.

"All okay under there?" He asked them in English, raising his voice as if the increase in volume might suddenly make them understand the foreign words. "Won't be long now... soon be over and done with. Try and get some sleep."

It was a ridiculous thing to say, but he decided that a few words, however meaningless, said in a friendly, upbeat tone, would be better than nothing for the poor inhabitants of this house who had found themselves unexpectedly caught up in the middle of a pitched battle.

"Corporal Green? Corporal Green?"

The sound of one of the soldiers outside floated through the hallway of the cottage.

"Here." Replied Green and quickly retraced his steps into the hall and back towards the rear door of the building.

Reaching the doorway, he paused and looked out into the garden. He could see one of the men he'd left there still covering across the scrubland towards the river and along the rear of the village. The other man was pacing up and down behind the opposite wall, apparently in a state of agitation, as he kept his gaze fixed back in the direction of the bridge.

"What's going on?" Green demanded from his place in the doorway.

The silhouette of the soldier went still as he heard Green's voice, and the man turned his head in the corporal's direction.

"There's something happening over near the bridge." The man hissed. "I can hear voices. Boots too; lots of bloody boots… Listen…"

The man went silent and Green saw him cock his ear to the breeze. Green did likewise. Sure enough, there it was; the unmistakable tramp and scrape of dozens of pairs of boots on cobbles, accompanied by a low murmur of conversation.

Green was out of the building and by the man at the back wall in an instant.

"That sounds like a lot of fucking people to me." He murmured, his senses alive once more to the possibility of a development in their situation.

"You don't think it's…" Began the private by Green's side, but he stopped in mid-sentence.

"What?" Green prompted him.

"There!" The soldier shot his arm out. "They're over there too; down by the crossroads near Mr Fox's mob. Look, you can see 'em moving…"

The corporal followed the soldier's outstretched arm as he pointed towards the junction of the two roads which sat barely a hundred and fifty yards away to the south of them. Green saw the movement of dark shapes; lots of them. His heart gave a little flutter of hope, but he forced himself to remain calm.

"Corporal Green?"

His name being called again, but this time by another voice. It was Mr Fox.

"Sir?" He shouted into the darkness, and saw a dark shadow suddenly veer away from the blob of other figures and head towards him.

"Over here, Sir; in the back garden."

The dark shape took on distinct form as it came closer, slowly transforming into a person. As the individual approached to within ten yards of the wall, Green waved his arm.

"Here, Sir. Behind the wall."

"Ah…" The well bred voice of Lieutenant Fox sounded. "There you are."

The officer came right up to the wall so that he could put his face close to Green's.

"Righto, Corporal Green, you need to prepare your chaps to pull back to the canal bridge."

Green was taken aback by the comment.

"Pull back, Sir?"

"Yes; but not until I give you the nod. And we need to make sure that we've handed over the position to these other chaps before we head back to the rest of the company. Once we've rejoined the company, we'll be put into a close defensive perimeter around the bridge itself."

Green was disoriented by the sudden flurry of instructions.

"Pull back?" He murmured again. "Why, Sir? What other chaps do you mean?"

Fox jerked his thumb over his shoulder, back towards the crossroads.

"That lot over there. That's the first contingent of 7 Para. They've just reached the bridge from their DZ. Apparently there's more coming up right behind them. They're going to take over the crossroads and start clearing out this village in order to expand the bridgehead. Our job now is to close on the bridge and act as an inner cordon."

Green felt his heart lift again, but he continued to fight the feeling down, not wanting to raise his hopes prematurely.

"7 Para?" He asked, his voice barely a whisper.

"Certainly is Corporal G. They're the first part of the relief force. All we need now are some Commandos."

CLOSE BY HEROUVILLETTE – HALF A MILE SOUTH OF RANVILLE, NORMANDY
TUESDAY 6TH JUNE 1944 – 0305 HOURS

They shook out quickly. There was no need for detailed orders, even though the tiny force was a mixture of men from different companies and battalions. The parachute battalions of Britain's new army were some of the most thoroughly trained units on the order of battle, and composed of a high percentage of early war veterans. They were fit, resourceful, and absolutely determined.

Dawes' little force advanced now; cautiously, quietly, yet quite purposefully towards the junction of the farm track with the road. Dawes, with Gilbert by his side, walked straight up the track on the axis of advance. A couple of men walked left and right of them across the grass, thus forming an extended line. Just out of direct sight on either side, a pair of soldiers advanced in line with the main group, going wide in order to cover the flanks. Harvey was one of the two men out on the left, closest to the village.

The line of paratroopers advanced at the walk, weapons up at the ready, eyes scanning the darkness to their front for the first sign of the enemy. Dawes had ordered a silent approach with, if possible, an attempt to capture the enemy soldiers on the junction if they proved to be just a couple of waifs and strays who weren't particularly alert. At the same time, if things did go noisy, he had ordered his men to assault the junction rapidly and aggressively, without giving the enemy a chance to gather their wits.

Suddenly, Dawes felt the stirring of familiar emotions; feelings that had lain dormant for several years since his last brush with the Germans during the withdrawal to Dunkirk. He knew that very shortly the night could be filled with deadly slugs of lead, the deafening crack of gunfire, and that men who were currently alive and breathing might very soon be dead; nothing more than lifeless lumps of meat, their souls taken in the blink of an eye. That feeling sent his pulse racing; his heart thumping inside his chest like a bass drummer gone mad. At the same time, additional feelings mingled with the tension and apprehension. These feelings were more comfortable; reassuring.

The last time Dawes had faced the Germans, he had been running away; along with the rest of the British Expeditionary Force and the French. The Germans had made a mockery of British and French military power. He and his parent battalion, the 3rd Grenadiers, had done their level best to beat the Germans back, but it had all been in vain. Every time they had stopped the Germans in one place, the bastards had found their way round the flanks somewhere else. And his old unit had paid the price during the Dunkirk campaign. Over two hundred men dead and as many wounded or missing. He'd cowered in trenches during ferocious bombardments, seen his friends and comrades vaporised by enemy shells in a heartbeat. He'd spent a whole day lost in a cornfield near the River Escaut, cut-off from his mates and playing cat and mouse with enemy assault troops. That memory helped to soothe his nerves and steel the non commissioned officer for whatever was about to happen. He was back in France, he was armed and ready for a fight, and there was no going back. It was payback time.

Dawes was suddenly aware of the minute details around him; the soft clump of his own boots on the mud of the track, the heavy scent of wet grass, the strong odour of cow dung. Then, just a few yards ahead, he saw the gap in the hedgerow where the track emerged onto the road. For a moment, he struggled to see anything else, but in no more than a heartbeat, a movement in the shadows by the opening in the hedge caught his attention. Two figures, side by side, ambled casually from behind the cover of the hedge and into full view on the cobbled roadway. They were talking; by the sound of it, without any particular sense of urgency or alarm. The language was unmistakable now however. They were German; no doubt.

Automatically, Dawes increased his pace, feeling the thrill of the moment surge through his veins.

"Keep going straight for 'em…" He hissed at Gilbert next to him.

Dawes splashed through a puddle on the track in his haste to get onto the road. They were barely ten yards away now.

"Wer ist da?"

The sudden call of alarm from one of the Germans on the road was all Dawes needed.

Without pausing or even breaking stride, Dawes squeezed the trigger of his Sten Gun and the skeletal little weapon clattered into life, shattering the comparative peace of the night.

"Forward!" He roared as he released the trigger for just a second, before firing another burst of three to five rounds.

They didn't scream or shout in the traditional manner of the pre-war infantry. Instead, the British paras simple surged forward, closing with the enemy, and searching for targets. Dawes concentrated on the figures in the centre of the road, letting off several bursts of fire at the two men as he thundered up the track towards them. Next to him, Gilbert, weighed down by the PIAT, struggled to keep up but emptied several rounds from his rifle into the hedgerow on the left hand side of the gap, working the bolt of the Lee Enfield furiously between shots. Somewhere to the right, another Sten Gun was in action, raking the right hand hedgerow with fire. Somewhere above the racket, Dawes registered a startled cry. As he emerged onto the road, bursting through the gap in the hedgerow, he saw that the two figures on the road were already on the cobbles, sprawled in a manner that suggested they had been hit by his initial bursts.

Instinctively, as he came through the gap, Dawes swung to his right and emptied the remainder of his magazine into the shadows along the hedgerow. He heard the sound of the bolt on his weapon lock to the rear with a hollow 'clunk' as he expended the last of the rounds and, as per his relentless training, he threw himself sideways into the cover of the nearest bush and began changing the magazine. As he was doing this, the corporal was vaguely aware of Gilbert and another man coming through the gap behind him and onto the road. He heard both the soldiers fire their rifles, work the bolts, then shout out the warning.

"Check the car!"

It was Gilbert's voice.

"Make sure there's no one hiding behind it!"

The sound of more running feet, and then more of his little group were emerging onto the road all around him. Bang. A single shot from one of the soldiers.

"There look! One of the bastards legging it!"

Dawes stood up as he completed the magazine change and snapped out an order.

"Stop the fucker!"

Before anyone in the immediate vicinity had the chance to act, there was bright flash about thirty yards down the road towards the village, the rattle of a Sten Gun firing, then silence.

"One Jerry down on the left!"

Dawes recognised Harvey's voice as the lance corporal signalled that they had taken care of the escaping enemy soldier.

"Spread out; search the hedgerows and the car. Make sure there's no more of the bastards hiding round here!"

He barked the orders out to the group, knowing they would sort the tasks out between themselves.

"Gilbert? You check those two dead Jerries on the road. Make sure they're done for and see if they're carrying anything of importance; maps, documents, the usual stuff."

It happened quickly; the result of a drill oft-rehearsed these last years and months. Within minutes, the group of paras were crouching in the shadows, spread out in a loose circle that provided all-round defence. At the centre of that circle, Dawes and Harvey crouched by the abandoned staff car, discussing their next move.

"Looks like we got them all; just the three. Some kind of checkpoint or patrol maybe?"

Harvey grunted his agreement with Dawes' analysis.

"Reckon so. Either way, they weren't expecting us to pop out of the night. I reckon the Jerries are still trying to work out what's going on; what with the bombing and dozens of parachutes all over the area." He gazed southwards. "No sign of life from the village so far. You reckon that's Herouvillette then, do you, mate?"

Dawes thought for a moment as he looked through the meagre haul from the pockets of the dead Germans.

"I think so, Harv'. Ranville should be straight up the road there in the opposite direction. And I think you're right about the Jerries. I reckon they're just as confused as us. I'm glad we're not the only ones running around like idiots in the dark!"

He stuffed the small German notebook and a wad of personal looking letters into his trouser pocket.

"Still, it won't take them long to sort out the confusion. I know what these bastards are like once they get their arse in gear. We need to get organised sharpish, because once they know where we are, they'll be coming for us alright. I just hope a few more of our lads appear before the Jerries do."

Harvey stared at the corporal through the darkness.

"We digging-in here then?"

Dawes nodded.

"That's what my orders were. The rest of our battalion should be up there in Ranville itself. You still happy to stay with us?"

Harvey grinned, showing his white teeth through the gloom.

"May as well. At least we're guaranteed to make ourselves a nuisance to the Jerries if we stay."

The lance corporal glanced briefly at the German car.

"I was thinking of maybe taking this and trying to drive to my battalion DZ, but on balance, I think it would make a bloody nice roadblock if we pulled it across the road here and turned it over."

Dawes shrugged.

"Your choice, mate. Not going to put pressure on you. If you think you can make it to your own lads in time then feel free to take the car. If not, well, I'll be more than happy to have you and the other boy with us."

Harvey sucked his teeth noisily as he calculated his chances of making it to his unit in time for their Zero Hour, driving through the night, in an unfamiliar landscape that was infested with trigger happy soldiers of various nationalities.

After a few seconds of deliberation, Harvey made his decision.

"At the end of the day, a fight's a fight, isn't it? We landed here, so we may as well start fighting here. Come on… Let's see if we can get this road blocked?"

THE DEBRIEFING ROOM, RAF DOWNHAM MARKET – NORFOLK
TUESDAY 5TH JUNE 1944 – 0315 HOURS

Hargreaves, along with the remainder of the crews, sat quietly as he listened to the Master Bomber describe the effect on target during the Main Force phase of the mission. Out at the front of the room, the debriefing officer scratched away with his pencil against the paper on the clipboard as he noted down the details.

Overall, the Master Bomber had been very happy with the mission. The Pathfinder crews, all of whom had returned safely, had dropped their markers in exactly the right place, which was a credit to them given the complexity of the split target. There had of course been the inevitable 'bomb-creep' from some of the Main Force aircraft, but that had been nipped in the bud quickly enough by the Master Bomber who had ordered his two reserve aircraft to mark the limits of bombing with additional markers. It had done the trick and the Master Bomber's estimate was that around ninety percent of bombs had dropped on target; which wasn't bad allowing for the fleeting cloud in the area and the unusual target layout.

The other crewmen sat patiently as the ritual of the debriefing unfolded, their eyes now red-rimmed and tired; the adrenalin rush of the mission long gone and the desire for food and sleep starting to dominate their thoughts. Eventually, the Master Bomber concluded his description of the effect on target and the debriefing officer mumbled his thanks.

"Alright then," The officer said brightly, glancing up from his clipboard. "moving on to the home-run... Raymond, you were first back..."

It was standard practice for the home-run to be reported in the order that the crews had returned, so Hargreaves sat up a little and stifled a yawn as he gathered his own thoughts.

"Yes, we came off target on orders and dropped down to around fourteen thousand feet, breaking due east for around twenty miles. We then turned north and cut the French coast somewhere between Le Havre and Dieppe, with a little light flak coming up at us, but nothing to worry about really. We gave the H2S a short burst as we crossed the Channel, then cut the English coast near Brighton..."

The debriefer was nodding as he scribbled away with his pencil.

"Anything on the radar when you gave it a burst?" He asked casually.

Hargreaves hesitated for just a moment before he replied.

"Yes... We picked up ships in the Channel; *lots* of ships in fact."

"*Dozens* of ships." The navigator chipped in from beside Hargreaves.

The debriefing officer paused in his scribbling momentarily and glanced up at Hargreaves and his crew.

"Mmm, well, the Navy are doing quite a lot of convoy moves by night at the moment..." He mumbled, shrugging his shoulders casually; too casually in fact.

"Bloody big convoy, then." The navigator countered. "The Channel was covered. Must have been two hundred ships at least..."

He left the insinuation hanging in the air.

"Yes, we got that too." The Master Bomber commented from further along the front row of chairs.

"And us." Declared another pilot.

"More like three hundred if you ask me. The Channel was packed." Another navigator added to the pot.

Out front, the debriefing officer had begun to flush a guilty colour of red. Hargreaves knew in that moment that their suspicions had been right all along. This hadn't been an ordinary op' at all. Tonight was the night. The big show was on. The debriefing officer clearly knew that, but was obviously under orders to maintain strict secrecy.

"Alright, pipe down everyone. Let's get on, shall we? I'm sure you're all keen to get some breakfast before you get your heads down."

He shot a look at Hargreaves once more.

"*Apart* from Royal Navy convoy operations… anything else to report from your home-run?"

Hargreaves fought a smile down.

"No; all quiet on the way back."

Around the room, the crew members from the various aircraft were exchanging broad grins, some shaking their head in disbelief at the debriefer's poor attempt at feigning innocence. Several men were chuckling quietly to themselves, whilst the tail gunner from the Master Bomber's crew gave a short bark of amusement. It was clear from the man's face that he had seen the host of shipping with his own eyes and was in no doubt whatsoever about what he had witnessed.

The debriefing officer pretended not to hear any of the bemused laughter and, with the crimson flush in his cheeks deepening by the second, looked across to the crew of the next aircraft.

"Okay Dennis, you next. Home-run…"

COMMAND POST 125TH PANZER GRENADIER REGIMENT – BELLENGREVILLE, NEAR CAEN, NORMANDY TUESDAY 6TH JUNE 1944 – 0430 HOURS

"So, we've identified a drop zone here too?"

Von Luck pointed the red pencil at the spot on the map and drew a small circle there.

"How many parachutes did you say?"

"First Battalion reckon about thirty, Major." Liebeskind confirmed.

Von Luck nodded and quickly wrote the number inside the circle. The map was now peppered with such circles; more than a dozen in fact. Some of those circles contained small numbers like five or ten; one of them boasted the figure of fifty plus. The information had been trickling in all through the night and the early morning from the various elements of the regiment who remained static in their holding areas.

The commander of the 125th Panzer Grenadiers stared at the map and frowned. It was clear that the landings were widespread now, with the little red circles filling the parcel of land between the River Orne and the River Dives.

"Oh, and they've found a glider in the same spot too, Sir."

Von Luck glanced up at his adjutant who still held the telephone to his ear.

"A glider?"

Liebeskind nodded.

Von Luck pursed his lips at the news and drew a small cross next to the latest symbol denoting parachute drops. Gliders. That was an interesting development. If only his regiment was let off its leash it would be able to find out what was going on for sure. The information trickling in at the moment was only the tip of the iceberg. There was much more going on out there in the night than they currently knew about; of that he was sure.

Liebeskind had barely put the telephone down on the First Battalion's command post when it rang again.

"Liebeskind; 125th." The adjutant had the phone back to his ear in a split second.

Von Luck glanced up from the map again and watched his adjutant's face. He saw the pulse ticking away in the man's left temple, and the sharp alertness of the lieutenant's eyes. Like everyone, the officer was wound up to fever pitch and fighting hard to control his frustration. Von Luck sympathised with the man, for he felt the terrible restlessness too. But he was the commander here, and commanders had to stay calm; at least on the outside.

As he watched his adjutant listening intently to the caller, von Luck noticed the sudden flicker in Liebeskind's eye. The lieutenant glanced at him momentarily, before speaking into the phone.

"Where are they now? Have you dealt with them?"

He paused whilst the caller replied to the questions. After a while, Liebeskind spoke again.

"Alright, just hang on the phone for a moment while I brief Major von Luck."

The adjutant placed his hand over the mouth-piece of the telephone and looked back to his commander.

"Sir, the Second Battalion say the bridge over the Dives at Troarn has been demolished; blown up by the Tommies."

It took all of von Luck's self control to prevent him from swearing out loud.

"How?" He asked instead.

"A group of British parachutists in a field-car have been driving around the local area, shooting up any checkpoints they pass through. Second Battalion think it was them who blew the bridge. The Tommies have driven off towards Escoville now."

Von Luck took several deep breaths, absorbing the information.

"Tell them to get a grip of the security in their area. I want their battalion area locked down tight, and every bridge needs a guard force on it. And if that Tommy car reappears then I want it stopped. I want prisoners too. Tell them."

Liebeskind relayed the orders down the phone whilst von Luck found the bridge at Troarn on his map. Struggling to move in a calm, measured way, he reached across the map and carefully drew a solid red square over the bridge to symbolise that this particular route across the Dives was now blocked. As Liebeskind was putting the telephone down on the receiver, it rang once again. Once more he answered and listened to the caller. It was Divisional Headquarters this time. There was no permission to attack towards the coast yet, but there was fresh information. Liebeskind placed the telephone back down and imparted the new intelligence to von Luck.

"Division confirms that British gliders have landed close to the bridges over the Orne River and the Caen Canal near Ranville. The Tommies have captured both of them."

Von Luck glanced down at the map and felt his stomach churn. It was obvious now. So obvious that it felt as if von Luck had been slapped around the face. He turned back to his adjutant.

"Liebeskind, take my car; get Beck to drive you to Divisional Headquarters. I need you to press the chief-of-staff there for permission to attack. Tell him everything of our situation. You know what to say; we're running out of time. General Feuchtinger may even be back from Paris by now. Tell him the same. We can't do much on the end of a telephone so go there in person and tell them. Tell them all... *we need that permission to attack.*"

Even as von Luck was tasking his adjutant with the vital mission, there was the sound of a commotion in the hallway behind. Both officers turned to see a soldier being ushered into the room. Dressed in mud spattered jack-boots and a greatcoat, the man was evidently a motorcyclist to judge by the goggles on his helmet and the leather gauntlets that he wore. He was also a member of the field police, as evidenced by the metal gorget of office that hung around his throat by a chain. Stamping into the room, his face betraying a harassed look, the policeman spotted von Luck and saluted.

"Major," He began without hesitation, "I have come from the checkpoint near Cuverville, just outside Caen; my sergeant told me to come straight to you with the message."

Von Luck felt the stirring of disquiet deep within his soul. He fixed the man with an even stare.

"What message?" He asked.

The policeman swallowed hard, before speaking again.

"Our checkpoint sits on high ground looking down into the Orne valley and out to the coast. It's starting to get light now so we can see for dozens of kilometres; right off to the horizon out at sea."

Von Luck felt his heart begin to thump inside his chest, more than it had done at any point yet thus far this long night.

"We can see ships, Sir." The policeman said.

Von Luck's mind was racing now. At the same time, everything else around him seemed to blur into insignificance. He was focussed entirely on the mud-drenched motorcyclist.

"Ships?" He asked. "What kind of ships?"

The policeman stared back at the regimental commander with wide, worried eyes.

"Fucking big ones, Major, by the looks of it. And there are hundreds of them…"

THE ROADBLOCK – HALF A MILE SOUTH OF RANVILLE, NORMANDY
TUESDAY 6TH OF JUNE – 0500 HOURS

"Are you 'C' Company?"

The question was uttered by the captain who, apparently, was in charge of the tiny group of four men. They had come down the road from Ranville, moving cautiously, just as the first light of dawn was beginning to creep across the fields of Normandy. After a tense couple of minutes, whilst both Dawes' men and this new group had established each others identities, the two commanders had finally come together to chat face to face in the lee of the overturned German staff car.

"We're mainly from 'C' Company, Sir." Dawes replied to the officer, who he recognised as the second in command of 'A' Company. "But we've got a mix of people from all companies to be honest, and we've even got a couple of lads from 9 Para."

The captain gave a mirthless laugh and nodded his head.

"Sounds about right. The whole drop seems to have been a bit haphazard. We've got a handful of men from each company in the village, but the bulk of them are from 'A' and 'B' Companies. There's no sign of the CO yet either. I reckon there are no more than ninety of us all up. How many blokes have you got up here?"

Dawes gave him the numbers.

"Right, well, at least you've got to the right place. 'C' Company are meant to be covering this whole set of junctions south of Ranville, aren't they?"

"Sir." Dawes confirmed.

The officer sucked his teeth for a moment, considering the situation.

"Well, you may as well stay here and get on with that job as best you can. I'm sure we've got a sprinkling of 'C' Company chaps up in Ranville, so I'll see about getting them sent down to you. What are you like for weapons?"

Mainly small arms, Sir, although we've got a PIAT and two bombs for it. We've also got a few Gammon Bombs and the explosive and detonators to go with them."

"That'll have to do for now, I suppose." The captain acknowledged. "Although, I'll see if we can spare you a Bren Gun. Now it's getting light we're going to scour these fields properly and see if we can find any more containers. We're also getting the engineer boys who are with us to start blowing some of those stakes out of the ground to make room for the follow up gliders when they arrive…"

He paused in mid-explanation.

"What's that?"

Dawes frowned at the question, but just a second later caught the noise for himself.

"Vehicle!" He cursed. Then, leaning around the end of the overturned car, he shouted across to his men who were crouching inside their hastily dug shell-scrapes on the verge. "Stand-to! Don't fire unless I give the order!"

The captain appeared beside him to stare around the road block.

"It's moving fast." He commented.

The vehicle was still out of sight around the bend in the road, but the noise of its engine came clearly through the morning air, gunning angrily as its driver forced it along at speed. Then, in the blink of an eye, the vehicle appeared; lurching round the bend with barely a drop in speed, wobbling dangerously to one side as it did so, before straightening up and coming straight for the two paratroopers crouching behind the barricade. They heard a shout of warning from the vehicle and, a second later, it skidded to a halt just fifty yards away. Dawes could now see that the vehicle was a British Jeep and, in addition to its driver and passenger, it was crammed full with yet more men in the back. There must have been at least eight men jam-packed onto the tiny vehicle, and all of them were garbed in the distinctive, drab parachute smocks of the British Airborne forces.

Before Dawes had a chance to react, the captain was stepping out from beside him onto the open road.

"Hey, ho!" He shouted in a jolly voice at the men in the Jeep, waving his hand as he appeared in full view.

At first, the men in the Jeep appeared to be startled at the sudden appearance of the officer from behind the upturned staff car, and more than one weapon came up to point in his direction. Just as quickly however, Dawes heard someone in the vehicle call out a warning.

"Easy boys, he's one of ours…"

The captain from 'A' Company was striding down the road towards the vehicle, so Dawes jumped up and jogged after him, falling in alongside the captain as he neared the vehicle and its occupants.

"Welcome to Ranville, gentlemen…" The captain called out brightly at the men in the Jeep, "temporary home of the 13th Battalion, The Parachute Regiment."

One of the men in the Jeep waved a hand at the two men walking up the road.

"Thank God we've finally found some friendly faces." He shouted back towards them.

As they neared the vehicle and passed the shell-scrapes of Dawes' little force, the corporal waved at his men to lower their weapons and stand-down. He'd already recognised one of the men on the Jeep; an old friend from 'D' Company, although the other occupants were unfamiliar.

"What are you chaps up to then?" The captain asked now as they reached the fully laden Jeep.

The man in the passenger seat replied, his voice tinged with a feint Scottish twang.

"We're from 3 Para Squadron, Royal Engineers, Sir; well, most of us anyway. We've just come from down the road there. We've been on a little adventure, so we have; just blew a bridge to smithereens down on the River Dives. Now we've come up here to get on with our second task. We're supposed to clear some lanes for gliders in the fields to the north-west of Ranville."

The captain gave the men in the vehicle an all encompassing smile.

"Well, you've come to the right place then. I don't suppose you've seen any Germans have you?"

The men in the Jeep began laughing.

"Oh, aye!" Replied the spokesman with the Scottish lilt in his voice. "That village we drove through to blow the bridge was packed full of the bastards! They were hopping mad with us for ruining yon bridge! They're proper pissed off now, mind, and I reckon they'll be on their way up here before long to vent their frustration on us."

The captain from 'A' Company gave Dawes a sideways glance.

"We'd better get organised then." He grinned. "Looks like the party's about to start!"

'THE CRUCIBLE' – NEAR CAEN, NORMANDY, FRANCE TUESDAY 6TH JUNE 1944 – 00500 HOURS

"Do you think they're after us?"

Kole stared across the telephone table at Gritz with a worried look.

The veteran sergeant major didn't reply immediately. Instead he just sat there, listening, wincing whenever one of the bombs came close enough to make the dirt fall from between the wooden supports of the command post. After a moment or two, he flicked his eyes away from the shuddering ceiling and looked at Kole.

"No." Gritz replied earnestly, giving his head a little shake. "I think they're after the Regimental Headquarters position and the gun battery there. The Tommies must know about it for sure; all that concreting that's been going on. I think we're just catching some of the strays."

The grizzled soldier paused for a heartbeat and emitted a grunt of wry amusement.

"On this occasion, Kole, I can't help praying that the Tommies are bang on target. Because... if they're not on target and we get a stray stick of bombs landing in the middle of our position..."

Gritz paused again, not wanting to finish the sentence.

"We'll be proper fucked." Kole finished it for him.

Gritz nodded grimly at the corporal.

"Pretty much." He agreed.

The sergeant major removed his helmet and ran a hand through his hair then pinched his nose between finger and thumb and closed his eyes.

"I'm bollocksed. What a fucking night..."

Kole knew what his commander meant. The bombing had been almost non-stop throughout the hours of darkness, making it almost impossible to sleep. On top of that, some of the sentries had reported seeing tracer and small arms fire off to the east, and that had worried Gritz even more than the bombing. As a result, the company had stepped up to fifty percent alertness and remained there until this latest bombing raid had brought the enemy's bombs far too close for comfort. Only then, just three quarters of an hour ago, had Gritz ordered a general stand-down with instructions for everyone to get under cover except the men who were manning the usual sentry positions.

"Hey, Kellerman?" Kole turned to address the nervous looking private who was curled up on his cot under a poncho. "Why don't you get that cooker fired up and get us all a brew on?"

Reluctantly, the timid soldier pushed himself upright and began pottering about with the canteens and a small field cooker. Kole looked back at Gritz, who was in mid-yawn.

"We'll have a hot brew, eh, Sergeant Major? Wake us up a bit. The Tommy planes will fuck off soon I reckon. They don't usually like bombing in daylight, so we should be able to catch up on some sleep soon enough."

Gritz, still yawning, nodded absently. That was when the phone rang.

The senior non commissioned officer looked up sharply as the field telephone rattled noisily on its cradle. Kole snaked his hand out and snatched the handset up.

"Command Post; The Crucible."

The corporal was silent a moment whilst the caller said something at the other end of the line.

"Yes..." Kole said a moment later. "This is Point 113; but the Corps Commander has told us that we are now to be known as The Crucible."

Another pause while the caller spoke; longer this time. Eventually, Kole gave a curt nod and mumbled into the handset.

"Yes, he's here in front of me. I'll put him on."

With that, Kole passed the handset over to Gritz.

"It's Regimental Headquarters over the way there; the Colonel wants to speak to you."

Gritz took the phone and put it to his ear.

"Gritz speaking."

There was no answer at first, but a couple of moments later there was a metallic click, and then a familiar voice came on the line; that of Colonel Krug.

"Hello?"

"Hello?" Gritz responded. "Gritz speaking."

"Ah, Gritz..." Krug's serious voice rasped down the phone. "Listen, there's something going on..."

"Yes, Colonel; we can hear it. Sounds like most of it's landing on top of you?"

"Mmm, yes, well..." Krug sounded agitated. "I think the Tommies are trying to knock us out. Fortunately they don't seem to be all that accurate at the moment. A lot of the bombs seem to be going wide, so keep your heads down Gritz because you might be catching some of them soon enough."

"Don't worry, Colonel; we're hunkered down over here."

Gritz heard the colonel take a deep breath.

"Good, now... listen, Gritz; there's something going on, apart from all the bombing."

The Regimental Commander paused for a moment but Gritz remained silent, so the colonel went on.

"There's been a commando raid over to the east of our position."

Now, Gritz did speak.

"Commandos?"

The veteran infantryman felt a chill run through his body. Although he'd spent most of the war on the Eastern Front, Gritz had heard about Britain's 'commandos'. They were, by all accounts, fearsome individuals; murderers and rogues according to some of the stories he'd heard; hence the Fuhrer's orders that all commandos were to be summarily executed if captured. Gritz had heard the story about the suicidal British commando raid on St Nazaire a couple of years back and there was no doubt that only the bravest, or most desperate of men would attempt such a daring feat.

"Yes." Krug confirmed, interrupting Gritz's thoughts. "They landed by glider just after midnight somewhere to our east. They have attacked the bridges over the Orne and the Caen Canal. I've got a couple of platoons trying to contain them and I've asked Divisional Headquarters for a mobile company to be sent up so we can launch a co-ordinated counter-attack in strength. The problem is that Division say they can't release any troops just yet, as there are reports of commando activities elsewhere. They're trying to work out what's going on."

Gritz thought he heard a hidden suggestion somewhere amongst the colonel's situation report.

"I've got barely half a dozen men who can walk without a limp, Colonel..." He began to explain, but Krug cut him short.

"Yes, yes; don't worry Gritz. I'm not going to ask you to take your bunch of cripples on a six kilometre march to attack Tommy commandos. That's a non-starter."

Gritz relaxed slightly.

"I just wanted to let you know that something is going on. I'm not sure what yet, but something's not right; believe me you need to stay sharp up there, Gritz; just in case there is more devilry to come."

"Don't worry, Colonel. I'll make sure we're ready if anything kicks off..."

Gritz stopped in mid-sentence as the sound of a commotion drifted down the phone line. He could hear other voices in the background behind Krug; excited voices; frightened voices. The phone clicked off for a moment, leaving Gritz with a dead line. A second later, the line went live again and the sound of agitated voices returned. Then, over the racket, Krug spoke again.

"Gritz? I've got to go... Something's happening... I'll ring you back. Stay alert..."

The line went dead. Gritz put the handset back down on the cradle. He looked across at Kole, who opened his mouth as if to speak, but he never got the chance.

"Sergeant Major Gritz? Sergeant Major?"

Gritz, Kole and Kellerman all turned and looked with alarm towards the curtain over the door at the sound of the urgent call.

"In here!" Gritz shouted, jumping up from the box on which he was seated and donning his helmet once more.

The curtain was pulled open almost before Gritz had uttered the words and a pale face wearing an over-sized helmet appeared from behind it.

"Sergeant Major; they need you up at the forward left platoon immediately! Sergeant Gunther says he needs you straight away!"

"What's up?" Gritz demanded, recognizing the face at the door as being that of one of the new boys.

"I don't know, Sir..." The young private stammered. "The sentry across the gulley is just shouting across for you... He says you need to come quickly..."

The hairs on Gritz's neck were standing up. He knew the feeling well. He was long accustomed to the subtleties of what he liked to call 'combat indicators'. On this occasion however, there was nothing subtle about the ominous chain of events that seemed to be unfolding.

"I'm on my way." Gritz snapped back at the man in the doorway, snatching up his MP40 machine-pistol as he did so. Then, turning to Kole, he said, "Kole; ring the checkpoint. Tell them there are Tommy commandos in the area. Tell them to stay sharp."

"Commandos?" Kole repeated.

But Gritz was already gone.

The veteran sergeant major moved as quickly as he could, striding through the damp undergrowth and feeling the moisture soak through his trousers in an instant. As he emerged from the cover of the trees of the knoll, he spotted the figure of a rifleman across the shallow gulley, crouching on the edge of the tree-line at that side.

"What's going on?" Gritz called out to the man as he began to descend the steep bank, down towards the ruins of the forge.

"Over here, Sir, quickly!" The man shouted back. "Sergeant Gunther wants you to see this!"

"See what?" Gritz shouted back as he negotiated the slope.

The rifleman's answer was lost to Gritz as the sergeant major lost his footing on the rain soaked turf and slid unceremoniously down the slope into the gulley, wrenching his bad knee as he went.

"Ahhh! You fucking fucker!" Swore the veteran as the sickeningly familiar pain shot through the muscles surrounding his left knee.

Sliding to a stop by the ruins in the small depression, Gritz lay there on his back for a moment or two, his face screwed up in pain.

"For fuck's sake!" He snarled in frustration; holding onto his injured limb. " Fuck, fuck, fuck!"

After several more profanities, the sergeant major rolled onto his right knee, pushed himself upright, and began hobbling around the ruined building and up the opposite slope towards the main position.

The rifleman had gone now; presumably back to Gunther's position on the forward left of the wood. Muttering with a mixture of pain and self pity, Gritz began struggling up the bank, holding onto branches and large clumps of grass for purchase as he did so. The sweat was pouring out of him now, despite the early hour and the damp air.

"This had better be fucking important!" The old warrior growled to himself as he staggered and slipped his way up the incline and into the cover of the trees.

Once up the slope he paused, gathering his breath on the more even ground. He got his bearings in the dull, dawn light and spotted the entrance to the communication trench that ran forwards through the wood to the forward left strongpoint. There was nobody manning the rear sentry position, and that pissed Gritz off. What the fuck was going on?

His foul mood became fouler still when there was a sudden flurry of large explosions just a few hundred yards away to the east, somewhere beyond the far side of the wooded ridge. Despite the distance, terrain and tree-cover, Gritz felt the shock waves rippling through the air as the ground trembled dangerously beneath his feet.

"This is fucking shit!" He snarled to nobody in particular then began hobbling towards the communication trench.

His passage forward, through the left hand side of the wood was easy enough. Nobody blocked his way or challenged him. It was as if the forward left platoon had just disappeared off the face of the earth. It was only when he reached the forward line of strongpoints that he understood why. Crowded into the forward fire-trench was a gaggle of about twenty men; the entire forward left platoon.

"What the fuck's going on here?" Gritz roared at the mass of soldiery. "Where's Sergeant Gunther?"

Two or three of the soldiers turned at the sound of Gritz's voice and he noted the look of fear and consternation on their faces, despite the gloom of the dawn's half-light. As they stepped back out of Gritz's way and pointed to the front of the fire trench, the sergeant major got the distinct impression that it was more than his foul temper that had them looking like death warmed up. He elbowed his way forward through the men, having spotted Gunther at the front of the group. The sergeant was staring out of the wood, across the fields and away towards the coast, a pair of binoculars raised to his eyes.

"Gunther? What the fuck is going on man?" Gritz demanded as he stepped up beside the non commissioned officer.

The sergeant lowered his binoculars and turned to Gritz. Gritz saw the ashen look on the man's face immediately and the hollow feeling in the sergeant major's stomach increased with sudden intensity. For his part, Gunther simply pointed with his arm towards the coast.

"There." He said grimly.

Gritz tore his eyes away from the sergeant and looked in the direction indicated. At first he didn't quite register the scene completely. He saw the open green meadows sloping gently downhill, the vast expanse dotted with the anti-glider posts that peppered the fields for kilometres around. He saw the intersecting hedgerows at the far side of the fields where the crossroads met, and beyond the crossroads, the distant grey roofs of several coastal hamlets and villages. Then he saw it.

Beyond the usual panorama was the sea; dull, grey and uninviting on this filthy, unseasonable morning. And out on that sea, unbelievably, and worryingly close, was a fleet of ships. A vast fleet; a fleet of the like Gritz had never imagined in his wildest dreams. Ships of every possible size, their outlines indistinct yet menacing in the damp haze of first light. The huge armada filled the horizon from left to right, appearing like some kind of huge dark wall sitting out on the ocean.

"My God!"

Gritz gasped the words aloud without thinking. He'd seen some sights in Russia, but he'd never seen anything like this. With a supreme effort, he turned his eyes to Gunther. The sergeant returned his gaze with a look of absolute dread. The two men just looked at each other in disbelief for a moment before the sergeant finally found his voice.

"They've come." He whispered.

FARMHOUSE PELLETIER, 300 METRES FROM POINT 113 – NORMANDY
TUESDAY 6TH JUNE 1944 – 0515 HOURS

"Is it morning yet?"

Madam Pelletier raised a weary head from the mattress that her husband had dragged into the cellar the evening before. Her husband, in whose arms she was snuggled and who had not slept a wink all night, glanced at his old pocket watch by the light of the oil lamp. He did so from habit, having checked the watch at regular intervals throughout that long, sleepless night. He knew the time before he even looked at the timepiece.

"Yes, almost. It's a little after a quarter past five."

Across from them, on another mattress, their son stirred from beneath his blanket.

"I think the bombing has stopped at last." He ventured.

Monsieur Pelletier cast a scowl through the gloom of the farmhouse cellar.

"Is this when it was supposed to finish?" He asked sarcastically. "Or was your contact in *The Resistance* not that specific?"

"Emile!" His wife appealed at her husband's implied reprimand.

This had begun the night before. Their son, Maurice, had returned from Mademoiselle Lisseur's the previous evening, late on; only just before the curfew was due. That in itself had been enough to both worry and anger his parents. They knew only too well that the Germans would not tolerate excuses for anybody caught roaming around the coastal zone after curfew, regardless of their excuse. Maurice had received a grumpy reception from his father in particular.

"You realise there are boys and girls your age in Caen prison for being caught out after curfew?" Monsieur Pelletier had rumbled, wagging his finger at his son across the kitchen table. "They're stuck in some cell and accused of spying! Can you believe it? Fifteen year olds in jail and accused of spying! The Germans could shoot them all if they felt like it; even if they don't have a shred of evidence against any of them. Suspicion is enough for the Boche. They have no mercy in these matters."

That had been just the start. When Maurice had suggested that they should spend the night in the cellar, because he had 'a strange feeling' that something was in the air, his father had detected the lie immediately, surprising the young man with his uncharacteristic shrewdness.

"What do you mean, 'a strange feeling'? What have you seen? Or, more to the point, what have you been told?"

Paling under his father's withering gaze, Maurice had made a pathetic attempt at concealing the source of his sudden desire for the family to sleep in the cellar.

"Er, nothing really, just... you know when you get that feeling that something isn't quite right..."

Monsieur Pelletier had once more surprised both his son and wife with his next, remarkably astute observation.

"She's in The Resistance isn't she?"

Maurice had drained of all remaining colour in an instant.

Monsieur Pelletier had risen from his stool, a simmering anger, or was it fear, bubbling in his voice as he spoke.

"How stupid of me! There was I, thinking that my son was obsessed with his young and beautiful teacher, simply because that is how all young boys are in the presence of beautiful women. There was I, thinking it was no more than a childish infatuation. But all along there has been more to it."

"Emile!" Madam Pelletier had appealed to her husband, but the farmer had ignored his wife and come round the table to lean over Maurice.

"I must have been blind. There's you, a young boy who hangs on the every word of his glamorous young teacher, and who lives in the defended zone near the coast; somewhere Mademoiselle Lisseur would never be allowed..."

Monsieur Pelletier had paused for just a moment.

"How does it work, boy? Do you get a kiss for every piece of information? A grope or a fumble maybe? Well?"

"Emile!" Madam Pelletier had cried out in protest now, but her husband was in no mood for her maternal instincts.

"Sit down." He'd ordered her in a flat, hard tone.

"What have you told her, Maurice?" He had asked his son in a low, dangerous voice. "And what did she tell you? Tell me everything. And in the name of God, boy, don't leave a single word out of it."

Maurice had cracked. He'd revealed everything that he'd ever told his teacher. His reports of the anti-glider posts being hammered into the fields; the establishment a fortnight ago of the check-point, and now of the Germans in the wood, up on the ridge above their farm. And then he'd told his father about Mademoiselle Lisseur's mysterious visitor, and her words of advice about taking shelter in the cellar.

His father and mother had listened in silence. At the end of it all, Monsieur Pelletier, rather than flying into a rage and slapping his son, had simply taken a deep breath. Watching him, both son and wife had realised in an instant that the man of the house was not so much angry, as frightened. Having controlled his breathing, Monsieur Pelletier had stood straight and spoken his next words in a tight, clipped voice.

"You will not see or speak to that woman again. None of us will ever speak to anyone about what has just been said. I am going to lock everything up. Maurice; you get the mattresses from the bedrooms and take them down to the cellar. Alice, you get some food and drink together and take it down there. And then we shall see what the morning brings. And pray to God that it isn't the Germans."

And that had been that. They had been down here all night, listening to the relentless bombing over towards Caen, and most recently, to the terrifying aerial bombardment that had been taking place even closer to the farm. God only knew what the British were trying to hit, but they were trying their damnedest all the same.

"She said to stay here until it was all over." Said Maurice weakly.

With a disconsolate grunt, Monsieur Pelletier struggled to his feet, shaking off the blankets. There had been no explosions for over fifteen minutes now, and in the eerie silence that followed, the sound of cows, lowing to be milked, drifted down into the cellar of the farmhouse.

"Stay here. I'm just going to take a look outside; see what's going on."

Neither Maurice nor his mother made any comment or attempt to stop the burly farmer as he cautiously ascended the stone steps of the cellar. They listened in silence as his footsteps disappeared into the kitchen. They heard the kitchen door open and the sound of the cows grew louder. Other than that, there was no sound of alarm that they could detect.

It seemed like an age before Monsieur Pelletier returned, and when he finally did rejoin his wife and son, his face was as white as a ghost. He came down the steps of the cellar slowly, carefully, as if unsure of his footing.

Coming at last to the bottom step, he regarded his family with a somewhat detached gaze.

"You two stay here for now." He said. "I need to milk the cows and let them out again."

Madam Pelletier, seeing her husband's somewhat distracted manner, looked at him with concern.

"Emile... Are you alright? Has something happened outside."

He stared at her for a moment before replying.

"The rain has stopped..." He said falteringly. "The storm has eased... You can see right out to sea... And the British..."

He tailed off, his larynx working overtime as he fought to maintain his composure.

"The British...?" His wife wondered aloud.

Monsieur Pelletier's face began to form the beginnings of a feint, disbelieving smile as he finished his sentence.

"They've come back..."

LANDING CRAFT INFANTRY 998 – 7 MILES OFF SWORD BEACH, NORMANDY
TUESDAY 6TH JUNE 1944 – 0525 HOURS

"Actually Sir, it's not quite as bad as I expected it to be. The way the Navy chaps were talking I thought we'd be getting thrown about all over the place."

Second Lieutenant Jeremy Willis smiled good-humouredly at his company commander across the dimly lit cabin.

Across from the upbeat young infantry officer, Dickie Smithson fought hard to keep his stomach under control and inwardly cursed the young sprog's child-like enthusiasm. Smithson was no sea-farer, and he'd hated every single moment of the trip across the Channel in the bowels of the heaving landing craft as it had bobbed up, down, and sideways on the storm-lashed ocean. Only by dint of stupendous effort and self discipline had Smithson not allowed his dignity to slip and join the majority of other men who had spent most of the night being routinely sick into an assortment of buckets and other receptacles.

The torment had been made no easier by the fact that young Willis, one of Smithson's platoon commanders, had been an accomplished yachtsman prior to the war and had whiled away the small hours regaling his superior officer with tales of his adventures under sail. Smithson was too well mannered to tell the likeable young officer to shut up, but now, after hours of enduring the hellish crossing, Smithson was on the verge of losing his patience.

"Still, we must be nearly there now, eh, Sir?" Willis blathered on. "It's half past five almost."

"Thank God for that..." Smithson mumbled through a mouth clamped tightly shut against the threat of a sudden projection of vomit.

"Yes," Willis smiled nervously, "be good to get onto dry land and take it to the Jerries after all these years. I bet you're itching to get stuck back in, aren't you?"

Smithson smiled back at the young ensign; a tight, grim smile. He understood what the fellow was going through. He had been like that once; young, idealistic, inexperienced, un-blooded. The boy was nervous as hell; that much was obvious. His endless chattering was nothing more than an attempt at self-distraction.

"Yes, Jeremy..." Smithson managed to squeeze out the words as he felt an ominous spasm deep in his stomach. "I can't wait to get back onto dry land."

"Morning, gentlemen."

The voice of the naval rating sounded buoyant and jovial as he popped his head around the door of the cabin that was crammed full of officers from the Hambledon and Moorlanders.

"The Skipper says it's okay for you to go up on deck now its light; get yourselves a bit of fresh air and take a look at the scenery."

Smithson felt a surge of relief at the news and he smiled a genuine smile of thanks at the weather-beaten sailor.

"Thank you. Thank you very much."

Willis was already on his feet.

"I think I might go up, Sir; take a look at the fleet if you don't mind?"

Smithson struggled to his feet, trying not to look too keen to be out of the cabin.

"Yes, I think I might join you actually Jeremy; stretch the legs a bit."

Around the cabin, there were sighs and groans of relief as the other sea-sick officers registered the message of salvation.

"After you, Sir." Willis opened the palm of his hand towards the doorway.

"No, please, Jeremy. After you old boy..."

Willis did as he was bade and stepped out of the cabin. Smithson waited until the young man was out of the room before he stepped up to a foul smelling bucket of stale vomit and emptied his stomach into it. There wasn't much to come out, because Smithson had eaten frugally the day before, and so he found himself retching over and over again, regurgitating nothing more than foul smelling fluid that gushed out of his body, stinging his throat and nostrils and making him gasp and cry out like a child.

As the wave of nausea subsided and Smithson fought to steady his breathing, he grabbed hold of a nearby shelf and straightened up, wiping his mouth and nose on the back of his sleeve. To his surprise, the cabin was empty. The remaining officers hadn't been the slightest bit interested in watching their company commander suffer the ignominy of throwing up in front of them. They were all too ill themselves and were already scrabbling up the stairs for the blessed fresh air of the open deck.

"Good God..." Smithson whispered to himself. "Never again..."

He picked up his helmet and put it on, then began making his way, somewhat shakily, along the gangway and up the stairs towards the upper deck. As he walked, his legs shook terribly; partly due to the after-tremors of vomiting that rippled through his body, and partly due to the awful heave of the ship as it lurched rather awkwardly through the choppy seas.

Climbing the steps, both hands gripping the rails, Smithson spat onto the floor, trying desperately to rid his mouth of the foul aftertaste. His nose detected the combined odours of puke, piss, salt-water and rusting metal as he progressed and this served to make him increase his speed; dreading the potential onset of a second wave of nausea. Thus, it was with some relief that he reached the top of the stairs and exited through a narrow doorway onto the upper deck of the landing ship. And there he came to a standstill.

It was dawn, perhaps a few minutes after, and despite the fact that he hadn't reached the guard-rail at the ship's side like the rest of the officers, he still had a perfectly clear view of the heart-stopping sight before him. He had no real idea where the coast of France was, or even if it was in sight yet, because his entire field of vision was filled with ships. Grey, dark, ominous looking shapes in the dull morning light, the surface of the water appeared to be filled with rank upon rank of troop ships; from the big landing ships like this one, to the ungainly, specially designed landing craft of the first wave assault units. Just visible, beyond the furthest lines of landing craft, were the slightly bigger silhouettes of the destroyer screen and minesweepers, clearing the water as the vast armada steamed inexorably onwards.

Staggered at the scene before him, and feeling instantly better as a sharp, salty, sea-breeze coursed by, taking away the fetid stench of the lower decks, Smithson walked slowly across the deck and came to stand beside Willis and the other officers from the battalion. They were standing in utter silence; each of them trying to take in the enormity of what they were witnessing.

"Ruddy hell!" Smithson finally managed to breathe; his voice tinged with awe.

Even as he spoke, the attention of everyone at the rail was diverted skyward as a dim, sonorous droning noise developed into something much louder, deeper, and ominous. The infantrymen squinted upwards into the slate-grey sky, where the worst of the storm clouds were breaking up now, like tiny snatches of dirty cotton wool being blown across the heavens by the prevailing wind. And up in that sky, between those ragged clouds, clearly outlined against the grey backdrop like a swarm of black crows, came the largest assembly of aircraft Smithson had ever seen.

He could see large, heavy bombers, arranged in neat groups of four, which were melded into bigger formations that seemed to fill the sky. Far above this mass of aircraft were yet more planes. Smaller planes, in slightly smaller swarms; the fighter escorts for their big brothers of the bomber arm. As the huge, aerial armada passed overhead, the air around the soldiers on deck seemed to be alive with the thrum of aero-engines.

"Ye Gods!" Willis murmured beside Smithson. "I didn't know the air force had so many planes...

Another voice spoke, just along the rail somewhat.

"Look at those beasts over there then..."

Smithson, Willis and every other person there followed the speaker's outstretched arm with their eyes, almost directly rearwards. This time, along with the sense of awe, Smithson felt an equally powerful sense of dread. Behind this massive assembly of landing craft, destroyers and minesweepers, were the battlewagons of the bombardment force. The capital ships of the Royal Navy, usually reserved for ship to ship engagements on the high seas, had today been brought here to the coast of Normandy to pound the defences of Hitler's Atlantic Wall with their huge guns. Although Smithson didn't know the identities of those big ships, the powerful bombardment force included such venerable warhorses as HMS Ramillies and HMS Warspite, both of them boasting massive fifteen inch guns.

Even without that knowledge, the mere sight of those huge ships, all of them now wheeled into formation on the bombardment line, was enough to make Smithson's pulse race. And, as the dumb-struck officers of the Hambledon and Moorlanders looked on, those big guns in their steel turrets began to rise up, like primeval beasts rearing their heads. The outline of those guns against the grey sky was a sight that Smithson knew he would never forget.

And then the ends of those big guns flashed orange; a startling, vivid orange that seemed to break the grey monotony of the dawn instantly. And a second later, the deafening roar of those fifteen inch monsters came rolling across the surface of the water and sent tremors of fear and excitement through the onlookers. And from that point onwards, the peace and tranquillity of the seas off Normandy was shattered with no hope of return; at least not on this momentous day. The first Allied shells of the long awaited 'Second Front' were hurtling through the air, screaming towards their German targets with a howl of vengeance that had been four years in the coming. It was D-Day, the 6th June 1944, and the liberation of Europe had begun.

'OBJECTIVE COD', SWORD BEACH - LA BRECHE D'HERMANVILLE, NORMANDY
TUESDAY 6TH JUNE 1944 – 0525 HOURS

It was their turn. Lehman had been dreading it all night. The bombing had started a little before midnight; well inland at first, over towards Caen and beyond. The raids had been widespread it seemed, for the entire horizon from the east, through south to the south east, had been illuminated by a constant, sickly glow; the glow that came from fire, flares, and explosions. The noise had been constant too; a distant tremble at first, that had grown into a continuous rumble.

During his time on sentry duty, Lehman had stood there gawping inland at the ominous light show, or up at the scudding cloud that was busily breaking up in the high winds that rolled in off the sea. Shivering in his greatcoat, the young man had once more thanked his lucky stars that he had been posted to a relatively non-descript stretch of shoreline that had no particular value; or at least, none that Lehman could identify. Heaven forbid that he ever got posted to guard a radar station or railway yard; the kind of place that the Tommies loved to target with their heavy bombers. No, the sandy dunes and requisitioned holiday villas of Le Breche would do him fine.

It had been with that mildly comforting thought that Lehman had finished his duty and returned to his bed in the early hours of the morning. Glad to be snuggling up under the blankets having got out of the damp sea breeze, the teenage soldier had managed to drift off to sleep; the steady, incessant rumble of bombing and anti-aircraft fire acting like a rhythmic lullaby to him. It had been a deep, surprisingly pleasant sleep, yet one that had been rudely interrupted just an hour before, when the air-raid alarm on the company's position had begun wailing.

Barely had Lehman sat upright on his cot when the first stick of bombs had exploded with unbelievable force just a couple of hundred yards away from the villa which acted as a billet for his platoon. The doors and window shutters had suddenly banged and clattered against the walls as the shock wave of the explosions had blown them inwards. The noise of the explosions had hammered at Lehman's ears making him cry out with the pain. It was, he'd thought groggily, like being in the very centre of a ground-based thunder storm.

He was already flat on his belly on the floor, scrabbling for his helmet, when Corporal Fuchs had burst into the room, half dressed and bootless.

"Into the cellar! Everyone; as quick as you can. Make sure you've got your gas masks and helmets with you; and your weapons. Come on, move it."

Lehman had reacted instantly and snatched at his equipment that was stored neatly at the end of his cot.

"What about the shelters?" Someone else in the darkened room had shouted above the sound of another series of explosions.

"There's no time for that!" Fuchs' had replied, crouching down against the doorway of the room. "There are bombs dropping all over the position! Just get into the cellar for now and we'll move out to the shelters if we get a clear spell. Now come on, shift your arses!"

And here they had been ever since; eighteen of them cowering in the cellar of the sea-front villa, surrounded by boxes of ammunition, grenades and mortar bombs. Not the ideal place to be sheltering, Lehman thought. The air was filled with choking dust, sand and the acrid fumes that resulted from the repeated detonation of dozens of tons of explosive. Lehman struggled to see the time on his wrist watch in the dim light, but he thought it must be some time after five in the morning.

"Sounds like that's the worst of it over…"

Corporal Fuchs' usually powerful voice sounded surprisingly weak in the silence following the lengthy bombardment. Even so, the words snapped Lehman out of his personal thoughts. The private rolled onto his side and cocked his ear, listening for the tell tale whistle of yet more bombs descending from the grey skies above. Nothing. Lehman realised that there had been no explosions for several minutes now and the sudden quiet after the constant pounding seemed strange; disconcerting.

"Should we try and get to the shelters now, Corporal?"

Gruber's voice came from a dark corner of the room, sounding decidedly shaky.

"I think we might as well…"

Fuchs stopped the soldier in mid-sentence.

"What's that?" He snapped.

At first, nothing came to Lehman's ears. All he could hear was the surreal silence that enveloped them all following the relentless pounding of the last hour. But then he caught it. Hard to distinguish at first, he soon realised it was the voice of Lieutenant Marder, their company commander. Somewhere outside the building, probably amongst the maze of communication trenches and dugouts, the officer was barking out orders with urgency. The officer's voice grew louder and more distinct.

"Come on, move your arses! Get to your positions!"

The last phrase was quickly followed by several shrill blasts on a whistle which made Lehman jump.

"Come on you fuckers!" Marder's voice was even closer now, as if he were right outside their building. "Stand-to! Stand-to!"

A sudden, heavy feeling of foreboding shot through Lehman. He wasn't sure why. Perhaps it was just those words? *Stand-to?* They just sounded deeply disturbing for some reason in the wake of the bombing.

"Come on, you lot!" Fuchs suddenly rapped out an order, scrambling to his feet. "Follow me. Everyone outside."

There was a frantic rattle and scrape of boots and equipment as the German infantrymen got shakily to their feet and began following their corporal up the cellar stairs. Even before Lehman had set foot on the steps however, he could hear Marder summoning them.

"Fuchs? Fuchs? Where are you? Get your men into position; move it!"

The corporal was at the top of the stairs and in the hallway now.

"We're here, Sir! We're standing-to now!"

Lehman staggered up the stairs, wishing he could pause for a quick drink of water. The dust and smoke was even thicker up here and it clawed at his throat, making him gag. Gruber was behind him, coughing and spluttering as the pair of them half ran, half fell up the steps in their haste.

Emerging into the hallway, Lehman found Corporal Fuchs and Lieutenant Marder together; the latter rapping out a string of orders.

"Get everyone into position quickly. All weapons to be made ready, and open up every bit of ammunition you've got; you're going to need it. I'll be back shortly; get it sorted..."

The lieutenant was in such a hurry that he didn't even wait for an acknowledgement from Fuchs. Instead he turned on his heel and disappeared out of the house. For his part, Fuchs turned harassed looking eyes on the men who had followed him up from the cellar.

"Lehman; Gruber; usual spot... Bottom left room at the front... go! Bauer; Foerster; Ostermann; front right, ground floor. Get that gun set up..."

Fuchs continued to rattle out the instructions as Lehman and Gruber groped their way through the dusty confines of the building towards their allocated stand-to position.

They could still hear the corporal's voice as they entered their allocated room, although his words were less distinct now as the two young soldiers crunched over bits of plaster and glass that littered the floor. Gruber headed towards the sand-bagged emplacement that had been constructed against the window that looked out onto the promenade, still coughing on the dust.

"The shutters have blown in..." Gruber squawked hoarsely. "I'll knock them back out. You get those ammo boxes opened up."

"Okay..." Lehman acknowledged and began searching around in the corner for the stock-piled rifle ammunition. He spotted the green containers covered in chunks of broken plaster and grabbed a pair of them by their collapsible metal handles. As he gripped hold of the two metal boxes, he heard the splintering of wood as Gruber smashed the shutters forwards and outwards from the window frame.

"Oh, my God!"

Lehman straightened up, an ammo box in either hand and his rifle slung over his shoulder.

"What's wrong?" He asked, turning towards the sandbagged position against the window.

Gruber didn't reply at first, but Lehman could see that his companion had succeeded in forcing the mangled shutters clear of the windows, and that the young man was now standing in the wide open space, staring out towards the sea, his upper body silhouetted against the pale, grey dawn sky.

"Tomas?" Lehman murmured, that sense of foreboding deepening even more.

"Oh, my God..." Was all Gruber could manage.

Lehman stepped across the room and came to stand beside his friend, following his gaze out of the window.

There was a large bomb crater in the middle of the road, right outside the house. The sea-wall ran across their front on the far side of the promenade, topped with barbed wire; and beyond it were the dunes and the beach. Beyond that was the sea. But something had happened to that sea. The vast, flat expanse of green-grey that Lehman and his friends had become used to was gone. Instead, the sea was black. Black with ships.

Those ships sat there, motionless it seemed; dark and ominous, like a ghost fleet that had arrived out of nowhere in the night. His jaw dropping open, Lehman tried to scan left and right to see the extent of the armada, but there was no end to the huge force it seemed. The ugly, menacing profile of warships of every description filled the soldier's field of vision for as far as he could see in either direction. The distant hills above Le Havre across to his half right were completely obscured by the wall of ships.

"They're here…" Gruber gasped beside him.

Lehman tried to speak, but found he couldn't. He just stared, mouth agape at the unbelievable sight before him.

And then, as if somebody had just flicked a light switch, that line of vessels seemed to sparkle and crackle with myriad tiny flashes of light. For a split second, Lehman and Gruber continued to stare at the spectacle, mesmerised by the sheer scale of what they were seeing. But then they noted the small clouds of smoke rising from the vessels, and a heartbeat later the terrible, thunderous roar of heavy naval guns came rolling across the lively surf, and this sound was quickly followed by another. This time it sounded like a giant, invisible freight train was running out of control, and coming straight for them through the very air above them. And that was when reality suddenly slapped both men into action.

"Shit!" Lehman cried out, dropping to his knees behind the sandbagged barricade as the ground beneath his feet seemed to heave and buckle. And then the shock wave from the first fifteen inch shell slammed into the house, ripping the mangled wooden shutters right off and bursting one of Lehman's ear drums.

It was dawn on D-Day the Sixth of June 1944. The Tommies had finally come. And they wanted a fight…

PART THREE
ASSAULT

LANDING SHIP INFANTRY EMPIRE BATTLEAXE – SIX MILES OFF SWORD BEACH, NORMANDY TUESDAY 6TH JUNE 1944 – 0530 HOURS

Downey looked down into the packed Landing Craft Assault, or LCA as they were commonly known, and hesitated. All around him was urgency. The air around and above them resounded with the hollow, deafening boom of the heavy naval guns of the bombardment force, and the howl and scream of those huge shells streaking overhead towards the enemy held coastline cut through ones nerves like a knife. Christ almighty, but Downey was glad he wasn't on the end of those shells. He'd been under shell fire before, but not from anything as big as the monsters currently hurtling through the dawn sky towards Sword Beach.

All about the ship's upper deck, the men of the 2nd Battalion of the East Yorkshire Regiment were clambering into their landing craft, ready to be lowered into the swollen waters of the English Channel before beginning their run in to this, the extreme eastern beach of the Allied landing. And these men, just a few hundred of them, along with a few hundred more from the South Lancashire Regiment, constituted the first wave; the men who would be the first British soldiers to throw themselves against Hitler's much vaunted Atlantic Wall.

He looked down at the men in his platoon, jam-packed into the little assault boat like sardines in a can. There were two non-commissioned officers apart from himself who had seen action before, along with Private Dawson in three section; an old soldier who didn't hold any rank simply on account of his propensity for getting into fist fights in pubs. Grimly, Downey realised that Dawson would get all the fighting he wanted today and more. He just hoped the little drama-merchant was up for it this time. Other than that, they were a pretty raw bunch. Well trained, Downey thought; superbly trained in fact. But un-blooded and raw all the same.

The surly Private Evans was there, jet-black haired and gypsy-like, from North Ferriby, just outside Hull; dour, reluctant and painfully slow at every task he was given. Wilberfosse was there too; a fair-haired, very Nordic looking lad from Wetwang who'd been to grammar school and could have probably been an officer if it hadn't been for his broad, Yorkshire brogue. Headley was there among them, the strapping farmer's boy from South Cave, who was balding on top, even at the young age of nineteen, and had the face of a man subjected to an eternity of desert sun. He was a happy, energetic lad, but slightly naive Downey thought. And then there was the platoon commander; a good, enthusiastic young man, doing his best to learn his trade and desperately trying to appear older, more confident and more experienced than he actually was.

They were the product of this long, costly war. Four years ago, this platoon would have been full of foul-mouthed, hard-drinking ruffians in their mid-twenties, but after the Dunkirk campaign, Norway, The Middle and Far East, not to mention the failed German invasion of Britain, the entire British Army now looked just like Downey's platoon. Absurdly young, with a sprinkling of veterans, this new army was equipped with new weapons and equipment too. The battle dress and webbing was still the same, but the helmets were a more streamlined design now, and covered with scrim-net which was in turn adorned with strips of coloured hessian cloth. The old Lee-Enfield rifle was still the staple weapon, but once again was a newer, sleeker model than before, its eighteen inch sword bayonet now replaced by the equally vicious looking pig-sticker.

And, like the German Army, the British now had their own sub-machine gun. It was nothing special to look at, but the Sten Gun did its job, and helped reduced the weight burden of the non commissioned officers and signallers. And as for tanks, well, apart from the fact that every infantry battalion now had its own platoon of deadly six pounder anti-tank guns, even here at platoon level, the British Tommy had the means of fighting back against the feared 'Panzers'. That came in the form of the PIAT; the heavy, awkward looking projector that was carried in platoon headquarters. It was a short range weapon, designed for a 'last-stand' against armour, but it was *something.*

Downey ran his eyes across the scene in the landing craft; across the grim, nervous faces of men who had spent an entire night of continuous, vomit laden hell; over the shovels, picks and Bangalore Torpedo tubes that were stowed amongst their equipment. Most of these men had no idea what was coming. Downey did. In a way, he just wanted to get on with it; finish the job that had been going on for so long now. Finish Hitler and his mob once and for all. But part of him wanted to stay here on the ship. Because he knew that once he had stepped into the landing craft there would be no going back.

This wasn't going to be like an exercise. There would be no umpires wearing white armbands, walking around and pointing at people with their sticks and saying 'You're dead.' Death would come instantly, suddenly, unexpectedly, and terminally. There would be no blowing of the whistle followed by the familiar cry of *'Endex'*. When a man was killed in battle, it just happened. One moment a man would be a living, breathing, functioning human being; the next, he would just be a lifeless pile of meat. No animation, no heroic last words. Just *'bang'*, and then he would be gone.

And it would be so indiscriminate too, Downey knew. There was no guarantee that anyone would live through the forthcoming battle. You could be the strongest, fittest, most professional soldier, and still be dead within seconds of the battle starting. On the other hand, you could be an utter coward who couldn't hit a barn door at twenty paces with a Bren Gun, yet you could come through a battle without a scratch and be hailed a hero. War was like that; so utterly, utterly random and unfair. So, there was no point worrying about it. If you survived; fine. If your time was up... well, you wouldn't even know anything about it.

"What's up Sarge? You not coming?"

The voice of Private Edmunds, the platoon joker, drifted up from the landing craft.

"I'm not sure if I'll be able to..." Downey replied in a voice betraying mock innocence. "You're such a bunch of fat bastards there's no room left in there for me! I might just have to wait here for another one to come along."

A ripple of nervous laughter came up from the men in the boat, as their platoon sergeant stepped carefully down into the laden assault craft. No sooner had Downey squeezed himself into position inside the boat, than the ships crew began to winch the landing craft over the side of the vessel and lower it towards the churning sea.

As the landing craft was cranked lower and lower over the ship's side, a sudden, powerful wave of apprehension swept over Downey. He took a deep breath and then held it, forcing the emotion back down.

"No going back now..." He whispered to himself.

"Sorry, Sarge? What was that?" Edmunds looked over his shoulder at Downey.

Downey forced a grin.

"I said, fart if you dare and I'll fucking throw you overboard, Edmunds!"

There was another ripple of laughter in the boat and Downey glanced at the side of the ship as they descended towards the water. He noticed every single rivet; every single spec of rust and chip in the paintwork. Strange that;

how you noticed such little things in times of stress, as if trying to drink in every last image of the world before it was gone forever.

There was a dull sploshing noise as the landing craft settled in the water, and then the crew of the small assault boat were releasing the drop-chains.

"Away boat!"

The cry of the coxswain came across the breeze from behind Downey and he heard the rumble of engines as the LCA started up and began to ease away from the mother-ship. Almost instantly, the craft began to roll and dip sickeningly. There was no panic. They'd done this enough times in training to know that the run-in would be a bumpy affair, especially given the apparent state of the sea on this occasion.

As per countless rehearsals, both with and without their troops, the LCAs swung purposefully into line-ahead as they passed forward of the landing ship flotilla before fanning out into assault formation. As the line of assault boats chugged steadily past HMS Largs, the Divisional Command Ship, a bugle sounded above the noise of gunfire and engines. All the faces in Downey's boat looked up at the clear, distinctive sound. It was coming from one of the LCAs in front; the sound of the 'General Salute'.

A cheer rose up from the men on the deck of the Divisional Command Ship and Downey saw people on the bridge of the big vessel salute the line of landing craft as they passed by.

"Here we go, boys!" Shouted the platoon commander from the front of Downey's LCA.

"Oh, yes..." Downey thought. "Here we fucking go..."

LANDING CRAFT TANK 178 – FIVE MILES OFF SWORD BEACH, NORMANDY
TUESDAY 6TH JUNE 1944 – 0535 HOURS

"Bloody hell, Corp'; I know we've done it in rough weather before but this is taking the piss!"

Private Stan Holloway of the 13th/18th Hussars, staring over the inflated flotation skirt of the Sherman Duplex Drive battle tank, regarded the dark, heaving ocean with a distinct sense of unease. As the driver, it was his job to drive the tank off the ramp of the LCT into the water and engage the propellers that would turn the heavy armoured vehicle into an amphibious tank. Amphibious was probably too grand a term to be honest. The DD tanks could 'swim', somewhat slowly, but were prone to being swamped in heavy swells. And of course, if the inflatable screen was punctured or if the engine cut out at any point, well… it wasn't even worth thinking about.

"Just give her everything you've got Stan and get ready to jump out the hatch as soon as you've got the prop-drive engaged." Came the encouraging words of the tank's commander, Corporal 'Peggy' Legg. "The Troop Commander's got off alright and he's got a crap driver. You'll be alright mate. Besides, we're two miles closer in than planned. At least we won't be in the water so long this time."

Holloway grimaced at the upbeat pep-talk. It was alright for Peggy and the rest of the crew, he thought; after all, they got to crouch on the rear decks of the vehicle throughout. If anything went wrong they would have plenty of time to get clear. Holloway, on the other hand, would have to really shift if he wasn't going to go under with a sinking vehicle.

"Marvellous." He grunted, then gunned the engine and began trundling the thirty ton metal beast over the lip of the ramp.

After a few seconds, the vehicle tipped forward as it descended the angled metal platform and Holloway took care to ease off, not wanting to plough the vehicle into the sea too fast. He took his eyes off the flimsy flotation screen for a second to look at the leading vehicle which was already in the water and about twenty yards out. He saw the faces of the crew peering over the rear of the buoyancy skirt and one of them, presumably the Troop Commander, waved an arm, beckoning him to bring his tank into the water and follow them.

"Here goes nothing…" Holloway sighed, and let the vehicle roll forwards at a steady trundle.

A moment later he heard the sploshing sound as the nose of the tank pushed its way into the sea, and the young driver kept his eyes fixed over the lip of the hatch to see if any water was going to get through the screen and come riding over the hull of the vehicle, drowning it before it managed to get seaborne. The front deck remained dry, and Holloway held his breath as the vehicle seemed to keep sliding forwards, further into the water.

Just as the driver thought that the tank would keep on nose diving until it was underwater, the vehicle suddenly lurched upwards at the front, throwing him back in his seat.

"You're off, Stan!" He heard Legg shouting over the noise of the engine. "Engage the props!"

Holloway needed no further prompting. He flicked the switch that changed the drive from track to propeller and heard the grinding of gears as the twin screws began to kick-in.

"We're moving mate; out you come!"

Legg's voice again, signalling that the propeller-drive was working. Holloway needed no further prompting. With his heart thumping heavily in his chest the tank driver hauled himself out of his cock-pit and up onto the front decks.

With a huge sigh of relief, he dragged himself upwards and fell against the turret, gawping across the top of it back towards the landing craft. To his surprise, the LCT was already some thirty yards distant and another Sherman was in the process of entering the water behind them. Across the turret from him, the remainder of his crew were grinning at him inanely.

"Well done, Stan!" Shouted Dennis Wells, the gunner.

Corporal Legg gave him a thumbs-up.

"Nice one, Stan. That's the hard bit done mate; nothing to stop us now. Just make sure you keep your eyes on that engine. Next stop Sword Beach."

Turning awkwardly on the lurching tank, Holloway gazed forwards over the top of the buoyancy screen. The coast of Normandy was somewhere in front of them. It was hard to actually see it at the moment because it was obscured by a massive bank of smoke and dust which was being added to every moment as shell after shell screamed overhead and slammed into the enemy held coastline. Lowering himself into a kneeling position, Holloway ducked his head into the hatch and reached an arm in so that he could ensure the engine didn't stall during the run-in.

"Sword Beach?" Holloway breathed to himself as he did so. "Or the bottom of the English bloody Channel?"

ON THE HIGH GROUND – 3 KILOMETRES EAST OF CAEN TUESDAY 6TH JUNE 1944 – 0545 HOURS

The scene was quite unimaginable. In his wildest dreams, and even his nightmares, von Luck had never imagined that the invasion would look like this. The scale of it all was breath-taking. Looking northwards through his binoculars, von Luck could see that the entire stretch of coastline from Ouistreham at the mouth of the Orne, westwards towards Arromanches and the Cotentin Peninsular was shrouded in the smoke of a heavy naval bombardment. 'Heavy' was probably an understatement for the pounding that was currently being given to that long coastal strip. 'Colossal' would be nearer the right word.

And beyond that bank of smoke and flame, out on the vast grey expanse of the English Channel, was a fleet of unbelievable size. The entire sea was covered from end to end with the dark silhouettes of ships of every size and function. And even in the furthest distance, out towards the horizon, yet more ships were approaching in successive waves. Above those ships hung large grey balloons, of the kind used to prevent low-flying aircraft from passing by, or the kind that could be used for observation. And then far above them, in great swarms like angry bees, there came wave upon wave of enemy aircraft. Von Luck was a dedicated, hard-fighting soldier, who would never admit defeat if he thought there was the remotest chance of victory, but gazing at this awesome display of combat power, he found himself wondering how Germany would ever be able to win this war now.

Slowly, he lowered his binoculars. The scene didn't change that much when he did so. The spectacle was so immense that even with the naked eye, it was impossible not to register the supreme strength of what lay out there on the ocean. Summoning a renewed sense of drive, von Luck began calculating the chances of success. Surely it wasn't too late to at least contain the Allied invasion; bring it to a grinding halt so that a more favourable tactical and strategic position could be arranged in Germany's favour?

In perfect clarity now, he saw the Allied plan on this, the eastern flank of the landings. These airborne landings were the hard shoulder of it all. They were the blocking force, dropped to prevent the Germans from occupying this high ground east of the Orne in strength, from where they could bring their artillery and tanks to bear on the invasion forces below. So, at least for now, these rolling hills between the Orne and the Dives were the vital ground. There was still time. The Tommy paratroopers and glider troops must still be in a state of disorganisation after the confusion of the night drop. They would still be trying to concentrate in force and would be short of heavier weapons and armour. Now was the time for von Luck to strike; indeed for the whole of 21st Panzer Division to roll into action. Only, they were forbidden to do so by a high command that had no idea of the scale of what lay off the coast of Normandy.

The commander of the 125th Panzer Grenadiers turned to his driver, Beck, and swore a small oath.

"We are running out of time, Beck. While higher formation is wringing its hands over what to do, the Allies are building up their strength. We've only got a limited time left to try and reverse our fortunes here… And it's running out rapidly."

Von Luck's faithful driver, who'd been with him for years, gazed back phlegmatically at his commander.

"What do you want to do then, Major?"

Von Luck climbed into the passenger seat of the staff car and jerked his thumb vaguely southwards; beyond where their field police protection squad were parked up in their own collection of cars and motorcycle combinations.

"Back to the command post I think... The Adjutant should be back from Divisonal Headquarters soon and he should have some proper orders for us. And I want to tweak the deployment orders for the battalions slightly, now that I know what we're up against..."

As von Luck was speaking, the sound of a large artillery shell sounded in the air above them. Neither the commander nor his driver made any sudden move. Instead they simply gazed upwards and followed the noise of the passing shell. As veterans of many campaigns, the two men knew instinctively when a shell was going to come dangerously close and when it was going to fly harmlessly past.

Sure enough, a couple of moments later, the shell landed about three hundred metres behind them in the middle of an open field, sending a huge pile of earth and smoke into the air in the wake of the bright flash of the detonation. Even though the shell had gone well over, the ground beneath the staff car trembled ominously and the sharp, concussive noise of the explosion came to the ears of the Germans with surprising force.

"That was a fucking big one..." Beck observed with only the faintest hint of worry in his voice.

"Mmmm..." Von Luck grimaced towards the cloud. "From the ships I reckon..."

"Jabo!"

The shout from one of the military police vehicles made the two men in the staff car twist round in their seats with alarm. They stared up in fearful expectation in the direction indicated, and saw the aircraft immediately. A small, single-seater and somewhat ungainly looking aircraft had appeared from behind one of the last snatches of lower cloud and was executing a wide turn overhead. Beck let out a sigh of relief when he set eyes on the plane.

"That's no Jabo..." He tutted contemptuously.

"No..." Von Luck agreed, eyeing the small plane with suspicion. "More like an..."

Boom!

The naval shell slammed into the ground to the north of their position, barely two hundred metres away; the concussive force of it similar to the last one. This time, von Luck and his driver ducked as bits of turf and hedgerow came flying through the air towards them, and their whole vehicle shook violently in the shock wave.

"Shit!" Swore the major of panzer grenadiers. "The bastard's bracketing us! It's a spotter plane!"

He slapped his hand onto the dash board.

"Drive, Beck! Drive! Get us out of here quickly!"

Without need for further prompting, Beck threw the vehicle into gear, revved the engine, then spun away in a tight turn and roared off past the stationary vehicles of the field police.

"Come on!" von Luck yelled at the men of his escort squad as his car sped past them. "There's more of that on the way and we're right in the middle of the target area!"

The military policemen needed no further prompting, and were following their commander within moments.

As von Luck watched the motorcycles and cars pull into column behind him, another shell exploded nearby, this one no more than fifty metres away from where he and Beck had been parked just moments earlier. Even above the noise of roaring engines, the sound of the explosion was deafening. The shock wave came rolling after them, forcing several of the motorcyclists to swerve and wobble dangerously on their machines. Fortunately, every one of them managed to stay mounted, and they simply ducked their heads and accelerated away from the seat of the explosion with renewed urgency.

"Bloody hell! That was a close one!" Beck yelled over the noise of the engine as he took the vehicle up another gear.

"Just a bit!" Von Luck shouted back. "And where's the bloody Luftwaffe when you need them?"

THE ROADBLOCK – HALF A MILE SOUTH OF RANVILLE TUESDAY 6TH OF JUNE – 0600 HOURS

"Good God, have you ever seen anything like it?"

The lieutenant, who was one of the platoon commanders from 'C' Company, shook his head in wonder at the sight of the huge demonstration of naval firepower that was unfolding just a few miles away to the north-west. Dawes, kneeling beside the newly arrived officer, shook his own head in muted wonder.

"Can't say I have." The corporal murmured. "I just hope they know who they're firing at. Tell you what though, Sir; the sooner they've got the rest of our boys ashore and up here, then the better I'll like it."

The officer, a young boyish looking chap by the name of Peterson, glanced at the corporal and offered a lame smile.

"Yes, well… I rather think I'm with you on that one. We're not exactly in an impregnable position here are we?"

That was certainly true; although in fairness, the situation was somewhat better than it had been a couple of hours ago. As promised, the captain from 'A' Company had tracked down some 'C' Company men amongst the defenders of Ranville and promptly despatched them southwards to help reinforce Dawes' roadblock, adding another six men to the tiny force that was currently fulfilling 'C' Company's task of blocking the road through Herouvillette towards Ranville. There had been a lance corporal amongst that group, which still left Dawes in charge of the position, but all that had changed about an hour ago, when a force of around twenty men, commanded by Mr Peterson and his platoon sergeant, had arrived en masse after a long night of wandering around in the dark having overshot their DZ.

Now the size of a large platoon, the force at the roadblock was a bit more to be reckoned with, and they were busily redeploying to cover wider arcs on either side of the road. The new arrivals had also brought two Bren Guns to the party, along with four more bombs for the PIAT, and thus the strength of this blocking position was growing steadily as the dawn developed into full daylight. Thus far, the Germans had been kind enough to stay away, and Dawes was beginning to hope that by the time the enemy finally woke up to what was happening, his entire company, and maybe even the entire battalion, would have finally sorted itself out and be ready to receive all comers.

For the time being however, the attention of the paratroopers was much distracted by the events out to sea and over to the north-west. There in the distance, just out of sight, lay their salvation, and so it was only natural to cast ones gaze in that direction from time to time. Thus it was that the approaching motorcyclist was only noticed at the last moment, just as he swung around the corner at full tilt.

Like the jeep full of engineers and paras before him, the motorcyclist screeched to a halt on spotting the overturned car in the centre of the road, pulling the front wheel of his machine around as he did so. The sound of the screeching motorcycle drew the attention of the British paratroopers back to the road and the route to the south-east. Dawes and Peterson turned their heads to stare at the motorcyclist, and heads popped up from the nearby shell-scrapes as the men defending the roadblock did likewise.

For his part, the motorcyclist just stared back towards them as he tried to work out what he was being confronted with. The man was garbed in a baggy camouflage smock, similar to those worn by the British paratroopers, yet *not quite* the same. His helmet, covered in a similarly camouflaged manner, was indistinct in shape at first. After a few seconds however, both the paras and the man on the motorcycle realised, almost simultaneously, that they were looking at the enemy.

It was the motorcyclist who responded first. With an experienced flick of his wrist and a kick of his heel, the German had the machine fully turned around and roaring away in a heartbeat, the exhaust belching a long stream of blue-grey smoke in the damp morning air. As the rider revved his machine and pulled away, back the way he had come, a Sten Gun chattered into life from somewhere nearby; a long wild burst reverberating around the narrow roadway. It was accompanied by the harsh report of several rifles. None of the shots seemed to find their mark however, for the German ducked low over his machine, increased the revs, then disappeared out of sight around the bend in the road just moments later. The firing stopped instantly, and within seconds, the sound of the motorcycle had faded dramatically as the rider sped away at full pelt.

Peterson glanced at Dawes and pulled a face.

"Well, I reckon that's let the cat out of the bag then…"

THE FIRST ASSAULT WAVE – ONE MILE OUT FROM SWORD BEACH
TUESDAY 6TH JUNE 1944 – 0710 HOURS

The noise was terrific. Downey had known battle before and remembered the chaos and din of it well; but this was something else. It was, he thought, perhaps the most complex and sustained bombardment in history. The big guns of the battleships and cruisers had sent tremors right through him in those first few minutes, and even once their landing craft had motored some way from the bombardment line, the sound of those great shells passing overhead continued to provide a continuous overture to the great adventure. That overture was supplemented by the sound of the smaller guns of the destroyers that were situated closest to the coastline, providing close in fire support. Even now, with the destroyer line some two miles behind them, the four and six inch shells came whooshing above the tiny assault boats at an ear-splittingly low trajectory.

And now there were the rockets. At first, the bigger landing craft that had followed the infantry assault boats towards the shore had seemed no different to those carrying the tanks of the supporting armoured regiments; but with only a mile or so to go before the assault troops hit the beach, the bigger vessels suddenly erupted in a huge bank of smoke and explosive noise, as line after line of high explosive rockets were launched from them. The great clumps of rockets streaked skyward, trailing dirty grey smoke, before reaching their culminating point and dipping together for their targets on the shore. It was, Downey thought, like watching a much bigger, high-explosive version of the English archer's 'arrow-cloud' at Agincourt.

The sergeant watched the first wave of rockets slam down onto the beach and seafront, directly ahead of his own boat. It was hard to see the specific detail, but a huge stretch of beach and coastline suddenly erupted in bright orange flame and black, bilious smoke. Indeed, the entire stretch of coast to his front seemed obscured by the fallout of the incessant bombardment, and judging by the waves of aircraft passing overhead towards France, Downey could only assume that the hinterland behind the beach was getting similar treatment from the combined Allied air forces.

The bombardment brought back memories of the story his grandfather had told him about the Great War. A South Yorkshireman by birth, his granddad had gone to war with the Barnsley pals and taken part in the infamous Battle of the Somme. As a young lad, Downey had heard 'Grandad Jack' tell of how the preliminary bombardment for that great battle had lasted for a full day and night; how the noise could be heard in London, and how the men of 'Kitchener's Army' had been told it would be a walkover; how nothing could survive such thorough artillery preparation. He also remembered how his grandfather had then described how his entire battalion had gone over the top at zero hour, only to find that the Germans were very much alive; as a result of which, the battalion had got no further than the first hundred yards.

'Grandad Jack' had been one of the lucky ones; wounded within seconds and thrown back into his own trench with the force of the bullet's impact. There he had lain, stunned and bleeding whilst hundreds of his lifelong friends had been massacred in the open ground as they struggled upslope through the mud towards the enemy trenches on the ridge. Downey shivered at the memory of the story and gazed towards the smoke shrouded shoreline. Were similar horrors waiting for these young men of the East Yorkshires, somewhere beyond that impenetrable veil of smoke, he wondered? He checked his watch. If the timings were all worked out properly then Downey would know the answer within the next twenty minutes.

HAWKER TYPHOON CG–M – APPROACHING THE FRENCH COAST
TUESDAY 6TH JUNE 1944 – 0715 HOURS

"Hornet Controller, this is Charlie George Leader; we're figures five from being on station. Do you have a target for us, over?"

In accordance with the very precise briefing he had received in the early hours of the morning, Squadron Leader 'Windy' Whittaker, commanding 1650 Squadron of the RAF's 2nd Tactical Air Force, checked in with the forward controller who was on board the command ship lying off Sword Beach.

They were less than ten miles out now, so Whittaker assumed that despite the unusually bad interference they were experiencing on the airwaves, he should be able to get through to the person responsible for tasking his squadron of rocket armed typhoons over Normandy. He waited for several seconds, but then, receiving no acknowledgement, he repeated his call. This time, after a few moments of silence, a metallic voice crackled over the air waves in reply.

"Hello Charlie George Leader, this is Hornet Controller, I have no targets for you at present. You should proceed to your secondary target, over."

Whittaker grunted to himself at the reply. It was partly good news and partly bad news that there were no targets for them over the invasion beaches. Good in the sense that he could only assume that the heavy bombers and naval guns had done their bit to perfection, thereby making it an easier proposition for the assault troops who were due to land any moment now. Bad in the sense that as his squadron's services were no longer required over the coast, he must now take his men further inland to conduct a low level attack against some enemy pontoon bridges that had been erected over the River Risle, east of the invasion area. That would probably mean lots of flak, unless of course Bomber Command had been true to their promise and flattened the entire area surrounding the bridges during the night. Either way, he and his men would find out very shortly.

"Roger, Hornet Controller." Whittaker acknowledged the instructions.

"Charlie George Leader, this is Hornet Controller, make sure you stay above five thousand as you pass over, as there is a lot of naval stuff flying about, over."

The second message came across the airwaves and Whittaker nodded silently to himself as he absorbed the direction. It made sense, especially judging by the enormous cloud of smoke that seemed to be enveloping the coastline. The air above those beaches would be alive with shells and rockets of every kind, and Whittaker certainly didn't fancy flying straight into the trajectory of a friendly barrage.

He acknowledged the message from Hornet Controller then spoke on the squadron frequency to his own pilots.

"Alright chaps, there's nothing doing over the coast, so we're going for the bridges. We'll peel off now in sections astern and cut the coast over the mouth of the Seine, then peel starboard after that towards the target. We'll go up to ten thousand to avoid any minor flak until we get over target."

He allowed a few seconds for any questions to come from his pilots, but there were none; each of his men accustomed to maintaining silence unless absolutely necessary. It was how he'd trained them. Since his experiences both in the air and on the ground during the campaigns of 1940, Whittaker had become an obsessive professional. Many people in the service regarded him as a touch dour, but at the same time, they understood that his quiet, serious minded approach to the business of waging war was probably what had kept him alive for so long; that and plenty of luck of course.

Instinctively, Whittaker reached out a gloved hand and touched the small brass cap badge that was tied to his cockpit canopy. The small badge was actually known as a 'capstar', and was the regimental emblem of the Coldstream Guards, the unit that had adopted him during the withdrawal to Dunkirk; the unit that had taught him the importance of discipline, in addition to raw courage. He wondered for a moment if they would be down there, amongst that vast armada; or would they be elsewhere? In Italy perhaps? The thought left him as the huge invasion fleet began to disappear from view below his aircraft.

"Okay chaps..." Whittaker spoke to his squadron again. "Sections astern, turning to port."

With a powerful, throaty growl, the Typhoon fighter-bomber banked gracefully to the left and curled away eastwards towards the mouth of the great River Seine. Like a pack of faithful hounds, the other eleven aircraft in the squadron did the same, and 1650 Squadron pulled away to play their part in the greatest adventure of history.

THE FIRST ASSAULT WAVE – 400 YARDS FROM SWORD BEACH
TUESDAY 6TH JUNE 1944 – 0720 HOURS

"Hard a-port! Hard a-port!"

The urgent cry from the young naval rating by the disembarkation ramp cut through the air, even above the noise of the shells which were still passing overhead. The men in the craft, Downey included, looked across at the man as one, their private thoughts interrupted by the obvious agitation in the man's voice.

Barely had the rating shouted the warning back along the small assault boat, than the craft suddenly heaved over to the left in a sharp swerve that sent the men in the boat falling against each other. The soldiers couldn't actually fall *over* because they were so tightly packed in, but the men of the left hand section cried out in alarm as the full weight of the remainder of their platoon fell against them, squashing them against the side of the craft.

For long, agonising moments, Downey thought that the craft was about to hit some underwater, anti-boat obstacle, of the kind they'd heard so much about. When no impact or explosion materialised, he was no less worried, for the heel of the boat was so extreme that he thought the heavily laden LCA might capsize in the churning sea. Just as he thought that they would surely go over, the craft suddenly tipped back to the right again, bounced heavily into the swell, then resumed its steady, bobbing course towards the smoke shrouded beach. There was a collective groan of relief amongst the soldiers in the boat, and the sound of retching accompanied it, as several men tried vainly to empty stomachs that were already devoid of contents and shrivelled from a night of endless vomiting.

The entire 3rd Infantry Division, to whom the 2nd Battalion of the East Yorkshires belonged, had trained rigorously with their Royal Navy counterparts of 'S' Force for months now, and so the crew of the tiny LCA were familiar friends to Downey's platoon. Now, the platoon sergeant threw a look across to the rating who had called out the warning that had resulted in the drastic manoeuvre.

"Hey, Frank! What the fuck was that all about?"

The rating turned his head slightly and shouted back over his shoulder into the packed landing craft.

"One of our swimming tanks was right in front of us! We nearly ran into the bugger! Couldn't see him until the last moment because of the swell! I think we managed to miss him though!"

Next to Downey, Edmunds looked sharply at his platoon sergeant.

"I thought the swimming tanks were supposed to land before us?" He asked worriedly.

"That'll be their reserve squadron." Downey replied instantly, though in truth, he knew he was telling a lie.

His mind began working overtime. Edmunds was right. The Sherman 'swimming tanks', sometimes referred to as DDs because of their duplex drive system, were supposed to hit the beach a few minutes in front of the assault infantry and the assault engineer teams in order to start suppressing the enemy positions and cover the men on foot across the open beach. But if this LCA was overtaking the swimming tanks, it meant only one thing. The rifle companies of the East Yorkshire and South Lancashire regiments were going to be facing the full fury of the Atlantic Wall's defences on their own; at least for the first few minutes. Downey felt his stomach go heavy as the reality sunk in.

"Gone a bit quiet, Sarge, mind you..."

The voice of Private Edmunds snapped the sergeant out of his dark thoughts, and Downey looked up, straining his neck so that he could see beyond the gunwales of their LCA.

'Quiet' wasn't technically the correct term, the sergeant thought, but he understood what the young private meant. After the tumult of the preliminary bombardment passing over them, there now seemed to be a calmer, almost peaceful dynamic to their surroundings. The shells still screamed overhead, but at a much higher trajectory now, going further inland and away from the beach itself. Even the close support artillery units behind them, firing their 105mm self-propelled howitzers from inside their own landing craft, had adjusted their fire onto the strip of land beyond the beach. The beach itself was hard to identify as the entire coastline seemed to be cloaked in thick, grey-black smoke.

Even so, Downey thought he saw strange, stick like objects protruding from the choppy waves, just a little way in front of them and felt his stomach tighten even more. Beach obstacles; they had to be...

"Four hundred yards; last few minutes lads! Get yourselves ready..."

The rating standing by the ramp was shouting back over his shoulder again. Unconsciously, Downey gripped his rifle a little tighter and rolled his shoulders, like a pole-vaulter limbering up for the jump of a life-time. Within the craft, the young men of his platoon were absolutely silent; their pale faces and wide eyes staring intently over the side of their craft at the approaching shoreline.

A sudden gust of wind passed across the top of the craft, and as it did so, it seemed that a great gap in that dense cloud of smoke opened up before Downey's landing craft, just for a moment, giving the men of his platoon a fleeting glimpse of what lay beyond. Downey stared fixedly at the scene, taking in every detail and processing it in a split second. Breaking surf; an unruly, dangerous, breaking surf, foaming white around a forest of strange looking posts and girder-like structures and, beyond it, a white strip of beach. That beach seemed surprisingly narrow, Downey thought, whilst beyond it he picked out the untidy tangle of barbed wire and the uneven profile of sand-dunes. Beyond all that, a long, low, grey band of something that resembled a wall, and even further in, the stark, black silhouette of a building that was belching smoke. Then the wind blew again and the smoke obscured much of the view once more.

"Stand-by…" Downey called out, without realising it.

And then it happened.

Out of nowhere it seemed, shattering the deceptively peaceful scene, came long, snake-like streams of bright coloured tracer from several different directions, the rapid 'crack-crack-crack' of the passing bullets assailing the ears of Downey and his men. Simultaneously, Downey heard the soft 'whoosh' of mortar bombs descending nearby and, a moment later, large geysers of water were erupting near to the tiny boat and drenching the occupants.

"They're bloody waiting for us!" Downey heard one of his men call out.

Of course they were, Downey thought. This was just going to be like Grandad Jack's big battle on the Somme. He'd always known it deep inside.

"Good!" He shouted out above the racket. "At least we won't have to go looking for the bastards before we kill them!"

His words sounded brave, but in truth they were born of despair. This was a stupid fucking war, and it was all because that bastard Hitler didn't know when he was beaten. And because of that, hundreds, if not thousands of men would now have to be slaughtered on a windswept beach in Normandy in order to bring the end of that war a little closer. The thought made him angry; so angry that he could have sobbed with the unfairness of it all.

But he couldn't sob, could he? Not here; not now. Not in front of his men. He was their platoon sergeant and one of the few men among them who knew how to fight. And if these young farm lads and factory workers from East Yorkshire were going to look to anyone in the next few hours it would be him. So he couldn't sob; he had to be strong. It was too late anyway. There was no going back.

The landing craft swerved to the right suddenly, then hard left again, and Downey saw a post go past them with something circular and metallic-looking tied to it.

"We're going in… One minute to ramp down… Stand-by…"

The sound of the naval rating's voice was edged with tension now.

"Here we go, stand-by…"

"Jesus…" Downey uttered the word under his breath and suddenly wished he hadn't dodged so many church parades.

There was a sudden, sickening jolt and a grinding sound, and Downey knew they had beached. The crack of bullets going past just a few inches away was continuous now, as was the sharp report of numerous weapons. The acrid smell of battle was already filling his lungs and the thud and tremble of exploding munitions could be felt, even within the tight confines of the LCA. No going back.

"Ramp down!"

The naval rating's voice cut through Downey like a bolt of electricity, and suddenly he found himself pushing hard against the rifleman if front of him, whilst simultaneously screaming out at the top of his voice.

"Gooo!"

CORPORAL LEGG'S TANK – 400 YARDS FROM SWORD BEACH
TUESDAY 6TH JUNE 1944 – 0722 HOURS

"Christ almighty! Look out!"

Why Legg was bothering to shout the warning he didn't really know, because there was little anyone could do other than watch the terrible spectacle unfold. From within the turret of his tank, and down in the driver's compartment, he heard the anxious calls.

"What is it Peggy? What's going on?"

The corporal didn't answer. He was too busy staring with horrid fascination at the LCA as it swerved at the last minute in a desperate attempt to miss the Troop Leader's tank. He watched, heart in mouth, as the grey and black assault boat somehow managed to avoid the low profile of the DD tank by executing an almost impossible turn to port at the very last moment. For a second, Legg almost cried out in relief as he saw the boat swing around his commander's tank with just yards to spare, but just as quickly the horror returned as he now watched the bank of water thrown up by the landing craft roll over the top of the tank's flotation screen.

The tanks had only just been managing to hold up to the fearsome swell of the storm lashed sea, but now the massive swell created by the landing craft's sudden manoeuvre in such close proximity to the Troop Leader's tank had sealed the armoured vehicle's fate just as surely as if the craft had rammed it. Legg stared helplessly as the surge of water crashed over the flotation screen of the tank. He saw a body appear from within the wave as it covered the tank completely and broke over the forward edge of it. Then, just for a second, he saw the tank again, clearly visible as the wave passed by, but with its nose dipped at a dangerous angle. And then the final, fateful bit of the tragedy unfolded as the forward edge of the flotation screen dipped below the surface of the water and the sea washed over the tank, drowning it within seconds.

If Legg was struck dumb by the awfulness of the sudden accident, he had no time to dwell on it, for the original wave created by the swerving LCA had not entirely broken up, and the backwash of it was even now coming towards their own tank.

"What is it, Peggy?" An increasingly animated voice shouted from within the turret.

Legg snapped out of his trance and leaned forward, shouting down through the commander's hatch.

"Big wave coming! Stand-by! It might swamp us, so get ready to… whoa!"

The backwash hit home against their tank and Legg had to grip onto the hatch to steady himself as the vehicle lurched up in the huge swell that now reared up underneath them.

"Oh, fucking hell…" He heard the gunner curse from within the turret.

The worst was yet to come, but the wait would only be a matter of seconds. And sure enough, it came as predicted.

"Jesus fucking Christ!" The gunner was yelling as the tank suddenly dropped off the passing swell and back into a trough.

As the vehicle came down, a small amount of water splashed over the top of their screen, soaking Legg through. He gasped loudly and spat the salty, sickly water from his mouth and blinked the remaining drops out of his eyes as he struggled to see if any more would come over their flotation aid. Nothing did, but from within the tank he could hear urgent shouting.

"Shit, shit, shit! There's water inside!"

"Get the pump going!" Legg spluttered, hauling himself upright and shouting into the turret again.

"There's water in the tank!" He could hear the co-driver's voice now.

"I know there is!" Legg roared down through the tank's fighting compartment. "So use the fucking pump on it! Quickly!"

He looked up, gulping in a huge breath and wiping his sleeve over his face which was still dripping water and snot. He paused for a moment, gathering his breath and staring straight ahead.

"Bloody hell…" He breathed quietly to himself. "We're almost there…"

After the long, tiresome run-in, which had taken even longer than Legg had expected, they were suddenly very close to the beach, the surge of the tide spurring them on at a faster pace now in the final stages of their approach.

He scanned the shoreline in front of him. To his forward right he could see the Troop Sergeant's tank, just yards away from the beach now, whilst right across his front, and on either side of his own axis, there were LCAs, weaving their way between the beach obstacles as they fought for their place on the shore. And coming towards that line of landing craft, was the most awesome demonstration of firepower Legg had ever seen. Great splashes of water were rearing up beside those little boats as mortar bombs and artillery shells came screaming down from above, whilst from that hazy, indistinct shoreline, bright tracer rounds came slicing across the beach in endless, weaving snakes of machine gun fire.

With a start, Legg realised that, very soon, he and his tank would be amongst the maelstrom.

"Stand-by to beach!" He yelled down into the turret. "Keep pumping; we're almost there! The infantry are already hitting the beach!"

"We're taking water, Peggy!" The gunner was still shouting.

"Just fucking pump!" Legg screamed back. "We're almost there! We're almost on the beach!"

LEHMAN'S POSITION, 'OBJECTIVE COD' - SWORD BEACH TUESDAY 6TH JUNE 1944 – 0725 HOURS

Such was the ringing in Lehman's ears that it took him a while to realise the shelling had stopped; or at least, moved away from their position. The young soldier felt the reduction in the tremors rather than heard the change in volume. He remained where he was for long, long moments; head covered by his arms, his breathing coming in short, rapid gasps. After some time, when he realised that bits of the house were no longer dropping around the sandbagged bunker he was sharing with Gruber, Lehman slowly pulled his arms away from his face and blinked through the choking dust and smoke that seemed to fill the room. Outside the sandbagged safety of the stand-to position, Lehman saw that huge chunks of ceiling plaster, brick and lengths of shattered wooden beam, lay scattered about the floor.

His left ear hurt like hell and his mouth was parched. Licking his lips, Lehman winced. They were dry, sore to the touch, and tasted of blood. He pushed himself upright a little more and scrabbled for his water bottle. Beside him, he saw Gruber begin to move. The other soldier reminded Lehman of a chrysalis. Covered in a layer of broken plaster and dust, Lehman's companion slowly opened his arms and legs, breaking the layer of debris away from his body as he emerged, wide-eyed into the devastating aftermath of the bombardment.

Lehman stared at his friend in fascination as he took a slug of water from his canteen, allowing some to spill out of his mouth and lubricate his cracked lips. Gruber's eyes seemed unusually wide and red-rimmed, and his pale, dust covered face carried two bloody trails from his nostrils down to his upper lip.

"You've had a nose bleed..." Lehman managed to croak to his friend.

Strangely, his own voice sounded distant, as if he were listening to himself from another room. Above the sound of his own weak voice, there was a constant, high-pitched whine.

"So have you..." Gruber mouthed back at him, then fell into a coughing fit.

Lehman offered his water bottle and his comrade accepted it readily as he fought to control his flurry of coughing.

Gruber glugged at the water bottle hungrily, then coughed again and promptly spat his mouthful of water over Lehman. Even so, it seemed to clear his throat because the young man suddenly drew in a huge breath and began rambling away, nonsensically.

"Oh, shit...Oh, my God... Fuck me..."

"I think it's stopped..." Lehman offered stupidly.

At that point, somebody entered the room and Lehman looked over at the doorway. The first thing he noticed was a pair of legs, at the end of which were feet clad in nothing more than an old pair of well-worn socks. As he raised his head, Lehman saw that the bootless feet and legs belonged to a surprisingly animated Corporal Fuchs.

"Hello Corporal..." Lehman muttered like a drunk.

Fuchs surprised Lehman by stepping inside the sandbagged shelter and reaching down to grab him by the arm.

"On your feet, man! You too, Gruber; for fuck's sake!"

Lehman allowed himself to be hauled to his feet, but grabbed at the parapet of the bunker as he did so to steady himself. His legs felt decidedly wobbly and he had a slightly dizzy sensation for the first couple seconds.

"Are you alright, Lehman?" Fuchs demanded as he grabbed the young man's discarded rifle and shoved it into his hands.

"Err, yes, I think so, Corporal..." Lehman ventured, banging a hand against his right ear in a vain attempt to get rid of the ringing sound. "My left ear hurts though..."

Corporal Fuchs ignored him and busied himself with hauling Gruber to his feet.

"Get your rifles ready…" Fuchs was jabbering at them. "Stand-to. Get ready for the Tommies…"

Something suddenly clicked inside Lehman's head.

"The Tommies!" He remembered suddenly. "The Tommies are coming…"

Fuchs, having pulled Gruber to his feet, gave Lehman a grim stare.

"The Tommies…" He growled. "…have *arrived*."

With that, he grabbed Lehman's shoulder and span him around so that he was staring over the parapet of the sandbags, out of the shattered windows, and out to sea.

He couldn't see the big ships anymore because of the thick smoke that seemed to hover everywhere, but he could see as far as the shoreline and, just out there, approaching the beach, were a dozen or more little assault craft; low in silhouette and a mottled black and grey in colour.

"Open fire when you hear me shout the order!" Lehman heard Fuchs bark out from behind him. "Shoot everything that comes off those boats! And keep shooting until there's nothing left to kill!"

Lehman knew he should have been scared, but for some reason his fear seemed to have evaporated. Not that it had been replaced by some kind of new found courage. Instead he felt as if he was in a dream. His mind and body were working mechanically, as if he had no real control over what he was doing. He registered the fact that he was checking his rifle, opening the bolt and sliding a round into the chamber. As if some unseen force was guiding him, Lehman found himself checking the sight setting on his rifle, and then he was brushing the debris off the parapet, wrapping the rifle sling around his left forearm and adopting a firing position.

Somewhere in his subconscious, Lehman realised that he was in shock; that the bombardment had left him completely stunned, his normal senses and emotions subdued by the numbing intensity of the shelling. He watched the little craft bobbing closer to the shore line; saw the white surf breaking around their squared off bows. Absently he noted that his field of fire would be limited by the anti-tank cubes that formed a wall of concrete along the promenade. He could shoot anything on the beach, but once a person was behind the dunes, they would be more or less hidden from his view unless they decided to come through the dunes and over the wall itself. Strange how he had never really considered that before.

Through his still ringing ears, he heard the sound of a sharp weapon report and glanced over to his forward right. A couple of hundred metres along the promenade and built into the anti-tank wall itself was a large concrete bunker, from where the strongpoint's 88mm anti-tank gun had begun firing. Lehman felt a nudge on his left arm and glanced in that direction. Gruber was there, nodding towards the beach, his own face showing that he too was still somewhat stunned by events.

"They're here…" He said calmly.

Then, from somewhere up above them on the next floor of the building, the two soldiers heard a voice shouting something incomprehensible. The shouting was followed instantly by an eruption of gunfire from inside the house, and added to by others manning the trenches outside in what used to be the wide, ornamental gardens of the villa.

Lehman looked back towards the shoreline. He saw long streams of tracer criss-crossing to his front and racing out like angry little tongues towards the oncoming Tommy landing craft. He saw large splashes of water where bombs were dropping into the surf, straddling the flotilla of small craft. Then he saw one of the boats come to a halt. He lined his rifle up on the boat and lowered his head so that he could peer through the weapon's sights. Just as he did so, the front door of the strange looking craft seemed to flop open, dropping down flat onto the edge of the beach where the swollen sea still bubbled and frothed. And then there were figures there in the grey dawn light; lots of figures clad in a strange brown-grey colour he thought.

And then Lehman pulled the trigger. He felt the weapon lurch in his hands and, as it settled, he automatically unlocked and opened the bolt, ejecting a spent cartridge case, before ramming the bolt forward and locking it again. It seemed so easy, he thought; easier than he would have imagined. All he had to do was aim and fire; aim and fire. It hurt his left ear every time the rifle barked in anger, but he kept on firing. It took no thinking about and he had been given his orders. So he worked the bolt and fired again.

DOWNEY'S PLATOON, QUEEN RED SECTOR – SWORD BEACH
TUESDAY 6TH JUNE 1944 – 0727 HOURS

"Ramp down!"

"Go, go, go!"

Everybody in the landing craft was screaming now. There was probably no need for it of course. The boat had beached; the ramp was down, and there was nowhere else to go but forward. To stay on the vessel was to invite death within seconds.

The men at the front of the platoon were bursting through the internal wooden swing doors and out onto the ramp now, like greyhounds out of the slips, forced on by the pressure of the men behind who were desperate not to get caught inside the tiny craft by a sustained burst of fire.

"Come on, get off!" Downey was calling out as he pushed forward against the man in front.

In his peripheral vision, the sergeant could see a line of tracer stitching its way through the grey dawn air towards another LCA off to their left. Part of him felt a pang of remorse and horror for the men coming off that boat, but a selfish voice in his mind told him that it was better that someone else drew the fire instead of his platoon. Later, he would have time to feel guilt over that emotion, but for now the desire for survival was foremost in his thoughts.

"Move! Come on! Before they switch fire onto *us*!"

Beyond the heads and shoulders of the file in front, Downey saw the long tubular outlines of the Bangalore torpedoes bobbing up and down as the men designated to carry them climbed onto the ramp and descended towards the water.

Crack–splat!

The sergeant registered the sound of the bullet as he felt something wet and sludgy slap into his face. At the same time, the man to his front suddenly became a dead weight, resisting Downey's forward pressure. Then the man fell to his knees, just as Downey got the first iron-like taste in his mouth. With a cry of disgust and horror, Downey realised that the man in front had been shot through the head, the bullet passing straight through and covering the NCO with blood, brains and bone.

As the unfortunate private collapsed face down in the vessel, Downey staggered over his prostrate form, rubbing his face with his sleeve in a desperate attempt to remove the offending bits of offal and fluid. Simultaneously, he felt a terrible dread rising inside him as he imagined that this was just the first bullet from a long burst of twenty or more that would come slicing into the packed ranks of his platoon while they struggled to get off their assault boat. No more shots came immediately after the first however and suddenly, like a dam bursting open, the wall of men to his front had gone, the internal swing doors of the vessel were banging off his elbow, and he was at the top of the ramp, staring down at the swirling surf.

One of his men was lying face down on the ramp, obviously dead, his head and shoulders underwater making his identity a mystery. Someone else was sitting down in the water, just a yard from the sand, looking stunned and lost as the surf broke over him. The remainder of his men were on the sand, fanning out into open order, passing between the strange collection of obstacles made from steel girders and wooden beams. All of this Downey registered as he lurched down the ramp in two strides and splashed into the thigh deep water. As he stepped forward through the frothing surf with his right leg, his foot went down in the expectation of finding firm sand. Instead it kept on going into a deep hole of some kind, tipping the sergeant off balance. With a cry of alarm, he staggered forwards another yard with his left leg then toppled face forwards into the water.

Instantly he tasted the sickly, salty water as it filled his mouth and nose, and in terrified desperation he pushed his arms down, forcing himself up so that his head came above water once more. As his head broke the surface, he let out an enormous sob as his lungs dragged the air into his body and he spat the salty sludge from between his lips. Staggering to his feet again, Downey saw the man still sitting in the surf, not more than a yard away, and recognised the face of Private Headley. The young soldier was staring wide eyed at the sergeant, a length of Bangalore torpedo laid across his submerged knees.

"Come on!" Downey blurted at him. "Get up!"

The young soldier just toppled backwards, his upper body splashing into the water, his arms flopping loosely to the sides as he did so. Downey stared at the man in surprise, but then flinched as a bullet cracked by him and smashed into the metal superstructure of the landing craft. With a cry of effort, Downey staggered onwards onto the sand, removing one hand from his rifle as he did so and reaching down to grab the Bangalore torpedo. His cold, macerated fingers grappled for the wide pipe-like object and managed to get a hold of it at one end. Thus in possession of the valuable piece of equipment, Downey staggered onto the sand and negotiated a metal obstacle, dragging the torpedo along behind him as he went.

He was wet through from head to toe, but it wasn't the cold or wet that was a problem, more the fact that his waterlogged clothing and equipment now felt like twice their normal weight. He realised that he'd gone no more than twenty five yards so far, yet already he felt like he'd run a marathon. His breathing was coming in huge sobs as he drew in the damp, salty dawn air, laced with the acrid taste of artificial smoke. His thighs and calves were already feeling the strain of sudden, intensive use, after so long standing in the cramped confines of the LCA. Somewhere deep inside, Downey had always known that it would be bad; but even so, the shock of his sudden emergence into the maelstrom of an assault beach landing was overwhelming. The only conscious thought in his mind right now was '*keep going*'.

It was the mantra he'd privately used these last few weeks, as he'd slowly realised that the time for training and telling war stories was rapidly coming to an end and that shortly he and his men would be holding their appointment with fate.

"Keep going..." He blurted to himself as he staggered up the beach dragging his torpedo with him. "Keep going..."

As Downey vaguely registered that he was now passing through the last belt of metal obstacles and that before him lay about a hundred yards of flat, bare sand, he glanced to his left. Through eyes still blurred and stinging with salt water, he saw the men from his platoon spread out amongst the obstacles, advancing quickly at a low crouch, their every step appearing laboured yet determined; faces strained in a rictus of physical effort. Beyond them, he saw the bright blur of tracer rounds cracking past towards a burning LCA; the occupants of that craft mainly laid face down on the sand, just above the waterline. Even as he took in the chaotic scene, that bright serpent-like stream of tracer seemed to weave and swing to the side; towards Downey and his platoon.

"Keep going..." He tried to scream above the clatter and thump of battle, but his voice seemed feeble and indistinct.

The line of tracer curved closer towards his platoon and he could see the first little explosions of sand where the high velocity rounds had begun slamming into the beach.

"Jesus..."

Then it was too late. The first glowing blobs of tracer were cutting between his men, and he saw at least two men go down in a manner that suggested they had not taken a deliberate dive for cover. The crack-crack-crack of the machine gun bullets was a continuous, terrible clatter now that caused his pulse to accelerate even faster. He knew he would be next. The tracer rounds were passing just feet away.

"Down!"

With a cry of desperation that was of benefit to no-one but himself, Downey threw himself to the ground with a sickening thud. He hit the beach hard, pressing his body as close to the ground as he could get it, instantly tasting the grainy ingress of sand in his mouth. At the same time, the deadly crack of passing bullets pricked at his ears and through a mouth full of sand, Downey began blurting a fervent, meaningless prayer.

"Oh Jesus... Jesus, Jesus, Jesus!"

Downey lay there expecting to feel the dull impact of heavy calibre bullets at any moment and wondered if he would live long enough to feel the pain or whether it would all be over too quickly, but even as he braced himself for his last moment of life, the thunderous hammering of machine gun bullets began to lessen in volume. Daring to twist his head up so that he could gaze across the beach, Downey saw that the stream of tracer had disappeared from his field of vision. He also noted that the sound of passing bullets had returned to the sporadic snap of rifle fire. All around him, the prone khaki bodies began to fidget, and one face after another looked up from the sand.

Despite everything, Downey was somehow able to recognise the features of Private Evans staring back at him from the other side of a metal 'hedgehog' obstacle. Through nothing more than habit, Downey found himself yelling the words at the young soldier.

"Keep going!"

Then, realising that he should perhaps be following his own advice, Downey began to push himself upright.

"Come on!" He managed to shout with more conviction now, not wanting to be the only person on his feet on that wide expanse of sand. "Keep going... Forward!"

To his amazement, he saw Evans pushing himself upwards too. With a jolt, Downey realised that his men might actually follow him through this living hell.

"Come on!" He roared now, fully on his feet and manhandling the Bangalore torpedo over his shoulder. "Get fucking moving! Up to the dunes!"

"Come on lads... follow Sergeant Downey!"

That came from Evans. He was shouting at the men around him as he too began staggering forwards, his soaking wet battledress covered in sand. The young man's words had a galvanising effect on Downey. He forgot his fear and remembered that his position demanded example.

"Come on!" He yelled again, lurching forward up the beach. "Follow me!"

He focussed on the grassy mounds of the dunes that he could now see beyond the coils of barbed wire, just a tantalisingly short sprint away. Maybe he could make it? Maybe they all could? Just eighty yards; a ten to fifteen second burst if he gave it everything. Crying out in sudden defiance of all the fates that had brought him to this slaughterhouse, Downey bent his head and forced his aching limbs across the beach.

"Keep going!"

CORPORAL LEGG'S TANK – QUEEN RED SECTOR, SWORD BEACH
TUESDAY 6TH JUNE 1944 – 0730 HOURS

"Ruddy hell-fire!" Legg swore as the machine gun bullets ripped through the canvas flotation screen and bounced off the front of the turret with a deafening whine.

Ducking down behind the turret, the corporal realised that he wouldn't last much longer outside the turret. His men were all safe, to a degree, within the confines of the Sherman, but Legg had no choice but to remain outside the protective armour until they had beached. It was his job to remove the wooden struts that supported the screen so that it could be lowered fully, thus allowing the driver to see, and the turret crew to operate the gun.

"We're almost there; get ready to go to action!" He yelled down through the turret, staying as low as he could.

Legg dared not look over the top of the screen anymore, for there was a tremendous amount of gunfire and noise saturating the shoreline now. They were only a matter of yards away from making it to the sand. Legg knew that because, some fifty yards out, they had identified their route through the obstacles and attempted the run in. Going blindly forward that final, short distance, had been terrifying. Not only had the strange looking amphibious tanks now started taking fire from the enemy positions onshore, there was also the danger that they would manoeuvre themselves straight onto a submerged obstacle that had been fitted with a mine. If that happened, the first thing they would know about it would be the lethal, explosive gout of molten steel bursting through the belly of the Sherman to vaporise the crew in an instant.

There was smoke drifting across the top of the vehicle now and Legg looked up at it. The smell of the smoke was quite distinctive. It was not the unusual, chemical smell of artificial smoke, but the thick, oily odour of a vehicle or boat that was 'brewing up' after being hit. Just at that point, Legg felt the first shudder as the tank nudged against something and he automatically held his breath. There was a pause of just a heartbeat, and then the Sherman moved forward again and once more encountered resistance. This time, Legg heard the tell tale grinding sound of a heavy metal beast pushing against loose shale or sand.

"We've done it…" Legg breathed, daring to hope.

"We're there!" Came the sound of Holloway, the driver, from down below.

"Peggy! We've hit the beach!" That was the gunner shouting.

"I'm engaging the tracks!" That was Holloway again.

Legg needed no further prompting. Turning away from the turret, he stepped gingerly across the rear decks of the tank and delivered a swift kick to one of the wooden struts that helped to brace the flotation screen. It snapped with surprising ease, making the tank commander wonder how on earth it had stood up to the rough swell of the sea. Without pausing too long to think about it, Legg repeated the process with the remaining strut at the rear before moving carefully around the side of the turret towards the front decks. As he traversed the side of the tank's hull, the engine gave a deep growl and the adapted exhaust louvers spat out a great cloud of black fumes. Simultaneously, the tank seemed to rear up slightly, forcing the corporal to grab hold of the gun barrel. Just a second later, a single bullet sliced through the front of the screen and bounced off the turret just inches away from him, causing him to lurch away from it with a yelp of surprise.

Somehow managing to stay on his feet, Legg snapped the third of the four struts before dipping under the main gun barrel and crawling across to where the last strut was holding up the rapidly deflating screen. He gave the final strut a kick, but the wooden pole simply leaned away from him under the pressure of his boot. Without any tension in the screen, he couldn't deliver enough force to break the thing. Without wanting to hang about too long on the ever more exposed front deck of the tank, Legg scrabbled at the retaining sheath for the wooden post and dragged it clear. As the strut came free, he tossed it carelessly over the side and then rolled onto his belly, intent on making a rush for the safety of his turret. The tank seemed to be at even more of an angle now as it ground its way out of the shallows onto the beach and Legg was forced to hold onto the barrel again as he struggled up towards the turret hatches.

As he went, he flung a quick look over his shoulder and caught his breath at the sight that was now presented to him. The screen was down now, revealing the scene of chaos on the beach. He saw a line of anti-boat obstacles that were not yet submerged. LCAs were level with his tank on either side and one of them was burning fiercely. Men in khaki, weighed down with weapons and equipment, were scurrying across the beach like giant soldier ants, whilst bright orange tracer rounds cracked through and around them, taking a man down here, another one there. He saw tanks too; a Sherman further down the beach, burning fiercely, and what looked like one of the Engineer tanks just beyond it, with a length of bridging unit folded back over its hull.

As Legg took in the sights, sounds and smells of Sword Beach, a long burst of machine gun fire hit the side of his tank again, the bullets ricocheting off at crazy angles once more, and one of them, a tracer, passing uncomfortably close to his head as it did so.

"Shit!" Legg cursed, and threw himself over the top of the turret and in through the commanders hatch.

"I'm in!" He yelled as he dropped through the hatch and into his seat inside the fighting compartment. "Hatches down!"

Then, turning to Private Wells, his gunner. "Dennis; you got one up the spout?"

"Yes mate." Wells responded. "What's it like out there? Looks like chaos?"

"It is." Legg confirmed. "The infantry are getting hammered. Start looking for enemy bunkers."

"Will do." Wells replied crisply and put his eyes to the gun-sight.

Less than a second later, he called out, depressing the gun's elevation as he spoke.

"All I can see is sky and smoke! We're on too much of an angle. Can we go forward a touch?"

"Take her forward, Stan!" Legg called down to the driver. "Not too far though; we don't want to run over any mines."

With a powerful roar, the Sherman edged forward, the sound of the battle outside now muted inside the steel turret as it ground its way up the sand. Wells was traversing the turret slowly to the right using the power-traverse gear.

"I don't even know if we've landed in the right place." Legg murmured as he placed his radio ear-phones on his head. "Not that it matters; everyone else has landed here and the Germans are obviously here too, so either way we've got ourselves a battle."

As he finished his sentence, Wells called out in reassurance.

"We're in the right place alright, Peggy; I can see those twin villas that were on the model and the air photographs. Three quarters right, look; through the smoke."

Legg pushed his own face into the goggles of the commander's sight and sure enough, leaping into stark view through the magnified viewfinder, he spotted the distinctive outline of the two large beachfront villas that marked the far right hand side of Queen Red sector of Sword Beach.

"Bingo!" He called out. "Let's get on with the war then shall we?"

"There's Jerries in them houses, Peggy;" Wells said. "I can see the tracer coming out of the second floor windows."

"We got HE up the spout or amour piercing?" Legg enquired.

"HE."

"Put it into the second floor then."

Wells needed no further prompting. Legg saw the sight move slightly, then settle, as Wells made the fine adjustments, then, just a second later...

"On... Firing now..."

Whoomph!

The Sherman juddered as the 75mm gun barked into life and spat its first round in anger at the German defences. Legg caught a brief glance of 'swirl', the vacuum of air caused by the shell's passing as it sped towards its target, then, just as the sight picture settled again, a bright flash and a ball of black smoke indicated where the HE round had smashed into the large building.

"Target! HE! Reload!"

Wells called out the prescribed words of the gun drill and opened the breech. Below and between Wells and Legg, Lance Corporal Roberts, the radio operator and loader, was sliding another HE shell out of the ready-to-use rack and up towards the breech of the main gun.

Clunk. Legg heard the breech close and lock over the new shell. He was busy staring at the target, assessing to see if they needed to put another round into it, or adjust their aim onto a different part of the two buildings.

"Wait..." He cautioned Wells.

"What's that?" The gunner murmured.

"Wait; don't fire yet..." Legg repeated, but Wells cut him short.

"No; I mean what's that, there... Bottom left..."

Legg switched his gaze to the bottom corner of the sight picture and spotted instantly what the gunner's source of interest was.

"That's concrete; switch target..."

Instantly the sight picture jolted off its axis and dropped down and to the left.

"Steady, on!" Legg ordered.

The sight picture settled and both the gunner and commander peered intently through the billowing smoke from another burning Sherman.

"Christ; that's another one of ours on fire..." Wells commented sourly.

"Look beyond it." Legg prompted. "Whatever it is, it's beyond that burning vehicle."

They peered even harder for several moments and then, for just a split second, the wind caught the smoke from the burning armoured vehicle and snatched it away to the left. As the view beyond the burning Sherman came into clear focus, the two men spotted the unnatural, squat dark outline of the bunker immediately. As they registered the dark grey concrete structure below the camouflage net, and the long, thin, horizontal dark slits of its firing ports, a bright flash lit up the enemy pill-box for a split second.

"Shit!"

Barely had Wells uttered the curse when their Sherman rocked violently and an explosion shattered the relevant peace of the fighting compartment.

"Fucking hell!" The voices of Holloway and his co-driver, Atkins came up from the forward compartment.

"Shit! Are we hit? Are we hit?"

Legg began twisting around in his seat, looking desperately for signs of fire."

"No!" Holloway's voice came up. "Near miss; forward right of us! Only by a gnat's knacker though!"

"Anti-tank gun in the pillbox!" Legg said to Wells unnecessarily.

The gunner was already adjusting his sights onto the spot where they'd seen the muzzle flash from within the bunker.

"Firing now!" He called out, and then jammed his foot down on the firing pedal.

Once more, the vehicle reared slightly as the gun launched its HE round towards the pill box. Barely had the shot been released however, than something big and green suddenly filled the viewfinders.

"What the fuck?" Legg creased his brow.

Even through the armour of the tank, they heard the throaty roar of another armoured vehicle nearby.

"Fucking hell, Corp!" Shouted Holloway. "You only just missed that bastard! He's cut straight in front of us!"

"Who has?" Legg demanded

"That engineer tank; one of those Churchills with the bridges on. He just went right past us. Looks like he's driving along the water's edge."

Legg's mind was working fast now. If the Churchill bridge-layer was going to their right, then it was driving straight into the arc of the anti-tank gun in the pillbox.

"Traverse right." He snapped.

Even as the breech clunked shut over a fresh round, Wells was power-traversing the turret right.

"Stop!" Legg called out just a split second later.

They had a perfect view along the length of the beach to their right now. Amongst the smoke, the flames and the chaotic activity at the water's edge, Legg could discern some kind of pattern to it all.

There were several other Shermans further along the beach and, as per their orders and much the same as Legg's tank, they were sitting on the waterline, acting as static fire support for the assaulting infantry as they hurled themselves up the beach. However, there were several burning vehicles and it was obvious that the enemy had anti-tank guns in action and that, one by one, they were starting to pick off the supporting armour. He could see a Sherman 'Crab' tank advancing up the beach, the vehicle's turret reversed whilst at the front of its hull, the large rotating drum span around and flailed the sand in front of the vehicle with its heavy steel chains, beating a path clear of mines. Behind the Crab, the Churchill bridge-layer was starting to manoeuvre itself into the cleared lane, ready to follow the mine-clearance tank up the beach towards the dunes.

"They're trying to open up an exit beyond that bunker!" Legg realised out loud.

"That bloody gun in the pillbox will get the poor fuckers first..." Wells said.

"Driver; neutral right, then forward along the waterline." Legg suddenly ordered. "Follow the bridge-layer. Maximum speed."

Legg had made his decision. If they sat where they were they would be picked off, as sure as could be. At the same time, it was dangerous to proceed up the beach in a vehicle due to the threat of anti-tank mines, so it took no brains to work out that the best chance of getting off the beach in one piece was for all the vehicles to pitch in together. The engineer tanks were clearly doing their bit to open a clear lane. Legg needed to support them as best he could. The Sherman was already lurching to the right and beginning to accelerate as he gave the next order to Wells.

"Traverse left, over to nine o'clock! Use the co-ax and spray that bunker as we drive along the water's edge. Keep the bastards' heads down. Let's go and open up this ruddy beach!"

1650 SQUADRON – AT 12,000 FEET, SOMEWHERE OVER NORMANDY
TUESDAY 6TH JUNE 1940 – 0735 HOURS

It was, Whittaker thought, the very last place on earth he had expected to find himself in a queue. Here he was, on 'D-Day', flying above the greatest invasion fleet in history as the Allies launched their long awaited liberation of Nazi-occupied Europe, and he was waiting in a queue, almost as if he were on Paddington Station waiting patiently in line at the ticket office. As bizarre as it seemed, Whittaker understood why he was being forced to circle widely over his allocated secondary target with the remainder of his squadron following his lead.

The skies over France were absolutely crammed full of aircraft; just as the sea had been crammed full with ships. Only now did Whittaker truly appreciate how far the Allied air forces had come since the dark days of 1940. Was this what it had been like for the Stuka pilots over Dunkirk? Hovering over their targets as they awaited their turn to wreak death and destruction? And was this how the Luftwaffe's Heinkel pilots had felt during the early days of the Battle of Britain? Surrounded by hundreds of friendly aircraft and wondering how on earth their enemies could even hope to stand against them?

Because, even though Whittaker knew it was foolish to assume that the Luftwaffe was toothless and unable to contend the ownership of the skies over Normandy, the fact remained that as far as the eye could see, the only aircraft visible were all British or American.

Flying along in great, ominous looking flocks, the heavy bombers could be seen going in at a relatively low level of between 8,000 to 10,000 feet in order to ensure that they could identify their targets beneath the low scattered cloud, where those targets now lay half hidden by the mass of smoke and dust caused by earlier waves of bombing. Far above the ceiling of the heavy bomber formations, right up at 18,000 feet and beyond, the top cover squadrons circled like carrion crows spying out their prey. The tiny silhouettes of dozens of sleek looking Spitfires, or the stubbier looking, but equally deadly Mustangs, circled high up in the grey heavens, just daring the Luftwaffe to interfere in this overwhelming display of air power.

And somewhere in the middle, cruising steadily along in the ever-rotating 'cab rank', were the fighter bombers. Squadrons of aircraft like the Hawker Typhoons of Whittaker's 1650 Squadron, patiently waiting their turn to lose height and dive in on their secondary targets. Whittaker had imagined that his first action that day would be to scream in low across the wave tops, just a couple of hundred feet above the leading assault landing craft, and plaster the enemy's coastal defences with a furious barrage of sixty pound high explosive rockets, eight of which each of the squadron's Typhoons carried on rails under their wings.

It was not to be however. It seemed that the waves of heavy bombers, backed by the powerful guns of the naval bombardment force, had the job of suppressing the enemy coastal defences well in hand; thus he and his men found themselves waiting for their turn to have a pop at the two enemy pontoon bridges that had been thrown across the River Risle, following the destruction of the original bridges a month before. He knew that the hinterland near the bridges had been plastered by heavy bombers during the night, which should, theoretically, have taken care of any close-in batteries of anti-aircraft guns, whilst also turning the approach routes to the bridges into un-navigable crater-filled moonscapes. Now it was the turn of the RAF's low level fighter bombers to make sure of the actual bridges.

Whittaker glanced down toward the silver ribbon of the River Risle, where a huge cloud of smoke and dust was even now threatening to obscure those two, stick-like bridges, as the preceding squadron of Typhoons, or '*Bomphoons*' as they had been christened, finished their own attack run. Hopefully, a good share of those deadly five hundred pound bombs would have found their mark and done for the bridges good and proper. Regardless, it was Whittaker's job to make sure that his own squadron made sure of the job, by following up their sister squadron and saturating the bridges with the equally deadly high explosive rockets.

A voice crackled over the intercom, informing him that the airspace over the target was now clear for 1650 Squadron to have their moment, and sure enough, as Whittaker surveyed the scene far below, he saw the last Bomphoons pulling away from the target to rejoin their own comrades, who were busily reforming high above the target area. Whittaker clicked on the pressel of his RT.

"Okay 1650, our turn now. Approach from the east in section astern, one at a time. Red Section with me first to have a look, then await my signal for the remainder to go in."

He tweaked the steering column and felt the heaviness of the controls as, with a powerful throb of its Napier Sabre engine, the awesome beast of an aircraft banked over to starboard and began losing height as Whittaker curled around for his first run in to the target. The remainder of his section followed suit, one aircraft following another, whilst the remainder of the squadron continued circling above, albeit in a slightly tighter formation, keeping their eyes peeled for enemy fighters. The approach wasn't perfect of course. Whittaker and his men had learned from long experience to attack their targets from directly behind, so that if they were hit by flak and the controls were damaged beyond use, at least the plane would keep heading in the direction of home until it finally gave up the ghost and plummeted earthwards. If nothing else, it gave the pilot the opportunity to get as close to home as possible before bailing out.

On this occasion however, there was little choice but to come in from a flank. The bridges were long, narrow targets, and so it made sense to attack them along their length to give a greater chance of hitting. Of course, the enemy would know that too. Whittaker could only hope that after the pounding the area had received over the last few hours, there would be little left on the ground that was capable of shooting at him. Aligning himself onto the southernmost of the two engineer bridges, Whittaker dropped the nose of his aircraft even more so that he could gather speed for his attack run. Although the Typhoon was a beast of a plane to fly, its power and speed made for a very steady and devastatingly accurate attack run.

He reached the required height and angle and gave the plane its head as it came out of its dive. The fields and trees whizzed past below the aircraft in a blur as Whittaker focussed all his energy onto aligning the Typhoon perfectly onto the distant bridge, which grew larger with every second. There may have been tracer coming up past his aircraft but he failed to notice as he concentrated on perfecting the very precise launch requirements for his rocket.

"Here we go..." He murmured to himself as the target bridge loomed up ahead and he registered that he was almost in the optimum position to release his rockets.

A heartbeat later he pressed the firing button and a mass of smoke engulfed either wing momentarily as his eight rockets exploded into life and streaked away towards the bridge. There was no jolt or buffeting as the rockets launched as the heavy aircraft afforded him a remarkably stable firing platform. The commanding officer of 1650 squadron waited just another split second to ensure all his rockets were gone, then banked sharply to starboard and powered away from the line of attack. As he did so, his mind caught up and began processing the information that his eyes had been feeding him.

He'd seen his rockets streaking towards the target bridge, seemingly on a perfect trajectory for a direct hit. In addition, Whittaker had also seen the prominent angle of the platforms and girders in the very centre of the bridge where they had been shattered by something big, leaving a gaping hole in the structure. As he banked his Typhoon left and right in an automatic evasive manoeuvre designed to dodge any ack-ack that might come up at him, Whittaker caught sight of the second bridge, the most northerly, as he roared over it at just a few hundred feet. It was intact.

"Hello all sections 1650, this is Red Leader; leave the southernmost bridge. Priority is the northern bridge. I say again; priority is the northern bridge. All sections acknowledge."

Whittaker sent the message over the RT as he finally pulled out of his corkscrew manoeuvre and brought the aircraft's nose up and gave the engine some throttle, fighting to gain height so that he could supervise the rest of the attack from an elevated position.

The remaining sections leaders in his squadron were already acknowledging his message and, as he began to bank round gently, climbing all the time, Whittaker saw the second and third aircraft from his own section pass straight over the target he'd just hit and begin banking round for a run-in on the northern bridge. Good men. The southern bridge itself was wreathed in dirty grey smoke, showing that his own rockets had indeed found their mark and added to the destruction already evident on that particular crossing.

A sense of cold, ruthless satisfaction came over Whittaker as he watched his well trained squadron begin their relentless assault on the German crossing points over the River Risle. Four years ago, it had all been so very different. And those four years had now passed, during which many of his friends had been killed or maimed for life, doing their utmost to put a halt to the seemingly inexorable creep of Nazi power.

But the balance of power had shifted, and now it was the turn of the Germans to feel the wrath of Allied air power, and to know the sense of dread that descended on one's soul at the first sound of an aircraft engine; knowing that it heralded imminent destruction. It was awful that he should think like that, Whittaker considered, as he watched his numbers two and three from Red Section launch their rockets in rapid succession against the northern bridge. Despite that, he could feel no pity; no qualms at all about the havoc he and his men would now wreak upon their enemies. After four years, the RAF was back over Northern France in force; and it was time to even the score.

THE DUNES – QUEEN RED SECTOR, SWORD BEACH
TUESDAY 6TH JUNE 1944 – 0735 HOURS

"Come on!" Downey was breathing like an asthmatic. "Come on!"

Crack-crack-crack-crack-crack-crack!

The machine gun was back in action again, spitting its deadly slugs across the beach towards the scattered group of khaki clad men who were struggling over the sand towards the perceived relative safety of the barbed wire entanglement lining the forward edge of the dunes. The sound of the passing bullets was deafening and Downey felt a strange thudding in his heart as each individual round cracked past him. Some of those bullets were invisible to the naked eye, their passing punctuated only by the ear-splitting whiplash noise they made as they sliced through the air. Others streaked past in a bright orange blur, like angry, luminous bugs.

The beach couldn't have been more than a hundred yards wide beyond the obstacle belt at the waterline, he thought, but it had seemed endless. His thighs, calves and lungs were protesting as if he'd just broken the world record for the mile sprint, and his words fell out of his mouth in a tumbling gasp; the same words repeated over and over again, like a man who had lost his wits. With a strangely childish sense of relief, Downey suddenly realised that the barbed concertina wire was just half a dozen paces away now, and that the gently undulating dunes were right in front of him. With an enormous sigh he fell, rather than dived, down against the modest cover that the edge of the dunes afforded.

"Down…" He gave himself the order.

He hit the sand with a grunt and took a huge intake of breath, desperately trying to control his ragged breathing. For several long seconds, he lay there, staring at the sand from very close quarters, his whole body shaking with the physical effort of trying to bring itself under control. Beyond the crack of passing bullets and the sound of explosions, all of which had blended into a constant, incoherent background symphony, he heard the thud of boots and bodies hitting sand and the sound of other human beings gasping for breath and retching with the effort.

He forced his head up and looked left, where he found himself staring at a line of men, perhaps a dozen or more, all of whom were laid prostrate, in a similar manner to himself, along the line of the dunes for perhaps twenty yards or more. The nearest of those suddenly looked up, straight at Downey, and the sergeant felt a pang of unusually fond recognition as he realised that it was the dour Evans, still alive and by his side after the dash across the beach. The young private's eyes were bulging in their sockets from the shock of the last few minutes.

"Fuck…me…Fucking hell…" The soldier was trying to speak as he gulped in huge lung-fulls of air.

For a while, Downey just stared back at the younger man, and all those who were stretched out beyond him, before casting a glance back across the beach. The scene was unbelievable. That great fleet was still there, but between it and Downey there was a chaotic mass of landing craft of various sizes being tossed about on the heavy surf. Some of those landing craft were on fire, whilst others manoeuvred, or were thrown between the forest of strangely shaped obstacles. There were tanks too; not many, but several of them on the beach, whilst others were trying to disembark from the bigger landing craft. Most of those tanks that he could see on the beach were on fire and, across the whole expanse of sand, there lay a scattering of limp, motionless khaki bodies.

"What now, Sarge?"

The question from Evans brought Downey back to the job in hand. He looked back at the young man beside him.

"You got any Bangalores or firing packs?" Downey blurted.

"No."

"Start shooting then." He ordered the soldier. "Look for bunkers or trenches and shoot at them... Keep your head down though..."

Evans nodded and, with an obvious effort, dragged his rifle up into position in his shoulder.

"I can't see a fucking thing..." The private gasped.

"Use your eyes..." Downey snapped back. "Look for the fuckers..."

With that, Downey dragged himself closer to Evans, then, taking care to keep low, climbed over the prone soldier so that he could reach out and touch the man beyond him.

"Who's that?" Downey demanded, finding that the strength was beginning to return to his voice.

The man rolled over to look at Downey and he saw that it was Private Winstanley, the platoon runner.

"Where's Mr Simmonds?" Downey asked.

"What?" Winstanley looked dazed.

"Where's the fucking Platoon Commander?" Downey snapped irritably.

"I don't know..."

Downey snorted in frustration but, understanding that the lad was in shock, he simply slapped him on the arm.

"Well... start looking for fucking Germans and then start shooting the fuckers!"

Then, throwing his voice beyond the frightened young man.

"Oi, you lot!"

A burst of machine gun fire came slicing through the air and the deadly bullets began slamming into the sand over a beaten zone of several square metres, right behind the next group of men at the edge of the dunes. The burst of fire caused the men nearby to enter into a flurry of excited shouting, which to Downey's ears sounded like nothing more than meaningless babble.

"Oi, you lot!" He tried again, but the combination of background noise and the shouting of the other men drowned out his words.

The platoon sergeant found his temper flare suddenly as the frustration and confusion of the moment welled up inside of him.

"Oi, you lot! Shut the fuck up!" He screamed at the top of his voice, the tendons in his neck going taught with the effort. "Shut the fuck up! Keep fucking quiet and listen to me!"

This time, it seemed to work. Several faces looked towards him, but he found he couldn't put a name to them.

"Who's that?" He demanded.

"Youngman." Replied the nearest.

"Corpora Saville." Shouted the other.

No.3 Platoon names he thought; not his men. The whole company had got mixed up on the way across the beach.

For just a second, the enormity of what confronted him almost overwhelmed Downey. This was chaos; absolute bloody chaos. But of course it was. What else had he expected? The image of a battle long ago flickered through his mind briefly. A burning, ruined farmhouse, defended by a motley collection of waifs and strays from the Regular Army, Home Guard, RAF, and even some civilians. The mass of hardened, determined German infantry, backed by armoured cars and half-tracks. The sheer impossibility of surviving the experience, never mind emerging from it victorious. And of course, there was the tall, grim, foul-mouthed sergeant with spectacles from the Coldstream Guards who would not admit defeat under any circumstances. In an instant, the memory was gone and Downey was back in the real world.

"Corporal Saville; get me some Bangalores and firing packs, sharpish! We've got one Bangalore over here already, but I want some more and I want some firing packs too. Go and find them and get them over here. Understand?"

The corporal strained his head to peer over Youngman's prone form and spotted the chevrons on Downey's battledress. A look of sudden recognition flooded over the NCO's face.

"Yes, Sarge!"

The man rolled over and began crawling off down the line of soldiers, as Downey turned his attention to Youngman.

"You; get hold of those fuckers there…" Downey shouted above the din, gesturing towards the other men lying prone, a little further on. "Get their smoke grenades off them and bring them here. When I give you the nod, I want you to start using them right in front of us and off to the side a bit too. I want you to get a smoke screen up and running and keep it going. I'm going to start cutting through the wire? Understand?"

The young soldier nodded back.

"Understand?" Downey growled again.

"Yes, Sarge; got it…" Youngman blurted.

"Good; now get it sorted, and tell the others I'm going through the wire. Tell them to get ready and follow me through."

Downey rolled away from the soldier and began to rummage inside his battledress jacket for the pair of wire-cutters he had opted to carry. It was easier said than done because he was constricted by the flotation vest that all the assault troops had been told to wear, in addition to the two bandoliers of ammunition that were hung around his body. As he struggled to reach the wire-cutters, he glanced up to see that Winstanley was staring stupidly over the sights of his rifle.

"Oi; why aren't you fucking firing?" Downey snarled at the stunned looking soldier.

"I can't see anything to shoot at..." The youngster replied in a piteous voice.

Downey was in no mood for weakness amongst his men today.

"Just fire at that fucking house over there then, you knob! Fire at the fucking windows and keep firing! Use your bloody head, man!"

Thus prompted, the soldier swung his rifle to the right and took aim on the dim shape of two large villas, that were situated perhaps a couple of hundred yards off through the smoke. Downey watched the young soldier fire a shot and then recock his rifle, before taking fresh aim. Satisfied that Winstanley was finally being useful, Downey returned to the struggle with his equipment and, with a series of foul oaths, finally managed to extricate the wire-cutters from within his battledress jacket.

"Sergeant Downey? What do you want us to do?"

Downey looked up and saw, to his relief, Corporal Jacobs with two other men on all fours beside him.

"We ended up down there..." Jacobs was jerking his thumb over his shoulder, grimacing as a burst of machine gun fire passed close by him. "In amongst Three Platoon. There's a couple more of our lads there; they're coming along."

There was a sudden high pitched 'snap' and then one of the men with Jacobs suddenly toppled sideways onto the sand and lay still.

"Shit!" The corporal swore as he and the third man flatted themselves as best they could against the beach.

Quickly, Downey explained the plan.

"I'm going through the wire with these. See if you can find any more Bangalores. There's a length just here, but we need a firing pack. And start organising these fuckers along here. I want a smoke screen where I'm cutting through the wire and I want everyone else suppressing the Jerries. Tell everyone to look for them. Those bullets are coming from somewhere. Follow the path of the tracer and look for vantage points. Start shooting back. Got all that?"

"Yep, got it Sarge..." Jacobs acknowledged.

"Good." Downey snapped. "Get on with it then, and let's get the fuck off this beach!"

LEGG'S TANK – QUEEN RED SECTOR, SWORD BEACH
TUESDAY 6TH JUNE 1944 – 0740 HOURS

"We're taking in water!"

Legg frowned as he heard Holloway's warning from below.

"Water?"

"Yeah; I think that shell that nearly hit us must have done something to the seals on the hull…"

It still didn't make any sense to Legg.

"We're on the beach though…"

"We *were* on the beach…" Holloway corrected. "That tide's coming in fast and we're now driving through the surf, even though we're going *across* the beach."

Legg jammed his eyes against the side periscope in the turret. The gun was traversed over the left side of the hull and thus the side periscope on the turret was now looking forwards along the axis of the vehicle's route. As soon as the corporal put his eyes to the viewing port, he saw what the driver meant. They were driving along the beach, side on to the enemy held shoreline, negotiating their way around obstacles as they went. The tide however, whipped up by the recent storm and high winds, was rising faster than anyone could have imagined, and thus the tank was ploughing its way through a good three feet of water again, despite having left the sea once already. Ahead of them, Legg could see the Churchill bridge-layer doing exactly the same thing. Even as he watched however, he saw the Churchill swing left and onto the churned up sand that had been turned over by the advancing flail tank.

"Just keep going Stan and follow that bridge layer up the cleared path."

"There he is…"

Rat-tat-tat-tat-tat-tat-tat!

The gunner made the exclamation at the same time that he pressed down on the firing pedal for the co-axial machine gun, and the automatic weapon chattered into life. Instantly, Legg changed his gaze from the side periscope to the commander's sight. The stark image of the square concrete bunker loomed into Legg's vision and he saw the small spurts of concrete dust where bullets where slamming into the solid enemy position. Curiously, he noticed that the firing ports they had seen on the bunker just a couple of minutes earlier were no longer visible.

"Stop firing!" He yelled, realising with a jolt that the bunker had a screen wall to its front that protected it from both view and fire from the seaward side.

The firing ports were on the sides of the bunker so that the weapons within could fire in enfilade along the beach, whilst being hidden from frontal view.

"You can't hit anything from this angle." Legg explained to the gunner. "You're just wasting ammo. We'll have to engage it from the side."

The Sherman slowed of a sudden and then swung to the left.

"Are we on the cleared path?" Legg called out to the driver.

"No! Just going around some dead bodies!" Came the reply.

"Oh…" The thought had never occurred to Legg up until now that there might be dead and wounded strewn about the beach, on which their tank already had so little room for manoeuvre.

"Bring the gun back over the front decks for a moment." He told the gunner. "I'm getting a bit disorientated."

Dutifully, Wells traversed the turret to the twelve o'clock position and Legg pressed his eyes to the commander's sight again. It didn't help any; the magnification of the sight was giving him a limited view of the beach and Legg decided that he needed to take a risk in order to get his bearings better.

"I'm going to pop my head out for a few seconds." He told Wells.

The gunner looked sideways at him.

"Fucking hell, Peggy; you want to be careful mate. There's all kinds of shit flying around out there…"

"I know…" Legg tried to brush the thoughts of death aside. "But I can't see a thing inside here. I need to get a quick look around and see what's going on. I'll only be a couple of seconds."

Wells nodded grimly.

"Just watch yourself, mate." He murmured.

Quickly, with trembling fingers, Legg unlocked the hatch levers and pushed upwards. The split hatch open up under the pressure of his hands and, slowly, carefully, the tank commander raised his eyes up to peer over the lip of the cupola. In an instant, the disorientation left him and the scene around him came into stark view. He saw the bodies laying on the beach, the line of khaki-clad men against the dunes, the burning vehicles and landing craft, and the outline of the twin villas just a couple of hundred yards away, looming up out of the battlefield smoke like a haunted house from some horror film.

He peered around the side of the hatch, straight up the beach, and saw the flail tank grinding its way forward, the sand flying in all directions as the heavy, metal chains thudded into the beach over and over again as the drum to which they were attached span rapidly on the end of its supporting arms. He saw an explosion within that blur of spinning chains, a huge pile of sand erupting with a roar as the buried mine detonated under the force of the beating flails. A small chunk of chain went flying through the air, but other than that, the explosion had little effect and the Sherman Crab edged closer to the wire entanglement at the edge of the dunes. Behind it, the bridge-layer had manoeuvred its way into the cleared lane and was following on, exactly as its crew had been trained to do.

"Hard left, driver!" He called abruptly into the tank's intercom. "Follow the bridge-layer. Hard left now; then forward."

Legg then threw a quick glance over his shoulder as the tank began to execute a tight left wheel. He spotted the low, camouflaged silhouette of the bunker and saw now that his vehicle was about to drive back into the arc of fire of the position. Sure enough, as the Sherman manoeuvred, the firing ports of the bunker began to appear once more.

Ping!

A single bullet hit the open hatch and ricocheted off, making Legg duck involuntarily. He had seen enough however, and took the near miss as confirmation that he no longer needed to pop his head up. Dropping down into the turret, he pulled the hatches shut again and flicked the locking levers across.

"Traverse left again, back over the side!" He ordered the Wells. "The bunker's coming back into view."

The gunner needed no further prompting. With a high-pitched whine, the turret swung left, before jerking to a stop at a right angle to the hull.

"Lay onto that bunker again; you can see the firing port again. Put some HE into the bastard!"

Legg shouted the command as he was settling his eyes into the commander's sight, and he saw the graticules within the viewfinder juddering as Wells made the final adjustments to the lay of the main gun. He sensed, rather than saw, Wells reaching out to change the firing switch from coaxial to main armament, and then, just a heartbeat later...

"Firing now!"

Whooomph!

"Target!"

Legg saw the bright flash and cloud of dark smoke as the HE shell slammed into the bunker just below the firing port.

"HE, reload!" The gunner was calling, whilst the loader was already in process of reaching up with another shell.

"Shit the bed!"

The exclamation from Holloway down below did not bode well, coupled with the Sherman coming to an abrupt halt.

"What is it?" Legg almost shouted down the intercom.

"The flail-tank's been hit! Something big! She's brewing up big style! Right by the bloody wire as well, poor bastards! They almost had us off…"

"Keep engaging that bunker…" Legg ordered the gunner as he once again threw himself to the side periscope.

The sight that greeted him was one of flame and oily black smoke. The Sherman was indeed brewing up, its entire hull seemingly engulfed in hungry orange flame. There was no sign at all of the crew making an attempt to escape from the tank and a shudder ran through Legg. Something, somewhere was picking the British tanks off one by one. The gun in the concrete bunker was on the opposite side to them now, so there must be a second anti-tank gun somewhere. They needed to get off this beach, and fast. The Churchill bridge-layer, which had come to a halt about twenty yards behind the burning Sherman Crab, jerked into life once more, and Legg saw that its commander was thinking exactly the same thing. Legg watched it execute a neutral turn right and then nudge its way past the burning flail tank, keeping the wrecked vehicle between it and the concrete bunker, just in case.

"The bridge-layer's going for it!" Legg gabbled.

"Shall I follow him?" Came Holloway's surprisingly calm voice.

"Yep. Do it. But don't get too close; give him room to manoeuvre." Legg ordered, then, glancing at the gunner. "Keep engaging that bunker with HE."

Whooomph!

The 75mm gun roared again.

"Stay inside the track marks of the bridge-layer!" Legg ordered the driver. "And try to position us as close to the brewed up flail tank as you can. We'll use the poor bastards to cover us from that bunker as best we can…"

The Sherman was already jerking into motion, trundling carefully forward over the sand.

"I'm going to put a smoke round into the ground in front of this bunker, Peggy…" Came Wells' voice.

"Roger; good plan. Do it." Legg responded, still watching the bridge-layer as best he could through his limited view in the side-periscope.

Moments later, the main armament roared again, heralding the launch of the first smoke round.

"He's reached the wire, Peggy." Holloway informed his commander.

"Okay, stay back from him until we can see what he's going to do…"

"I think he's going to drop his bridge…"

"Peggy?" The radio operator tapped the corporal on his knee. "I've got Sergeant Saddler coming over the net; he's trying to contact us and the Troop Leader."

Legg glanced down momentarily.

"Tell him the Troopy's tank is drowned and that we're okay. Tell him we're to the right of the big bunker, next to the burning flail tank. Tell him we're following a bridge-layer."

"Roger." The radio operator nodded and began relaying the message.

Jamming his eyes back against the periscope, Legg found that they had come to a halt by the rear-right of the burning Sherman Crab. Beyond the ruined tank and just to the right of it, he could see the bulk of the Churchill tank of the Royal Engineers, its hull pushed right up against the barbed wire, whilst its folded section of Bailey bridge was in the half open position.

"They're trying to span the minefield with the bridge…"Legg murmured absently.

"They'll never reach right over those dunes…" Commented Holloway.

The commander of the Churchill must have read Holloway's thoughts because, just a moment later, the bridge paused in mid opening. Then, seconds later, the Churchill began grinding its way forward over the wire entanglement.

"Christ Almighty!" The co-driver, breathed. "He's driving into the minefield!"

Sure enough, deciding that this might be the moment to make the supreme sacrifice, the crew of the bridge-layer were pushing their vehicle as far into the minefield and the dunes as they dare, hoping they could get far enough to lower their bridge across the remaining distance.

Legg, Holloway and the co-driver, watching through their apertures, watched in silence as the Churchill trundled forward, ever deeper into the dunes which, according to intelligence reports, would be even more heavily mined than the beach itself. They watched as the tank progressed more than its own length beyond the wire, holding their breaths and not daring to make a comment.

Whoomph!

Wells fired another smoke round in the direction of the bunker. The Churchill slowed to a halt. Then, carefully, its bridge began unfolding again.

Still, nobody spoke. The three members of Legg's crew who could see the spectacle sat staring in desperate fascination as the portable bridge section slowly folded out into the semblance of a full bridge-span.

"Ruddy hell, they're going to make it…" Holloway breathed eventually. "The far end is just going to reach those dragon's teeth."

The *'dragon's teeth'* to which Holloway referred were the strange, almost pyramid like concrete blocks that had been erected along the promenade beyond the dunes by the Germans; their purpose to serve as an anti-tank wall across the entire frontage of the beach. The wall thus created resembled an endless row of giant grey teeth, and had been reinforced with another barbed wire entanglement to keep the infantry at bay too.

"Nearly there..." Legg murmured.

A moment later, the far end of the now extended bridging unit bumped down to rest, only just, on a stretch of the anti-tank wall at the far side of the narrow dunes. Without any prompting, a collective cheer went up within Legg's tank.

"Woohoo! You little dancer!" Whooped Holloway.

"He's only gone and done it!" Came the co-driver's jubilant voice.

"Okay, stand-by to go over! Traverse right! Bring the gun back to twelve o'clock!"

Immediately, Wells swung the turret back over onto its frontal axis, and as he did so, Legg sat back and wiped the sweat from his face. It was getting hot inside the tank now, and the pungent fumes created by the use of main gun were adding to the general discomfort. The corporal would be glad when he could open up the hatches again, but just now that really wasn't a good idea.

"Sergeant Saddler's trying to find us..." The operator said from his position below and between Legg and Wells.

"Tell him the beach is open!" Legg blurted, suddenly becoming animated and realising that he needed to get the message out. "Tell everyone you get hold of. Between the concrete bunker with the anti-tank gun and the twin villas, there's a brewed up flail-tank. Next to that there's an engineer bridge over the dunes and the wall. Tell them we're going over now."

Again, the operator began relaying the information.

"The Churchill's backing out for us Peggy." Holloway warned him.

Jamming his head to the forward periscope, Legg saw the ungainly looking tank trundling rearwards now, as it made to clear the approach to the bridge it had just laid.

"As soon as it's out of the way, go for it, Stan. But make sure you're properly lined up or else we'll be off the side and into the dunes..."

Legg had barely got the words out of his mouth when disaster struck.

Boom!

The Churchill, almost fully out of the dunes now, had begun to wheel to its rear right as it attempted to pull back behind the flattened wire entanglement, and as it did so, something big exploded under its right hand track. Legg saw the tank rock violently, and for a moment thought that it might flip completely over, but after a split second of being half in the air, the heavy armoured vehicle thumped back down onto the sand the right way up. Thick black smoke began pouring from the far side of it.

"Bollocks!"

Legg echoed Holloway's sentiments.

For a moment, nobody spoke as they watched the Churchill become enveloped by the cloying, oily smoke. Just as Legg was beginning to assume the worst however, the hatches on the vehicle began opening, and several heads emerged from within.

"Thank God!" Legg breathed. "It looks like they're all okay…"

Okay, but obviously stunned and disorientated by the mine-blast, because the crew of the Churchill didn't so much climb out of their disabled tank, as fall out. The men came tumbling out of the burning vehicle coughing, spluttering, sliding and falling without ceremony off the decks of the tank and onto the sand. Amazingly, one of the crew, presumably the commander, managed to straighten himself up and look directly towards Legg's Sherman. With one arm, the man gave a very definite and very urgent indication that Legg should stop hanging around and get over the bridge. With a jolt, Legg realised that despite the immobilisation of the Churchill, there was enough space left between it and the burning flail-tank for his own vehicle to get through. It was tight, but it was do-able.

"Forward, Stan." Legg snapped. "Squeeze past them and onto the bridge."

With a sudden rush of understanding, Legg realised that up until now, he had been following other people. Now however, all those people had been taken out of the equation and it was his turn to lead from the front. His tank, right here and right now, was about to lead the break-out from the beach and drive straight into the jaws of the enemy.

"Alright lads, here we go!" He said over the intercom. "Keep it steady over the bridge, Stan, and get ready for the drop as we come off the wall at the other side. Once we're over, turn sharp right and head towards the twin villas. The rest of you, stand-by to open fire as soon as we come off the bridge. We're going into France, so let's go in with all guns blazing…"

THE TWIN VILLAS, OBJECTIVE COD – SWORD BEACH
TUESDAY 6TH JUNE 1944 – 0745 HOURS

"Walther? Are you alright?"

Lehman looked up from where he was crouching on the floor of the sand-bagged bunker. As he did so, he saw that the room outside the confines of their little strongpoint was piled high in rubble, wooden beams, bits of plaster and God only knew what else. The thick fog of plaster dust had once more been swirled up by the most recent explosion which had taken place somewhere directly above the bunker occupied by Lehman and his colleague Gruber.

"I... I think so..." Lehman stammered as he rose unsteadily to his feet. He could barely hear his friend's words now. Everything apart from the sound of gunfire and explosions seemed like it was coming from a great distance away and Lehman's ears were now subject to a permanent high pitched whine.

"That shell hit the room right above us..." Private Gruber intoned in a voice choked with fear. "They've got tanks, Walther... Tanks! They're not supposed to have tanks! Not yet... the Lieutenant told us so. He said it would take hours before the Tommies would be able to get tanks ashore..."

Lehman shook the dust and plaster off his rifle and looked at his friend directly.

"They swam ashore, Tomas. I saw one come out of the sea. They've got swimming tanks. It's alright though; the anti-tank guns will get them. Come on... we've got to keep shooting..."

Lehman glanced to his left slightly as he reached into a pouch for a fresh clip of ammunition. As he did so, he froze. In the corner of the room, protruding from a pile of debris that had collapsed from the upper floors, Lehman saw an arm, clad in a field-grey tunic, the hand seemingly frozen in some kind of desperate grasping position, like an animal's claw. The young soldier looked away quickly.

"Come on..." He said again, grabbing Gruber by the sleeve and guiding him back to the parapet. "We've got to keep firing..."

Lehman slid the fresh clip of ammunition into the grooves above the open magazine of his rifle and pushed the five rounds down into the belly of the weapon. Removing the clip, he slammed the bolt forward and locked it in position, feeding a round into the chamber as he did so.

"Where've they all gone?" He heard Gruber ask.

Squinting through the smoke and dust beyond the sand-bagged parapet and the shattered window frame, Lehman saw that the beach was now a confused mess of burning tanks and boats, but the mass of khaki figures that had been flooding across the sand seemed to have disappeared of a sudden.

"Gone to ground perhaps? By the dunes?"

"Maybe they're all dead?" Gruber asked hopefully.

"Maybe... Just keep looking and shoot anything that moves." Lehman replied.

As if to follow his own advice, the young soldier scanned the beach beyond the wire and the concrete anti-tank wall and the undulating sand dunes. He could see bodies laid on the beach. Far down that beach, by one of the few remaining steel hedgehogs that had not yet been swallowed by the incoming tide, he saw a crouching figure, moving around beneath the criss-crossed metal girders. He levelled his rifle, aimed towards the distant figure through the fleeting smoke of a burning Tommy tank then squeezed the trigger. The KAR 98 rifle lurched in his grasp, and Lehman automatically worked the bolt, ready to take a second shot.

"Shit, here they come again!" Gruber suddenly cried out.

Lehman looked up in alarm as he rammed his rifle bolt closed again. He saw the danger instantly. From amongst the burning assault craft that bobbed about on the surf, more craft, undamaged ones, had appeared and were even now lowering their ramps. In an instant, another flood of khaki figures were spilling into the water and up the sand.

Bang!

Gruber's rifle barked out and, a second later, Lehman's rifle barked too.

The two soldiers aimed and fired; aimed and fired. They didn't know how long they were there for, shooting at the new wave of attackers, but Lehman suddenly found that his pouches were empty and he began dipping his hand inside the ammunition box to retrieve the reserve clips. All the while, shells of various sizes smashed into the upper floors and peripheries of the building in which their strongpoint was situated. Eventually, the beach seemed to empty of moving bodies again, although the amount of smoke seemed to be increasing, giving everything an indistinct ethereal appearance.

"What are those things!" Gruber gasped as he surveyed the scene on the beach. "There, look… Big boats coming in closer."

"God knows…" Lehman muttered as he stared with red-rimmed eyes at the next wave of landing craft that were edging closer by the second.

"Just keep shooting, Tomas. Keep shooting…"

Just as he uttered the words, there was a series of sharp explosions just off to his forward right. Crump-crump-crump-crump!

Snapping his head in that direction, he spotted the bright flashes, all in a line, as something in the shape of a snake seemed to explode from within a bank of smoke in the middle of the sand dunes.

"What the fuck was that?" Lehman asked of nobody in particular, and forgetting himself by using such foul language.

"Something in the dunes…" Gruber murmured. "Looked like an exploding pipe or something?"

Lehman peered into the thick cloud of smoke created by the explosions, trying to establish the cause of the unusual blast. The smoke itself had belched upwards in a linear shape, like a strange black hedge running from the beach, right across the dunes towards the anti-tank wall almost. And then he saw them.

Faces. Pale faces; staring out from between funny shaped helmets and khaki bodies, coming through the smoke towards the anti-tank wall.

"Tommies!" Both Lehman and Gruber called out together.

Instinctively, both men swung their barrels towards their right of arc and began snatching off shots in rapid succession towards this latest threat.

"Don't let them get over the wall!" Gruber was shouting now as he reloaded his rifle.

Lehman was parched; his mouth so clogged with dust that he could barely speak anyway, and his whole body was drenched in sweat. His fingers, already cut and bleeding from the repetition of loading and firing, felt like big fat sausages as he clumsily tried to maintain his rapid rate of fire.

"Don't let them get over..." Gruber called again, his voice taking on a desperate, almost childish tone.

And then it appeared, completely unexpectedly. Just as Lehman fed another fresh clip of ammunition into his rifle and slammed the bolt shut, the big, green, funny shaped tank clattered into view from the right hand side, directly in front of their position, no more than thirty metres away. For a second, Lehman just stared at the thing as it clattered into full view, his mouth hanging open stupidly as he noted the slightly angled front of the big metal beast, its fat, round little turret, and its stubby little gun that was pointing straight at him. And then it fired.

The machine gun bullets began slapping into the outside of the building just a heartbeat before several more came flying straight through the window and into the bunker. Lehman's mind must have computed the danger with unbelievable speed because he was already ducking below the sandbags when the burst of fire cracked through the gap between the parapet and the overhead protection of the strongpoint. Gruber was nowhere near as quick. He simply toppled backwards, falling onto the floor beside Lehman with a dull thud.

There were no final words, no cry of pain, just a flop, a thud, and then Gruber was dead. Lehman, pushed hard up against the sandbagged front wall of the position, stared in horror and disbelief at the face of his friend; or at least at the half of his face that was still recognisable. The tissue and bone and blood that had constituted the remainder of Gruber's head was now splashed out across the rubble and debris at the rear of the fighting position.

Lehman felt the panic suddenly well up inside him, almost like a feeling of nausea, but a feeling that was infinitely, infinitely worse.

"Tanks!" He let out the word in a strangled voice from between cracked lips. "Tommy Tanks!"

THE DUNES – QUEEN RED SECTOR, SWORD BEACH
TUESDAY 6TH JUNE 1944 – 0750 HOURS

"Shit, shit, shit!"

Downey had changed his mantra to the single expletive, which he repeated over and over again, every time a fresh bullet cracked by or slapped into the dunes and kicked sand up into the air in his immediate vicinity. It was even worse when the occasional, yet exceptionally terrifying air-burst artillery shells detonated over the beach. Even when the explosions were some distance away, the shock wave that hammered through the air, driving the red hot steel splinters before it, made Downey's whole body shudder with unimaginable fear.

The sergeant was on his back, and to some degree, in his own little world; enveloped as he was in the acrid grey chemical smoke that was being generated by the No.77 Smoke Grenades that the men behind him were throwing, one at a time, every minute or so, to try and keep him obscured from enemy view. The Germans weren't daft of course. They realised that a smoke screen only meant trouble, and so their snipers were making a point of firing blindly into the artificial fog in the hope of hitting somebody with their speculative fire.

Downey tried not to wonder how long the supply of smoke grenades might last and continued cutting the wire as fast as he could. It was gruelling work. He and his men had practiced these techniques over and over again in training these last few years but, even so, doing it under fire, and whilst physically and emotionally drained, was a different matter.

The sergeant bent the latest loose end of wire back carefully, trying not to get his sleeve caught up in the process, before raising his knees slightly, digging in his heels and then pushing himself another couple of feet along the sand. He felt the rough sand slipping under his battledress jacket as he pushed himself along, where it would irritate and chafe his sweat lathered and salt-water drenched skin. Something caught on the scrim net of his helmet and Downey arched his neck, staring upwards and forwards. Another strand of wire.

He reached up with the wire-cutters, the lanyard of which dangled loosely beneath, tickling his nose. With aching arms, the NCO opened the jaws of the cutters and slid them either side of the wire strand. He made sure the strand was firmly lodged in the angle of the jaws and then pressed the cutters together. He felt the slight resistance as the steel cutting edges closed around the soft metal strand, and then… snip. With a jerk, the cutters sliced through wire and Downey turned his face away as one loose end of the wire, complete with barb, rebounded towards his eyes. Grabbing the end of the wire like it was a poisonous snake, the sergeant began folding the strand back where it wouldn't be able to bounce up again and snag on his equipment.

This particular barb was exceptionally springy and really didn't want to stay down, so Downey was forced to curl it around another length of wire nearby and fashion a kind of hook to secure it in place. It was then he spotted the mine.

"Shit!"

It was some way off, perhaps three yards or more, and lay just beyond the stretch of concertina that he was in the process of cutting through. Nothing much was visible, but the distinctive rounded edge of something metal and circular was enough to make Downey realise that cutting the wire was just half of the problem. He rolled onto his side and twisted his head round so that he could get a proper view of the dunes beyond this jungle of barbed wire. The dunes weren't that wide he supposed; perhaps twenty yards until they washed up against the jagged profile of the anti-tank wall? But that meant twenty yards of minefield. Trying to clear that stretch under such intense fire would be like trying to climb a mountain with your feet tied together.

"Sarge! Sarge!"

The shouting from behind caught his attention and he looked back towards the beach. He could see the face of Corporal Jacobs and Private Evans peering at him from behind the tufts of sea-grass at the edge of the dunes.

"We've got the stuff!"

"What?"

"We've got all the stuff for the Bangalores!" Evans was shouting.

Jacobs waved something in the air.

"We've got the firing pack!" He emphasised.

A surge of sudden relief flooded over Downey.

"Thank fuck for that!" He breathed to himself, and began pushing himself backwards through the partially cut avenue in the wire entanglement.

As he went, his sleeve caught on loose ends of the cut wire, as if they were tentacles of some mythical creature trying to drag him to his death. Blowing out hard with the effort, Downey shrugged off the barbs and emerged, arse first from within the wire entanglement. He slid down the bank and rolled over onto his back, gasping with exertion.

He was surprised to find even more men crowded in against the dunes than before, and he noticed that several more bodies lay motionless in the sand; their arms and legs thrown out at curious angles.

"We've got the firing pack!" Jacobs' excited face was right in front of Downey now.

"Doesn't matter..." Downey gasped. "We got other problems... there's mines in the Dunes..."

Jacobs' face straightened for a moment, but then became animated again.

"It's alright, we've got more stuff! More Bangalores! There's about five or six of them."

Downey blinked, trying to calculate the length of five Bangalores slotted together.

"If we lay them at ground level..." Jacobs was continuing, "they should detonate any mines underneath."

"Will it reach though?" Downey asked, slowly managing to regain his breath.

"Near as damn it..." Jacobs was nodding enthusiastically.

"Do it then..." Replied the sergeant, struggling up onto his knees and reaching out to recover his rifle from where he had left it, beside Private Winstanley. "Get it put together. I'll get everyone ready to follow me through when it blows."

The corporal scuttled away on all fours and began shouting instructions to the press of men who were starting to gather by the proposed breach in the enemy obstacles. Quickly, Downey checked his rifle over and began calling out instructions to those not involved with putting together the Bangalore Torpedo.

"Alright, listen in. When you hear Corporal Jacobs give the warning, put your heads down and wait for the bang. As soon as the thing goes up, get on your feet and follow me straight through the gap. Don't fuck about and don't stop for anything. Just keep going until you reach the other side of the dunes. There's a concrete wall about chest high at the other side. Get down behind it and start looking for Jerries. Shoot anything you see and wait for us to get through the last belt of wire. Everyone understand?"

Downey cast his eyes around the faces nearby. The men were all looking at him with grim expressions. Not frightened any more, not shocked; just grim. That was good. They were getting over their baptism of fire now. Even so, it was a motley collection of men. He recognised some of his own platoon, but many other faces were less familiar to him; the ones from the other platoons in the company. Some of the faces were complete strangers, but he had no time to reflect on the matter. The important thing was to get everyone moving; get out of the killing area on the beach.

"Stand-by!"

The initial warning from Jacobs sounded above the noise of battle.

Downey watched as three soldiers carefully guided the first two lengths of torpedo through the half-cut path in the barbed wire, then beyond the entanglement and out into the minefield of the dunes. A third length of torpedo was added and then the long explosive filled tubes were pushed further yet. It was, Downey thought, a rather absurd, yet very clever invention. Essentially just a whole load of drainpipes filled with explosive, about three yards long each, capable of being clipped together at either end, the Bangalores were capable of clearing a gap through the thickest of barbed wire entanglements and also of detonating mines directly beneath the seat of the blast. Please be long enough, Downey silently prayed as the fourth, and then the fifth length of torpedo was joined to the rear of the long metal snake.

It was taking all the strength of the three men to push and manhandle the ludicrously long explosive device across the undulating humps of the dunes towards the far side, and Downey saw that even with five lengths fastened together, they would still fall a few yards short of the distant concrete wall.

"We'll give it a final push forward once we've popped the fuse..." Jacobs announced, looking back over his shoulder to Downey.

"Okay; get on with it." The sergeant ordered, then, throwing his voice in either direction. "Get ready to move! Single file and follow me; just as soon as the Bangalores have gone up!"

"Heads down!" Jacobs was shouting.

Downey heard the hiss of the safety fuse and caught a small puff of smoke from the rear of the torpedo as the three handlers shoved it forward with one final push.

"Down!" Screamed Jacobs, pushing himself flat into the sand beside the three handlers, and Downey did likewise, suddenly realising the size of explosion that five lengths of Bangalore would create.

Cruuump!

The torpedo erupted some ten to fifteen seconds later with a resounding and highly satisfying thump. Smoke billowed over the heads of the men laid against the dunes and a shower of fine sand and sea-grass rained down upon them. Downey felt his heart lurch with a sudden burst of energy.

"Come on!" He yelled as he pushed himself to his feet and stepped into a thick cloud of foul smelling smoke. "Follow me! Stay on the blast area!"

Without a clue as to whether anybody was indeed following him, the sergeant thrust himself forward and into the fog shrouded dunes.

Crack... crack... crack...

The bullets came slapping past Downey's ears within seconds, although he had no idea from which direction they came. The world was an indistinct mix of dirty smoke, sudden glimpses of sand or clumps of grass, and a knee-jerking, shin-jarring tumble across the uneven dunes at the edge of the beach. Suddenly however, the smoke seemed to evaporate before his eyes and he found himself staring at a wall with an unusual, serrated profile, which was just a few yards in front of him, whilst beyond it he could see a scattering of small houses that were spread out between wide gardens and meadows, and he realised, with a sense of incredulity, that they had almost achieved the impossible. He vaguely registered that those last few yards could be strewn with undetonated mines, but it was too late to worry about such things and so, with a roar of determination, he bent his head forward and leapt across the last few yards of sand and grass and threw himself down in the lee of the anti-tank wall, just as the first bullets began to slap into those self same blocks of concrete.

Downey's first instinct was to stay there, hugging the concrete, chest heaving, whilst he regained his composure, but something deep inside kept reminding him that he was a commander and that it was his duty to keep things moving. He couldn't indulge himself at all; there was, quite simply, no room for self-pity. Still drawing in huge gulps of air, the sergeant twisted round so that his back was against the concrete and looked back the way he had come.

Private Evans was already throwing himself down against the wall next to his platoon sergeant. Another man followed him out of the dissipating smoke and ducked down into cover behind the wall. More men came; another three in rapid succession, followed by a man on his own carrying a Bren Gun. The bullets cracked past even faster now. Not the machine gun from earlier, but the rapid, repeated crack of many rifles firing from different directions, as the enemy in several positions saw the danger and began to concentrate their fire.

Jacobs came next with the men of his Bangalore party. As they crested the highest part of the dunes, the man behind Jacobs suddenly dropped sideways to the sand and lay still. There was no shout; no cry of pain, and no theatrical end to the man's life. He just dropped to the sand and died. As the increasing number of men from the East Yorkshires began to crowd in behind the concrete wall, Downey started shouting instructions.

"Spread out! Don't bunch up! Spread out! Corporal Jacobs; get them all spread out and get them firing back at the Jerries. Look for the depth positions and start returning fire!"

Downey looked back across the dunes as something caught his eye. Three men, one of them Winstanley, were staggering over the uneven humps and bumps of the sandy tufts of grass; not in single file but three abreast, each of them trying to overtake the other two in order to reach the safety of the concrete wall.

"Single file!" Downey roared at the three men above the racket of small arms fire and explosions. "Get in single fucking file and stay on the…"

Pop.

Before Downey finished the sentence, a puff of smoke billowed out from beneath Winstanley's foot and a second later, something small, dark and cylindrical jumped out of the sand as if attached to an invisible spring and hovered at waist height just behind the three soldiers.

Crump!

The anti-personnel mine exploded with a dull thump and all three men were thrown forwards and face down onto the sand. Small bits of shrapnel whizzed in all directions causing at least one person by the wall to cry out in pain. Winstanley and one of the other men in the trio were motionless on the ground where they had been thrown; the third was writhing about on his stomach, sobbing in a pitiful voice.

"Fuck me!" Downey breathed in shock.

He had heard about the 'Bouncing Betties' or 'De-bollockers' as the battle-school instructors liked to call them, but this was the first time he had ever seen one do its deadly work.

Another line of men came stomping over the dunes, led by a lance-corporal.

"Stay in single file!" Downey yelled at them. "Spread out! Keep low!"

The men needed no advice on the matter as they slunk over the dunes at a low running crouch, weapons at the trail. As he came across the two dead soldiers and their sobbing comrade, the lance-corporal paused in mid-stride.

"Leave him!" Downey yelled. "Get into cover!"

Obediently the young NCO leapt over the three khaki bodies and, followed by his men, made a final dash for the protection of the anti-tank wall.

A few rifles were barking in anger nearby, and Downey turned his attention to the men who were fanned out on either side of him.

"Come on, get some fucking fire down. You lot on the right; start engaging that house! Fire into the windows! You lot on the left; look for the trenches between the buildings! Start giving it back to the bastards!"

As more weapons began to snap back at the enemy, Downey glanced up at the barbed wire lining the top of the dragon's teeth that formed the anti tank wall. It was double banked again, but one well placed torpedo would do the trick; if they could find anymore of the obstacle clearance explosives of course.

"Who's in charge here?"

Downey swivelled round at the sound of the upper class voice.

He was immediately presented with the sight of more men streaming over the dunes in a long single file. At the front of that line was a red faced young private sporting a double set of ammunition pouches on his webbing braces, betraying his role as the No.2, or ammunition carrier, for a Bren Gun. Directly behind the heavily laden soldier came another figure, dressed in minimal battle order and sporting nothing more than a revolver.

"Who's in charge?" The man with the pistol demanded again as he closed on the wall, ducking low.

"Over here, Sir!" Downey shouted, waving his hand. "Over here!"

The man with the pistol spotted Downey's flapping arm and veered towards him and slid down onto his knees in front of the sergeant.

"Who's that then? Downey isn't it? From 'A' Company?"

"Yes, Sir." Downey replied, recognising the Company Commander from 'B' Company instantly.

"Have you seen your OC?"

"No, Sir."

"What about your Platoon Commander then? Or the Company 2 i/c?"

"Not seen, Sir."

The major pulled a face.

"Oh, right... Well, it looks as though you and I are running this battle for the time being then. I'm going to get my chaps to blow this wire just along here on the left, and then I'm going to break left and clear out these trenches around that little cottage there. I'm also sending a platoon along the wall here to sort out that bloody great pill-box further down. You get all your blokes together and start clearing through the position to the right, and take care of those two big houses on the right there. I'm sure everyone else will catch us up in due course. Happy with that?"

Downey was somewhat stunned to be told that he was now responsible for orchestrating an attack on his company's entire objective, but there was nobody else but him to get on with the job, so he simply nodded his head in acknowledgement.

"Yes, Sir."

"Tank!"

The shout from somewhere along the wall made both Downey and the 'B' Company Commander look round sharply. For a second, Downey's pulse went into overdrive. Tanks? He hadn't expected German tanks on the beach? Where was the PIAT, he suddenly wondered? He hadn't seen Private Atherton, charged with carrying the weapon, since coming off the LCA. What the hell were they supposed to do against a tank without a PIAT to hand?

"It's one of ours!"

The second voice called just a heartbeat later.

"They've got a ramp over the dunes for the armour!"

Instantly, Downey felt the blessed surge of relief wash over him.

"By Jove! So they have..." The OC of 'B' Company was peering carefully over the wall. "It's one of our Shermans and he's brassing up the trenches over yonder!"

The major looked back at Downey and gave him a curt nod.

"I reckon that'll be our cue then Sergeant Downey, eh? Let's go get stuck into Objective Cod shall we?"

Without another word to Downey, the officer rose to his feet and, at a low crouch, began jogging down the length of the anti-tank wall.

"Alright 'B' Company, follow me..."

LEGG'S TANK – OBJECTIVE COD, SWORD BEACH
TUESDAY 6TH JUNE 1944 – 0750 HOURS

"Ruddy hell, Peggy! I reckon they've noticed us then!"

Legg was inclined to agree with the gunner's comment. The very moment their Sherman had emerged from between the burning flail-tank and bridge-layer, and ascended the portable section of engineer bridging that now spanned the dunes as far as the anti-tank wall, the bullets had been bouncing off their vehicle's armoured hide thick and fast. Up to now it had been the constant ping and whine of small arms fire, as inexperienced enemy soldiers wasted their ammunition pointlessly against the British tank. Soon enough however, something bigger and infinitely more dangerous was going to come racing towards them, and Legg didn't want to be a sitting duck on the engineer bridge when it did.

"Keep going steady as you are, Stan..." Legg coaxed the driver as they trundled carefully forwards over the steel-girder construction.

Crossing an engineer bridge was a difficult job at the best of times, with hardly any room for error. Doing it closed down, with restricted views, and whilst being shot at, made for a trickier than usual operation.

"Almost there; a few more yards and we're at the end. I can see the promenade now..."

Crack!

"What the fuck..." Legg, Wells and the loader-operator, all gave a collective start.

The sudden, and surprisingly loud high-pitched crack, came to the ears of the crew even through the thick armour plate of the tank.

"Anti-tank gun..." Legg realised out loud. "Must have missed us by inches... Come on then, Stan; let's get off this bloody bridge!"

"Stand-by then..." Holloway warned the rest of his crew. "I've lost sight of the bridging unit and the wall. All I can see is barbed wire and road. We'll be dropping off the wall any second now, so hang onto your hats..."

The turret crew needed no further prompting. The three tank men grabbed hold of any piece of equipment that would give them purchase, with Legg folding his arms over the eyepiece of the commander's sight and bracing his feet against the side of the turret cage. There was silence on the intercom for a couple of moments before Holloway's voice cut in again.

"We're going down..."

Legg felt it at precisely the same moment that Holloway warned them. A sudden tipping of the tank's front end, followed by what seemed like a kind of floating feeling, as if the vehicle was in mid-air, and then finally, a heavy, violent thump as the tracks and running gear slammed down onto the cobbles of the road.

Legg felt the forward, downwards pressure as the tank came off the anti-tank wall, and he felt himself begin to slide off the seat. At the same time, he fancied he could hear the sloshing of water from down below in the driver's compartment.

"Big bump behind now..." Called Holloway as he inched the tank carefully forwards.

Just as Legg began reaching out to adjust his grip, the rear end of the tank dropped off the wall.

"Uurgh!"

With a sickening bounce and thump, the Sherman's rear end dropped several feet onto the road, throwing all three turret crew members back against the rear of the fighting compartment, and Legg felt a painful jolt in his back.

"Christ all-fucking-mighty!" Wells cursed as he was thrown around the inside of the turret.

"Sorry about the slight bump!" Holloway apologised, not sounding remotely sincere.

"Don't worry…" Legg snapped. "Just go hard right and drive; quickly!"

The driver responded instantly and the big tank swung to the right and gathered speed, the tracks rattling noisily on the cobbles. After the subdued churn of the sand beneath the tracks, the stone cobbles seemed excessively noisy, yet somehow reassuring too. Hard ground at last. That meant the tank would be able to manoeuvre more efficiently, and at speed too.

"Gunner, traverse left…" Shouted Legg, re-adjusting his position once more.

"Start searching for targets. Driver – straight on towards the twin villas."

"Got it." Holloway responded.

The turret began to swing sideways, accompanied by the profanities of Wells, the gunner, as he offered his thoughts on Holloway's driving ability.

"Trenches…" He murmured as the turret slowed and then came to a stop under Wells' control.

The gunner was already reaching for the firing switch as Legg responded.

"Seen. Co-ax… Suppress them as we go by…Go on."

Rat-tat-tat-tat-tat!

Wells was already pressing the firing pedal as Legg finished the sentence.

And off they went. The first tank off Sword Beach was now driving across the frontage of Objective Cod, peppering the maze of trenches with its machine guns as it went, and serving the very useful purpose of distracting much enemy fire away from the dunes and the beach, where the remaining armour and infantry of the assault waves were still looking for a way off. With his eyes pressed up against the side periscope now, Legg tried to assess where the main points of enemy resistance were. He was pretty sure that the two big houses just a couple of hundred yards away were hiding a significant strongpoint.

"Bunker!"

Legg threw himself back behind the commander's sight as soon as he heard Wells call out.

"Fuck!" The gunner swore a split second later. "He just…"

Boom!

The vehicle rocked slightly as a shell hit the road just a yard or two away from the tank and exploded, showering the side of the vehicle with debris.

"Stop!" Ordered Legg sharply, and a moment later the Sherman rocked forward on its front drive wheels and then settled back down as the suspension reasserted itself.

"Lay on. Co-ax. Engage when ready."

Legg stared into the sight as he gave the orders.

He saw the sight picture move left, stop, come back right a touch, then rise slightly and settle as Wells made the adjustments. Instantly, the corporal spotted the threat. Sitting halfway along a trench line was a built up position made from sandbags and wooden beams, camouflaged with turf sods and netting. And poking out of the narrow firing slit of that bunker was the snout of an anti-tank gun.

Rat-Tat-tat-tat-tat-tat-tat!

The first burst of fire streaked across the flat grassland towards the position and Legg saw at least two tracer rounds bracket the bunker.

"Again!" He snapped.

Again, Wells pressed on the firing pedal and the co-axial mounted machine gun spat its bullets towards the position.

The constant training of the preceding months was kicking in now, and Legg was rapping out orders in quick succession.

"Gunner, stop! Driver, reverse back twenty yards, move!"

Legg knew that the crew of the anti-tank gun would be relaying onto them with all the speed born of desperation, and at just three hundred yards, it was essentially point blank range. They couldn't afford to sit still for more than a couple of seconds.

The engine revved suddenly and the Sherman jerked into action, rolling back rapidly the way it had come.

"What's up the spout? HE?"

"Roger; HE." Wells responded to his commander's enquiry.

"Switch to main arm'; stand-by to engage...Driver, stop!"

Once again, the Sherman rocked to a sharp halt.

"Lay-on and engage when ready; HE!" Legg snapped in business like fashion.

He was sweating profusely now; the perspiration running down his face like a mini-waterfall.

"Firing now!"

Whoomph!

The 75mm gun roared. At such short distance, there was barely time to register the shot. Legg caught a slight swirl in the air, then a bright flash of impact followed by a cloud of black-brown smoke.

"Shit and bollocks!" Wells was swearing. "Reload!"

They had missed. The shell had slammed into the earth twenty yards short of the bunker.

"Driver, reverse!" Legg shouted, his pulse racing now; knowing that they were in a race against time with the enemy gun position to see who would be able to lay and fire the fastest, and the most accurately. Legg did not intend to make it easy for the Germans.

Boom!

Even as the Sherman began rolling back again, a German shell flashed past the front of the Sherman and slammed into the sea wall with a bright flash and resounding thump.

"Reloaded!"

"Driver, stop! Forwards, full speed!"

Holloway was hard at it now; listening to his commander's instructions and throwing the vehicle backwards and forwards in order to keep jockeying and thereby disrupt the lay of the German gunners.

"Stand-by gunner..." Legg warned. "Driver, stop! Gunner, lay-on... engage!"

Wells was already adjusting the lay of the main armament as the vehicle bounced to a halt once more. With rapid, feverish movements of his hands, he adjusted the fine elevation and deflection gears of the gun, correcting his aim after the earlier miss.

"Come on, Wellsy..." Legg whispered, as he watched the aiming marks in the gun-sight flicker slightly.

"Stand-by..." Wells murmured in an anxious voice, face dripping with sweat.

"Come on mate..." Legg hardly dared breath.

"Firing now!"

Whoomph!

"Driver, forward!"

Legg wasn't going to sit still any longer.

"Driver, stop!"

"Bingo! Take that you fucker!"

Wells thumped the top of the breech block on the main gun.

"Reload!"

As the gunner and loader-operator went through the drill, Legg focussed his eyes on the scene presented in the commander's sight once more. There was lots of black smoke again where their shell had struck home, only this time it was gushing from within the collapsed bunker.

"Well done gunner! Bang on!" The corporal barked in satisfaction. "Driver, forwards!"

They lurched forward, the tracks clattering on cobbles once again.

They continued on their original route; towards the twin villas which were now emitting smoke from their upper floors, as if they were starting to burn. As they went, Legg ordered the gunner to switch back to the machine gun and continue with the suppression of the trench system which, it now became obvious, was extensive and a good three hundred yards deep. After a short while, the twin villas loomed up through the commander's sight as the tank rumbled by, and Wells automatically increased his rate of fire, pumping several long burst into the buildings.

"That's fucking full of Jerries, that is!" He commented enthusiastically.

"Go left, driver!" Legg shouted. "Round the side of these houses. Let's see what's behind them…"

Obediently, Holloway swung the vehicle left whilst, on Legg's orders, Wells traversed the turret back over the front decks. As the vehicle nosed around the side of the buildings, it began crushing the line of single concertina wire that had been placed along the frontage of the gardens. Beyond that, another maze of trench systems was evident, connecting the various little holiday homes that were dotted along this part of the coast. Immediately, the co-driver opened fire with his own machine gun, engaging the nearest trenches which lay just forty yards ahead.

"Bloody hell, Peggy! This is going to take some clearing out!" Wells commented as he began depressing the gun in order to engage the trenches before them. "We could do with those infantry boys getting up here, sharpish."

"Well…" Legg acknowledged. "Let's see if we can give them some cover while they do. Start spraying those trench lines. Work your way along."

Boom! Boom!

"What the fuck was that?" Legg cursed, looking up in fear at the hatch above him.

"There's Jerries still in these houses to our left, Corp'!" Holloway was calling up. "The bastards are dropping grenades on us from the top floor!"

Legg cursed inwardly as another explosion sounded outside the vehicle. Grenades were no serious threat to their armour, but they could do damage to running gear or observation slits if they fell in the right place.

"Okay gunner, traverse hard left and put a HE right through the side of this bloody house…"

"We're only ten yards away…" Wells glanced at his commander.

"I know…" Legg replied, a look of resolution sitting squarely on his sweat-drenched features. "I want you to bring this ruddy house down around their ears. Let's clear the fucking place out good and proper shall we?"

Wells raised one eye brow, but nodded all the same.

"Whatever you say Peggy..."

He began traversing the turret.

DOWNEY'S GROUP – QUEEN RED SECTOR, SWORD BEACH
TUESDAY 6TH JUNE 1944 – 0800 HOURS

"Smoke! Smoke!"

Downey repeated the order several times, throwing his voice left and right. His collection of men from his own platoon and other stragglers from the company totalled around sixteen men with two Bren Guns now, as more and more men began to find the breach in the wire and thread their way across the cleared path in the dunes. Some way off to his left, a large group of men from 'B' Company, under their company commander, were now assaulting some of the bunkers positioned along the anti-tank wall whilst others had blown open the wire and were racing through it to cross the open road and into the first line of trenches beyond.

Around Downey, his men began lobbing all the remaining smoke grenades they could muster into the open ground, beyond the line of concrete obstacles. Meanwhile, a three man wire cutting party were tearing away at a section of the concertina fence that reinforced the anti-tank wall.

"Come on, lads, get that fucking wire open!" Downey urged the men, who immediately began snipping and yanking at the entanglement with renewed vigour, cursing all the while as they were lashed by the sharp barbs on the sprung coil.

Off to the right, the two Bren Guns were chugging away, putting burst after burst into the nearby villas. The smoke was building up now, creating a half decent screen immediately to their front, but Downey knew it wouldn't last much more than a minute.

"Come on!" He urged the wire-cutting party.

"Yaagh!"

Evans, who had wordlessly volunteered himself to assist the cutting party, gave a cry mixed with frustration and pain as he grappled for several loose ends of wire and began dragging part of the coil aside, suffering numerous cuts from the rusty barbs in the process.

"That's it! You've got it!" Downey yelled, seeing the gap open before his eyes. "Keep pulling!"

"Yaagh!" Evans yelled again as he gave the wire another huge tug.

And there it was; a gap. Big enough for two men at a time if that, but it was a gap all the same.

"That's it! You've done it! Hold it steady!" Downey shouted, slapping Evans on the shoulder.

"Come on, 'A' Company! Everyone through! Into those trenches! Follow me!"

And with that, Downey leapt up from behind the cover of the wall and into the breach.

The two other men from the cutting party were already in front of him, leading the way through. Even as they began to move, a rattle of individual rifle shots came cracking blindly through the artificial fog. One bullet cracked very close by and, with nothing more than a grunt, one of those leading two men span round to his left and toppled face first into the wire, where he hung, quite motionless. His companion, Lance Corporal Ingham, carrying a Sten Gun, ducked his head a little lower and went on. Downey followed him.

"Come on!" The sergeant yelled over his shoulder.

Downey and Ingham lurched into the smoke and felt their hobnailed boots rattle on a cobbled surface. Seconds later, they heard more feet behind them; and then the two NCOs were emerging from the smoke to find themselves staring at wide open lawns that were criss-crossed with trenches. Almost immediately, a machine gun opened fire on them and a stream of tracer cracked hard by them; bullets passing to either side but miraculously missing them both. A startled cry from behind them suggested that somebody following had not been so lucky.

"Into that trench!" Downey was shouting breathlessly.

Ingham needed no prompting. He was sprinting for the nearest trench line, head down, weaving from side to side. Somewhere to the right of the two British soldiers, the friendly tank fired its main armament and the two infantrymen felt the concussive blast-wave that burst sideways from the gun barrel with a mighty crack. Within just a couple of heartbeats, both men were hovering over the parapet of long trench that ran parallel with the dunes and the beach. It appeared to be empty, and without hesitation they jumped in.

Both men landed heavily, and as they did so, Ingham's Sten Gun chattered into life. The bullets slammed into the earth just a yard away from Downey, kicking up bits of soil.

"What you fucking firing at?" Downey roared, stepping sharply to one side.

The lance corporal, barely pausing for breath, began pushing past his sergeant.

"Sorry, Sarge! Caught the trigger by mistake!"

Downey just shook his head and scanned left and right. To the left, the trench was a dead end; to the right, it ran for about twenty yards then turned sharply inland.

"I'll check round the corner…" Ingham stated as he passed Downey and advanced down the narrow subterranean corridor.

More men began dropping into the trench around Downey now, and he shouted out a warning to Ingham.

"Don't go round that corner yet; let's get organised first…"

"I'll just have a quick peek round the corner…" The young lance corporal replied.

Downey saw Corporal Jacobs drop into the trench beside him.

"Jakey; get the lads organised into pairs, with HE grenades ready to go. We'll fight our way along this trench and pick each enemy position off as we go. Organise a link man to guide in anyone following up…"

Crack-crack-crack!

Downey looked sharply along the trench to where Ingham was leaning against the corner of the dog-leg. The lance corporal looked back down the trench at him and shouted out a warning.

"Jerries round the corner, Sarge! Couple of the bastards with rifles by the looks."

"Okay; hold on there. We'll get organised then flush the bastards out."

He looked back at Jacobs.

"Jakey, get those assault pairs ready, mate. We're going to go through this fucking strongpoint like a dose of salts!"

THE TWIN VILLAS, OBJECTIVE COD – SWORD BEACH
TUESDAY 6TH JUNE 1944 – 0745 HOURS

Lehman, already stunned beyond belief, could hardly believe what was happening when the wall at the side of the room suddenly imploded. He could not have described what had happened if he tried. One moment he was on all fours, staring at his dead companion; and the next moment he felt as if he was being lifted off the floor by some giant, unseen hand and flung against the sandbagged wall of his fighting position. The world descended into a maelstrom of noise that caused excruciating pain in his already damaged ears, and his only picture of what was happening was of a thick grey fog that surrounded him and threatened to choke him to death with its cloying dust.

He lay there for long moments, wondering if he were dead. The world was nothing but grey billowing dust; almost like clouds, and the only thing he could hear was that high-pitched ringing in his ears, only now it was even louder. Just as he assumed that he must be dead and was on his way to the next life, a dark figure appeared from among the grey miasma. The man's face was familiar in some way, but Lehman couldn't get his mind to put a name to it. The stunned soldier just stared at the wild eyed man as he reached down and grabbed hold of him by his collar.

Lehman felt himself being pulled up and saw the man's mouth moving as if he was trying to speak to him, but the poor young German could only hear the whining noise. The other man was highly animated; his teeth flashing and his mouth curled back in a snarl. Lehman stared stupidly at the other man's face and, as he did so, a name came into his addled mind. Fuchs.

"Come on Lehman, for fucks sake!" The corporal bellowed at the young man, dragging him to his feet. "Back to the second line! The Tommies are right outside! They've got tanks with them!"

Lehman couldn't hear what Fuchs was saying, but his mind was slowly catching up, and the corporal's agitated manner suggested that he wanted Lehman to go with him somewhere.

Somehow managing to balance himself on his feet, Lehman accepted the rifle that Fuchs thrust into his hand wordlessly, and when the corporal turned and began struggling over the piles of rubble and debris that were now heaped around the room, Lehman followed him. He stumbled clumsily over the bricks and plaster and bits of furniture and wood, using his rifle almost as a walking stick. He followed the corporal into what looked like a hallway but one where the staircase had almost been totally ripped apart. Following Fuchs' example, Lehman struggled over a door that lay at an angle across the hallway, forming a partial obstruction. He saw three more figures appear in the hallway; faces that also looked vaguely familiar. Comrades?

Even if his mind hadn't been completely numbed by the devastating events of the last couple of hours, Lehman would have struggled to identify the frightened looking faces that peered out from what looked like oversized helmets. Every one of them was covered in a thin grey sheet of plaster dust, obscuring the details of uniform and facial features. The only things that Lehman was able to focus on were the men's eyes. Their eyes, every one of them, were filled with terror; bulging from sunken, red rimmed sockets in disbelief at the events that were unfolding around them. Somehow, Lehman knew that his own eyes looked the same.

He staggered on, following Fuchs towards the stark outline of the doorway at the rear of the building. The three other men came on behind him. As he emerged into daylight, Lehman felt his sense of disorientation lift slightly, although he still felt a little detached from reality. He could hear noises above the high-frequency whining now, but they were muffled and indistinct. Fuchs was clattering down the steps of the house, then down some more sandbagged steps into a trench. Lehman followed him, vaguely registering the green carpet of grass lawns that surrounded the building, and somewhere in the distance, several more individual buildings.

Then, in an instant, that image was swallowed up and he was hemmed in by wicker-revetted earth walls as Fuchs led him along a thin communication trench. The corporal, cradling a machine-pistol, kept looking over his shoulder and shouting something which Lehman couldn't hear. He assumed he was being encouraged to move faster. They staggered on, and moments later came across a junction in the trench. Another trench broke off left, whilst this particular one went straight on. Fuchs was pointing straight on and stepped forward onto the junction. Then, the corporal did something strange.

He seemed to take a small shuffling step to his right, then another. And then he span around to face Lehman suddenly. The corporal's mouth opened wide, as if he were about to shout something at Lehman. However, rather than words spilling forth, a great gob of dark red blood suddenly spilled down over the man's chin and, without further ceremony, he toppled backwards onto the floor of the trench. All of this seemed to happen in slow motion and Lehman, utterly dumfounded, stepped towards the falling corporal in horrid fascination. Then, for some unknown reason, Lehman decided to look sideways down the other trench.

He noted several bodies on the floor of the trench, maybe ten metres down it, slumped against a pile of boxes. Beyond those bodies, he saw upright figures coming towards him. He registered brownish, dun coloured clothing, dirty faces beneath helmets covered in some kind of camouflage. Then he was overcome by the feeling that his left leg had suddenly disappeared and, with utter astonishment, he began to collapse. He didn't dive, or topple; he just collapsed. Hitting the ground with an impact that he knew should really be painful, Lehman stared up in dumb astonishment as the three other men from the house began jumping over him. Something was hitting the side of the trench above him because bits of wicker cane and soil kept dropping into his face.

The young man twisted his head and saw his three comrades run along the trench several more metres and then duck inside a doorway. Why were they going in there, he wondered? At about the same time, he realised that his left leg was getting extremely hot. He glanced down and saw that his entire leg was drenched in blood. It made no sense. He felt something hard kick his right hand and he instinctively let go of the rifle he was holding. Looking back up, Lehman saw that a face was staring down at him. One of those dirty faces, belonging to the men in brown with the funny helmets. The eyes in that face were staring down at him fiercely; hard, brown, uncompromising. More men in brown pushed passed this first one, who continued to point a short, stubby looking gun at the wounded German soldier on the floor.

Lehman found he could hear more noises now. The sound of gunfire was there in the background. Voices too; almost too indistinct to understand. He heard one word; not a German word, but strangely familiar to him all the same. Was it '*grenade*'?

The ground shook beneath him, and Lehman felt a shock wave and loose soil wash over him. The man standing above Lehman hardly flinched. The young German, convinced he was now in some kind of dream, twisted his head once more and saw a cloud of dirty black smoke belching from the shattered doorway just along the trench where he had seen his friends disappear just moments earlier. The men in brown were all around the doorway now, pointing their weapons inside and firing into the smoke shrouded interior.

"Oh, my God…" Lehman whispered.

Just as Lehman's mind finally began to catch up with what he was witnessing, he passed out…

THE TRENCH SYSTEM - OBJECTIVE COD, SWORD BEACH
TUESDAY 6TH JUNE 1944 – 0850 HOURS

Downey quickly totted up the numbers on his note pad. Twenty two men all ranks. If he was honest, the figures were better than he had been hoping for. This meant that two thirds of his platoon were still in one piece. Just half an hour ago, the platoon sergeant had been of the opinion that maybe half of his platoon or more had become casualties, but since then, in small groups, more and more men from both his own platoon and the rest of their company had appeared amongst the maze of trenches and bunkers that constituted Objective Cod.

Thrown into dispersed chaos during the initial rush up the beach, the men from the assault companies of the East Yorkshires had fought their way through several small breaches in the obstacle belt in the dunes before breaking into the main enemy strongpoint. Now, the small groups of men were starting to reform into recognizable sub-units and the initial assault on

Cod, beginning as an opportunistic rush, was developing into a co-ordinated and methodical clearance.

That clearance was now being co-ordinated by the battalion's senior officers, including the Battalion Second in Command, who now stood in conference with Downey's own company commander and another officer from the South Lancashire Regiment; the battalion that had landed alongside the East Yorkshires and assaulted Cod from the right flank.

Downey looked up from his notebook and nodded to Corporal Jacobs.

"Thanks, Jakey. Get around the lads and make sure everyone's bombed up again. We'll be moving on again in a couple of minutes just as soon as the Company Commander gives us the nod."

The section commander nodded and doubled away. In the background, the sound of small arms fire rose to a sharp crescendo as another platoon from the East Yorkshires launched an assault against the next stretch of trenches.

Downey considered how he might use his reassembled platoon for the next phase of the operation. Looking at the numbers, and given that two of his corporals and one of his lance corporals were still missing, he thought it would be best to amend the platoon's order of battle into two rifle sections, with a small command group under himself. He considered the fact that he was now in sole command of the platoon, and that prompted him to shout along the trench to where his men were reorganising themselves.

"Has anyone seen the platoon commander at all?" He enquired. "Anyone seen him at all, since we landed?"

Nearby, two private soldiers looked up at Downey and shook their heads as they pushed fresh clips of ammunition into their rifles. Just beyond them, Lance Corporal Bryce was also shaking his head.

"Not seen, Sarge..."

Another voice shouted back down the trench towards Downey.

"He's dead."

"What?" Downey snapped, a bit too abruptly. "Who said that?"

A head appeared from amongst the crowd further down the line of crouching infantrymen.

"He's dead, Sarge." Came the voice again, which Downey recognised as belonging to Private Thompson. "He got hit as soon as the ramp went down. I saw him go face down on the ramp as we came ashore."

Downey instantly saw an image in his mind's eye; the image of the khaki body lying face down on the ramp of the LCA, the head and shoulders under water in the frothing surf. Bollocks.

A flurry of activity to his right made Downey glance over towards the junction of the two trenches. A pair of British medics were checking over an injured German whose leg was covered in blood. The young German was wailing like a child in his delirium. Next to the wounded man and the two medics, lay the body of a dead German defender. Curiously, the dead man wasn't wearing any boots. One of the medics was wrapping a large broad-fold bandage around the wounded prisoner's bloody leg, whilst the other medic held the limb carefully.

"Missed his artery by the looks..." The medic holding the bandage was saying. "But his leg's proper smashed up. Don't need to worry about this chap doing a runner..."

Above the clatter of nearby small arms fire and the continuous background noise of shelling and mortars, Downey detected another, very alien sound. He frowned slightly, cocking his ear to the wind as he struggled to identify the unusual noise. It was, he decided, some kind of wailing noise; almost like that of an air raid siren starting up. He listened intently for another moment. Then it came to him.

"Bagpipes?" The sergeant creased his brow. "Who the fuck is playing bagpipes?"

There was no mistaking it now. Downey could hear the lilting, irregular tune being played on the instrument. He recognised the tune but couldn't name it.

"Ruddy bagpipes..." He murmured to himself again, shaking his head in disbelief.

"Sergeant Downey?"

The sergeant looked up from the curious vignette as he heard the Company Commander calling him.

"Yes, Sir?"

"How are you doing over there? Is your platoon ready to go?"

"Yes, Sir." Downey replied. "We've got twenty two all ranks, Sir; split into two sections. I'm afraid it looks like the Platoon Commander might be dead though, Sir..."

"Looks like it's your show then, Sergeant Downey." The major replied matter of factly. "I'm going to launch you and your lads against the last stretch of trench in a few minutes. The South Lancs are going to settle that concrete bunker at the rear right of the objective. Ready to move in two minutes if you please?"

"Right, Sir."

Downey took a deep breath. His platoon had survived the murder and chaos of the initial beach landing, but had lost a third of its strength in the process. Now they had to clear the final part of Objective Cod. But that too, was only just the beginning. Once this strongpoint was cleared out, their battalion had orders to move inland and capture two more enemy strongpoints; Sole and Daimler. It was going to be a long day Downey thought, and as he pushed his notebook and pencil back into his battledress pocket, he suspected it was going to be an exceptionally bloody one too.

HIDE LOCATION, 21ST PANZER DIVISION – NEAR CAEN, NORMANDY
TUESDAY 6TH JUNE 1944 – 0900 HOURS

"What do you reckon is going on Herman?"

Private Hartmann looked across the circle of tank men towards the commander of the second tank in the platoon.

"Fuck knows." Corporal Bauer shook his head. "Something big though. There are hundreds of planes up there this morning and I don't reckon any of the bastards are ours."

"Not by the sound of all that bombing…" Chimed in Private Wesser, the gunner in Hartmann's tank. "The Tommies were going at it all night. I reckon Caen got hit, big style."

"I'm amazed the Tommies are even flying in this weather…" Hartmann pulled a sour face as he gazed up through the dripping canopy of leaves above the little cluster of panzer crews.

Epstein, the driver from the platoon's third tank put in his own thoughts.

"I reckon it's the invasion."

Bauer scoffed.

"In this weather? The Tommies might be able to drop bombs in the dark but can you imagine them trying to get an army across the sea in these conditions? I'm no sailor but I bet the English Channel is a pretty crap place to be right now."

"Well…" Continued Epstein confidently. "I saw a despatch rider come in earlier, asking for directions to Battalion Headquarters. I heard him say something to the sentry about paratroopers."

"Paratroopers?" Hartmann's ears pricked up.

"Probably just bailed out bomber crews…" Bauer insisted.

"Well, we'll know for sure in a minute, boys…" Wesser nodded towards a figure striding urgently through the trees, coming in the direction of their platoon's hide. "Here comes the boss."

Weimer was moving briskly, his map case in one hand and a grim look on his face. As he approached the gaggle of tank crewmen, they all turned to look at him.

"Alright, men..." The staff sergeant announced even before he had entered the clearing in the wood. "Cam-nets down; all gear stowed. We've got to come to immediate notice to move by 0930 hours."

The members of his tank platoon exchanged worried glances.

"What's going on, Staff Sergeant?" Bauer asked, frowning.

Weimer came to a halt amongst his men and threw a serious look round the group.

"We're going into action. The Tommies have dropped paratroopers over a wide area to the east of Caen. The Orne River and Canal bridges near Ranville have been captured by enemy glider troops, and there's talk of all the bridges over the River Dives being destroyed by commandos or resistance fighters; although that hasn't been confirmed yet. We've been ordered to advance northwards on the east side of the Orne and secure Ranville, before recapturing the Orne bridges. We should link up with elements of the 125th Panzer Grenadiers on the way."

A collective murmur of alarm ran through the assembled tank crew.

"You see? I told you there'd been a parachute drop..." Epstein commented.

"That's only half of it." Weimer continued, preventing an outburst of debate amongst his men. "There's also a large fleet off the coast opposite Cabourg and Ouistreham. That bombing you can hear? Well, not all of it *is* bombing. Some of it is naval gunfire. The coastal defences are being shelled too."

"A fleet?" Hartmann wondered aloud, but his question faded away as the whole group went utterly silent. More than a dozen pairs of eyes were now fixed firmly on their platoon commander.

"Yes... a fleet." Weimer confirmed in a calm, dispassionate voice. "It's the invasion. It's here. It's happening."

The silence continued for what seemed like an age. Eventually, after a few moments, Weimer cleared his throat and slapped his map case against his leg, breaking the spell that had fallen over the group.

"Right, that's all there is to it. It's time to fight. Everyone get back to your vehicles and get packed up. I want everyone ready to move in twenty five minutes."

PART FOUR

ADVANCE

HEADQUARTERS ALLIED 21ST ARMY GROUP – BROOMFIELD HOUSE, NEAR PORTSMOUTH, ENGLAND TUESDAY 6TH JUNE 1944 – 1045 HOURS

Haldane entered the ante-room to Montgomery's office and paused at the door, scanning the room. He quickly saw that the room was relatively quiet; just Montgomery's ADC sitting behind his desk, writing away quietly in a large, leather-bound journal and, standing by the window, staring out into the garden, was the Army Group's Chief of Staff, Major General Freddie de Guingand.

When Haldane entered, both men looked up sharply. The suddenness of their movements brought Haldane to an immediate halt. There was an air of suppressed anxiety in the ante-room which was palpable.

"Jamie?" de Guingand tried unsuccessfully to hide his concern.

"Morning, Sir." Haldane responded. "Sorry to bother you. We've got the first signals from the Army Commanders. I thought you and the Army Group Commander would like to see them straight away, Sir?"

The Chief of Staff turned away from the window and walked into the middle of the room in a brisk, nervous manner.

"Yes. Show me…" Then just as quickly, he remembered himself and smiled at Haldane. "If you please, Jamie…"

Haldane walked fully into the room and came to stand in front of de Guingand. He could see that the Chief of Staff was exercising huge self restraint, physically pinching the side of his trousers with both hands to prevent him from reaching out and snatching the handful of signals from the young major in his eagerness to discover what was happening across the English Channel.

Not wanting to drag out de Guingand's agony, Haldane presented the small clutch of despatches promptly.

"There are reports from all the sectors, Sir, including the airborne units; although the American reports are a bit on the sketchy side."

The Chief of Staff reached out his hand and took the signals from Haldane, eyeing the staff officer with an enquiring look.

"Everything in order?" de Guingand asked, trying to sound conversational, knowing that the young staff officer would have already scanned the signals from front to back.

Haldane cleared his throat and replied cautiously.

"I think so, Sir. The reports from our chaps sound very encouraging, certainly…"

The Chief of Staff held the younger man's gaze for a moment and then looked down at the bundle of signals. He began to read. Haldane, watching the major-general sifting through the signals, silently ticked off each one in his mind. The Chief of Staff read the signal regarding the operations by the British 6th Airborne Division first and gave just the faintest grunt of approval. Next he flicked to the signal from Sword Beach. This time de Guingand let out the smallest of sighs; a sound of undeniable relief. Then he flicked to the signal from the Canadian beach; Juno. No noise this time, but a sharp little nod of the head. Quickly, de Guingand flicked the paper and began scanning the signal from Gold Beach. More nodding and another little sigh of relief. Then he flicked over the paper to start reading the signal from Omaha Beach; the first of the two American landing beaches.

The Chief of Staff was absolutely still and absolutely silent. He stayed on that particular signal for a while, no doubt reading it several times over, just as Haldane himself had done. After what seemed like an interminable period of time, de Guingand flicked over once more, this time scanning the report from Utah Beach. He read it in short order, made no comment then flicked over the paper one last time to read the signal concerning the drops made by the American 82nd and 101st Airborne Divisions. Again, he dwelt briefly on this signal, before flicking back to the Omaha sheet, which he scanned at length yet again. Eventually, he looked up.

"Yes… It does seem quite encouraging, don't you think?" He said, his eyes studying Haldane intently.

"I thought so, Sir, yes…" Haldane ventured.

After a moment, de Guingand murmured, "We'll need some more detailed updates from Omaha in due course I think…"

"Yes, Sir." Haldane replied quickly. "I've told the Signals Room to send any information from Omaha straight through the moment it arrives."

The Chief of Staff nodded.

"Good…"

He handed the signals back to Haldane.

"Well... the Army Group Commander is in his office having tea. Let's go and tell him the news shall we?"

And without further comment, de Guingand turned towards the double doors of Montgomery's office and walked over to them. Haldane thought that de Guingand's gait looked a little more relaxed than a few moments before. Only a tad mind you. The Chief of Staff knocked on the door and then opened it just a touch, then leaned his head inside the room beyond.

"Sorry to bother you, Sir. I've got Jamie Haldane here with the first reports from the beaches. Do you want me to show him in straight away?"

Haldane heard the crisp, affirmative reply from within, and de Guingand turned back to look at him, giving the major a beckoning jerk of his head.

"Come on then, Jamie..."

Together, Haldane and de Guingand entered Montgomery's office. The man himself, General Sir Bernard Law Montgomery, Commander of the 21st Army Group, was sitting calmly behind his desk, writing a letter. He was, unusually, dressed fairly smartly on this particular occasion; in standard battledress with shirt and tie beneath. As the two staff officers entered the room, Montgomery placed down his pen, removed his glasses, then sat back in his leather writing chair and regarded them both impassively.

"Jamie; you have news." The comment was a statement, rather than a question.

"Yes Sir. We've now got the initial reports from the Army Headquarters and the airborne divisions."

Montgomery said nothing, simply giving the slightest nod for Haldane to proceed.

Clearing his throat, the major from the Army Group Staff began his briefing.

"Reports from British 6th Airborne Division indicate that all objectives have been achieved more or less on schedule. Both the Orne River and Caen Canal bridges have been captured intact and the bulk of the division is now consolidating its positions east of the Orne. The reserve brigade will fly in to reinforce them later this evening."

He paused, should the Army Group Commander wish to comment, but Montgomery remained impassive and continued to stare at him, so Haldane went on quickly.

"Reports from Sword, Juno and Gold are all pretty similar, Sir. They report initial heavy resistance but in all three cases the assault brigades have fought their way clear of the beaches and are now eliminating the strong points in depth. The reserve brigades of each Divisional Group are about to land and begin exploitation of the beach-head."

Again he paused and glanced at Montgomery. The small General, with his foxy looking nose and little moustache looked as calm and confident as ever, although now Haldane thought he detected the faintest twinkle in his icy blue eyes.

"And the American sector?" Montgomery prompted gently.

Haldane flicked through to the clutch of signals from the various US Headquarters and gathered himself.

"In the American sector, General, we know that the US 82nd and 101st Airborne Divisions were dropped as planned, although there is good reason to believe that the drop may have been somewhat dispersed. Having said that, we know that both divisions are on the ground and fighting hard. On Utah, the landing went ahead against light opposition and a good lodgement has been made. Follow up units are now landing and the exploitation has begun."

Haldane had reached the part he had been dreading.

"In regard to Omaha, Sir..." He made a pretence of examining the signal from Omaha as if he had no idea of the contents.

Glancing up briefly, Haldane saw that Montgomery remained in the same, calm, sitting position; hands clasped comfortably in his lap.

"The report is rather brief and the details a little sketchy, however..." The major took a deep breath. "The commander at Omaha reports that there is extremely heavy enemy resistance and that the first wave of assault troops has sustained heavy casualties. The second wave has been landed and they are currently attempting to fight their way off the beach..."

Haldane's voice tailed off and he looked up once more, just as Montgomery made his first gesture of any kind in response to the reports. He gave a tiny, curt, almost imperceptible nod, as if to say *'I told you so.'*

After several seconds more, Montgomery took a deep, yet unhurried breath and gave several more nods in rapid succession.

"Good." He quipped. "Very much as I expected. All is going to plan. The first few hours of any battle are always rather intense and it will take a good while for all the fine detail to come through. I suspect that the Americans may suffer from the lack of specialised armour for obstacle clearance and I have no doubt that the American soldiers on the ground will pay a heavy price because of it. Besides, they have a tough stretch of coastline to attack. However, they're a good bunch, you know? The Americans will do it. They know what has to be done. They are going to have a hard day of it, I am sure; but they'll keep at it and do it none-the-less."

Montgomery mulled over his own words for a moment or two, allowing his gaze to wander across his desk top briefly. Within a heartbeat however, he had snapped out of the small lapse and looked up quickly at both Haldane and de Guingand. He smiled, pleasantly.

"Thank you, gentlemen. I see no reason why we should not proceed with our plan of embarking the Tactical Headquarters this evening and sailing to Normandy during the night. If you could bring me an update on matters around mid-afternoon, that would be fine. In the meantime, I have a recording to make for the BBC, so in the unlikely event that you need me urgently, I shall be in the garden..."

LANDING CRAFT INFANTRY 998 – SWORD BEACH
TUESDAY 6TH JUNE 1944 – 1100 HOURS

The scene that met Smithson's eyes as the large landing craft manoeuvred carefully towards the beach was not dissimilar to a painting he'd once seen, back in his days at Cambridge. That painting had been a Victorian artist's attempt to portray the Day of Judgement, and the gaudy, vivid, horridness of that painting was now being played out in real life it seemed, right here on the coast of Normandy.

The landing craft was nosing its way gently through a very narrow gap in the almost completely submerged obstacle belt so that it could land its troops as far up the beach as possible. The beach, it seemed, was not especially wide. There was probably no more than a hundred yards of sand between the tumbling waves and the grassy hillocks of the dunes, and all of that space was crammed with vehicles and men. Most of the men were queued up in long lines, whilst others were laid in a variety of unnatural poses at random intervals across the sand. With a sense of dismay, Smithson realised that they were the unlucky ones; the men of the assault wave who had been killed within the first few minutes, if not seconds, of this great enterprise.

Many of the vehicles on the beach were on fire, and a low, dense pall of smoke from the destroyed tanks mingled with the grey, artificial smog that had been laid by the invaders themselves. Beyond the beach, Smithson could see the vague outline of buildings through the shifting smoke, and several of these were on fire too; long, hungry looking orange flames licking from shattered windows and collapsed roofs. He glanced over the side of the landing craft as it negotiated the deadly underwater obstacles, some of which had been reinforced with anti-tank mines. Something bobbed in the water, making Smithson blink and stare a little harder. The strange, khaki coloured object seemed to roll over in the back-wash of the landing craft and, with a startled cry, the infantry company commander found himself staring down at a pale, bloated, and clearly lifeless face of a drowned soldier.

"Good God!" He exclaimed, averting his eyes, only to find that as he did so, he immediately caught sight of at least another half dozen bodies lolling in the water, between the protruding metal posts of the obstacle belt.

"Oh, my word..." He whispered, taking a deep breath.

He looked back towards the beach, deliberately making a point of not scanning the shoreline where the waves were breaking noisily. He had, Smithson reflected with a rising sense of distaste, forgotten exactly how terrible a business battle could be. And this battle, he reflected, was a bloody big one. The flames from burning tanks and houses seemed to flare higher just then, perhaps caught on the wind, but seeming to emphasise just how extreme the destruction had been on this beach.

"And the sea shall rise up and swallow them all..." He mouthed the words almost unconsciously.

"What's that, Sir?"

The question from Lance Corporal Haines, his radio operator, made Smithson jump.

"What? Oh... nothing. I was just saying... It looks like bloody chaos to me..."

The NCO murmured his agreement, hitching up his radio pack and adjusting the straps as he did so.

"Looks like *somebody* knows what's going on though, Sir." Haines commented, pointing towards the beach.

Smithson followed his radio operator's indication and immediately spotted the man in khaki battledress who was using a pair of signalling flags to guide their boat into its disembarkation point. Behind the man, two more soldiers were conferring in animated fashion. Even through the scrim netting on their helmets, Smithson could see the broad white band that had been painted onto the metal, indicating that they were men from the specially formed Beach Group. Based on an infantry battalion and reinforced with experts from the Royal Navy, the Beach Groups were responsible for bringing order to the chaos of the landings. Smithson remembered the briefing on this particular point quite clearly.

'The Beach Groups are in charge of anything between the water and the promenade. Anything or anybody that moves on that beach must follow their instructions to the letter, as if it were the word of God.'

"Yes." Smithson agreed with Haines. "And it looks as though we'll be going ashore any moment."

Even as he made the comment, Smithson felt the underside of the landing craft begin to grind against the sand. He risked another look down at the water's edge and frowned when he saw that there was still a good twenty yards of water between the end of the boat and the first stretch of sand.

"I hope they can get us a bit closer, mind you…"

They didn't. There was another loud, grating noise, a small jolt, and then a flurry of shouted orders being exchanged amongst the Royal Navy crewmen of the vessel. Moments later, one of the two naval ratings standing in front of Smithson looked over his shoulder and grinned at the Army officer.

"That'll be us then, Sir. I'll just extend the ramp as far as it'll go and then you can be off."

And with that, the young rating, in unison with his companion, began to slide forward the ramp that ran alongside the bow of the vessel. On the opposite side of the ship, the same was being done by another pair of crewmen.

Smithson watched as one of the ratings threw a rope down to the man with the flags who was standing by the very edge of the water now. As the end of the rope coil splashed down into the water at the man's feet, the other two members of the Beach Group who were standing beside him came forward and retrieved it, and then began hauling on it enthusiastically.

"Stand clear!" One of the ratings near Smithson called out as he and his comrade began sliding the ramp forwards.

It took less than a minute to extend and then drop the ramp at a steep angle towards the beach, after which the ratings fixed the locking pins into the top part of the metal gangway. Eventually, when all was done, the first rating turned and gave Smithson the thumbs up signal.

"Okay, Sir. We're all good to go. Follow me, please?"

Just at that point, a large shell screamed down out of the sky and slammed into the water about thirty yards to the right of the landing craft, showering Smithson, his company staff and the lead platoon in a great blanket of water.

"Bloody hell!" Chimed Lance Corporal Haines, grimacing from beneath his dripping helmet. "Here we bloody go!"

And so they went.

Smithson followed the two ratings down to the bottom of the ramp, and was followed in turn by his men. At the end of the ramp, Smithson and the two sailors both stopped and stared down at the water.

"I'm afraid we're still a bit short, Sir." Said one of the ratings. "Just watch how you go when you go off. There's a couple of feet drop into the water and

I reckon it's about waist deep when you're in. Make sure you keep a hold of this rope to steady yourself."

The infantry major looked down at the swollen waves that churned menacingly beneath the ramp. He'd practiced this drill a number of times already, but even so, the sea state today was particularly unruly, and he had serious doubts about the sailor's estimate of the water's depth.

"Do you want me to go first, Sir?"

Smithson glanced behind him to see Private Morrison, his batman and runner, taking a voluntary step forward. Like every other private soldier and NCO in the company, Morris was loaded up to the eyeballs. In addition to his webbing and bulging large pack, he had several bandoliers of ammunition hanging around his neck, a container of mortar bombs strapped to his large pack, and a sandbag packed full of composite rations stuffed down the front of his battledress jacket. The tiny little life-preserver that was slung around the young man's body looked ridiculous against the huge load he was carrying. Smithson allowed his eyes to run up the gangway. All his men were there behind Morrison, similarly burdened with the paraphernalia of war.

"No, it's alright thank you, Morrison. I'll go first."

He turned back to look down at the water, gave a quick sideways glance at the impassive sailor, then stepped off the ramp.

Smithson entered the water with an almighty 'splosh'. Instantly, he realised that the water was deeper than waist height. For a terrible moment, he thought that the sea was bottomless, although that was preposterous of course, because he was only a few yards from the beach. Even so, it felt to Smithson as if he was going to carry on sinking forever. After a terrifying couple of seconds however, Smithson felt his boots hit the sand beneath the churning sea. And then the coldness of the water hit him like a thunder bolt.

"Ugh!"

He cried out involuntarily in shock as he fought to stay upright, almost wrenching his arm from the socket as he clung onto the rope for dear life. He was gasping for breath, rapidly and repeatedly, as he steadied himself in the surging tide. When he finally got his balance, he realised that he was up to his chest in water.

"Go... careful..." He gasped up towards the ramp, twisting awkwardly in the surf to look up at Haines and Morrison. "It's... quite... b...bloody deep..."

He took a huge gulp of air and tried to steady his voice.

"Help each other down..."

Haines didn't hesitate. The radio operator lowered himself into a sitting position on the end of the ramp, grabbed hold of the rope as far down as was possible, then pushed himself off.

Splosh!

Like his officer before him, the radio operator entered the water with a resounding splash. Smithson blinked water out of his eyes and spat the salty liquid from his mouth as he reached out his free hand to grab hold of and steady the lance corporal. After a moment, Haines, just like Smithson before him, emerged from the water spluttering and gasping for breath.

"Well done..." Smithson gabbled, his chin wobbling uncontrollably due to the water temperature. "Come on then... Next one..."

Smithson turned back towards the beach and began wading ashore.

It seemed much harder than on the exercises they'd done. The current in the water was stronger then he'd experienced hitherto, and the ebb and flow of the tide sent him staggering from side to side as he slowly waded up the beach and emerged from the water. As he forced his way shore, Smithson glanced left and saw that the first men from No.2 Platoon, led by Captain Roy Chislehurst, his second in command, were also coming off the ramp at the other side of the vessel's bow.

He was almost there now. The two men on the beach who were holding the rope had begun to peg it down into the sand. The man with the flags had disappeared. Smithson looked behind him and was rewarded by the sight of Lance Corporal Haines coming on behind him, followed by Morrison, whilst the leading men from No.1 Platoon were dropping off the ramp behind them. Satisfied, he turned and began wading the last couple of yards towards the sand.

"Help me..."

Smithson hardly registered the voice at first, but then it came to him again; louder, and with more desperation in its tone. "Please... mate? Help?"

Smithson stopped dead, the water still lapping around his ankles. He cast his eyes around looking for the source of the appeal for help. At first he thought that one of his own men must be floundering in the water, but when he looked back, everything seemed to be going fine at the ramp. Then he spotted the man in the water.

The soldier lay about fifteen yards away to Smithson's right. He was flat on his back, right beside a metal hedgehog obstacle, and he was about to drown. The man, presumably from the first or second waves, had obviously been wounded and immobilised whilst crossing the beach, but now, with the tide coming in fast, it was not bullets or shrapnel threatening the man's survival. Even as Smithson stared in surprise at the supine khaki figure, a wave came rolling in and washed over the man, momentarily covering him, before receding again.

"Help!" The poor man suddenly screamed with surprising volume and force, spluttering in fear and panic. "Help!"

Haines and Morrison were beside their officer now and staring towards the man in horror.

"Give me a hand." Smithson ordered, changing direction to splash through the shallows towards where the stranded man lay screaming for rescuers to come to his assistance.

Haines and Morrison splashed after their officer, threading their way through the scattering of obstacles and the detritus of battle that washed up in the surf.

"Hold on, old chap..." Smithson called to the man as they hurried across to him. "We'll have you out of here in a jiffy."

They reached the bedraggled looking soldier just a moment later. Just a quick glance told Smithson that the man belonged to one of the assault engineer companies that had landed with the assaulting infantry. He was fully dressed and kitted out with a bulging demolitions vest, whilst both of his legs were loosely wrapped in blood stained and badly secured bandages.

"What happened, old boy?" Smithson enquired of the pale-faced, wide-eyed sapper.

The man rolled terrified, exhausted eyes upwards to look at Smithson.

"Shot through the legs..." The young engineer gasped, his voice betraying the approach of unconsciousness. "Tried... to crawl..."

His voice petered out and he shook his head weakly, indicating that he couldn't even find the energy to talk.

"Grabs his arms, quickly." Smithson instructed Haines and Morrison. "Drag him up here onto the sand. Get him clear of the surf."

Even as Smithson was speaking, another wave came rolling up the beach and washed over the stranded soldier, forcing Haines and Morrison to grab the man by his demolition vest and lift his upper body clear of the water.

"Come on, drag him." Smithson prompted the other two, grabbing hold of the man's collar and beginning to step carefully rearwards.

"Don't worry, old chap..." Smithson spoke lightly to the injured soldier as they pulled him up the sand. "We'll get you well away from the shoreline and find a medic to have a look at those bandages. We'll soon get you sorted."

They had managed to drag the man about twenty yards by now, and Smithson instructed the others to pause for a moment so that they could adjust their grip on him. At precisely that point however, their little rescue mission was rudely interrupted.

"What the bloody hell are you arsing around at? Leave him and get off the damned beach!"

Smithson stood up and looked round in surprise. A major, wearing the distinctive identity badges and white helmet band of the Beach Group, was storming down the beach towards them.

"Are these your men, here?"

The new arrival was gesticulating wildly towards where Smithson's company were now starting to congregate at the waters edge.

"Er, yes..." Smithson responded, slightly taken aback. "Why? What's the matter?"

The major came to a halt in front of Smithson. He was extremely animated to say the least.

"We're trying to get this beach open, that's what the matter is. You need to get your men moving, now. There's no time for pratting around down here. Get your company moving up to the dunes and through the cleared lane. There's enough confusion down here as it is, and I don't need another hundred men adding to it!"

Smithson felt his temper flare momentarily, but he forced it back down and replied in a calm, but forceful manner.

"We are not *pratting about*. This man is seriously wounded and he was drowning in the surf. I can't believe the poor man had just been left there..."

If Smithson was hoping to shame the officer from the Beach Group, then he was disappointed. The major simply narrowed his eyes and delivered a sharp reply.

"It's the job of the medical teams to deal with the wounded. It's *my* job to get this beach cleared and keep everything moving..."

The officer half turned and pointed towards one of the burning buildings at the far side of the dunes.

"And it's *your* job to get your arses over there and start killing Germans. Now, get your men moving; up the beach until you reach the wire, then turn left and follow the wire until you reach the clear lane through the dunes. Get moving."

With that, the irate Beach Group officer turned on his heel and stomped off along the sand, calling out more blunt, peremptory orders to anyone who looked as though they were idling. Smithson, somewhat taken aback by the rather harsh treatment, turned to look at his companions. Morrison was shaking his head, a dark look on his face.

"Rude little fucker..." Smithson heard his batman comment.

Lance Corporal Haines on the other hand simply blew out his cheeks and raised his eyebrows.

"Welcome to France... Mind the bloody gap..."

WEIMER'S HEAVY TANK PLATOON – 2.5 MILES SOUTH OF RANVILLE
TUESDAY 6TH JUNE 1944 – 1130 HOURS

"Have they seen us?"

Wesser's voice was filled with apprehension. That was understandable. Even though the gunner had several years experience of intense armoured combat on the Eastern Front under his belt, this was a whole new dynamic. In Russia, the air situation had generally been one of parity between the Luftwaffe and the enemy, but here in Normandy, there was only one air force in the sky today, and that was the Allied one.

"I don't think so..."

Weimer didn't sound especially confident on that point.

Somewhere above the apple trees, flight after flight of single-seat Allied fighters roared past; the throb of their powerful engines reverberating through the humid summer air.

From the cupola of his Panzer Mk IV, Weimer peered up through the foliage at the deadly looking aircraft as they zipped past. He couldn't work out whether they were British or American, but one thing was for sure; they certainly weren't German. He caught sight of the curious black and white striped markings on the wings of the aircraft as they flashed by and knew that such colour schemes were not in use by his own air force.

It had been damned close he reflected. Their company, the lead company of their battalion, had been threading its way northwards for almost two hours now; heading towards the supposed concentration of enemy paratroopers and glider troops around Ranville. The journey had been unbelievably slow and frustrating, with all manner of frustrations adding to the chaos of the morning's advance. Every major junction or crossroads seemed to be peppered with bomb craters, whilst telegraph poles and half collapsed cottages littered many of the main routes. There was also the continuous to'ing and fro'ing of their own troops, mainly from various headquarters or support groups; clogging up the narrow lanes of Normandy with staff cars, bicycles and all manner of unnecessary vehicular movement. And then of course, there were the Jabos.

Twice before now, the column of heavy tanks had been forced to pull into the side of the road and take shelter beneath the overhanging branches of the trees and hedgerows, as waves of Allied heavy bombers passed by, several thousand feet above them. But then, just two minutes ago, the company commander had suddenly ordered the entire column to pull off the road and veer right, straight into a large orchard, and then go firm and await further orders. Barely had Weimer's platoon, at the rear of the column, squeezed itself into the shade of the exceptionally crowded orchard, than the first enemy Jabos had come roaring overhead at just a couple of hundred feet.

There had been an initial surge of panic amongst the tank commanders who had voiced their fears over the radio net, but after a few seconds the Company Commander had cut everybody short with a sharp radio order to *'shut the fuck up'*. In the long, agonising seconds since that order had been delivered, the tank crews had sat there under the heavy branches of the apple trees, cringing in terror lest the swarm of enemy fighter-bombers suddenly wheel round and dive into the attack.

As the last flight of enemy aircraft thundered past however, Weimer was desperately beginning to hope that the enemy Jabos had more important targets waiting for them elsewhere. He had little time to dwell on it though because, at precisely that moment, the radio crackled into life, and the Company Commander's voice ordered all vehicle commanders to dismount and close in on his tank.

"Okay, wait here..." He told his crew, then pulled off his headset and began hauling himself out of the turret. Then, just before he slid out of the cupola completely, he looked down at Wesser.

"You stick your head up here, Wesser. Keep your eyes peeled for Jabos. I won't be long."

With that, the tank commander lowered himself over the side of the tank's hull and jumped down into the soft, lush grass that carpeted the orchard. It was a beautiful little orchard to be fair, and under any other circumstances, would be a wonderful place to laze on a muggy summer's day. Today however, the gloom beneath the trees, coupled with the heavy, humid atmosphere that threatened more rain, just seemed oppressive. Weimer shrugged off the feeling as best he could and began threading his way through the regular lines of apple trees towards where he guessed the Company Commander's tank would be parked. As he went, he glanced to his left and saw Corporals Bauer and Metzger, the other two tank commanders from his platoon, jogging across to join him.

"Fuck me!" Bauer called, even before he'd caught up with Weimer. "That was close!"

"We only just got into the orchard before they came over…" Metzger added, looking especially pale. "If we'd been just a few seconds later they'd have spotted us; no doubt."

"The Tommy aircraft are all over the fucking place." Bauer commented sourly as he fell in beside Weimer. "Where the hell is the Luftwaffe?"

"Forget the Luftwaffe." Weimer answered bluntly. "They aren't playing today."

The two corporals exchanged a quick look and then changed the subject.

"What's the Company Commander want, d'you reckon?" Bauer asked.

"God knows." Weimer replied. "But this is taking the piss. We've done less than five miles in two hours. I never thought I'd say it, but give me the Russian steppe again any day."

Falling into a brooding silence, the three tank commanders joined a group of men dressed in black overalls who were gathering around the company's command tank. The Company Commander was sitting on the edge of the tank's hull, his map spread over his legs, frowning deeply as he stared at it.

The lieutenant, who commanded the eleven tanks of the heavy panzer company, glanced up when he saw Weimer and his corporals join the group then threw a gaze around the expectant faces of his NCOs.

"Right, listen in; change of plan. The Tommies have indeed got paratroopers sitting all over Ranville and the Orne bridges, and 125th Panzer Grenadiers have been sent in to shift them. And the Tommies are indeed launching a seaborne invasion, but…"

And with this, the lieutenant's face darkened somewhat.

"They're not coming ashore at Cabourg. They're coming ashore to the *west* of the River Orne and Ouistreham."

The lieutenant used his pencil to point to the strip of coastline further west of the mouth of the Orne on his map. Amongst the group, the individual tank commanders began frowning at their own maps.

"Basically, this business up here with the Tommy paratroopers looks like a bit of a side-show. It seems that the main attack is coming ashore at the far side of the Orne. Therefore, we have been ordered to go over to the west bank of the river and form up, ready to launch a counter attack against the beaches there. The Regimental Commander is moving there now to get a brief from the Corps Commander. The problem is, the only bridges left in our hands are those in Caen itself. So, the whole regiment has been ordered to turn around and head back the way we came."

A sudden wave of groaning came up from the assembled vehicle commanders, and the lieutenant held up his hands to stem the flow of subdued murmuring.

"Yes, men... I know it's bollocks, but we are where we are. There's nothing we can do about it. The Tommies are blocking our route across the river at Ranville so we've got no choice but to go back around them. We can't waste our strength fucking about with a bunch of paratroopers when the Tommies are trying to land tanks, guns and infantry on the beaches up towards Lion-sur-Mer."

The officer took a deep breath.

"So, there we have it. There's no point moaning. We were at the front of the regiment. We're now at the back. As soon as we get word that everyone else has turned around and got moving then we'll be moving off ourselves. Go and brief your crews."

The Company Commander suddenly grinned down at his NCOs.

"And keep smiling, men. It's going to be one of those days..."

THE ROADBLOCK – HALF A MILE SOUTH OF RANVILLE TUESDAY 6TH OF JUNE – 1145 HOURS

"What? They want us to move?" Dawes asked, taken aback.

The corporal and Mr Peterson looked at the runner in surprise. The young private had just come doubling down the road from Ranville, to where Dawes and his scratch force, supported by Mr Peterson and his platoon, had established their tiny little blocking position. Centred on the Y-junction just to the north of the small village of Herouvillette, Dawes and Peterson had planned to block any potential German counter-attack along two converging axis. Now however, they were being given fresh orders.

"Yes, Sir." The runner from Battalion Headquarters said, glancing from Dawes to Peterson. "The CO says that the battalion is too thinly spread at the moment, and some of the other units have been widely dispersed, so we've got to draw everybody into a fairly tight perimeter. The remainder of 'C' Company have already been directed to the new position on the southern edge of Ranville. If you come straight back up this road you'll walk right into them. You won't have any trouble finding them."

Peterson and Dawes exchanged a frustrated look. Their ad hoc force had been digging-in furiously for several hours now as they desperately tried to increase the strength of their position. Now they were being told to abandon it and pull back. Both men, despite feeling disappointed at the news, were professionals however. They knew that they were just a small part in a much bigger machine.

"Well..." Peterson gave a deep sigh of resignation. "They did warn us it would be chaos..."

He looked back at the runner.

"Alright, no problem. Thank you for the message. Get yourself back to the battalion and tell the CO that we're on our way. We'll be right behind you. It'll just take us a few minutes to get everyone called in; then we'll be moving off."

The young paratrooper from Battalion Headquarters nodded his thanks and doubled away. As the sound of his hobnailed boots clattering on the cobbles began to fade, Peterson turned to Dawes.

"Bit of a bugger that! Still, it all makes sense I suppose. We'd best get going because the Jerries can't stay asleep all day."

Little did the young officer realise how prophetic those words would be.

He was just in the process of struggling out of the recently dug slit trench when the strange whisper sounded in the air above. Dawes, who had heard that noise several years before, immediately reached up and grabbed hold of the lieutenant's webbing straps and yanked the startled officer back into the trench.

"Down!" Yelled Dawes as he and the officer collapsed heavily onto the rough earth floor.

Crump! Crump! Crump!

The belt of three mortar bombs exploded with a resounding thump less than fifty yards away.

"Bloody hell, Corporal D!" Peterson shouted as clumps of soil and turf rained down into the trench. "Thank God you washed your ears out this morning!"

The two paratroopers struggled up into a kneeling position and Peterson regarded the corporal with an excited grin.

"Do you think that means the Jerries want us to move as well?"

Crump! Crump! Crump!

Another salvo of mortar bombs slammed into the ground nearby, and this time some of the falling detritus from the blasts included stone cobbles.

"The fuckers have got us marked!" Dawes observed bitterly.

"Do you think it's worth taking the risk and moving now? Or should we wait for it to calm down a bit?" Asked Peterson.

The decision was made for them, because even before Dawes had a chance to consider the question, the steady chug of a Bren Gun erupting into life shattered the brief silence between the explosion of mortar bombs.

"Stand-to! Stand-to!" Some one was shouting.

"Here they come! Loads of the fuckers!" Another English voice roared out.

"We'll talk in a minute shall we, Sir?" Dawes shouted above the sudden flurry of small arms fire as he struggled to his feet.

Rat-tat-tat-tat-tat-tat-tat-tat!

The burst of machine gun fire that cracked low over Dawes' head as he peered over the lip of the trench was not from one of their own Bren Guns. For a start, it was coming from the wrong direction, and secondly, it was firing way too fast. He'd heard that kind of machine gun fire before, and he knew without even looking that it was German.

"Stand-by, Sir..." Dawes murmured to Peterson as he brought his Sten Gun up into the shoulder, aiming along the right hand of the two roads. "Looks like you're going to have your first battle..."

The young lieutenant did likewise, his eyes searching for any sign of the enemy.

"Which way are they coming from?"

Dawes grunted a reply.

"Not sure... The right hand fork I think?"

And then they were there. In the blink of an eye, a camouflaged car sporting a machine gun, followed by an armoured car and a half track came rolling steadily around the bend in the road that led off to the right. It wasn't just the car that was armed, for both of the armoured vehicles that came on behind it were bristling with machine guns, and all of them were spitting out deadly bursts of fire at an unbelievably rapid rate. Without speaking, Dawes squeezed the trigger of his Sten Gun and it chattered into life, making Peterson jump in surprise. Just a moment later however, the officer recovered from the slight shock and began firing his own weapon. The hedgerows on either side of the wide, Y-shaped junction erupted as almost a dozen British paratroopers opened up on the enemy vehicles with everything they had.

For just a moment, it seemed to take the Germans by surprise, for the car swerved to one side and the vehicle mounted machine gunners in all three enemy vehicles appeared to duck down, and Dawes detected a distinct pause in the constant crack of incoming fire. But, in typical German fashion, the enemy recovered within moments. The armoured car and half-track pushed forward level with the car; all three vehicles squeezing in next to each other to fill the entire lane from one hedgerow to another and spitting fire towards the hidden British paratroopers all the while.

The enemy gunners were, perhaps, using searching fire; for a long snake of tracer came flashing along the hedgerow to the left of Dawes' trench, ripping great chunks of foliage from the undergrowth, and then, inevitably, it came straight towards the corporal's trench. Dawes noted the spurts of soil to his front at the last safe moment and threw himself to the right, slamming into Peterson so that both of them fell sideways into the trench again. Just as they did so, several high velocity rounds slapped into the turf covered spoil at the front of the trench with a deafening series of cracks.

"Watch yourself, Sir!" Dawes cautioned as he levered himself upright again. "The bastards have seen us!"

Carefully, the two paratroopers raised their eyes to the parapet of the trench once more. The bullets were cracking past and above them now in every direction. The air was filled with the cacophony of an intense small arms battle, with the rapid crack-crack-crack of the German 'Spandaus' mixing with the steady chug of Bren Guns, the noisy clatter of Stens, and the solid, hollow thump of Lee-Enfields.

The German vehicles were still there, forming a solid wall of metal as they advanced slowly, yet inexorably towards the junction. Dawes and Peterson opened fire again with their Stens. Even the crude little sub-machine guns couldn't fail to hit the large target at just seventy five yards, and Dawes unconsciously registered the ping and whine of bullets ricocheting off metal superstructures. Then, amongst the din, there came a different sound. It was a strange, hollow sounding 'pop', which made Dawes wrinkle his brow in confusion. But then he saw a large, dark blob sailing through the air in an ungainly fashion, as if somebody had just thrown a great boulder towards the enemy vehicles, and he realised that he had heard the sound of the PIAT being fired.

He released the pressure on his trigger for a moment as he watched, fascinated, as the large projectile arced down the narrow road towards the oncoming enemy vehicles. Unfortunately for the Germans, their tactic of advancing like an armoured wall was now their undoing. The big, cumbersome projectile, which reminded Dawes of a giant gnat, reached its culminating point then dropped heavily towards the centre vehicle; that being the half-track. There was a sudden flash as the two and a half pounds of explosive detonated with a heart-stopping 'thump' and then all three enemy vehicles were enveloped in a cloud of dirty grey smoke, whilst Dawes blinked and looked off to the side as the blast wave came back at him.

"Good shot!" Peterson enthused, whilst from both flanks, the sound of British small arms fire intensified.

Dawes watched with fascination as blobs of orange tracer streaked through hedges and disappeared inside the dark cloud of smoke, before emerging again as ricochets, flying off in every direction. As the smoke began to clear slightly, the sound of revving engines came through the sound of gunfire and Dawes saw that the small car and the armoured car were both now reversing back along the road. The half-track was immobile; its square bonnet sprouting hungry looking flames whilst all around the vehicle, bodies lay strewn on the cobbles, excepting one that was draped over the side of the vehicle. The British gunfire increased to an even higher pitch as the defenders of the roadblock scented victory.

"They're retreating!" Peterson laughed out loud beside Dawes.

"Maybe..." Dawes replied, not entirely convinced. "Maybe not..."

The two surviving enemy vehicles were now starting to disappear back around the bend in the road and the British fire was slackening accordingly. Just as it did however, the tell-tale whoosh overhead sent the defenders ducking for cover once more.

Crump! Crump! Crump!

The enemy mortars brought down another deadly accurate bombardment on the junction as they attempted to cover the withdrawal of the vehicles and once more Dawes and Peterson were forced to drop to their knees inside the trench as lethal splinters of red hot shrapnel sliced through the air.

"I knew the peace and quiet wouldn't last forever!" Peterson joked.

Dawes, busy changing the magazine on his Sten Gun, regarded the young officer with serious eyes.

"It's going to get even noisier soon enough..." He grunted. "That was just a recce party. They'll come back again soon enough, and this time they'll be mob-handed. And that little mortar bombardment was just a taster. Wait until they get their big stuff out of the cupboard..."

The corporal stuffed the empty magazine away in his pouch and jerked his head towards the rear of the trench.

"Come on, Sir. There's no time to hang about. We need to get back to the main position before the Jerries put in the next attack. Let's get the boys together and get the fuck out of here..."

1,000 YARDS INLAND FROM SWORD BEACH – NEAR HERMANVILLE
TUESDAY 6TH JUNE 1944 – 1250 HOURS

"I can only assume that the Germans aren't too happy about having us here then?"

Bunty Brown, the Battalion Second in Command, ducked down as another salvo of German artillery shells slammed into the countryside just a hundred yards away and grinned at Smithson from beneath his helmet.

Although the shelling was quite close, the large wood in which Smithson's company was sheltering, gave the impression of relative safety. Smithson, staring out from within the wood, got the idea that the Germans were targeting the road that ran from the village of La Breche on the beach, up to Hermanville.

The two officers, along with Archie Newbold, the Company Commander of 'C' Company, were crouching beside an ancient looking tree at the northern tip of the wood that had been designated as the Battalion RV. The whole battalion was ashore now, with 'B' and 'D' Companies spread out amongst thick hedgerows and small orchards on the other side of the Hermanville road, but as yet they hadn't moved any further inland. Their Commanding Officer had been summoned by the Brigade Commander, and now the senior officers from the battalion were sitting around waiting for the order to advance. They had been told that their objective was to 'make a dash for Caen', but at present there seemed little urgency.

They had come ashore amongst organised chaos. The beach had been crammed full of stranded vehicles, queuing to enter the clear lanes through the dunes. The only problem was, not all of the planned lanes were open, and the tide was much higher than expected. As a result, dozens of tanks and other vehicles, along with hundreds, if not thousands of men, had begun to build up on the ever-narrowing strip of sand. All the while, the Germans shelled the landing area and the Royal Engineers continued their valiant struggle to blow open gaps in both the waterline obstacle belt and the minefield in the dunes.

For the Hambledon and Moorlanders, the initial wait on the beach had been relatively short. Several narrow lanes had been blown through the minefield by the assault troops; just wide enough for men to pass through in single file, and so after just a few minutes Smithson and his company had been ushered off the sand. The scene around them as they had progressed proved sobering. Every few yards they had come across the dead body of a British soldier from the assault battalions. These poor men, killed and, in some cases, literally ripped apart during the first crucial minutes of the invasion, lay strewn about the beach and in the dunes, exactly where they had fallen. Some of the dead faces registered looks of shock or surprise. Others just seemed to be asleep. Others still were unrecognisable.

It seemed unbelievably callous that these casualties of war had been left where they had fallen, ignored by everyone as the Beach Masters ruthlessly went about their business of clearing the incoming troops off the sand. At the same time, Smithson understood the imperative. This was war in all its ugly glory. The niceties of the human spirit were subordinate to the mechanical, functional needs of military efficiency. There was no time for grieving now. Not here. The most that any casualty could expect in the way of dignity was for some passing soldier to pause just long enough to throw a ground sheet over them. The thoughts fermented inside Smithson's head and he felt his shoulder begin to ache once more.

In an attempt to shake off the dark thoughts, the young major scanned around the interior of the wood. He could see his men, spread out amongst the trees in groups of two or three, sorting their equipment out or else taking the opportunity to consume just one more can of the ubiquitous self-heating soup. At least they had been given the chance to lighten their loads. Shortly after they had exited the beach, and as they had progressed through the body-strewn ruins of an enemy strongpoint, Smithson's company had come upon a stores centralisation point, where they had been ordered by members of the Beach Group to dump their sandbags full of rations and non-essential ammunition. At least when the advance began properly they would not be as weighed down as previously. Smithson checked his watch. 1250 hours. Christ almighty, they were wasting time sitting here.

"Hello? Here comes the CO, chaps…"

Newbold's comment snapped Smithson out of his private thoughts and he sat up expectantly as Colonel Blair, their Commanding Officer, clambered over the small fence that separated the wood from the nearby road, assisted by the unit's adjutant, Captain Jimmy Hollins.

"Right, gentlemen…" Blair announced as he successfully negotiated the fence. "It's time we got cracking."

The colonel came directly across to where the three officers were sitting and plonked himself down next to Brown. He was surprisingly young for a colonel; just twenty seven years old. But that of course was the same story throughout the British Army in this, the sixth year of the war. The grey haired, very distinguished old men of the pre-war regular army were largely gone; put out to grass and replaced with younger, more dynamic individuals. In fact, at a mere twenty nine years old, it was Bunty Brown who was the 'old man' of the group.

Without any preamble, Colonel Blair unfolded his map case and spread it on the ground in front of the others. Hollins, now over the fence himself, came to kneel beside the colonel.

"I'm sorry there's been a bit of a delay," Blair began, "but as I've just discovered, everything is a bit of a bugger's muddle at the moment. The beach is absolutely choc-a-block with men and vehicles and they're having real problems getting everything off. They had to close the beach to landing craft for an hour or so, but they've re-opened it now and things are starting to sort themselves out a bit."

The colonel produced a pencil from his jacket pocket and began tapping at the map.

"The Suffolks from 8 Brigade have apparently run into some tough opposition up front. I'm led to believe that they've captured Objective Morris, but that they're only just making a start on Hillman. There is, by all accounts, some pretty strong resistance coming from that particular objective which is a bit of a pain because it interferes with our plans slightly."

His pencil began tracing lines on the map.

"As a result, the Shropshires, who are meant to be advancing on our left flank, will need to swing around that objective to the west as they by-pass it. That means they're going to squash up against us a bit, and we can't go any further right because we've got the Ulster Rifles from 9 Brigade on that flank. Does that make sense so far?"

The collection of officers nodded.

"Good. Now then, because we're going to have a constrained frontage, we won't be able to advance with two companies up as originally planned. We're going to have to move off in echelon; one company after the other. We might as well keep it simple and go in company order, so Dickie..."

He glanced up at Smithson.

"Your chaps will be the point company to start with."

Smithson nodded his understanding.

"The battalion axis is now your company axis too..." Blair continued. "In other words, straight up this side road here, right past point 113, then onwards to Periers, down past Beuville and through Lebisey to the very outskirts of Caen. It's a good five miles at least over some undulating terrain, so we're going to have to get a shift on."

The colonel tapped his pencil at a small crossroads below point 113 on the map.

"You'll remember that recent intelligence reports indicated that the Germans had established a temporary checkpoint just here, near point 113, but I daresay the handful of men who were manning it have buggered off back to their parent unit by now. Either way, there's nothing that we know of in the form of fixed defences along this route, so we should be able to make good progress. We'll need as much daylight as we can get when we get to Caen. Clearing a built up area in the dark won't be easy so speed is of the essence now if we're to get back on schedule. Hopefully, by the time we reach Caen, the tanks and guns will have caught up with us."

At this, all of the officers in the group looked up sharply at their CO.

"Which brings me onto the next point..." Blair went on, a slight hesitance in his voice. "The tanks that were supposed to be supporting us are still snarled up in that chaos on the beach. What's left of the assault tanks from the 13/18 Hussars who managed to get off the beach are being used to help take care of the remaining strongpoints along the coastal strip. The Brigade Commander is going to try and cadge a few of them and send them our way. The Staffordshire Yeomanry, when they finally get off the beach, will follow on after the Shropshires. In terms of guns, the Royal Artillery boys have established a gun-line on the beach and they're going to send a FOO party up to join us shortly. I'll keep them with Battalion HQ as we advance. Once the exits from the beach are cleared the gun-line will move forward to keep pace with us."

The other officers were all making notes now as Blair went through the detailed instructions for the advance to Caen.

"I'm afraid our own Anti-Tank Platoon is also snarled up on the beach for now, but I've briefed Alex and he will come forward as soon as he's off. The Mortar Platoon has likewise got its carriers stuck on the sand, but they're leaving their drivers with the vehicles and the remainder of the platoon is going to man-pack the mortars forward. That means they'll be slightly limited for ammunition for the time being."

Blair pointed his pencil at Newbold.

"Archie? Your chaps, along with 'D' Company, need to retrieve the mortar bombs they've just dumped and carry them forward as a second line reserve. Once the carriers can get off the beach, you'll be able to offload them again."

Newbold nodded his understanding.

"Now then..." Blair went on, pulling back his cuff and checking his watch. "I make it a couple of minutes before 1300 hours. We need to get going sharpish. So Dickie, I want your company ready to move by 1325 latest. Okay?"

"No problem, Sir." Smithson replied, glad to be on the move at last. "We'll be ready to go."

"Good man." Blair smiled. "And don't forget, we can't afford any hold ups, so if any Germans get in your way, just plough straight through them before they know what's hit them."

"Will do, Sir." Smithson acknowledged.

A brace of artillery shells slammed into the field nearby, and the shrapnel came rattling through the branches above the heads of the officers from the Hambledon and Moorlanders, whilst the ground beneath them shook violently. As the tremors subsided, the pitter-patter of heavy rain drops began slapping against the tree canopy. Blobs of water penetrated the heavy foliage and began drizzling down on the group.

"Here comes the rain again..." Observed Bunty Brown.

"Yes..." Remarked Colonel Blair, glancing up at the dripping leaves with a frown. "I wish I'd brought my umbrella..."

13TH BATALLION THE PARACHUTE REGIMENT – RANVILLE DEFENSIVE PERIMETER TUESDAY 6TH JUNE 1944 – 1255 HOURS

"Come on! Keep fucking going! Get hold of it!"

Dawes was screaming at the other men holding onto the improvised stretcher, his voice nothing more than a hoarse grating noise after almost an hour of constant shouting.

The withdrawal of their small force from the roadblock just north of Herouvillette had been a fraught one. One man had been killed and three injured during the first German attack against the roadblock, and even as the tiny force of paratroopers began to pull back towards their battalion's main defensive position, the enemy began to saturate the surrounding area with mortar fire. Thankfully, two of the wounded had minor injuries to the upper body and were able to walk, but the third man had serious shrapnel injuries to both legs and so the decision had been made to carry the man back on an improvised stretcher made of rifles and groundsheets. Now, Dawes, who was gripping onto the forward right of the makeshift litter, was swearing and cursing at his sweating companions to get a grip of their own corners as they made the dash along the last couple of hundred yards of road into the small village of Ranville.

The German mortar fire had thumped down around them for several hundred yards of their forced march before finally petering out. That was no blessing however, for it simply marked the start of another German thrust with their armoured vehicles. As Dawes and his small band of waifs and strays concentrated on lugging the casualty, Peterson and the remainder of his platoon had brought up the rear, fighting off any pursuit by the enemy. There had been no time for dawdling. It was obvious that the Jerries had finally realised the scale of the British operation and now they were throwing a considerable weight of men and machines against the beleaguered British paras. As Dawes wiped another wave of sweat from his eyes with the sleeve of his smock, he reflected on how fortuitous it had been that they had been ordered to withdraw from their exposed position. They wouldn't have lasted there very long at all he now understood.

"Come on fellas; not far... Keep hold of it; just another couple of hundred yards..."

Dawes was gasping now, his breathing laboured and ragged from the near sprint of almost half a mile whilst hauling the dead weight of a casualty on the improvised stretcher. It wasn't just the weight of the man that was sapping the energy of the stretcher party. Each of them was still carrying his own full battle load of equipment and ammunition. The sweat poured from them, despite the overcast sky and occasional spot of rain, and their weapons, helmets and water-bottles clunked and clanked noisily as they raced along the cobbles. Dawes felt as if his fingers and left arm were on fire, the feeling in them all but gone. He gnashed his teeth together and gave a growl of effort as he stumbled onwards, ignoring the crack of half spent bullets that flew past his ears every few seconds. Somewhere behind, the crackle of small arms fire told him that the enemy were still following them up with vigour.

As he looked up, grimacing with strain, he thought he saw somebody on the road up ahead. Pushing his helmet up and wiping more sweat from his stinging eyes, the corporal spotted two figures in Denison Smocks beckoning his stretcher party onwards.

"We're nearly there..." Dawes gasped, hardly able to get his words out.

"Yaaagh!" One of the men at the rear of the stretcher roared out in painful defiance as he pushed himself onwards.

The sound of hobnailed boots on cobbles rang out with urgency as the small group of men forced themselves on the last few yards. Dawes was beginning to register more detail of his surroundings now. He noticed small, quaint looking cottages dotted amongst clumps of trees, many of which were heavily laden with apples. There were low yet sturdy looking stone walls and thick hedgerows separating small fields. He stumbled past a shell-scrape that had been so well camouflaged he hadn't noticed it until he went by it. Inside the small position, two men crouched over a PIAT, and didn't even look up at the passing stretcher party.

"Where are the others?"

The two men were coming towards them now, just ten yards away, and Dawes recognised one as the Company Sergeant Major of 'C' Company.

"Back there..." Dawes tried to answer, his voice more of an exhausted sob. "The Jerries are following us..."

The Company Sergeant Major flicked his gaze down the country lane towards Herouvillette momentarily before falling in beside the stretcher party.

"The Company Aid Post is just along there about fifty yards..." He directed, pointing straight up into the village. "Second building on your left. Drop him in there and then get back out here. I'll show you where to go..."

Dawes nodded vaguely, feeling his strength begin to drain away.

The Company Sergeant Major dropped away from the group and as Dawes steered his party and their burden towards the cottage in question, he heard the warrant officer bellowing orders.

"There are more of our boys coming up the road still! Don't shoot until you know what you're shooting at. Don't fire on our own blokes! There's Jerries right behind them mind, so stand-by!"

Dawes reached the door of the cottage in question and saw that a tactical sign denoting a medical post had been pushed into a flower pot by the side of the entrance. The black and white sign with its very military looking symbol appeared somewhat ridiculous surrounded by a variety of pink and purple flowers that were in full and glorious bloom. The door was already open and, slowing to a halt, the four men carrying the wounded paratrooper began to manhandle the casualty across the threshold and down a narrow corridor. A face appeared at the far end of that corridor, nothing more than a dull silhouette in the dark interior.

"Stop!" The voice shouted authoritatively.

Dawes looked through the gloom towards the figure and tried to gather his breath for a reply. Before he could even respond however, the dim figure came towards them and pushed open a side door off the corridor. Dawes vaguely registered the red cross on a white arm band that the man wore on his sleeve.

"Put him in there." The medical orderly told them. "Then take all his kit and weapons and get back out to your positions.

Dawes had no idea who the bossy medic was, but he was too exhausted to worry. Compliantly, the stretcher party bundled their charge into the room.

It had once been a bedroom, but now the gloomy space had become a waiting room for casualties. Several other men lay spread around the small space; two occupying a bed each, whilst three more were squeezed in side by side on the floor.

"Down here..." Dawes told his companions as he gulped in the air and tried to calm his breathing.

Without ceremony, they dumped the man heavily onto the boards, causing him to emit a weak moan through his delirium.

"Get the weapons..." Dawes couldn't even finish his sentences yet. His lungs felt as if they were going to burst and the muscles in his buttocks twinged as if he was about to lose all bowel control and shit himself.

Breathing like a band of asthmatics, the four men dragged the rifles from inside the buttoned groundsheets and rain-capes as quickly as they could.

"Outside then; let's have you!" The medical orderly was instructing them.

Wordlessly, obediently, Dawes and his companions left the building.

They emerged into chaos. Out on the road, Peterson and his men were pelting like madmen along the cobbles, their faces twisted with the agony of physical effort, as the Company Sergeant Major pointed and waved towards the hedgerows and walls to his right.

"Come on! Hurry up! Get into cover!"

The warrant officer turned his head and spotted the four erstwhile stretcher bearers stumbling out of the cottage onto the road again.

"You four!" He shouted towards them. "Get into those trees there. Join Ten Platoon."

The four men shambled into a run again, heading towards the trees on the left hand side of the road. As they went, the sound of renewed small arms fire erupted from not very far away.

"Here they come!" Somebody shouted.

Dawes hauled his Sten Gun up from beside his right leg and took a firm grasp of it once more, adjusting the sling around his body for comfort. He glanced at the weapon and saw that he hadn't yet re-cocked it, so reached along and grabbed hold of the bolt and dragged it to the rear. It locked in the cocked position and he flicked the safety catch into the *'on'* position. These weapons had a nasty habit of going off unexpectedly if given a hard knock whilst cocked.

Just as the corporal ducked his head under the first overhanging branch of the small copse, the first enemy mortar bomb thumped into the fields about seventy yards away to his right, on the very forward edge of Ranville. He heard the rattle of shrapnel and earth in the leaves above him and gripped his Sten Gun even tighter as he plunged through the trees in search of a fire position.

"Here they come alright…" He murmured to himself. "Here they fucking come!"

HEADQUARTERS 125TH PANZER GRENADIER REGIMENT – BELLENGREVILLE, NEAR CAEN, NORMANDY TUESDAY 6TH JUNE 1944 – 1230 HOURS

"Liebeskind, what's going on?"

The adjutant of the 125th Panzer Grenadier Regiment looked up from the map as his Regimental Commander entered the room, a grim look etched on his face.

"Ah, Sir… you're back. We've had new orders, Sir…"

"What kind of orders?" von Luck asked brusquely. "Who from?"

Liebeskind stood straight and passed a hand-written note across to the major.

"It's come from Headquarters 7th Army, via Divisonal Headquarters. They have cancelled General Feuchtinger's original orders to attack with the whole division east of the Orne. 7th Army now orders the division to split in two and attack on both banks of the Orne, with the majority of armour on the west bank. Our regiment is to form the nucleus of a battle-group under your command, Major, and take the east bank."

The serious faced von Luck took the proffered note and scanned it with knitted brow. At length he grunted.

"Mmm, well… I can understand why. I've seen the enemy fleet. It's huge Liebeskind. You cannot begin to imagine how many ships are out there on the water. I have no doubt the Tommies have already made a lodgement on the beaches. This business on our side of the Orne is a blocking action. The Tommies are protecting the vulnerable flank of their landings whilst capturing the vital ground and bridges that they will need in order to launch a break-out. Even so…" He looked up and regarded his adjutant with serious eyes. "This order means more reorganisation, and consequently more delay. We have just hours left to reverse our fortunes, Liebeskind. If we can't push the Tommies back into the sea by nightfall then we never will."

Liebeskind tried to sound upbeat.

"The armoured reserves will be here soon, Major. The 12th SS Panzer Division isn't far away. And the other panzer divisions will surely make haste? Once they're all concentrated we must surely be able to smash such a small beach-head?"

Von Luck gave a wry smile.

"It is a great theory Liebeskind, but the fact is that the Tommies rule the skies. I haven't seen a single Luftwaffe aircraft yet. The enemy planes are swarming like bees, everywhere you look. And when the weather clears completely, they will have nothing to obstruct them. As for their naval guns… Well, I've just had a close call with some of them and I tell you, we have nothing to compare with such firepower."

Remembering himself, von Luck broke off his lamentation and looked back down at the notepaper.

"So…" He continued, adopting his business-like tone once more. "We have our own regiment, the assault gun battalion, the reconnaissance battalion, and a platoon of 88's? It's a decent force on paper, but trying to get it assembled and launched in time is going to be difficult…"

He looked up from the paper once more.

"We'll leave it until 1500 hours Liebeskind; no later. I'll issue quick battle orders at 1500 and then we'll attack at 1600. We'll just have to go with what we've got. Start assembling these units…"

Von luck tapped the paper with his free hand.

"Do what you can Liebeskind. Do what you can…"

BY OBJECTIVE COD – SWORD BEACH
TUESDAY 6TH JUNE 1944 – 1325 HOURS

"Have you seen anyone else from the Regiment?" Sergeant Titch Saddler asked Legg as he clambered down from the turret of his Sherman Firefly.

"You're the first ones, Sarge. How did you get off the beach?"

The sergeant jumped down onto the cobbles of the road and jerked his thumb back along the sea-front.

"Same way as you; over that bridging unit. We followed one of those Centaur jobs from the Royal Marines. I think we were the last ones off the beach using that route though. We've just driven past it and the bridging unit is fucked. Must have been hit by a bloody big shell because it's snapped clean in half, and it's all mangled up."

He looked back at Legg.

"What have you been up to since you came off the beach?"

The corporal indicated the still smouldering pair of villas behind him.

"We came straight for this place. There was a shitload of Jerries inside it giving our infantry a hard time so we put a few rounds through it. Then, when we got right up against it, we realised that it was right in the centre of Objective Cod. We've spent the last few hours helping the East Yorks and the South Lancs to mop up all the trenches and bunkers in depth. We got as far as Hermanville up the road there, but decided we'd better come back down here and find out what had happened to everyone else."

Saddler grimaced and looked back towards the beach.

"I reckon that most of our surviving tanks are still on the beach. They've just blown a bloody great breach through the dunes so they should be able to get off pretty soon; those that are still in one piece of course."

He shook his head in wonder.

"You want to go take a look at that beach, Peggy; it's bloody chaos mate. The tide's come right in and there's got to be at least two hundred vehicles sat on that sand waiting to get off. Packed on there like sardines they are. Just as well that Jerry artillery isn't coming in too heavy."

"What do we do now?" Legg enquired.

Saddler pulled a face.

"I'm not sure. I think we just spend a few minutes getting our tanks sorted out and throw a brew down our necks, and I'll take a walk back onto the beach through one of the infantry lanes to see if I can find any of our officers."

The comment reminded Legg of their terrifying run-in to the beach earlier that morning.

"You know the Troop Leader's dead, Sarge?"

Saddler looked round at Legg, sharply.

"You sure?"

Legg nodded sombrely.

"Pretty sure. His tank got swamped by a landing craft on the run-in. It nearly ran into him but veered at the last moment. Even so, the backwash went right over his screen. The poor buggers went down in seconds. I didn't see anyone get out..."

Saddler took the words in without comment. After a few moments of contemplation, he finally spoke.

"Well... I think quite a lot of us made it ashore, all the same. I just think they all got stuck on the beach. Once that traffic jam clears I'm sure the rest of the lads will start to turn up."

He rubbed a hand over his dirty, sweat streaked face and yawned.

"Righto; nothing for it then. You wait here and try to get a brew or some soup organised. I'll go take a quick look around the beach and try to track down our mob..."

"Which unit are you from?"

The question came from an unnoticed arrival and cut Saddler short. As one, the sergeant and corporal both turned toward the voice and found themselves staring at a captain carrying a notebook in one hand and a map case in the other. Something about his stance and minimal equipment suggested that he wasn't one of the officers from the assault infantry units.

"Er... 13th/18th Hussars, Sir..." Saddler blurted out, throwing up a hasty salute. "We're just trying to find the rest of our regiment, but I think they're still stuck on the beach..."

"They are." The captain replied in a very matter of fact way. "As is just about all the armour we've got ashore at the moment. Which makes your two tanks somewhat unique."

Saddler and Legg exchanged a knowing look. Both men realised that their plan to take a breather was about to be scuppered.

"The reserve brigade is coming ashore and starting its advance on Objective Poland…" The officer paused momentarily, appeared to give consideration to something in his mind, then continued. "That's the code-name for Caen by the way. Anyway, they've had to get cracking as there's no time to lose. Trouble is, as I've said, all of their supporting armour is still struggling to get out of that bugger's muddle on the beach."

The captain paused again briefly as he stepped in between the two tank commanders and unfolded his map case.

"The KSLI are advancing straight up the way there, directly for Caen by the shortest possible route. They're on their own at the moment but very shortly the Staffordshire Yeomanry will be coming off the beach and we'll send them to catch up and give support."

He looked from Saddler to Legg in order to make sure they were following his brief. Both men nodded their understanding. It was obvious now that they were talking to someone from the Divisional Group Staff.

"Anyway…" The staff captain continued, pointing up the road towards Hermanville. "The Hambledon and Moorlanders are moving up to the right of the KSLI, with an axis that takes them through Point 113 and around the side of Periers. At the moment, they're also without tank support, so until we get more armour off the beach, I need you two to head on up the road there and support their advance. As soon as we round up the rest of your regiment we'll send them on after you. Any questions?"

There was little that the two tank men *could* ask. They were being given clear orders from the Divisonal Group Staff.

"The Hambledon and Moorlanders you say, Sir?" Saddler asked.

"That's right." The captain nodded. "Their First Battalion. You're looking for a chap called Colonel Blair."

Saddler nodded his understanding, his face pensive.

"Okay then, Peggy…" He said throwing a grim smile in Legg's direction. "You heard all that. Let's get mounted up…"

THE CAEN CANAL BRIDGE
TUESDAY 6TH JUNE 1944 – 1330 HOURS

"Get your bloody hands up! Come on; *hande hoch*…"

Green was no linguist, and his German pronunciation was not especially polished, but the gesture he made with his Sten Gun was clear enough to the terrified German soldiers.

The two pale-faced youngsters had nosed their way cautiously out of a clump of thick gorse bushes just yards away from Green's trench only seconds ago, their eyes wide with fear and their arms spread equally as wide. The two men must have been hiding in the bushes all night, Green surmised. The thought made him suddenly paranoid. How many other Jerries might have escaped during that initial assault? There could be a dozen or more lying low in the surrounding area. If the enemy mortars took a break from their relentless bombardment, he would send some men out on a small clearance patrol, Green decided.

As he was considering all this, a German mortar bomb exploded with a dull crump on the far side of the canal, not far from where one of the gliders lay flopped over to one side. The two German prisoners cringed at the sound, but Green simply ignored it.

"Give those buggers the once over." He ordered Private Cartwright.

Immediately, the young soldier to his left stepped forward, slinging his Lee Enfield over one shoulder and began rifling through the pockets and equipment of the two Germans. They remained perfectly still, allowing Cartwright to pull everything out for inspection, and all the while they kept their eyes on the barrel of Green's Sten Gun.

"Poor bastards." Green commented to nobody in particular.

These individuals were certainly no Nazi storm-troopers; rather, they were just a couple of frightened teenage boys.

Green watched as Cartwright yanked out clips of rifle ammunition and tossed it away carelessly into the grass, before removing both of the men's bayonets and doing likewise. Eventually, Cartwright came to an end of his search and nodded to his section commander.

"They're all clean, Corp'. Nothing on 'em…"

The private stopped mid-sentence.

"What's up?" Green frowned.

"Listen…" Cartwright said.

Green listened.

Crump, crump. Two mortar bombs landed in rapid succession at the far side of the canal again. Somewhere in the distance he could here the rattle of small arms fire.

"Just the Jerries having a pop…" Green answered, but Cartwright shook his head.

"No, not that. Listen…"

The two British glider-borne soldiers stood there silently for a moment, their heads cocked to one side as they strained to listen to the myriad sounds that constituted the background symphony of war, whilst their two prisoners stared at them with nervous, confused faces. After a moment or two, Cartwright's face brightened.

"There! Did you hear it?"

"Shh…" Green hissed.

The corporal creased his brow as he tried to identify the strange sound that was barely audible above the rumble of battle.

"No way…" He gasped suddenly as the wind caught the strange noise and carried it clearly to his ears. "No bloody way…"

Bagpipes. He could hear them clearly now. So could the German prisoners, because they exchanged puzzled glances, not quite understanding what was going on. For those not familiar with bagpipe music, it is an alien sound at the best of times. To hear them in the middle of an all out battle is quite bizarre. The four men; two Germans prisoners and their two British captors, turned their bemused faces towards the line of houses that marked the nearby village of le Port as the skirl of pipes became more distinct. The noise from the strange Scottish musical instrument was taking on more structure now, transforming from a tuneless wail into a lilting, upbeat jig. And then the first men from the long column of infantry came into sight.

They emerged from the village of le Port and marched steadily onto the junction for Benouville before turning the corner towards the bridge; heading almost directly towards Green and his companions. Green squinted and picked out the staggered files of men clad in khaki battledress. Some of the men wore soft, floppy berets, whilst others wore scrim-covered helmets. All of the men had large Bergen-style rucksacks on their backs and lugged copious amounts of weapons and ammunition.

At the head of this column of heavily-laden infantry were two unusual figures. One was out in front by some way, and was, rather strangely, wearing a white, woollen, roll-neck sweater instead of a battledress jacket. Just behind him came a soldier armed with a set of bagpipes, into which he was blowing lustily. Green, Cartwright, and their two prisoners watched open mouthed as the column of men from No.4 Commando, led by Brigadier Lord Lovatt and his personal piper, Bill Millin, came tramping down the road towards the Caen Canal Bridge having fought their way through from Sword Beach to relieve the beleaguered troops of the 6th Airborne Division. They came on quickly, with a spring in their step; as if they were out on a pleasant route-march through some Scottish glen.

Cartwright looked towards Green and shook his head slowly.

"Bugger me…" He said.

THE GROCERY STORE - MAIN STREET OF LE PORT, CLOSE TO THE CAEN CANAL BRIDGE TUESDAY 6TH OF JUNE 1944 – 1330 HOURS

Krause wasn't quite sure what had woken him up. It could have been the shouting, or it might have been the strange wailing sound; he wasn't sure. Neither was he sure if he was just tired or delirious through loss of blood. All he did know for sure was that his mouth was as dry as a bone and his right leg hurt like hell. It felt as if it was made out of lead and he had the sensation that it was three times bigger than it should be. When he squinted at his lower limbs through blurry eyes he could see that both of his legs appeared to be of normal proportions, allowing for the extensive bandaging that was evident on his right leg. Even so, he couldn't shake off the sensation that the injured limb was badly swollen. It didn't really make sense, but there again, nothing that had happened over the last twelve hours or so made sense to him really.

"Bollocks!"

Through his disorientation, Krause recognised Corporal Lang's frustrated voice.

"We're fucked now! There's dozens of the bastards coming up the road from Ouistreham. They must have broken through the beach defences…"

There was the sound of worried muttering elsewhere in the room and hazy, shadowy figures scurried about. Krause heard another voice speak in a low, urgent voice.

"We can't fight them off from both directions. Not that many. If we stay here any longer we'll get caught like rats in a trap; right between both groups. I say we get the fuck out of here…"

There was more whispering and more scuffling about in the room, followed by the sound of feet coming down the wooden stairs in a hurry. The next thing Krause knew, he was being shaken roughly by a hand that was gripping his shoulder.

"Krause? Krause? Are you still alive?"

The young German soldier opened his heavy-lidded eyes as fully as he could and found himself staring at the dark silhouette of someone with a worried looking face.

"Ah… you're still with us then?"

It was Lang's voice again. He tried to nod and realised that he was jerking his head like a badly handled puppet.

"Right, listen in Krause, lad. We've got to go; okay? We've got to pull back. The Tommies are closing in and there's no way we can hold them off. There's just too many of them. We're going to have to bug-out…"

Krause was acknowledging each piece of information with more clumsy nods. His mouth was just too dry to speak.

"We can't take you with us…" Lang said hesitantly. "You can't walk and we haven't got time to manhandle you. Besides, you'll be better off waiting here. The Tommies have good doctors and they're a decent lot. They'll look after you, no worries. You might have to live on cucumber sandwiches and some of that other shit they like to eat but they'll look after you all the same…"

Krause managed an exhausted, lopsided grin.

Lang was patting him on the shoulder now.

"Good lad. Hang in there. You'll be alright. No more fighting for you son."

And then Lang was on his feet; whispering curt, urgent orders to the other men in the room. There was a scurrying of feet, the rattle of equipment, then silence. Comparative silence anyway. Krause's mind had long since accepted the dull rumble of artillery and bombing as the natural state of things. After what seemed like a few moments, a strange sound came to the semi-conscious soldier. It was a sound like he'd never heard before. He had no idea what it was. Something high pitched, but with a deep undertone. The weird, almost musical notes were arranged in a fashion that suggested it was some kind of tune, yet to Krause's befuddled mind it was no tune that he could fathom. He blinked.

It seemed that what had begun as a blink had ended up as a short nap, because suddenly Krause was jerking awake at the sound of a splintering crash, His mind told him that it was the sound of a door being broken open. He remembered the strange wailing sound from before and listened for it. It had disappeared completely.

A shadow appeared above him.

"Look at this fucker here."

The words were in a language that Krause couldn't understand.

"Is he dead?" Came another voice, again speaking the strange language.

The shadow developed into a distinct shape; a man with a blackened face and big, enquiring eyes, squatting down in front of the wounded soldier. Krause slowly opened his drooping eyelids to study the stranger with the foreign accent.

"No; he's still alive. His leg's smashed up pretty badly though. The bandages are caked in blood. I reckon he's lost a fair bit of claret already."

Krause stared stupidly at the man with the blackened face. Something told Krause that he should be scared by a man with a blackened face, but despite that he detected a sense of kindness in the other man's eyes, and the feeling of fear evaded him. Rather, he just felt terribly tired.

"Right." Said the other foreign voice. "Let's search the rest of the house, then we'll get the medics to take a look at him."

The squatting man stood up and moved away. Krause felt quite calm and very relaxed. It was all going to be okay. Corporal Lang had said so. He knew what he was talking about did Corporal Lang. Krause sighed gently. He closed his eyes and went back to sleep...

SOMEWHERE ON THE ROAD TO CAEN
TUESDAY 6TH JUNE 1944 – 1400 HOURS

"Who is it?"

Smithson asked his Company Sergeant Major, who was still breathing heavily after his dash up to the front of the company column from his place at the rear.

"It's Lawton, Sir; from No.3 Platoon. It hit him smack in the side of the head."

Smithson tried not to remember what a head looked like when it had been hit by a high velocity bullet.

"Is he dead?"

"I'm afraid so, Sir."

Smithson cursed inwardly. The proposed 'dash for Caen' had proved to be anything but, thus far. In fact, to Smithson's mind, it was a painfully slow advance. When he compared it to the speed the German Army had once moved, way back in 1940, the snail's-pace progression of his own, heavily laden company gave rise to an uncomfortable feeling of inadequacy.

"Was it a sniper?" Smithson now asked the Company Sergeant Major; a small, wiry man by the name of Frampton.

"Hard to tell, Sir. It just came out of nowhere. The poor bugger was just a few yards in front of me. There's that many rounds flying around it's hard to tell what's just a stray and what's intentional."

Smithson nodded his understanding. Frampton was speaking the truth there. The fact was that there were thousands of men crammed into a few square miles, who were all firing at each other with everything they had. The laws of physics said that anything that didn't hit its intended target would keep on travelling through the air until it either hit something else or dropped out of the sky, its energy spent. And so his company had been advancing in this stop-start fashion for almost two hours now. One minute they would be tramping along, making good progress, then the next moment the young, inexperienced men of the Hambledon and Moorlanders would be throwing themselves into the hedge bottoms and ditches as a flurry of shots came cracking past them. So far, up until the unfortunate Lawton had taken a round through his head, nobody had been hurt, and those odd stray shots had been nothing more than an inconvenience.

Now, the constant up-down and stop-start dynamic was beginning to rattle the young infantrymen before they'd even got into battle properly. Smithson suspected that many of the random shots were coming from Objective Hillman, which the Suffolks from 8th Infantry Brigade were in the process of tackling and he was keen to get his men up and moving again. The sooner he could break out of the increasingly crowded beach-head and find some elbow room in the open country, the better.

"Right..." He decided, addressing Frampton. "There's not much we can do. Strip his essential kit off him and spread it amongst his platoon, then make a note of where he fell so we can pass it onto Battalion Headquarters later. There's no time to hang around. We need to get going."

Frampton nodded his understanding.

"Got it, Sir. I'll go sort it now and we can get cracking."

With that, the warrant officer jumped up and loped off back down the company column, keeping at a low crouch as he went.

Smithson watched him go for a moment then turned to his signaller.

"Alright Corporal Haines; tell One Platoon to get moving again. I want to be past Point 113 and heading into Periers by 1430 hours."

Haines nodded his understanding and immediately relayed the message over the company net. Amazingly, the radios seemed to be working quite well for a change and sure enough, just a couple of minutes later, the soldiers of No.1 Platoon, leading the company advance, began struggling to their feet again. Shaking off their aching limbs and adjusting their large packs, the men of the point platoon began tramping along the narrow road in the direction of Caen once more.

After a while, it was the turn of the company's headquarters to move off, and Smithson motioned to his small tactical headquarters group to follow on. As he stood up and looked beyond the thick hedgerows once more, Smithson noted how orange, green and red tracer was flying in all directions above the grey, drizzle-veiled landscape. Much of it was way over to his forward left and so he assumed that the Suffolks were still hard at it trying to secure Hillman. Somewhere in the middle distance, he could see drab, khaki figures trudging across the open fields in arrow-head formation; the Shropshires no doubt, making their own, careful way forward.

He forgot about everyone else now apart from his own company. He wanted to get them shaken out in a more dispersed formation just as soon as possible. Looking ahead, he could vaguely make out the slight ridge a few hundred yards in front, part of which appeared to be wooded. Point 113 he assumed. That would be the place, he reckoned. They would sweep over the small crossroads that lay hard by the small wooded knoll, and then shake out ready to occupy the ridge in strength. From that vantage point they would be able to get a first class view of the landscape beyond; perhaps all the way to Caen itself? Then they could advance on a broader front, with plenty of room for manoeuvre, and make a concerted attempt to clear a path all the way to the ancient city that was their objective for the day.

The pace picked up a little as the column got into its stride again, and Smithson began to hope that this time they would get going without being brought up short for no good reason. Smithson was desperate to impose his will on this battle today. In his last engagement with the Germans, some four years earlier when he was a brand spanking new ensign, Smithson had fallen victim to every possible friction of war imaginable. He had learnt in a hard school that war was filled with unpredictability, chaos, and just sheer bad luck. For years however, first whilst recovering from his wounds, then whilst training his men for this great expedition, Smithson had promised himself that next time around things would be different. This time it would be him, Smithson, who dictated circumstance. He would turn events to his own advantage and create his own opportunities; his own luck. That was the plan anyway, and as he squinted into the sudden flurry of drizzly wind that blew across the open fields of Normandy, he made a fresh resolution to keep his promise to himself.

Smithson was so busy turning all this over in his mind, that at first he didn't notice the sudden eruption of gunfire several hundred yards to his front. It was only when he saw Morrison, his runner, stop dead and turn around to look enquiringly at his officer that Smithson snapped out of his private thoughts and realised what was going on. Hearing the gunfire, Smithson stopped too. It was different this time. Instead of a lone 'crack' or a short burst of stray fire, there was the unmistakable sound of multiple weapons engaging in a rapid, ferocious exchange of fire. Then, just a second or two later, the first stray bullets came slicing through the air past Smithson.

Crack, crack, crack!

"Shit!" The young company commander let out a surprised yelp and dropped to one knee against the hedgerow.

All around him, the remainder of his Tactical HQ did the same.

Smithson frowned in the direction of the point platoon, from where he could hear the rattle of several sub-machine guns, the solid, dull report of rifle fire, and the chug-chug-chug of at least one Bren Gun. This was different, Smithson realised. This was very different. This sounded familiar. It sounded like a real battle. His thoughts were confirmed just a second later when Haines suddenly sat up sharply in the hedgerow nearby and clamped a hand over one ear piece of his headset. The lance corporal's face creased in concentration for a moment as he listened intently to something coming over the airwaves. Then, eyes alive with excitement, he looked up sharply, straight at Smithson.

"Message from One Platoon, Sir..." He shouted above the clatter of small arms fire. "Contact... Wait... Out..."

THE CRUCIBLE – POINT 113
TUESDAY 6TH JUNE 1944 – 1430 HOURS

"They're coming."

Gritz repeated the comment for about the twentieth time that minute. He was scanning the terrain over to his forward right with binoculars, concentrating on where a ferocious battle was obviously taking place in the vicinity of the regiment's headquarters position. The sergeant major lowered the binoculars and glanced at Sergeant Gunther who was standing beside him.

"They're definitely coming. There's Tommy infantry swarming all around the Colonel's position. If they come within range we will engage them with our machine guns; but only when we get a good line of sight. I don't want to reveal our position until the last moment, and our first shots need to count."

The commander of 'The Cripples' ran worried eyes along the line of trenches and improvised bunkers that had been constructed just inside the tree-line of the small wooded feature here on Point 113. It was the nature of things he realised, that when the enemy finally presented himself in front of your position, you became suddenly aware of that position's shortcomings. The thin strands of barbed wire that had been laid out in an irregular pattern between the trees and bushes on the edge of the wood line now seemed pathetically feeble. The neat trenches and bunkers, constructed from logs and wicker hurdles and covered over with packed earth, seemed laughably weak. If the concrete fortifications and thick belts of metal obstacles and wire on the coast hadn't managed to stop the enemy assault, then how was his little position?

Just as quickly, Gritz checked his negative thoughts. He'd been in these situations before; countless times in the frozen wastes of Russia, with waves and waves of T-34s and sub-human Siberian infantry charging towards him. And he'd held them hadn't he; every time? His left knee began to throb at the memory of his last close quarter engagement and for a brief moment a thrill of terror ran through him as he pictured the stinking, barbarian looking Russians pouring into the trench-lines of his company position; their teeth bared in ignorant, savage rage, and those big T-34 tanks rolling over the protective wire entanglements. Christ almighty, but that was what you called a desperate situation.

In his mind's eye he saw the dozens of Russian bodies that had been cut down on the bare white plain by his company's machine guns; remembered the brutal hand to hand battle as he and his men had risen up from their defences to meet the cheering enemy. He recalled the dull, sickly sound of bayonets and shovels biting into flesh; the crunch of bones and skulls as they were trampled and bludgeoned with rifle butts. And of course, he remembered the look in the eyes of the Russian soldier that he had strangled to death with his bare hands. Coming freely from his previously suppressed memories now, he remembered with enormous admiration how his young soldiers had thrown themselves physically against the enemy tanks, placing Teller mines by hand right in front of the lumbering metal beasts, often at the cost of their own lives.

"Do you think we can hold them?"

Gunther's question shook Gritz from his trance. The sergeant major looked directly at the platoon commander.

"Of course we can hold them." He said. "We've held the Ruskis back for three years; so a few Tommies shouldn't worry us. We can dominate the whole area from here. Besides; they don't even know we're here yet."

Gritz looked back out of the wood, across the gently sloping fields that were peppered with anti-glider poles, right down towards the coast, which was still partly obscured by smoke.

"I think it's time we brought the squad at the checkpoint back in. We'll use them to cover the approach from the left flank, where the track runs up to the ruins. Gunther, get one of you men to…"

Rat-tat-tat-tat-tat.

The sound of gunfire from just a few hundred yards away stopped Gritz in mid-sentence.

"That was close." Gunther said, scanning the fields beyond the wood.

"It came from the checkpoint." Gritz said tightly, clapping his eyes back against the binoculars and searching the surrounding countryside.

The first burst of sub-machine gun fire had been joined by the bark of rifle fire. After just a few seconds, the flurry of gunfire had transformed into a cacophony of weapon reports. Gritz had stopped scanning with his binoculars and was now staring directly down towards where the checkpoint was situated on the crossroads. Small wisps of gunsmoke rose from behind the thick hedgerows that bordered the narrow lanes and a single tracer round suddenly ricocheted directly upwards into the air from the same location.

"It's the checkpoint." Gritz snapped irritably. "Shit, shit, shit, it's the checkpoint..."

"Tommies." Gunther grunted from beside him.

"Where?"

"There, look. Just along the road towards Hermanville, just where it drops over that little false crest... About four knuckles right of the checkpoint as you look at it..."

Gritz thrust out his fist and peered along the length of his arm, using his knuckles as a measure in order to align himself onto the area described by Gunther. He squinted at the point on the ground that presented itself. There. Shit.

He saw the gunsmoke first; little puffs of it coming up from the undergrowth and hedgerows, and his ears picked up the sound of a machine gun firing at an unusually slow rate. A sudden flurry of movement caught Gritz's eye and he spotted the two khaki clad figures running at a low crouch where the road crested the first part of the ridge. They were here. Too late now. No time to redeploy or conduct any remedial work on his defences. There was no point in worrying now; it was time to fight. Just like in Russia, Gritz thought.

He lowered his arm and turned to Gunther.

"Cancel my last. The checkpoint squad will have to make their own decisions now. The Tommies are here; and that bunch down there are just the first few of a shit load more. We need to get ready for action. Pass the word... Stand-to and prepare for immediate action..."

LEGG'S TANK – HALF A MILE SOUTH OF HERMANVILLE TUESDAY 6TH JUNE 1944 – 1430 HOURS

"There's another Sherman look; over on the left! I think it's one of ours!"

It was Wells, the gunner, who spotted the tank, coming in from the left along a connecting road. Legg swung his gaze in that direction, and spotted the distinctive turret of the vehicle as it trundled along behind the thick hedgerow bordering the hidden road. The tank's commander was sitting up in the cupola, as was Legg, and the corporal saw the man waving cheerily towards them. In front of Legg's tank, Saddler, also up in his cupola, was waving back at the new comer.

Saddler's tank suddenly gave a spurt of exhaust fumes and juddered into life; rolling forward towards the junction just ahead. Within moments, Saddler's tank and the new arrival had met, nose to nose by the T-junction. Legg saw Saddler removing his headset and begin hauling himself out of his turret. Legg decided to follow suit.

"Wait here." He told his own crew. "I'm going forward with Titch to see who that lot are."

Quickly, he removed his ear phones and dragged himself over the edge of the cupola, slid down the turret, then dropped off the hull and onto the road.

As he began to walk somewhat stiffly towards the junction, he checked his watch, which by now was removed from its protective contraceptive wrapping and back on his wrist. It was smack on half past two.

"Bloody hell!" He murmured to himself, surprised at how quickly time had moved on and how slowly they seemed to be making progress.

In some ways, that wasn't too much of a surprise. If the beach was clogged up, the area just beyond the beach was just as bad. Not only was the landscape dotted with huge shell craters, piles of rubble, collapsed walls and fallen telegraph poles and trees, but the fields, roads and woods just inland of the coastal strip were clogged with infantrymen, engineers and every kind of staff officer, all of them trying to bring order to the chaos as they jostled for elbow room and established RVs, checkpoints, collection points, stores and ammunition dumping points, casualty and prisoner collection points, and God only knew what else.

Over the last hour or so, Legg and Saddler had slowly trundled forwards through Hermanville, trying to locate the Hambledon and Moorlanders, the infantry battalion they had been told to support. Instead, the two tank commanders had come across just about every regiment of the line other than the Hambledons. They'd found the exhausted survivors of the South Lancashire Regiment, who'd come ashore in the first wave and stormed the beach defences with the East Yorkshires. They'd found the Kings Shropshire Light Infantry, or at least the back end of them. They'd even bumped into the Quartermaster and Battalion Headquarters of the Suffolks, but as yet they'd still not found the Hambledons. They must have really got cracking, Legg reckoned.

He broke from his consideration of this point for a moment as he passed Saddler's tank and came up to the nose of the third Sherman. Instantly he recognised the painted symbols on the turret and realised that he was looking at a vehicle from 'C' Squadron. A moment later, he glanced up past Saddler, who was already clambering up the hull of the tank, and recognised the face of a young troop leader from that squadron; a fairly new young gentleman by the name of Mr Barratt.

"Hello, Sir…" Saddler was greeting the second lieutenant. "I thought for a moment we were the only ones who had got off the beach."

The young officer moved his headset to one side and wiped a hand across his tired, dirty face.

"Yes, we thought the same…" The officer replied, the stress of the last few hours evident in his voice. I think we might be the only one from our squadron. Three of us got off the beach behind a couple of engineer vehicles, but the other two got knocked out quite quickly by some anti-tank guns that were in depth of the beach. Then the breach got blocked behind us when two more vehicles got knocked out, right in the middle of it. We've been helping No.4 Commando clear the villages down the way there…" He turned and waved back down the road. "What about you chaps? What are you up to?"

Saddler quickly regaled Barratt with the details of his and Legg's exploits thus far that day, and finished with explaining their latest orders.

"Some captain from the Divisional Staff told us to follow this road and link up with the 1st Hambledon and Moorlanders, but we can't find the buggers anywhere. We've found just about every other unit, but no sign of the Hambledons."

At Saddler's words, the officer brightened.

"Ah! I can help you there. I got given a similar order to you and I've been blundering about trying to find them too. I've just bumped into their second in command, his tactical headquarters and one of his reserve companies just back here, about two hundred yards. Their point company is up that road there, exactly where you're heading. He says they can't be more than half a mile in front, and their colonel is just a little way behind them with his tactical headquarters and another reserve company."

Saddler let out a sigh of relief.

"Thank God for that. I thought we'd never find 'em."

He looked back at Barratt.

"So, it looks like the three of us then, Sir?"

Barratt grinned.

"Strength in numbers, eh?" He laughed; an ironic sound, Legg thought. "Well, I suppose we'd better make sure we can all talk to each other before we go any further. Are you two both on the same net?"

Saddler confirmed that both he and Legg were on the same squadron frequency.

"Alright then..." Barratt said. "We'll net in to your frequency for now. Once we've got it sorted we can push on."

He glanced across to Saddler's tank which, unlike his own or Legg's, sported a long, deadly looking 17 Pounder gun instead of the standard 75mm short barrelled gun.

"Nice to have a Firefly on the team." Barratt grinned. "Haven't seen any Jerry tanks yet but I'm sure they'll have some hanging around the place."

"Let the fuckers come, Sir." Saddler grunted. "Let the fuckers come..."

It was as the three tank commanders were conferring that the sound of fresh small arms fire filled the air, somewhere to the south of their position, and just a few hundred yards by the sound of it. The exchange of fire began as a few desultory thumps and a rattle of machine gun fire then quickly escalated into what sounded like a rather vicious fire fight. The three tank men immediately looked off in the direction off the gunfire. Beyond the hedgerows and patchwork of fields, they could vaguely make out a low ridge, perhaps a mile or more in the distance. Somewhere between that ridgeline and their present position, somebody was having a good scrap, as evidenced by the little blobs of tracer that kept shooting off into the air in various directions.

"I reckon we just found the Hambledons..." Saddler commented.

"Yeah, and so have the Jerries by the sounds of it..." Legg added grimly.

Barratt looked first at Saddler, then down at Legg, then back to Saddler again.

"I suppose we'd better march to the sound of the guns then?"

THE POINT PLATOON – 'A' COMPANY, 1ST BATTALION, HAMBLEDON AND MOORLANDERS
TUESDAY 6TH JUNE 1944 – 1430 HOURS

Second Lieutenant Jeremy Willis nearly jumped out of his skin when the first burst of gunfire came cracking past his ears so unexpectedly. He'd never been in action before and, regardless of all the training and the battle inoculation exercises, the feel of his first real battle was decidedly unnerving. Prior to all of this, there had been the long, boring and highly frustrating waiting period aboard the landing craft, followed by the chaotic shambles of the beach itself. The mass of men and vehicles, combined with the sight of real dead people, the stench of smoke and blood, along with the fog of war, had all combined to create a sense of disorientation for Willis.

Even after they had cleared the beach area, sorted themselves out at the Battalion Assembly Area, and commenced their trek towards their key objective for the day, the sense of disorientation had continued. The enemy didn't seem to be behaving in the way Willis had assumed they would. Instead of remaining conveniently static in a series of very obvious defensive positions, the enemy were nothing more than fleeting figures in the distance; an odd man here, two fleeting figures in a hedgerow there. The enemy shelling and mortar fire had been random and inconvenient, whilst the gunfire had consisted mainly of sporadic shots that caused the company to pull up short each time, before carrying on nervously towards Caen. All in all, it had made the nervous young ensign even more jumpy than he already was.

It was just as Willis was beginning to settle down and get accustomed to the nature of his first military operation, that he learned the same lesson that generations of soldiers before him had also had to learn; normally the hard way. In war, life is often dull; the time dragging on endlessly with nothing more than the occasional, mundane task or fatigue to punctuate the boredom. But then, when the mind is lulled into a false sense of security, it happens. There come those few minutes, sometimes several hours, of absolute frantic and bloody chaos, that leaves the mind stunned by the sudden whirlwind of events, one upon the other. And that was exactly what Willis was experiencing now.

The first flurry of high velocity rifle shots cracked through the air, the sharp sound assaulting the young officer's ear drums as he gave a yelp of surprise. Before he had the chance to register that these shots were much closer than anything yet experienced, a rapid burst of automatic fire followed, the half dozen bullets slicing past the officer as he dived, unceremoniously, into the ditch and hedgerow to his right.

Suddenly, all was noise. The constant, menacing crack of bullets permeated the air above Willis' head, backed by the sharp report of rifles and machine guns thumping away. The sheer volume of the gunfire made Willis realise that the enemy on this occasion were much closer than previously experienced. What was more, they seemed to be smack bang in front of his platoon, shooting straight down the length of it.

The young platoon commander hit the shallow ditch with a thud that knocked the wind out of him, and he felt his signaller drop heavily beside him. Across the road, he saw his runner throw himself almost head first into the ditch opposite. The sound of frantic shouting came from just up ahead, and as Willis pushed up the rim of his helmet and arched his neck back to get a proper view of the road ahead, he spotted two khaki figures lying on the cobbles of the road about fifty yards ahead. One of them was flat on his back and perfectly still, his rifle lain across his chest. The second man, also on his back, was flapping his arms around heavily, like a drunk trying to get up after falling in the gutter.

Even as the young officer began to take in these details, he heard more weapons begin to join the cacophony of the fire-fight. A Bren Gun was in action somewhere up ahead, chugging away in its stolid, reliable fashion, and the metallic chatter of a Sten Gun also punctuated the heavier background noise of rifles. He rolled over onto his right shoulder and looked back at his platoon signaller. The private soldier, who was no older than Willis himself, was dripping with sweat. Despite the dull skies and occasional cloudburst of rain, it was uncomfortably humid. The man's eyes were wide and his face pale as he pressed himself in low against the grass bank of the ditch. Willis suspected that he probably looked very much the same as his radio operator at this point in time.

"Selby; tell the Company Commander we're in contact. Enemy front, about a hundred and fifty yards!"

The signaller nodded and immediately began speaking into his microphone.

Willis took another quick look up the road. He could see the scrim-camouflaged helmets of the men from No.1 Section as they popped up from amongst the long grass of the verge to return fire back down the road. Other than that, he could see little of what was beyond, and certainly no enemy. That they were just a little way ahead wasn't in doubt. The crack and thump of gunfire was constant now, with not a second of quiet between individual shots or bursts. The noise was so loud that he could barely make his voice heard as he shouted across to his runner.

"Naylor? Naylor?"

The man couldn't hear him above the din, so Willis took a deep breath and shouted as loud as he could, his vocal chords protesting at the strain.

"Naylor!"

The young soldier's face swung towards him, peering through the grass on the opposite verge.

"Get over here!" Willis shouted.

The young man just stared at him dumbly for a second, before shouting something back. Willis couldn't hear the man's voice, but he saw his lips move.

"What?" The young soldier was mouthing.

"Come over here!" Willis shouted again, and this time reinforced the order by placing the fist of his right hand on top of his helmet, then removing it and pumping the same fist up and down in mid-air several times; the infantry field signal for *'on me, at the double.'*

The sudden change of expression on Naylor's face, from one of confusion to one of utter shock, told Willis that his runner had finally understood the order. Despite the young man's obvious distress, he gathered himself for a dash across the road never-the-less. Willis looked on as Naylor prepared to crawl over the cobbles; but the runner then appeared to change his mind and levered himself up onto all fours.

"Come on; quickly!" Willis pressured the man.

A moment later, the soldier sprang up and leapt across the road, almost bent double as he raced over the exposed stretch of highway. Naylor was moving so fast and bending so low, that just as he reached the grass verge on Willis' side, his bodyweight carried him beyond tipping point and he half fell, half dived, headfirst into the ditch between Willis and Selby.

The poor soldier tumbled head over heels, kicking Willis in the head as he passed by him, and collapsed into the bottom of the ditch in a jumble of arms, legs and equipment. Rubbing his ear which was stinging from the impact of a hob-nailed boot, Willis reached down with the other and grabbed hold of Naylor by his webbing braces.

"Are you alright, Naylor?" He asked, pulling the soldier upright, terrified in case the man had been hit by a bullet as he dashed across the open ground.

To Willis' relief, Private Naylor pushed himself up awkwardly and looked round at his platoon commander.

"Yeah..." The young man was breathing as if he'd just run a five mile sprint. "I think so..."

As Naylor struggled to adjust the ammunition bandoliers that were threatening to strangle him, Willis began issuing instructions to the sweating runner.

"Listen; there's some kind of problem up in front. It sounds like we've walked into a bunch of Jerries. I want you to go forward and find the section commander of the point section. Find out what..."

Before Willis could finish his sentence, his signaller was tapping him on the arm and pointing up the road.

"Someone's coming back, Sir."

Willis broke off and twisted round to look back up the road towards the point section. One of the men from that section was indeed coming back towards them; moving along the shallow ditch and scrambling over his fellow soldiers on all fours. Willis saw the man's helmet and equipment swinging from side to side as he struggled through the undergrowth and past the other men until, after a moment or two, he spotted the single chevron on the man's battledress sleeve.

"It's Lance Corporal Vincent." Willis realised out loud.

Seconds later, Vincent, the second in command of No.1 Section, dropped down alongside Willis heavily, his face bright red and pouring with sweat, his breathing ragged and laboured.

"Contact..." The lance corporal managed to gasp. "Up front... about a hundred yards to our front... right on the crossroads..."

The man paused slightly as a spasm ran through him and he fought to control his breathing. It was scary how fit, young men could be reduced to exhaustion so quickly under the weight of full battle order and the stress of close contact with the enemy, Willis reflected. Suddenly his own stomach felt empty and his limbs weak.

Vincent recovered his breathing and went on.

"They're on the junction... the crossroads. Don't know how many... but... they've got a machine gun of some sort and we're getting hit from a couple of different directions... We've got two men hit and we're pinned down... What do you want us to do?"

The question hit Willis like a slap in the face. He had come to Normandy excited, nervous, but generally confident that he was as well trained for what lay ahead as he could be. But this was it. Somehow, the starkness of reality took him by surprise. They were *really* in a battle; his men were *really* getting killed and wounded. And he was *really* in charge. There would be no whistle to signal the 'end of exercise' this time; no closing-in for debrief and a discussion on tactics. No words of advice from an umpire. This was for real and the only umpires were wearing German uniforms. Willis was in charge, and now his men were looking to him for an answer. What *were* they going to do?

COMPANY HEADQUARTERS – 'A' COMPANY, 1ST BATTALION, HAMBLEDON AND MOORLANDERS TUESDAY 6TH JUNE 1944 – 1440 HOURS

"Ask them what on earth is going on?" Smithson snapped at Haines. "I can tell they're in contact; but I want to know what they're doing about it?"

The corporal nodded and immediately began talking into the microphone again, demanding a more detailed situation report from the point platoon. The bullets had been cracking past them and overhead for more than five minutes now, almost ten, and still there was no information coming back from the point platoon. In a few more minutes, Smithson fully expected the Commanding Officer to be pressing him for information in turn.

"Where's the Company Commander?"

Smithson twisted round at the sound of the voice. He saw a private soldier doubling along the lip of the ditch, coming towards him from the direction of the fire-fight.

"Over here!" Smithson shouted at the soldier who was bending over almost double. "Oi! Over here!" He waved his arm madly to get the man's attention above the racket of small arms fire.

The soldier glanced up, spotted Smithson waving at him, and came running directly towards him. As he got near, a rattle of three rapid gunshots cracked close by the young man and he literally skipped sideways into the ditch, and began scrambling the last few metres on hands and knees.

"Message from Mr Willis, Sir!" The private shouted at him as he got up close.

The runner from the point platoon slumped down against the bank next to Smithson and leaned back against the earth, pushing his helmet rim up and loosening his chinstrap as he gulped in air like a drowning man.

"What is it?" Smithson demanded. "What's going on?"

The runner from No.1 Platoon took several deep breaths, gathered his thoughts, then delivered his message in one long burst.

"He's tried to pass a message on the radio but he doesn't think you've got it because it keeps breaking up. Contact front, Sir; about a hundred yards to our front, right on the crossroads. He thinks there are a couple of trenches maybe; one on either side of the road. Our point section got hit at close range and they've got two men down. Mr Willis has asked for permission to attack, Sir. He wants to go left flanking."

His message delivered, the soldier went silent and awaited the response. For a couple of moments, Smithson just stared back at the man, feeling a little flabbergasted.

"Why's he asking me for permission? Of course I want him to bloody attack!" The major suddenly blurted, his thoughts coming out unintentionally.

Smithson saw the slight look of surprise on the runner's face and instantly regretted his own words. What else could he expect? These men weren't veterans after all. This was all new to them.

"Listen…" He began again, taking the edge out of his voice. "Go back and tell Mr Willis that he has my permission to attack. Tell him I want him to launch his attack immediately. I don't mind if he goes left flanking or if he just rushes the crossroads; I just want him to take out those enemy trenches as quickly as possible. We can't afford to get bogged down every time we bump into a small pocket of enemy. Does all that make sense?"

The runner nodded back vigorously.

"Yes, Sir; got it. You want him to attack immediately."

"Quite so." Smithson confirmed.

The major thought for a second, then reached for his notebook.

"Here, take him this note…"

Removing his notebook and pencil from his battledress pocket, Smithson quickly scribbled down a brief note in block capitals.

LAUNCH IMMEDIATE ATTACK <u>NOW</u> AND CLEAR CROSSROADS OF ENEMY. DO NOT WAIT FOR FURTHER ORDERS. <u>ATTACK NOW</u>. REPORT BACK WHEN CROSSROADS CLEARED. <u>GET MOVING</u>!

Smithson quickly scanned the words he'd written. They appeared a little peremptory; sharp even. But this wasn't the time for fatherly advice and pleasantries. The battalion advance was already behind schedule and they needed to plough on through small scale opposition such as this. Smithson ripped the page carefully out of his notebook and handed it to the runner.

"Take this back to Mr Wills and show him. Tell him what I've just said. No more delay. Attack now and drive on…"

THE POINT PLATOON – 'A' COMPANY, 1ST BATTALION, HAMBLEDON AND MOORLANDERS
TUESDAY 6TH JUNE 1944 – 1450 HOURS

Willis looked from one section commander to the other, then to Sergeant Askey, his Platoon Sergeant.

"Everyone got that?" He asked.

The three men nodded and assured him they had. They were keyed up; their faces serious, eyes bulging from sockets in anticipation of the coming fight.

"Alright, go and get your men ready to move. As soon as you've briefed them, No.2 Section can lead off. My group will drop in behind you."

Without further discussion, the small orders group broke up and the three NCOs began scrambling away towards their own sections, keeping as low as possible in the process.

Sergeant Askey, along with his light mortarman and a medic, pushed past the officer and began crawling forwards towards where No.1 Section was still fully engaged in a close range fire-fight with the enemy on the crossroads. Willis watched the three men go, festooned as they were with mortar bomb satchels and bandoliers of small arms ammunition. He was starting to feel as though he was gaining control of the situation now. Just a few minutes ago he had received the Company Commander's categorical, written instruction; ATTACK NOW. That had been reinforced by the verbal brief that his runner relayed to him.

At that stage, the training from the battle school had started to kick in and Willis had begun putting together his plan of attack. Judging by the amount of stray rounds that continued to fly past them along the road, there was no chance of just rushing the enemy, and so Willis had decided to take his rear two sections left flanking, crossing the fields to their left until they reached another road that ran back towards the enemy held crossroads. His point section, reinforced by the Platoon Sergeant's group, would keep the enemy occupied whilst he and the remainder of the platoon hit the crossroads from the flank. The more he thought about the plan, the neater it seemed in his mind.

"Okay, Sir; we're ready to go!"

He turned and saw that Corporal Lewis, the commander of No.2 Section, was giving a thumbs-up signal from where his men were now lined up behind him in the ditch.

"Righto; wait for the smoke…" Willis replied.

He turned away momentarily and nodded to his runner.

"Alright Naylor, you can throw it now."

The young soldier needed no further prompting. He lifted the cylindrical, pale-green No.77 Grenade and began preparing the device. Just moments later, Willis watched the runner lean back, arm outstretched, then hurl the smoke grenade through the air towards the centre of the road a little way in front. The small object arced through the grey afternoon light, the long priming tape flowing behind it, and then just a moment later it bounced onto the cobbles.

Instantly there was a loud 'pop' and a cloud of thick white smoke billowed out of the device, hiding it from view in a moment and filling the roadway with a dense, artificial fog. Almost immediately, Willis heard the scraping of boots on cobbles and turned back towards No.2 Section. They were already out of the ditch and racing across the road as individual bullets sliced through the smoke screen and cracked off towards Hermanville. Amazingly, all of the men from No.2 Section got across the road without being hit and, suddenly remembering the order of march to their forming up point, Willis struggled to his feet, ready to follow them over.

"Come on, chaps..." He shouted over his shoulder to Selby and Naylor, and they too began scrambling to their feet, following on behind.

Willis was across the road in seconds, followed swiftly by his runner and radio operator. No.3 Section followed them almost instantly so that now, the ditch on this side of the road was chock full of men. That would not last however for No.2 Section were already forcing their way through a gap in the thick hedgerow. Willis could see white smoke billowing up above the line of the hedge from the field beyond, showing that Corporal Lewis was taking no chances as he led the platoon across the field towards the next hedgerow. This was more like it. At last, everything was falling into place as it should do as part of the platoon battle drill. As Willis clambered to his feet and made for the gap in the hedgerow, he noticed that the riflemen in both of his rear sections had fixed their spike bayonets.

Now at the gap in the hedgerow, the young ensign reached up and grabbed hold of the bushes on either side of the narrow cutting. Gripping the thorny branches with both hands, he hauled himself up out of the ditch and over the slight berm on which the hedgerow was situated. He tumbled through the gap and into the next field, fighting to keep his footing as he did so. White smoke filled the field and the figures of No.2 Section flicked in and out of the artificial fog like ghosts as they ran across the open pasture in the wake of their section commander. Willis followed them, noticing that the smoke screen seemed to me moving with them. With a little spark of surprise, Willis realised that Corporal Lewis must be kicking the smoke grenade along the ground in front of him as he ran. Clever that, he thought absently.

As he raced through the thinning smoke, Willis glanced back over his shoulder and saw Selby following him, his face contorted with effort as he lumbered along with the heavy radio. Behind Selby, Naylor followed close on his heels, muttering encouragement to the signaller. Willis looked forwards again and saw the hedgerow that bordered the next road suddenly loom up beyond the remains of the smoke screen. He could see the men of No.2 Section lining up against the thick undergrowth whilst Corporal Lewis and another rifleman tore at a slight gap with their rifle butts, battering the branches and foliage aside as they fought to make an exit from the field. Within a few more seconds, Willis, Selby and Naylor were all in line behind No.2 Section, with the men from No.3 Section now crossing the last few yards of open ground to peel in behind the column of men.

The young platoon commander noted with satisfaction that there didn't seem to be any fire coming towards them as they crossed the open field and began their approach towards the enemy position. His plan was working. As long as the point section could keep the Jerries occupied for a couple more minutes then he would be ready to swoop down on the crossroads from the left and roll the enemy position up in a short, tidy little attack. Even as he planned the next phase of his attack, the men in front of Willis began moving again. One by one they disappeared through the gap in the hedge made by Corporal Lewis. Beckoning to his radio operator and runner, Willis stood up and began to follow on.

He was very quickly through the hedge and found himself on another road, very much the same as the one on which his platoon had been contacted. As he emerged onto the road, he glanced to his right and spotted the crossroads about a hundred and twenty yards away. Gun smoke drifted across the open roadway and the thump of rifles and clatter of machine guns told him that the enemy still occupied the position. At the far side of the crossroads, the road disappeared off at a diagonal up and across the ridge and out of sight.

Within a couple of minutes, both of Willis' sections were through the hedgerow and formed up in staggered file on either side of the road. Quickly, he called his two section commanders together.

"Right chaps; we'll move down towards the crossroads in staggered file with Two Section in front and Three Section behind. As we get closer to the junction we should be able to pinpoint the Jerry trenches. As soon as you see the first one Corporal Lewis, you get straight in there with your lads. Corporal Armstrong; you wait for me to give you the nod to pass through and assault anything that's in depth. All clear?"

They nodded. It was perfectly clear. It was familiar to them. The platoon battle drill was designed to make things easy during the chaos of battle. It was a set sequence of procedures that could be superimposed onto any situation in any terrain and would allow for a variation in circumstance. So far, everything was going to plan.

Unfortunately for Willis and his platoon, the enemy at the crossroads were not on their own. The enemy's small position was just an outlying post; a checkpoint, of a larger and very well sited position, just three hundred yards away on Point 113. Not only that, the man who commanded that position was a veteran of several campaigns, including three years on the Eastern Front. That commander had seen every type of battle drill you could care to mention and understood the use of ground like a fox. And now that commander was up in the wood-line on Point 113 and had decided that the time had come to spring his trap.

The first thing Willis knew of that was when something red, wet and with an iron-like taste spurted into his face and Corporal Armstrong gave a surprised grunt, before slamming face down onto the cobbles with a loud thud. That strange occurrence was followed in less than a second by the unbelievably rapid crack-crack-crack-crack-crack of machine gun bullets ripping through the nearby hedge at a breathtaking rate. More men went down in both sections; some unintentionally whilst others threw themselves flat in terror as the hedgerow that lay between themselves and Point 113 suddenly erupted as if it was alive.

Shocked and half-blinded by the blood that had spurted across his face, Willis toppled sideways onto the cobbles and tried to roll onto the verge as he realised with horror that he and his men had just walked into an ambush. Bullet after bullet ripped through the hedgerow, slamming into flesh or dirt, and ricocheting off the cobbles with a fiendish whine, as the men from Willis' platoon tried to press themselves as far into the ground as they could.

Crack-crack-crack-crack-crack-crack-crack-crack!

Above the deafening, ceaseless cracking of bullets, Willis registered another sound; a distant, unusual noise, not dissimilar to the ripping of canvas. Although he hadn't yet realised it, this was a noise that Willis and his surviving men would get to know very well over the coming days and weeks in Normandy. It was the sound of the MG42 general purpose machine gun, the German Army's outstanding medium machine gun that would be referred to as the *'Spandau'* by some, or *'Hitler's Buzz-saw'* by others. Whatever its name, it was deadly, and right now, it was doing its terrible work with relish.

"Take cover…" Willis heard himself shouting. "Take cover!"

THE CRUCIBLE – POINT 113
TUESDAY 6TH JUNE 1944 – 1450 HOURS

"Gunther? Send one of your men up to the command post. Tell Corporal Kole to ring the checkpoint. I want him to tell them to withdraw. Tell them to disengage and withdraw up the track towards the ruins of the forge. They are to occupy the fall back trenches on the slopes of the saddle. Understand?"

He tore his eyes away from the fire-fight down by the crossroads and fixed the sergeant with a serious look.

"Got it." Gunther nodded to him, his face equally grim, and turned away, shouting for one of his men.

Gritz looked back out across the slopes toward the crossroads. He was still cursing himself inwardly. He should have withdrawn them earlier. Still, it was too late to worry now. At least he knew that the Tommies were here for certain. He must now try to pull the checkpoint squad back to the main position and then begin orchestrating the defensive battle that would surely develop. He wanted to keep the Tommies guessing; make them dance to his tune and put themselves into his killing areas. If only he had a mortar…

"It's sorted."

Gunther was back beside Gritz again.

"I've sent someone. Do you think it's worth ringing the Colonel's position and seeing if we can get some artillery or mortars brought down?"

Gritz pulled a face.

"You must have been reading my mind. Mortars would be useful; artillery too. Not yet though. We can't see exactly where the Tommies are. I suspect that eventually they'll start to pile up behind that false crest beyond the crossroads. Once we've got a nice big bunch of them in one place we'll see if we can get the Colonel to rustle something up for us. At the moment however, I think he's busy enough…"

Gritz broke off in mid-sentence. He was staring back down the slope towards where the fire-fight raged amongst the hedgerows. He had spotted something.

"Smoke." Gunther observed.

"Yes…" Gritz watched as the fluffy white cloud of artificial smoke began to rise above the thick hedges that bordered the road towards Hermanville.

"If it's just an advance guard of reconnaissance troops they might be pulling back over the crest?" Gunther suggested.

"Possibly…" Gritz murmured, raising his binoculars once more and focussing them on the area concerned.

"They're certainly up to something..." The sergeant major mumbled to himself; then, "Hello? What's this?"

The smoke seemed to be increasing in its footprint. Originally confined to the roadway that was hidden between the thick shrubbery of the bordering hedges, the smoke seemed to be spreading now; off to the right hand side as Gritz looked at it. There was smoke in the adjacent field to the road, and it seemed to be rolling closer and closer by the second.

"They're putting in a flank attack on the crossroads." Gritz snapped suddenly as he realised what the British were doing. "They're covering their move round... They're heading for this nearest road right in front of us...."

Next to Gritz, Gunther gave a snort of grim amusement.

"It's nice of them to mark their route for us." The sergeant observed.

"Yes..." Gritz was studying the lay of the smoke screen, estimating where the enemy were headed for. "They're well drilled, but not very experienced. They should have smoked off their whole frontage. Instead you can literally trace their route. Look..."

He pointed towards the nearest road that ran left to right in front of The Crucible.

"They'll cut this road almost right in front of us. Their commander intends to follow this road down to the crossroads using the hedges as cover and then assault our checkpoint from the flank. It's straight out of the textbook."

Again, Gunther snorted.

"Textbook is predictable." He commented.

"Exactly." Gritz snapped, lowering his binoculars. "So we'll have to give them a lesson in tactics they'll never forget. Prepare your platoon to open fire on my order at the rapid rate. Get the 42 to lay onto that telegraph pole there..." He pointed downslope towards the relevant spot. "And then they can traverse right after each burst when I give the order."

Gunther smiled wickedly and acknowledged the order, before stepping away and rattling out a string of fire control orders to his men. Just off to the left of Gritz, the three man crew of the MG42 unlocked their gun and began aligning it onto the designated aiming point. Gritz put the binoculars back to his eyes.

He could see them now. Feint, indistinct figures, heavily laden and jogging clumsily across the field, only half hidden by the pale, drifting smoke. They looked as if they were running straight towards him, and one by one they disappeared behind the hedgerow that ran laterally across the front of his company position.

"Stand-by..." Gritz rapped out, staring intently towards the distant field.

The last enemy soldier appeared to have crossed the field now and the last of the smoke was dissipating quickly.

"Straight through the hedgerow; not too high... aim low." He called out to the men around him.

The sergeant major took one last look at the hedgerow, lowered his binoculars then counted silently to five; just enough time to let them all get through the far hedgerow and onto the road.

"On my order... rapiiiid..." Gritz raised his voice as he judged his moment.

He paused for just one more heartbeat as he felt the old familiar thrill of battle rise up within.

"Fire!"

The trenches that lined the forward edge of the wood erupted with the deafening roar of concentrated small arms fire, and Gritz watched with professional satisfaction as the first lines of tracer sliced down the slope and disappeared through the dark, leafy wall of the hedgerow. The killing had begun.

THE POINT PLATOON – 'A' COMPANY, 1ST BATTALION, HAMBLEDON AND MOORLANDERS TUESDAY 6TH JUNE 1944 – 1500 HOURS

"Oh, Christ!"

Willis was laying flat on his stomach, staring at the prostrate bodies of Corporal Armstrong and Private Naylor, both of whom lay dead in an ever growing pool of blood on the nearby road. Somewhere along the hedgerow, another member of his platoon was screaming hysterically as a comrade tried to calm him down and apply dressings to his wounds. Willis was completely stunned. His orderly line of men were now piled up against the hedgerow; some wounded, some dead, the remainder utterly stunned by the deluge of fire that had just ripped through the foliage and torn through their ranks.

"They're up on the fucking hill!" Somebody was shouting.

Willis barely heard the words. The crack of passing bullets was constant and so loud that he could hardly hear himself think.

"Mason! Get that fucking Bren Gun in action! Littelwood! Get your rifle up and start firing at the fucking tree-line on the hill!"

Somewhere behind Willis, a voice was roaring out orders, attempting to compete with the racket of small arms fire. The young second lieutenant managed to tear his eyes away from the two dead men on the road and twist round to look behind him.

Corporal Lewis was there. Good old Corporal Lewis; dependable as ever. The young NCO was crawling along the bottom of the hedgerow on all fours, yelling at his men and physically getting a grip of them. One by one he was dragging them up from the floor and pushing them into fire positions against the earthen bank on which the hedgerow had been planted. In addition to the crack of passing bullets, Willis could also hear the dull thud of rounds slapping into the far side of the earth bank. Ignorant to the danger of imminent death however, Lewis was making his way back and forth along the verge, growling, threatening, cajoling the men into action.

"Come on you fuckers! Get up against the bank and start fucking firing back! The Jerries are on the hill; in the wood-line. Rapid fire at the wood-line on the hill!"

The corporal seemed to be possessed by some kind of primeval warrior spirit, his face almost purple with exertion as he exercised his grip over the terrified soldiers of No.1 Platoon.

"Corporal Darwin! Corporal Darwin!"

Lewis had reached the end of his own section and was trying to get the attention of Lance Corporal Darwin, the second in command of No.3 Section.

"Corporal Darwin! Take over Three Section! Corporal Armstrong's dead; you're in charge! Now get some fucking fire down on that wood-line!"

The corporal turned around and began scrambling back along the hedgerow towards Willis. Midway, he paused and delivered a harsh slap against the side of one young soldier's head. The private looked round in surprise, his face etched with fear.

"Oi!" Lewis raged at the man. "Stop fucking wasting ammunition! Get your eye up to that rear-sight and aim that fucking rifle properly!"

His rebuke delivered, Lewis scrambled onwards, coming quickly up to Willis.

The corporal dropped from his 'monkey-run' position and flattened himself on his belly next to Willis.

"Bastards have ambushed us, Sir! That position on the crossroads is just bait. Their main position is up on that hill inside the trees. We're sitting ducks down here. I reckon we've got three dead and maybe a couple more wounded on top of that…"

The corporal was pouring with sweat and he wiped his battledress sleeve across his face irritably, before squinting at Willis.

"What we going to do now, Sir?"

The stark query hit Willis like a slap in the face. For the second time that morning he had been asked that dreaded question; the one that all military commanders find themselves faced with in battle. The question to which their men will always expect an answer. Willis wracked his brains. What the hell *were* they going to do now?

He looked sideways to where Private Selby lay pressed flat against the grass verge, his radio set strapped to his back making him look like a giant khaki and green snail.

"Selby!" Willis managed to find his voice and shouted over the din of gunfire. "Get hold of the Company Commander on that radio. Tell him I need to speak to him… urgently…"

COMPANY HEADQUARTERS – 'A' COMPANY, 1ST BATTALION, HAMBLEDON AND MOORLANDERS TUESDAY 6TH JUNE 1944 – 1505 HOURS

Smithson looked over his shoulder at Captain Tom Winters, the Mortar Platoon Commander, who had been sent up to join his company.

"Bloody hell, Tom; I don't like the sound of that!"

The sudden eruption of heavy small arms fire to the forward left indicated that No.1 Platoon had either launched their assault on the crossroads or had run into trouble. Smithson, who had fought the Germans before, and even used one of their machine guns, recognised that the sound of the gunfire indicated more enemy weapons in action than British.

"I don't blame you Dickie." The captain replied. "Look at all that…"

Smithson followed the other officer's outstretched arm and looked southwards towards where the ground rose gently towards a ridgeline. The crest of that ridge was only just visible above the tall hedgerows, but even so, the flash of tracer coming down from the tree-line on the crest of that ridge was evident enough.

"Bugger me!" Smithson exclaimed. "The Jerries aren't supposed to be up there in any strength. There were just meant to be a couple of checkpoints along this road…"

As soon as he'd said the words, Smithson realised how naive they sounded. He'd fought the Germans before and he knew how adaptable they were; how thorough. Why *would* they leave a perfectly good elevated position free of troops? Did he really think that British intelligence would have discovered *every* enemy position prior to the invasion?

"Message from No.1 Platoon, Sir…"

Corporal Haines' voice snapped him out of his thoughts.

"What is it?"

"From their Sunray, Sir. He's gone left flanking and been ambushed by a large enemy force on the hill. They've taken casualties and they're pinned down on the next road."

Smithson felt his stomach tighten. It was happening again, just like back in 1940; events were starting to spiral out of control. He felt his shoulder begin to throb. He realised there and then that he had just minutes to get a grip of things before they descended into chaos, and bloody chaos at that. He snapped his head back round to look at Winters.

The captain was already studying his map and reading off bearings and grid references to his own signaller. He paused briefly, looking up at Smithson.

"I'll get some mortar fire brought down on that hill, Dickie; give you a bit of time to think and take the pressure off Jeremy's platoon."

Smithson felt a wave of gratitude sweep over him at the Mortar Officer's comments. That was swiftly replaced by a sudden determination. He wasn't on his own this time. He had firepower behind him today. Smithson ground his teeth together as his mind raced. No; this time it would be different.

"Company Sergeant Major!" He bellowed. "Send the message down the line. Company Sergeant Major to the Company Commander at the double!"

Moments later, he heard his order being repeated down the line. Meanwhile, he began looking at his own map and quickly began sketching out the dispositions of both the enemy and his own men. As he studied the terrain, his mind registered how effectively he and his men had been lured into the killing area. Point 113 was a perfect defensive position. Elevated yet not obvious, with thick tree cover and a sweeping view over the surrounding area, Point 113 was the ideal place for the Germans to block this particular route towards Caen.

"You bloody fool Smithson..." The major cursed himself.

"Sorry Sir?"

Smithson looked up to see the Company Sergeant Major kneeling beside him.

"Ah, just the man..."

"You seen all the fire from up on that ridge, Sir? There's a shit load of Jerries up in that wood."

"Yes, we've seen it. The buggers have got Mr Willis and his platoon pinned down further up the way there and things are getting a bit hairy. Captain Winters is sorting out a fire mission onto that hill, but in the meantime I want you to get the two inch mortars from the other two platoons and bring them as far forward as you can. Start bringing some smoke down on that slope in front of the wood as quick as you can. Hold the HE back; let the mortar platoon use their big stuff. Got all that?"

"Yes, Sir." The Company Sergeant Major nodded and made to depart.

"And send the two rear platoon commanders up to me as well please, Company Sergeant Major?"

"Right, Sir." The warrant officer acknowledged as he doubled away back down the column.

"We'll be in action in about three minutes, Dickie." Winters informed Smithson as the Company Sergeant Major hurtled off on his task. "We'll range the bombs in as quickly as possible then saturate that tree-line with HE for about two minutes."

Smithson nodded his thanks.

"Cheers, Tom; very kind of you. I've asked the Company Sergeant Major to get our light mortars into action and put a smoke screen between the wood and where Jeremy's platoon are pinned down."

"Got that." Winters acknowledged. "Just be aware that our ammunition is limited until the carriers get off the beach with all the reserve bombs."

Smithson nodded back.

As he and Winters were discussing the fire-plan, two more officers came running up the road. One after the other, the two platoon commanders from Nos.2 and 3 Platoons slid down into the ditch between Smithson and Winters.

"Right then gentlemen, I'm afraid we've got a bit of a sticky problem up in front." Smithson fixed the two young subalterns with a grim expression. "Things are about to get rather busy."

Quickly, as succinctly as possible, Smithson outlined what was going on; showing the two officers how both No.1 Platoon and the Germans were deployed. As he was briefing the two men, he heard the sound of a mortar bomb thump into the ground several hundred yards away and, immediately afterwards, the sound of Winters sending corrections to the mortar line via his signaller. Smithson continued with his orders.

"Tom is organising a fire mission onto that wood-line on the ridge, and the Company Sergeant Major has been tasked to take your light mortars and start laying a smoke screen in front of where Jeremy is pinned down. Charlie; I want your platoon to stand by to go straight up this road. Basically, as soon as that wood starts to get hit with HE, I want you to take your platoon down both sides of this road, straight over the point section from No.1 Platoon, then rush that crossroads and take it by storm. I'm afraid we haven't got time to mess about. The longer we faff around, then the more Jeremy and his boys are going to get cut up. Got that?"

Lieutenant Charles Normanton, commanding No.2 Platoon, confirmed that he understood what was required. Just at that point, they overheard Winters speaking to his signaller.

"That's smack on! Stand by to fire for effect for two minutes on my order..."

Having briefed his radio operator, Winters looked over at Smithson's little orders group.

"We're ready to go, Dickie." He said, his voice calm and even. "As soon as you give us the nod."

Before Smithson had the chance to reply, a sudden revving of engines caused all the men in the vicinity to swing their heads around and look back along the road towards Hermanville. Appearing over the crest of the ridge like some exotic beast rising from a swamp, a Sherman tank suddenly wheeled into view, its tracks clattering loudly on the cobbles as it trundled steadily towards the head of the 'A' Company column.

"Well bugger me backwards!" Winters commented. "Just in the nick of time!"

LEGG'S TANK – 500 YARDS NORTH OF THE CRUCIBLE TUESDAY 6TH JUNE 1944 – 1510 HOURS

They'd found the Hambledon and Moorlanders at last. The leading tank, commanded by Mr Barratt, had come across the battalion's commanding officer and another of their rifle companies just a few hundred yards further on from where the three tank crews had met up with each other. According to their colonel, it seemed that the Hambledons were starting to make some progress southwards towards Caen and their lead company were trudging inexorably on towards Point 113 and the village of Periers beyond it. Having explained their orders from Divisional Headquarters, and received the colonel's thanks, the trio of Sherman tank commanders had spurred on up the road on the heels of the Hambledons' point company.

As the three tanks trundled steadily forwards, keeping a good thirty yard gap between each vehicle, Legg popped his head out of the turret to try and get his bearings. He didn't put his head too high of course. That was a lesson he'd already learnt today. There were snipers everywhere, taking pot shots at vehicle commanders, and even when there weren't any snipers about, there were enough stray rounds and bits of shrapnel to make life exceptionally hazardous.

As they began to climb a very slight gradient towards what looked like a false crest, Legg started to register the sound of intense small arms fire some way ahead, even above the noise of the tank engines. They climbed a little higher up the gradient and began passing soldiers; British infantrymen who were crouching expectantly in the ditches and hedges on each side of the narrow lane. They looked tired already, Legg thought, weighed down as they were with large packs, digging tools, weapons, and at least two frontline scales of ammunition. He noted the tactical recognition flashes on their sleeves and recognised the 3rd Division insignia, an inverted red triangle on a black pyramid background, sitting just above the regimental flash. The infantrymen looked up at the three Shermans as they rumbled past and the corporal saw the expressions of relief wash over the young, tired faces. Here and there, the odd soldier waved as the trio of armoured vehicles ground on up the slope.

"Right lads..." Legg spoke into his microphone. "Looks as though we've caught up with their lead company. Better stay sharp now; we can't be far off the front line..."

From inside the turret, Wells made a comment over the intercom.

"Not by the looks of all that we're not, Peggy. Look at all that bloody tracer mate..."

Legg scanned the ground in front and instantly spotted the glowing orange dots that zipped across the distant fields, several hundred yards in front.

"Bugger me!" Legg observed. "Somebody's having a good old scrap!"

"Looks all one way to me though..." Wells observed.

Legg remembered that his gunner would be viewing the battle through the telescopic gunner's sight and would thus have a close up view.

"I think that wood on the hill is full of Jerries by the look." The gunner elaborated bleakly.

Legg scanned the ridge line where it rose to a small wooded point, just over to the left of the road. It did indeed look as though there was a considerable enemy presence in the wood, judging by the constant flash of tracer that seemed to emanate from the trees.

"Tanks stopping." Holloway warned as he began to slow their own vehicle down. Sure enough, just up ahead, both Barratt's and Saddler's tanks had come to a halt. The long, menacing looking barrel of the 17 Pounder gun on Saddler's tank swung half left and stopped, pointing over the fields towards the ridge-line like an animal sniffing out its next meal.

Legg's tank came to a stop, with Holloway maintaining the thirty yard gap between vehicles. As their Sherman jerked to a halt, Legg noticed a khaki clad infantryman emerge from the hedgerow further up the road and run across to Barratt's stationary tank. Within moments, the figure had clambered up behind the turret of the lead Sherman and begun conversing with the tank's commander.

"Looks as though we just found whoever is in charge of the footsloggers." Legg told his crew. "I reckon we could be in action pretty soon, so stay sharp."

Legg watched as the man on the back of Barratt's Sherman gesticulated in various directions in animated fashion, whilst Barratt himself leaned out of his cupola, keeping himself pressed as flat as possible as he listened to the infantryman's words. After just a minute or so, Legg saw Barratt nod his head in acknowledgement, after which the infantryman slid down from the tank and disappeared into the hedgerow again. Up ahead on the ridgeline, several explosions shook the earth and made the trees in the wood-line sway. They were followed by several more; short, bright flashes amongst the dimness of the wood, followed by dark, grey, ominous clouds of smoke billowing out from the seats of the explosions. A smokescreen of some kind seemed to be shrouding much of the slope in front of the wood.

"Hello chaps; Barratt here..." The voice of the young lieutenant in the front vehicle crackled over the airwaves, dispensing with the usual signals protocol. "We've found who we've been looking for and they're having a spot of bother. There are Jerries in that wood to our forward left on the ridge; roger so far, over..."

In sequence, Saddler then Legg acknowledged the message thus far. After a slight pause, Barratt went on.

"They're bringing mortars down on that position, but they've got a handful of enemy dug in on the crossroads just in front, about two hundred yards or so; just over the lip of this little crest we're on. We're going to plough straight onto the crossroads and shoot the buggers up. One of the infantry platoons will follow us forwards. When we get onto the crossroads, we'll start to engage any targets we can see up in the wood while the footsloggers get themselves reorganised. All clear, over..."

Again, Saddler and Wells acknowledged the orders.

Beside Legg's tank, the infantrymen were beginning to struggle to their feet as NCOs ran up and down the hedgerows, chivvying men along.

"Okay chaps, baton down and get ready to go on my order."

Legg responded to Barratt's instructions and slipped back down inside his turret, pulling the hatch closed behind him and locking it in place with the lever.

"Alright men; get ready to go." Legg warned the crew. "Look out for trenches on the verges when we get to the crossroads. "Gunner, traverse half left and depress as far as you can; switch to the co-ax. We'll brass up anything we see that aint British. Co-driver? You get your machine gun ready and cover the right hand side. You'll probably be the first to spot anything. Stand-by..."

Legg stuck his eyes against the forward periscope and watched for any forward movement by the other vehicles. He was starting to sweat again and he could feel his pulse picking up. This was going to be a close-in business. Nasty.

"Alright, chaps, here we go; stand-by..." Barratt's voice came over the net. "Three, two, one... Forward!"

Almost as one, the three Shermans revved their engines, their exhaust louvers spewing out dirty brown smoke, and then with a jerk, the trio of tanks juddered into life and began rolling towards the crossroads, gathering speed every second. At last, the British were attacking.

THE CRUCIBLE – POINT 113
TUESDAY 6TH JUNE 1944 – 1515 HOURS

"Here it comes! Stay low!"

Crump – crack!

The second mortar bomb landed in close proximity to the first, almost directly in the centre of the main position. Like the first, there was a bright flash and simultaneous thunderclap of the explosion, followed by a shockwave carrying bits of wood and undergrowth with it in addition to the red hot shrapnel. Additionally, just a split second after the initial blast which sent tremors through the ground beneath the defenders' feet, there came the crack of a large tree splitting wide open. That was followed in turn by the strange groaning sound and muffled crash of a large portion of the said tree toppling over.

For Gritz, the experience was nothing new. Even so, the immediate shock of being under bombardment sent a familiar spark of dread through his entire body. Perhaps it was worse for him than for the raw, inexperienced soldiers he commanded. After all, Gritz knew that once the enemy had your range there was little escape from the deluge of indirect fire. It was really a case of how many mortars or guns the enemy could muster and how much ammunition they had. A third mortar bomb whooshed through the air, rattled through the tree canopy and then exploded in mid air, having struck the large limb of a tree on its way down. The resulting airburst was even more terrifying than the ground-burst explosions.

"Gunther! Drop the rate of fire down a bit. Get your riflemen to keep up a harassing fire on that hedgerow. Conserve the machine gun ammunition and get people to stay low…"

Gritz shouted the orders above the noise of battle, even though the sergeant to whom he was giving the orders was just a few metres away. Gunther turned and nodded at the sergeant major.

"But make sure they keep their eyes on their arcs!" Gritz added. "I don't want them sticking their heads in the dirt. Keep their chins up and ready to fight, Gunther…"

Again, the sergeant commanding this part of the position nodded, then turned away to start passing the orders.

Gritz meanwhile looked left to where the MG42 crew were still blazing away with their weapon. The newly arrived soldier with the phosphorous burns, a veteran of Russia, had assumed command of the gun by natural selection. The wizened veteran was rapping out sharp commands to the two conscripted men who were manning the gun in the No.1 and No.2 positions.

"Ignore it!" The veteran soldier was telling the other two. "Keep firing. Start traversing left again, back to the start point."

Gritz felt a momentary flush of satisfaction. At least he and Gunther weren't the only experienced men in the company. It was the handful of veterans like this one who would hold the company together during its first proper taste of combat.

Gritz shouted over to the gun crew.

"Stop firing! Stop firing! Hauser; that will do for now! I think we've got them pinned down. Save your ammo for another big target. Watch and shoot."

Hauser, the veteran who was acting as the gun controller, glanced towards Gritz and nodded curtly; understanding the logic. Gritz watched as the man calmly ordered his crew to cease firing and change the weapon's barrel. Once the barrel change was completed, he instructed the No.2 to begin reloading the ammunition belts from a box of loose rounds. Happy that Hauser was on top of things in the gun pit, Gritz raised his binoculars once more to study the battlefield.

The binoculars were of limited use. In addition to the mortar bombs that were now starting to fall inside the wooded area of the main position, smoke bombs were starting to drop into the field to Gritz's front. He saw the thin white trails of smoke as the mortar bombs plummeted down from a great height to thump onto the green sloping pastures, where they continued to emit the thick, acrid smelling artificial fog. Within less than a minute, half a dozen of the bombs had landed in a well spaced belt, resulting in a near impenetrable wall of smoke.

"They've certainly been reading their manuals, haven't they?"

Gritz lowered his binoculars and glanced to his right where Gunther had joined him once more.

"They certainly have." Gritz smiled grimly at the sergeant. "So what do we think they're going to do next? Will they try to extract their men down there in the killing area, under cover of smoke; then pull right back and just plaster us with mortars and artillery? Or will they use it to push a bit harder? And if so, which way will they come?"

Gunther considered it for a moment.

"Mmm. Hard to say. The Tommies are usually quite cautious; methodical. That said, they might not be proper Tommies..."

"What do you mean?" Gritz frowned "Americans?"

Gunther pulled a non-committal face.

"Maybe... Or maybe they could be Australians? The Tommies used Australians out in the desert. Bunch of stubborn bastards they are; and they aren't shy about attacking either. They come charging at you with these bloody great bayonets on their rifles... Not nice..."

"Sounds a bit like the Ruskis." Gritz commented, studying Gunther's face.

It was clear that the sergeant had some personal experience of Australian troops from his time with the Afrika Corps in North Africa.

Gunther spat into the dirt at the bottom of the trench.

"If they keep laying smoke down, then my money would be on an attack."

Whoosh...Crump-crack! Crump-crack! Crump-crack!

Both NCOs ducked hurriedly as a belt of three HE mortar bombs sliced through the tree canopy and exploded inside the wood.

"Or they might just shell the shit out of us all day..." Gunther added as lumps of soil and bits of broken branch pattered down on top of them.

The sharp smell of burnt explosive and chemical smoke was thick in the air now and a hazy grey fug hung in the air amongst the trees and further out in the fields, lying close to the ground in the humid atmosphere of the damp summer's afternoon. Gritz peered over the top of the trench carefully and saw that the smoke screen to their front was beginning to thin a little. He was about to raise his field glasses for another scan of the ground when he froze.

He cocked his head to one side, straining to hear the sound that he thought he had just detected. After four years of war, Gritz was aware that his hearing was getting worse, and now he held his breath, attempting to suppress any sound that might intrude on his concentration.

And then he heard it. The unmistakable squeal of metal on metal; backed by a strange clattering noise.

"Panzers..." He breathed, his heart sinking.

"What?" Gunther looked at him sharply.

"Panzers!" The shout of alarm from a neighbouring stretch of trench saved Gritz the job of repeating himself. "Tommy Panzers!"

Gritz narrowed his eyes and pressed them into the binoculars, directing his gaze down towards where gunfire still rang out in the vicinity of the crossroads. At first, all he could see was the indistinct solid outline of the thick hedgerows through the gradually thinning smoke screen but then, as he swung the binoculars to his right, following the line of the Hermanville road, he saw it.

The enemy tank came rolling along the road, straight towards the crossroads, its strange, bulky hull and little turret appearing through the fog of war like a prehistoric beast rising out of the mist. Its main gun appeared to be short and stubby, but a sudden series of flashes told Gritz that the vehicle was employing its machine guns as it rushed towards the German troops defending the road junction.

"Sergeant Major; we can't get through to the checkpoint! Nobody's answering the phone!"

"Huh?" Gritz turned at the sound of the voice to see a private soldier crouching between him and Gunther, breathing heavily. With a start, Gritz remembered the runner they had sent back to the command post.

"Corporal Kole has been ringing them over and over, Sir, but he can't get them to answer..." The soldier went on. "He's sent a runner down the track to give them the message face to face."

"It's too late..." Gritz began, thinking out loud.

The squad from the checkpoint were just as pinned down as the Tommies were. They were lost to Gritz now, unless he could do something to make the Tommies back off. With a surge of adrenalin pumping through his body, Gritz turned away, ignoring the runner, and began sprinting along the trench to where the 47mm anti-tank gun had been positioned between the two forward platoons. As he ran through the revetments, he roared out a warning order to the anti-tank gun's crew as he closed on the gun pit.

"Tank action!" He screamed at the top of his voice. "Tank action!"

THE CROSSROADS – HARD BY THE CRUCIBLE
TUESDAY 6TH JUNE 1944 – 1515 HOURS

The crossroads was a surprisingly short distance ahead. Legg had assumed that the enemy must be ensconced further along the road by the side of Point 113, but the four-way junction was some two hundred and fifty to three hundred yards forward of the high feature. Thus, within less than a minute of revving their engines and lurching into a headlong charge up the road, the three British tanks found themselves on top of the surprised enemy.

Barratt's tank was leading and hurtled straight over the crossroads, both of its machine guns chattering away madly. The road straight ahead, the one that led onto Periers and Caen, was blocked by three wooden knife-rest barriers that had been hastily constructed from local timber and reinforced with barbed wire. The barriers were designed to bring small motor vehicles, cyclists or pedestrians to a halt, and were no obstacle whatsoever to a tank. Barratt's Sherman simply smashed straight into the first barrier and pushed it back into the second and third. As the three barriers began to create resistance against the onward force of the armoured vehicle, the massive weight of the tank began to tell.

At first, the caterpillar tracks snapped the single strand barbed wire and began biting into the wooden frame. After just a moment of pressure there was a loud snapping noise and then the barrier broke in two. The Sherman lurched ever so slightly as its tracks churned up the splintered wood and barbed wire of the first barricade and then ploughed on into the second and third. In a matter of seconds, the three barriers were no more than a messy pile of matchwood and shredded wire, and all the while, the two machine guns in Barratt's tank raked both hedgerows and verges with automatic fire.

Two small objects tumbled out from behind a particularly overgrown section of grass verge and bounced along the road, disappearing under the tank. A split second later, the two stick grenades exploded with a dull crump. Smoke billowed out from beneath the vehicle but the chunky green metal beast continued to churn forward through the remains of the barricade, spitting death from its guns. The driver in Barratt's tank spotted the place from which the two grenades had been thrown and the co-driver, doubling up as the bow machine gunner, swung his weapon onto that precise spot and fired several long burst straight into it. Bits of grass and camouflaged sandbag flew into the air and a moment later, a dark figure toppled sideways from behind the foliage.

Not wanting to take any chances, the driver swung the tank to the right so that his right hand track was on the verge itself, and then he ran the tank forward, straight towards the danger area. The tank lurched up ever so slightly on one side as the right hand track rolled over the parapet of the shell-scrape to the horror of the two surviving Germans within. The two unfortunate defenders only had chance to stare up at the huge steel beast in horror before it dropped down on top of them. Their terrified screams could barely be heard above the roar of the Sherman's engine as it ground the two Germans into a bloody mass of flesh, bone and blood; tearing them to pieces and grinding them into the dirt. The shell-scrape became the grave of the Germans as the parapet caved in on top of their dismembered bodies.

Up in the turret, Barratt's gunner had been busily raking the opposite hedgerow. Now, he saw the gap in the hedgerow where the track emerged onto the road from a nearby field. Crouching in the gateway, a look of terror frozen on his pale young features, was a German soldier. The man was simply kneeling there, like a frightened rabbit, unable to move or react as he saw the big British tank appear before him. Barratt's gunner was in no mood to give the German any more time. He traversed the sight picture onto the man, locked off the gear quickly, then stamped down on his firing pedal. The co-axial machine gun burst into life once more and at a range of less than forty yards, there was no way the weapon could miss.

A long burst of twenty rounds slammed into the ground around the German soldier, who had just come running down to the crossroads with fresh orders for the checkpoint commander. Spurts of soil and grass erupted all around the exposed soldier, just a split second before two more bullets sliced straight through his chest, flipping him backwards into the grass.

Coming up hard on the heels of Barratt, Saddler brought his tank onto the junction and then ordered the driver to swing right. The tank turned sharply onto the road that led off westwards and its machine guns conducted a similar sweep to those of Barratt's vehicle. On this occasion however, it was merely a formality. It appeared that there were no enemy dug in on this particular branch of the crossroads.

Following along in third place, Legg ordered his own driver to swing left at the crossroads. Holloway did as ordered and brought the tank round to the left in a tight curve.

"Bloody hell! Right there!" The co-driver yelled, before opening fire with the bow machine gun.

There was a shell-scrape containing several men on the very corner of the crossroads, and Legg's tank drove right past it in less than a heartbeat.

"Driver – stop!" Legg screamed out. "Reverse back!"

With impressive speed and much jerking of gears, Holloway brought the tank up sharp and then threw it into reverse. Inside the turret, Legg, Wells and the loader/operator grabbed for a purchase on various fittings as they were thrown around the fighting compartment.

Legg was desperately trying to see out of the forward periscope, and when he judged they had retraced their tracks just enough, he yelled another order.

"Driver – stop! Go firm! Can you see that position?"

Another burst of fire from the bow machine gun suggested that the co-driver had indeed spotted the shell-scrape. The machine gun chattered noisily several times, until there was the sound of a small explosion just outside the vehicle.

"What was that?" Legg asked pressing his eyes to the periscope.

"Jerry with a grenade!" Shouted the co-driver. "I just shot the fucker and he dropped it in his own trench! The whole thing just went up!"

"Good." Legg snapped curtly. "Scan the verges for more positions. Watch out for any of our boys coming along from the rear…"

Legg's words were drowned out by the sound of a large, sharp explosion.

"What the fuck was that?" Legg swore, feverishly scanning the terrain outside, searching for the source of the noise.

"Fuck knows…!" Wells grunted, swinging the turret to the right.

"Shit!"

Legg had found the answer. He was staring through the side periscope block and could see the smoke pouring from the side of Barratt's tank which was visible from the top decks upwards, above the line of hedges.

"Mr Barratt's tank has been hit by something…" He murmured, trying to understand what had happened to it.

The next moment, Legg registered a bright flash, followed by a large black cloud, which occurred so suddenly that he pulled back from the periscope in shock.

"Fucking hell!" He cursed, even as the sound of the second explosion reached the ears of his entire crew.

"What is it?" Wells was asking.

Legg jammed his eyes back to the periscope and emitted a pained cry.

"Jesus Christ!"

Barratt's tank was now on fire. The cloud of smoke was now a dense, oily black fog, at the heart of which greedy orange flames licked up the side of the stricken tank.

"Anti-tank gun!" Holloway shouted. "Up on the hill! I'm sure of it!"

Even as Legg was taking in the news, he saw the turret hatch of Barratt's tank flick open. A figure emerged from within, indistinct amongst the pouring smoke and flame. As the individual struggled out of the burning tank, bright blobs of orange tracer appeared out of nowhere and bounced off the burning vehicle with a howling whine. The figure busily escaping from the tank suddenly toppled forward onto the deck of the burning vehicle, disappearing from sight in the smoke.

"Peggy!" Holloway shouted. "There's an anti-tank gun up in that wood! I saw it fire! Positive mate!"

Legg's mind made a hurried calculation. How long to traverse a gun from one target to another when both targets were only yards apart, he wondered? Seconds, was the answer he came up with. The corporal yelled into the intercom with terrified urgency.

"Driver – forward! Forward!"

COMPANY HEADQUARTERS – 'A' COMPANY, 1ST BATTALION, HAMBLEDON AND MOORLANDERS TUESDAY 6TH JUNE 1944 – 1520 HOURS

Smithson's shoulder was throbbing like hell now. Hardly surprising, he thought, because the current situation was horribly reminiscent of his last encounter with the Germans back in 1940. In short, everything was chaos; smoke-obscured, ear-shattering, bloody chaos. As he ran up the road at a low crouch, followed by the ever faithful Haines and Morrison, Smithson tried to take stock of the situation as it presented itself to him.

His first encounter was with the tired, shattered looking men from the point section of No.1 Platoon. This handful of men had been in close contact with the enemy for the best part of an hour now and the look of relief on their faces was obvious. Smithson passed two men from the Bren Gun team laying flat on the verge; the gunner busy filling an empty magazine, whilst his No.2 was in the process of changing the steaming hot barrel. A pile of glistening, expended brass cartridge cases sat beneath the weapon, showing how intense the prolonged fire-fight had been.

A little further up, Smithson saw the face of Sergeant Askey appearing from the shallow ditch at the side of the road.

"Everything alright?" Smithson called out as he approached.

The sergeant gave a shake of his head.

"We're in a bit of a state, Sir… Going to take as a few minutes to get organised. Corporal Oliver's badly wounded and we've got two more dead from this section. Lance Corporal Vincent has taken over as section commander. I don't know what's happened to Mr Willis and the rest. They went left flanking and I haven't seen them since…"

Smithson paused and knelt down by Askey.

"I'm afraid they've run into trouble over on the left. They got hit by all that fire from the wood-line and they've been pinned down. Hopefully they'll be okay now we've taken the crossroads. I want you to get all this lot together and follow me up to the junction. When we get there, deploy your men in the hedgerow down the left hand road and start suppressing that wood. Oh, and get a runner to go further down that road and try to find Mr Willis. Tell him that your whole platoon is now fire support until further notice. Got that?"

"Aye, Sir." Askey nodded, his face creased with the stress of the last hour's fighting.

"Good man." Smithson reached out and clapped the NCO on the shoulder. "Give your lads a pat on the back, but keep them going. This is just the tip of the iceberg by the looks of it."

"Marvellous…" Askey murmured, pushing himself upright.

Smithson was already on the move however. Waving for his signaller and runner to follow him, the company commander began jogging along the cobbles once more towards the crossroads. Not that he could really see the crossroads of course. The entire junction was wreathed in smoke; a mixture of the white, artificial smoke from mortar bombs and the black, pungent, oily smoke from a burning vehicle. The flames that were visible through that smoke confirmed Smithson's worst fears that at least one of the Shermans had been hit. At least one was still in action however because he could hear it clattering along one of the roads to the left or right of the junction, somewhere amongst the smoke.

Bullets continued to crack through the air; sometimes a single shot, and every now and then a short burst of machine gun fire. The orange tracer rounds snapped through the smoke like angry, lead fireflies, seeking out soft human flesh on which to inflict their fatal bite. As Smithson came to the junction itself, he was able to see deeper into the shifting smoke and, with a sinking heart, he saw the burning Sherman at the far side of the crossroads, up on the right hand verge. Bits of broken wooden post lay across the cobbles with loose ends of single strand barbed wire, and empty cartridge cases glistened on the cobbles.

Crack-crack-crack-crack-crack!

The sudden burst of fire sent Smithson running for the hedgerow by the left corner of the junction. He reached the verge and immediately spotted the tell-tale hump of a shell-scrape's parapet, reinforced with sandbags. Immediately, he made as if to jump into the handy piece of man made cover, but then pulled up short. The bottom of the shallow trench was filled with bodies; or rather, the remains of bodies. It was hard to tell exactly how many men there had been originally, for the earthen floor of the shell-scrape was a jumble of limbs and torsos that seemed to be disjointed and tangled in some mad arrangement. Bizarrely, Smithson thought that they looked like a bunch of scarecrows that had been ripped apart and then thrown haphazardly into a ditch together. The only difference was that on this occasion, it wasn't straw that spilled out from within, but blood and entrails and other mangled bits of human tissue.

"Jesus!" The former student of theology swore, and threw himself down on the flat, grassy verge instead, hastily taking his gaze away from the awful sight.

Haines and Morrison thumped down into the grass beside him as he scanned around the smoke covered junction.

"Don't go in this hole, chaps." He shouted to his signaller and runner during a brief pause in the gunfire. "It's a bloody awful mess inside."

The major scanned the surrounding hedgerows and spotted a lance corporal from No.2 Platoon.

"Where's Mr Normanton?"

The NCO looked up at the query; searching for the voice that had made it.

"Over here!" Smithson gave a little wave. "Where's the Platoon Commander?"

The corporal's expression changed to one of recognition and he pointed towards Smithson.

"Behind you, Sir… He's there look…"

Smithson turned to look back towards the burning Sherman and saw Lieutenant Normanton running towards him through the billowing smoke.

"Charlie! Over here!"

Smithson waved at the young officer then placed his fist on his helmet. Instantly, Normanton swerved towards him and came running across. Without ceremony, the lieutenant slid down onto the grass beside his company commander.

Smithson was just about to question him when the roar of an engine made him jump with surprise.

"Stay back Dickie…" Normanton cautioned.

Even as Smithson swivelled his head again, a Sherman tank came rolling backwards through the smoke.

"They're moving backwards and forwards constantly…" Normanton explained. "There's an anti-tank gun up in that wood. That's what did for this poor bugger!" He jerked his thumb over his shoulder at the burning tank.

Smithson took the information in quickly.

"Okay; what's the situation here then? Is the crossroads secure?"

Normanton nodded vigorously.

"Yes, we've taken the crossroads no problem. Turns out there were only a few Jerries here in two or three trenches. Looks like they were manning some kind of temporary checkpoint. The main position seems to be up in that wood. Like I say… they've got an anti-tank gun up there and at least two of those bloody quick firing machine guns."

Normanton paused as a group of soldiers turned into the road, their hobnailed boots clattering on the cobbles as they ran clumsily round the junction; their packs, digging tools and tin mugs rattling madly.

"Down there and line the hedgerow…" Smithson shouted at them, recognising Askey and his group. "Start firing up at the wood… And try to link up with the rest of your platoon!"

He turned back to Normanton.

"What's it like up the road? Beyond the burning Sherman?"

Normanton's face brightened momentarily.

"It's not too… Fucking hell!"

Both officers pushed themselves flat into the grass and clamped their hands over their ears as the nearest surviving Sherman fired a round from its main armament. The shockwave and crack of the shell passing almost directly overhead nearly popped Smithson's ear drums.

"Jesus bloody Christ!" The major swore as his ear drums rang in agony.

The Sherman's engine revved again and, within a heart beat of firing its shot, hurtled forwards again, clattering past the two officers and back along the side road.

As the vehicle moved away once more, the two officers took their hands away from their ears. Both of them were grimacing; still shocked by the ferocity of the report from the Sherman's main gun.

"As I was saying, Sir…" Normanton continued. "It's not too bad beyond the junction. The road runs over a little ridge then disappears. But there's a track that comes off the main road and snakes its way up towards the rear of that wood by the looks. It's got big hedges and banks either side of it too. I reckon it's a good option for a flank attack on the wood-line. You ought to come and have a look. The sooner we get off this junction the better."

As if to reinforce Normanton's suggestion, a long burst of machine gun fire cracked through the hedgerow a few yards away and smashed into the centre of the crossroads. Bullets bounced off the cobbles and ricocheted away, howling as they went.

Before Smithson had time to recover however, the Mortar Officer and his signaller appeared on the crossroads, spotted him lying by the corner, and ran across to join him. A few seconds later Winters slid down beside Smithson and Normanton.

"Ruddy hell, Dickie..." Winters commented laconically, catching his breath. "It's a bit cheeky up here isn't it? Getting a bit crowded too. I think I might push straight over the junction and up past that brewed up tank, so I can get a better look at that wood; see if I can zero right in on the buggers."

Smithson nodded his understanding.

"That's fine, Tom. You can come with us. Charlie's going to show me what's up ahead. Apparently there's a possible way into the flank of that position in the trees." He stopped abruptly and looked hard at Winters. "How are you doing for ammunition? Can you keep bringing fire down on the wood for us?"

Winters nodded calmly.

"Oh, yes; don't worry about that Dickie, we've got it sorted. I've just had word. Our carriers have finally got off the beach and caught up with the mortar line, so we've got a shed load of extra bombs now. I've already asked for a repeat shoot. Once we get through this smoke I'll sort a fresh fire mission out. We'll mix some smoke in with it too; take the pressure off your two inchers."

"That's brilliant Tom, thank you..."

"Major Smithson, Sir?"

Smithson found himself once more the most sought after man on the battlefield. He looked up at the call from a powerful, authoritative voice and this time saw none other than the battalion's Regimental Sergeant Major on the far corner of the crossroads, shouting across the cobbles towards him.

"RSM? Yes, over here..."

Like a gun-dog, the RSM's head turned at the sound of Smithson's voice and zeroed in on the major. Kneeling proudly against the hedgerow opposite, the battalion's senior warrant officer gave the impression of a faithful Labrador, awaiting its master's word before racing into action.

The RSM's eyes narrowed in on Smithson, ignoring those of irrelevance that surrounded him.

"Major Smithson, Sir; the CO would like to speak to you immediately, please. He's just back here, Sir."

The politely phrased request was clearly more of an imperious command.

"I'm on my way, RSM; two minutes..." Smithson held up two fingers in a victory sign to emphasise his words as a flurry of rifle shots cracked over the crossroads.

"Two minutes..."

The RSM gave a brief nod of acknowledgement then twisted away and raced back down the Hermanville road.

Turning to his companions, Smithson rapped out some quick instructions.

"Right, chaps; it *is* getting very crowded here, indeed, and we don't want to tempt Jerry to use his own mortars on us, so let's get shaken out. Charlie, you take Tom with you so he can start organising his revised fire mission. Keep your own platoon poised and ready to exploit on my orders. I'll see what the CO wants, then I'll be back in a couple of minutes to confirm the next step. Happy?"

"As a pig in shit, old boy." Winters smiled.

"Happy." Normanton nodded.

Even as his two fellow officers replied, Smithson felt a pang of envy at how calm Winters seemed to be. Regardless of the chaos around him, the captain from the Mortar Platoon seemed to be coolly competent; the very image of phlegmatic professionalism. Smithson decided that he should be the same; after all, he'd already seen combat before, had he not?

"Off you go then. I'll catch up with you shortly." Smithson dismissed the two officers, trying to create the same impression of urbane detachment as Winters.

They were away instantly. Smithson rolled over to look at his own tactical headquarters.

"Corporal Haines? Try to get hold of the Company 2 i/c and tell him to hold Three Platoon just short of the crossroads. Be prepared to feed them forward from reserve when called for."

"Sir." The radio operator responded crisply.

"Morrison?" Smithson switched his gaze to his runner. "Get yourself along this lateral road to the left and find Sergeant Askey; then go further along and see if you can find Mr Willis and the rest of his platoon. Tell Mr Willis... In fact, *bring* Mr Willis back here so I can give him new orders. Also, tell him to get his platoon linked up together along this side of the road and put some coordinated fire down on that wood-line on the hill."

"Sir." Morrison nodded.

"And keep low, Morrison." Smithson called after the young private as he began working his way along the bank and hedge that lined the side road.

Having got things moving within his own company, Smithson gathered himself to run back along the Hermanville road to see what the CO had to say.

"Wait here, Corporal Haines." The major ordered, then launched himself over the cobbles and sprinted back across the junction.

As he went, there was another large report nearby as one of the two surviving Shermans returned fire at the wood with its main armament again. Not two seconds later, an enemy anti-tank round cracked through the air somewhere off to Smithson's right but didn't appear to explode or hit anything. How long the Shermans could continue dodging the enemy fire he didn't know, but suddenly, a pang of guilt rang through him.

What was he waiting for? He had a platoon over the crossroads, with the Mortar Officer for company, and there were two Shermans still in action. He should have ordered them to just launch themselves at Point 113 straight away, without any faffing around. That's what the Germans would do he thought. Of a sudden, every second of delay in getting the attack going was a weight on Smithson's mind and so the major ducked his head and ran faster.

"Dickie!"

The CO called out to him as he almost ran past the gaggle of men from Battalion Tac' HQ who were mixed in with the rear men of No.3 Platoon.

Smithson pulled up sharply and dodged back onto the verge and down into the shallow ditch from where the lieutenant colonel's head and shoulders protruded.

"Dickie? How's it going up front? I gather you've bumped into something pretty substantial?"

Fighting to regain control of his breathing, Smithson rapidly informed Colonel Blair of the situation thus far; how the checkpoint was actually just an outpost for a major enemy position on Point 113, a position that appeared to be well supplied with machine guns and at least one anti-tank gun. The CO's brow furrowed as Smithson elaborated on the stiff nature of resistance currently being encountered. When Smithson had finished, Blair gave a little shake of his head.

"Sounds like duff intelligence to me, Dickie. There was nothing about a major position on our line of advance in our orders."

Smithson nodded his agreement.

"No, Sir; it rather caught us on the hop a bit too. Not to worry though; I'm about to launch the next phase of the attack. We'll soon have it dealt with."

Blair eyed Smithson with concern.

"Are you sure, Dickie? Sounds like your point platoon has taken a bit of a mauling..."

He left the question hanging in the air, but Smithson was already nodding his head vigorously.

"Yes, Sir; we can do it. My other two platoons are both good to go and we're in the perfect position to hook round and attack the position from the right. We've got two Shermans in support still and Tom Winters is up front with Charlie Normanton adjusting a fire mission onto them now. We'll be ready to go in minutes..."

Blair considered Smithson's words for a moment before nodding his agreement.

"Alright, Dickie; you seem to have it all in hand. I've got the FOO from 7th Field Regiment just back here. I'll get him to come up to the crossroads and help you sort out your fire plan. No point being thrifty with the artillery when we've got some to spare, eh? It'll make up for the lack of tanks..."

At that point, Blair paused, appeared to have a brief moment of concern, then spoke again, this time in a guarded voice.

"You've not seen any Jerry armour yet, have you?"

"No, Sir." Smithson shook his head. "Nothing of the kind."

The CO seemed reassured.

"Good... Well, I'll leave you to get on with it then. I'm going to push 'C' Company out to the left and get them to provide some long distance harassing fire onto that wood-line with their Brens; just to try and take some of the pressure off you. Try to pull in that left hand platoon of yours so they can get a clear shoot. I'll bring 'B' and 'D' Companies up behind you, nice and close, just in case you get bogged down and need them to push through and take up the reins."

"Thank you, Sir..." Smithson nodded. "But I think we'll be fine."

Blair favoured Smithson with a paternal smile.

"I'm sure you will, Dickie, but just in case, we're right behind you ready to give you some added punch. And we've got the anti-tank platoon on the way too, Dickie. They've finally got clear of the beach, so if you spot any armour then just whistle us and we'll get them sent up to you."

The CO paused and looked at his watch.

"Anyway... It's 1530 now. How long before you can launch?"

Smithson responded instantly, feeling his confidence and determination surging.

"Five minutes, Sir."

Blair nodded and smiled.

"Let's say 1540 then? You'll need time to brief those tank commanders too."

He looked back at Smithson.

"Off you go then, Dickie. Get a wiggle on... And the best of luck, old boy."

THE CRUCIBLE – POINT 113
TUESDAY 6TH JUNE 1944 – 1540 HOURS

"Bollocks! The Tommy bastard moved again!"

The commander of the 47mm anti-tank gun swore in frustration as he watched the latest armour piercing shell from his gun slice through thin air and disappear into the field beyond, having missed the Sherman by a whisker. Three hundred metres for an anti-tank gun was as good as point blank range, yet the continuous, shifting smoke screen and the fact that the enemy vehicle kept moving backwards and forwards at high speed every few seconds made getting an accurate shot off exceptionally difficult.

"Stop wasting your time with that fucker!" Gritz shouted at the gun commander as another enemy mortar bomb landed nearby, bringing yet more branches and natural debris down into the trenches and gun pits. "Switch fire onto that other one; it's hiding right behind the first one you knocked out. Try and sneak one just past the burning vehicle and get him."

Before the gun commander was able to respond to that order, a series of high pitched cracks rent the air around them, and several bullets slammed into a large tree just a couple of metres to the right of the old French anti-tank weapon that had now been pressed into German service.

"I think they've spotted us..." The gun commander observed, shrinking behind the bullet shield of the gun.

"It's just searching fire!" Gritz snapped irritably. "Now lay that gun onto the tank with the long gun and take the bastard out!"

Leaving the gun commander to get on with the business, Gritz exited the gun pit and followed the communication trench along the front edge of the wood. He passed the rear of three small bunker positions before he reached the MG 42 position. On arrival, he found Gunther directing the weapon's fire towards the crossroads, but instead of engaging in long, rapid bursts, the gun was now rattling off short, selective bursts, changing its point of aim each time. Behind the gun, kneeling on the floor of the pit, two riflemen were refilling expended belts with loose rounds from a nearby ammunition box.

Gunther turned as Gritz entered the pit.

"Nice shot on that Tommy tank!" He grinned.

Gritz spat onto the floor and gave his aching knee a rub.

"Not bad..." He grunted. "But those fucking gunners can't hit a barn door at the moment! Too busy playing chase with that tank that keeps moving up and down the road!"

"Not to worry..." Gunther commented. "I reckon we've got the bastards pinned down anyway; they don't seem too keen to come any further forward.

We could do without this bloody mortar fire mind you. They were pretty quick getting that brought down; I'll give them that."

Gritz didn't answer. He was up against the parapet with his binoculars to his eyes. He studied the scene below. The last skeins of the enemy smoke screen had almost disappeared, though the burning Tommy tank still billowed out oily, black smoke by the crossroads, and the gusting wind pushed it across the slope in front of The Crucible. Here and there, he saw occasional movement in the hedgerows, but overall the Tommies were hugging the undergrowth and keeping themselves out of sight. The small arms fire from the enemy was increasing in tempo now; not dramatically, but enough to suggest that the enemy were recovering from their initial shock.

"They're up to something…" Gritz said.

"They're taking their time then…" Gunther murmured.

As the sergeant was speaking, a new sound came through the air to add to the crump of mortar bombs and the staccato chatter of machine guns. This sound was one that both he and Gritz were familiar with. It was some time since they had both heard it, but nevertheless it was unmistakable. Apart from the battlefield, the only other time you would here such a noise was on a railway station platform as an express train hurtled through at top speed. If the soft whoosh of incoming mortars wasn't enough to chill the blood, then the infernal scream of incoming artillery shells was.

"Down!" Both Gritz and Gunther yelled simultaneously, and pressed themselves in against the parapet of the gun pit.

Crump! Crump! Crump! Crump! Crump! Crump!

The salvo of shells sliced through the tree canopy and exploded with ear shattering volume, enveloping the entire company position in pungent smoke in the wake of the fearsome explosions and shrapnel laced shock waves. Lumps of soil began to fall into the gun pit, finding their way through the wooden revetments, as the ground beneath shook violently under the onslaught of the heavy artillery bombardment.

For a second after the salvo landed, there was almost a complete silence, as everyone in The Crucible's garrison gathered themselves and wakened to the dread realisation that they had become the target of a vastly superior force. Crouching within the gun pit, Gritz turned his eyes towards Gunther.

"Looks like they've made their decision then…"

And as he spoke, the scream of yet more artillery shells cut the afternoon air above them.

ASSEMBLY AREA 21ST PANZER DIVISION – NEAR LEBISEY VILLAGE, 1.5 MILES NORTH OF CAEN

The low growl of tank engines filled the air, reducing the sound of widespread fighting to a subdued, background noise. Amongst the copses, orchards and small woods that lay between the villages of Lebisey and Herouville, the bulk of the 21st Panzer Division's armoured power had been concentrated after much frustration and friction. Both battalions of the 100th Panzer Regiment, equipped almost entirely with Panzer IV tanks of varying models and quality, were formed up here amongst the trees. On the left of this armoured task force, the 1st Battalion of the 192nd Panzer Grenadier Regiment were also forming up in their half-tracks and armoured cars.

Amazingly, all of these formations had managed to reach the assembly area as designated by their divisional headquarters, despite the almost continuous waves of enemy heavy bombers and Jabos that had filled the skies throughout this long, gloomy day. Standing on the edge of an orchard, looking due north towards Periers and the coast, General Erich Marcks, the commander of the German 84th Army Corps, studied the clouds of smoke that obscured that distant coastline. Although the coast itself was hidden behind the curtain of artificial fog, from this elevated position, the wide vista of the English Channel beyond was clearly visible, and that vast expanse of water was covered in ships.

Marcks stared impassively at the sight, his keen, clever eyes taking in every detail; from the observation and barrage balloons that floated defiantly above that huge fleet, to the constant stream of tiny craft plying to and fro the beaches that were hidden beneath that blanket of battlefield smoke. He had always known they would land here. He had told everyone; even though they said he was mistaken and that the Tommies would attack in the Pas-de-Calais. Marcks was an able general and possessed of a considerable intellect. A thorough analysis of the situation had told him that Normandy would be the place for the Allies to attack. On top of that, he'd felt that his conclusion was correct because his gut had been telling him so for several weeks now. And now the enemy had come; to precisely the place he had forecast they would. The only thing was; the high command still wouldn't believe him.

If any of those fools at Army Headquarters, or even from the Fuhrer's own staff, could stand here now and view this terrible spectacle, then even they would have to admit the truth of it and release the panzer reserves. Instead they procrastinated and delayed, worried lest they incur the wrath of Hitler for releasing the panzers without his personal authority. And every hour that was wasted, every minute, would push the chance of victory beyond their grasp, whilst bringing the prospect of defeat ever closer. Well, Marcks was no obsequious Party sycophant, but he *did* know his duty, and he was an experienced field commander. This *was* the real invasion, not just some diversion; and he would not stand idly by and let it happen under his nose. His divisions were fighting well, especially over in the west where it appeared the Americans were landing.

Here though, here was where the outcome of the day would be decided. The British were down there in front of him somewhere. Thousands of them, with new weapons and new attitudes; bent on revenging themselves after those long dark years following Dunkirk. Behind him lay Caen, the crossroads of Normandy, and a pivot point for all troop movement. Caen must be held, and the Tommies driven back into the sea. If the Allies got a foothold in the west, well he could deal with that in good time. But here? No, the Allies must be defeated here. These few square miles of rolling farmland, woods and villages were now destined to be the scene of the greatest struggle of the war to date. As Marcks scanned the middle distance with his binoculars, he saw that Point 113 was under bombardment; small orange flashes giving way to large, grey-black clouds of smoke.

He remembered the veteran sergeant major who commanded there; the man he had met just yesterday during his tour of local strongpoints. That man would do his best, Marcks was sure. But he could certainly do with some help. The general remembered the conversation he'd had with that grizzled veteran of the Eastern Front, just over twenty four hours ago as they had stood on the parapet of the gun pit, looking down the slope towards Hermanville, Lion sur Mer and la Breche. It had all turned out exactly as they'd discussed. So here they were, all of them… in the crucible of fate. He chuckled to himself, despite the enormity of the task that lay before him.

"Happy birthday, Erich, old boy…" He murmured.

"Sorry, General?"

Marcks turned and looked at the young, determined looking figure of Colonel von Oppeln-Bronikowski, the commander of the 100th Panzer Regiment. Clad in his black tank overalls, the colonel was standing just behind Marcks, along with the Corps Commander's small staff.

"I said… are you ready to advance now Colonel?"

The panzer commander nodded his head vigorously.

"We are, General. We've been driving all day to get into position. We just want to get stuck into the Tommies now. The men are eager to be off."

Marcks nodded thoughtfully.

"Good." He snapped. "Then get moving. You know your orders. Drive hard and fast and sweep everything before you. The troops at The Crucible are still holding out by the looks of it, but they are under heavy attack. There isn't a moment to lose; so go... Go now."

Colonel Oppeln-Bronikowski snapped to attention and saluted.

"At once, General. And thank you for giving us this honour."

He turned to head back to his tank.

"Oh, and Oppeln..." Marcks called after him.

The colonel stopped and turned back to face the stern looking general.

"Make no mistake Oppeln, how critical and onerous a task I have given you. You may not wish to thank me too heartily. For if you do not succeed in driving the British back into the sea by last light... then we have lost the war..."

COMPANY HEADQUARTERS – 'A' COMPANY, 1ST BATTALION, HAMBLEDON AND MOORLANDERS TUESDAY 6TH JUNE 1944 – 1545 HOURS

Yet again, Smithson was reminded how time consuming even the simplest task could be in battle. He was already five minutes late for his H-Hour and his men were still shaking out into position. There had been so much to organise that should have been a matter of a few brief words, yet under the stress and dislocation of close combat, those straight forward conversations and orders had required considerable elaboration; none more so than in the case of the deeply shocked Lieutenant Willis.

The young commander of the badly mauled No.1 Platoon had been waiting on the crossroads alongside Corporal Haines when Smithson had returned there following his conversation with the Commanding Officer. Of Morrison, the company runner, there was no sign. Willis, pale faced, glassy-eyed, and clearly stunned by his first experience of battle, had mechanically informed Smithson that the unfortunate Morrison had been hit by an enemy sniper just after passing on Smithson's summons. The young second lieutenant had then gone on to inform Smithson that No.2 and 3 Sections from his platoon had been badly cut up over the course of the last hour, with three dead and four more wounded, including Corporal Armstrong; almost a forty percent casualty rate.

Thankfully, it seemed that Sergeant Askey had begun to make his presence felt now that the composite parts of No.1 Platoon were reunited, and there was a distinctly more regular and coordinated sound of gunfire coming from the nearby hedgerows as Willis' depleted force began to settle into its role of fire support. Having briefed Willis several times over to ensure the disorientated lieutenant had got the message, Smithson had arranged for the Company Sergeant Major to resupply No.1 Platoon with the remainder of the company's ten percent ammunition reserve. Then, leaving Willis with his new task, Smithson had moved off to brief the other commanders within his company group.

That had involved briefing the two remaining platoon commanders and the Mortar Officer, before finally flagging down one of the two surviving Shermans and holding a decidedly uncomfortable conversation with its commander on the exposed hull of the vehicle as it continued to jockey backwards and forwards in the vicinity of the crossroads. Finally, he had managed to track down Captain Roy Chislehurst, his company's second in command, and bring him up to speed with the situation. They very quickly agreed that Chislehurst should remain on the crossroads to keep an eye on the shaken Willis, and liaise with the Forward Observation Officer who was being sent forward from 7th Regiment Royal Artillery. The said FOO had appeared just moments later, clattering onto the junction in a carrier sporting a long radio antenna. After just a few brief words of wisdom, Smithson had left the gunner officer with Chislehurst and then doubled off, with Corporal Haines in tow, to get his company attack moving.

Crouching by the gateway where the track joined the road, Smithson now looked about him to make a final check that all was set. Barely two yards away from him, a youthful looking German soldier lay dead; spread-eagled on his back with two small, neat bullet holes punctuating his field grey tunic. The material around the holes had been stained a dark red and a large pool of thick red blood had soaked the grass and earth beneath the man's body. The poor German looked ridiculously young and, somewhat disconcertingly, his eyes were neither open nor closed. Instead, his lids had frozen in a half closed position; almost as if he was peeking at Smithson and feigning death.

The company commander ignored the body, temporarily inured to the abhorrent sights, sound and smell of traumatic death as his mind worked overtime, trying to coordinate his force within this realm of chaos. He glanced back along the road and saw the expectant, nervous faces of No.3 Platoon staring back at him, lining the verges on either side of the two large, green, bulky Shermans that were queued up ready to advance, though still jockeying back and forth as they waited. Looking up the track, his lead assault platoon, Normanton's, was formed up in similar fashion to No.3 Platoon, but on the right hand side of the track only. The plan was for them to use the Shermans as moving shields on their left hand side during the initial thrust up the track and into the flank of the wood.

Beneath Smithson, the ground shook and trembled continuously as the mortar fire from his own battalion's mortar platoon was now joined by the 105mm shells of the 7th Regiment's self propelled artillery. There was precious little fire coming back at them now. Either he had formed his company up in a blind spot to the enemy, or they were being almost completely suppressed by the combined mortar and artillery bombardment.

Smithson was beginning to feel more confident now. He remembered, for the hundredth time that day, his last encounter with the Germans in 1940. It had been a similar experience then. That initial shock of contact and the terrible confusion as one's mind attempted to make sense of the noise, the confusion, the conflicting emotions and vague reports from subordinates, followed eventually by an acceptance of chaos as the normal state of affairs. Once that process had occurred within one's mind, it was possible to start imposing your own will on the battle. On the last occasion however, Smithson had only had a short while to do just that before events had finally overwhelmed him. This time, he resolved, it would be different. As every minute went by, his ability to dictate events increased in line with his combat power. Today was the day when he could at last take the fight back to the Germans on his own terms. It would be exhausting and brutal, he knew, and he would have to run around and brief people several times over; shout at them, encourage them, threaten them. But he would prevail today. His men would be the victors on this occasion; he had sworn this to himself.

As it had done all day; Smithson's shoulder began to twinge once more. He allowed a grim smile to cross his grimy features. That twinge was his body telling him that it was time for action once more. He twisted round and beckoned to the leading Sherman tank. A moment later, the Sherman gave a throaty roar of its engine then lurched forward. Thirty yards behind it, the second Sherman, the one with the shorter gun, also began to roll forwards. Happy that his two supporting tanks were on the move, Smithson raised his Very Pistol and aimed it high in the air, in line with the track that was to serve as the axis of their advance. He squeezed the trigger and experienced a slight jerk of his wrist, accompanied by a gentle 'pop'.

The green Very Light sailed upwards before curling over and descending again in a broad arc. Even before that first flare had begun to drop earthwards again, Smithson was breaking the pistol open, ejecting the spent cartridge and placing a fresh one inside. He snapped the pistol shut and repeated the process. As the second green light soared upwards, the first Sherman rumbled past him, showering him with churned up mud, grass and cow dung. Amongst the cacophony of exploding shells and mortar bombs, Smithson fancied he could hear an increase in the rate of fire from Willis' platoon, who had been ordered to switch to the rapid rate on seeing the green flares.

The men from No.2 Platoon were on their feet now, moving at a low crouch and a fast walk, bunching up behind the protective silhouettes of the two tanks. Up on the hill, the first of the smoke shells exploded as the FOO adjusted his fire mission. Smithson clambered to his feet.

"Okay Corporal Haines; tell the CO we're attacking now."

With those words, he beckoned with his arm again, this time to No.3 Platoon behind him.

"Alright then 'A' Company; let's go take that hill shall we? Forward…"

LEGG'S TANK – THE CROSSROADS BY THE CRUCIBLE, POINT 113
TUESDAY 6TH JUNE 1944 – 1545 HOURS

"Back." Legg called out over the intercom.

By now, his voice had lost a lot of its urgency. The continuous jockeying backwards, forwards and around the corners of the crossroads to spoil the aim of the enemy anti-tank gunners had become second nature. Holloway, the driver, understood the drill now too, and could almost anticipate his commander's orders. This simple form of manoeuvring had already spared them direct hits from the said gun on at least two occasions. Even so, Legg was aware that it was only a matter of time before the German gunners would get lucky and correctly guess Legg's next manoeuvre.

It had come as something of a relief therefore when Saddler had spoken to Legg via the radio to inform him that the infantry had finally decided what to do about the enemy strongpoint on the hill. There was, it seemed, a considerable bombardment imminent on the German held wood-line and, while that was occurring, the infantry commander was planning to continue over the crossroads, up the Caen road for about one hundred yards, before swinging left onto a track that approached the flank of the enemy position. The track would become the axis of advance with Saddler's tank leading and suppressing the rear-most section of the wood, and Legg's tank following up a little way behind, bringing fire down on the forward edge of the wood as it progressed. The infantry would run alongside the tanks initially, using them for cover before breaking into attack formation and launching an assault into the trees. So far, so good.

"I wish the bloody footsloggers would hurry up!" Wells grunted from the gunner's seat next to Legg.

The corporal responded to the comment phlegmatically.

"Won't be long now; they're just sorting themselves out and waiting for the fire mission to come in. Just make sure we've got plenty of ammo ready to go for when we start moving."

It was at least the fourth time that Legg had reminded his gunner about ammunition conservation. They had already used more than half of their machine gun ammunition since landing on the beach earlier that day, and almost two thirds of their HE. The two natures of which they still had a full complement were smoke and armour piercing.

"As long as we don't end up like the poor buggers in Mr Barratt's tank..." Wells murmured.

Legg made no reply. There was no need. The same concern was on everybody's mind. They had all seen Barratt's tank get hit by two shells in rapid succession. The first had smashed his vehicle's running gear and immobilised it; the second had smashed into the hull of the vehicle and set it on fire. The speed with which Barratt's tank had been engulfed by flames had shocked Legg's entire crew. In truth, Legg had noticed the same thing on the beach. Even when other Shermans had been hit by shells that might not have ordinarily been enough to destroy the tanks outright, the vehicles had all caught fire quickly and burned fiercely. The thought of being trapped in a burning tank was terrifying and Legg tried to forget the image of Barratt's charred, dead body, draped over the hull of his still burning vehicle.

"Looks like we're going, Corp..."

The co-driver warned Legg.

The tank commander put his eyes to the periscope and saw Saddler's tank rolling forwards and swing left through a gateway in the hedgerow. On the verges, heavily laden infantrymen were struggling to their feet.

"Well, that bombardment is certainly getting heavier..." Legg remarked.

Even inside the armoured confines of the Sherman's turret, the reverberation of the shells and mortar bombs exploding on the hill could be felt.

"That should keep the bastards heads down..." Holloway added.

"Green flare!" Wells snapped.

"That's it then!" Legg became animated. "We're off, for sure. Driver – forward; follow the Troop Sergeant... And watch out for the infantry; we don't want to squash any of our own blokes."

Legg settled himself as Holloway began to roll the vehicle forwards. As he did so, he heard the sound of Saddler's radio operator telling him to follow on. Moments later, they turned sharp left through the gateway and then half right again as the track veered in that direction, heading uphill and across the meadows at an oblique angle. As he stared through his front periscope, Legg watched Saddler's turret swing to the right, the long, deadly 17 Pounder gun projecting over the heads of the infantrymen who ran alongside his tank.

"Okay, gunner..."Legg ordered. "Traverse left... steady... on... Watch and shoot..."

THE CRUCIBLE – POINT 113
TUESDAY 6TH JUNE 1944 – 1550 HOURS

Even a veteran like Gritz had to admit that things were starting to get serious. The sudden intensification of the bombardment certainly matched his experiences of Russian artillery and Gunther, crouching beside him, commented without any sign of humour that it felt like the night before the big Tommy offensive at El Alamein. The ear shattering explosions were backed by shock waves that went right through the body, and it felt as if the ground beneath the wood were some kind of living beast. Huge, foliage laden branches were being ripped from the trees and thrown down over the trenches and bunkers, and the inside of the wood was now filled with an eerie white mist that floated at waist height in the damp, humid, explosive filled afternoon air.

Despite this, the two German NCOs continued to stare out from the machine gun pit towards the crossroads; hoping to work out what the enemy's next move might be. The answer came when the two enemy tanks made a simultaneous move to the left, as Gritz looked at it, disappearing one after the other beyond the destroyed Sherman which still burned fiercely despite the feint drizzle.

"Where are they going then?" Gunther shouted over the racket of shellfire. "Looks like they're moving up the Caen road to our left."

Instantly, Gritz felt his stomach go heavy. Yet again, he felt a sudden pang of regret.

Caen; of course. The British had been learning from the Germans for four years, and now they were going to put those lessons into practice. Why make a frontal assault on the position when you could just by-pass it? This hill, in the big scheme of things, was only of tactical value. The city of Caen was a strategic target, and now the Tommies were going to ignore the German defenders at The Crucible and plough on past them in a race for the bigger prize. Hence the bombardment.

"I should have put the anti-tank gun here on the corner..." Gritz spoke, almost to himself.

"What?" Gunther leaned in close to him.

Gritz looked into the sergeant's eyes, his own showing alarm and urgency.

"They're by-passing us! Gunther, get half of your platoon together and bring them back to your rear left positions! Send a runner to the forward right platoon and get their MG34 sent over here too; with as much ammo as they can carry!"

Gritz paused momentarily, his mind working. They would never be able to move the anti-tank gun in time.

"Panzerfausts too! As many as you can find, and quick! The Tommies are trying to just drive right past us whilst we're pinned down under this bombardment. We've got to stop them!"

Gritz saw the look of realisation dawn in Gunther's eyes.

"We're not important enough are we?" The sergeant said out loud. "They're going for Caen..."

"They are..." Gritz shouted back above the deafening barrage. "Now get your men moving back to the rear left as quick as you can, and find me some fucking Panzerfausts... We're going tank-hunting!"

PART FIVE
ATTRITION

THE ORCHARD – SOUTH EDGE OF RANVILLE
TUESDAY 6TH JUNE 1944 – 1555 HOURS

W hoosh – crump! Whoosh – crump! Whoosh – crump!
The mortar fire came in again, but this time it was heavier; more sustained.

"Sounds like they mean business this time?" One of the young privates next to Dawes, a Midlander named Hulme, suggested.

"I reckon so." The corporal agreed. "Keep your eyes peeled on those hedgerows across the way there. There are plenty of lads covering that road; we don't want the bastards coming in across the fields when we're all looking the other way."

Whoosh – crump!

Another mortar bomb landed, but this one closer by; in the pastureland just forty metres in front of Dawes' position. Not for the first time in the last couple of hours, the corporal and his three comrades thanked their lucky stars that they'd been allocated the orchard as their defensive position. The large apple grove was bordered by a stout dry-stone wall, a three yard stretch of which the group had promptly disassembled in order to open up their field of fire. The stones that they had stripped away had been used to build a small parapet around the sides and rear of the slit trench they had dug in the opening in the wall. Thus, they were now firmly ensconced and ready for the fight which, they assumed, must be imminent.

All of the men were dog-tired. They'd been awake for well over twenty four hours now, and during that time experienced a terrifying, disorientating night drop; following which they had been pushed and pulled from pillar to post in the process of locating their battalion. Now they were finally settled, the fatigue was looming over them heavily. Even the dull crump of exploding mortar bombs, once gotten familiar with, became a kind of audible, rhythmic, sedative. Now however, Dawes recognised the change in tempo of the barrage. The enemy had switched from a steady harassing fire to an intensive bombardment, and as Dawes knew from his 1940 experiences, that generally meant one thing.

"The bastards are getting ready to attack." He muttered.

As if reading his mind, several enemy machine gunners opened up just a heartbeat later. The high-speed staccato of automatic fire cracked through the air, off to the right of Dawes' trench, and he spotted the bright blur of tracer rounds zipping above the hedgerows bordering the road, before slamming into the first building on the edge of the village.

"Here they come!" Hulme said, swinging his rifle towards the road.

"No!" Dawes grabbed the stock of the young soldier's Lee Enfield and dragged it back to face into the field. "Remember what I said; stay focussed on our own arcs. Don't get distracted by what's going on over there..."

The corporal's words were drowned out by the growl of engines as several enemy armoured cars and half tracks emerged from behind a copse just two hundred yards down the road. From his position in the trench, Dawes was looking obliquely at them across the field. He could see the flash of the pintle mounted machine guns, whilst the rattle of the vehicle tracks on the cobbles added to the racket of the gunfire and the noise of engines.

"There they are!" Hulme shouted excitedly.

"Watch your arcs!" Dawes reminded his three men once more.

Crump!

"Jesus fucking Christ!" One of the other privates swore, pushing his face into the dirt alongside Dawes and the others.

The mortar round had landed less than ten yards away, right against the dry stone wall which, thankfully, took most of the blast. Even so, the noise was deafening and the blast wave, directed sideways, was breathtaking.

"Fuck me! That was almost right on top of us!" The fourth paratrooper in the trench called out.

As the noise subsided, the pungent smell of burnt explosives drifted through the air, and further to the right, the sound of small arms fire intensified. A few seconds later there was another large explosion from the direction of the road, and this time even Dawes couldn't resist a sneaky peek. The convoy of enemy vehicles had come to a halt about a hundred yards from the village and the leading half-track was on fire; pouring bilious looking smoke from its hull.

"Nice shot, somebody!" Dawes observed.

As he watched the flames lick up around the bonnet of the burning half track, something caught his eye.

Flicking his gaze to the left, back into his own arc of fire, the corporal spotted the indistinct figures behind the distant hedgerow.

"The fuckers…" He yapped in surprise. "There trying to flank us! I told you they would! The cunning little bastards!"

Then remembering himself, he shouted out something more practical.

"Two hundred yards… hedgerow to front… enemy moving right to left behind it… rapiiiid… fire!"

He emphasised his own order by levelling his Sten Gun and letting off three short bursts in rapid succession. At nearly two hundred yards range, the cheap little sub-machine gun would be far from accurate, its stubby little 9mm bullets spreading out across a wide area, but on this occasion it was simply about spraying the hedgerow with as much fire as possible.

There was a loud report from Dawes' left hand side which made his ears ring, as one of the privates opened up with his rifle. A heartbeat later, Hulme and the other paratrooper opened up with their rifles too. For long moments, the world erupted into a crash of gunfire as all four paratroopers raked the distant hedgerow with fire, trying to bring down the men beyond it.

"Magazine!" Dawes yelled as his weapon's bolt shot rearwards and locked open with a hollow pop.

He dropped low in the trench and fumbled for a new magazine, exchanging it for his empty one just as fast as he could.

"What the fuck is that?" He heard one of his men shout above the gunfire.

"What's what?" Demanded the corporal as he completed his magazine change and popped back up into a fire position.

"Tank!" Hulme shouted in response.

"What fucking tank?" Dawes yelled as his head came up above the parapet once more.

It was a rhetorical question, uttered out of surprise more than anything, for the corporal's blood was already running cold at the sound of the word '*tank*', and there was no mistaking the great, bulky silhouette that now loomed up above the far hedgerow, almost directly in front of his position.

"Shit!" He cursed as his eyes took in the sight.

It was a *sort* of a tank; more like some kind of self-propelled artillery piece on the back of an armoured hull. He deduced that much from the fact that several heads were clearly visible above the metallic screen from which the evil looking gun protruded. A series of bullets slammed into the nearest piece of standing wall with resounding cracks, and one of them ricocheted off with a loud whine, causing all four men to duck involuntarily.

"What the fuck do we do now?" Hulme was shouting above the maelstrom of gunfire and explosions in the immediate vicinity.

Dawes' mind was working overtime and his limbs felt as if they were being given a pulse of electricity. He barely noticed the small, ungainly looking aircraft that wheeled overhead as he desperately wrestled with a plan.

The corporal's eyes settled on the three Gammon Bombs at the foot of the trench. As if a veil had been lifted, Dawes suddenly knew what to do.

"Hulme, you get these Gammon Bombs prepared! Make sure they're ready for immediate use! We'll try and pick the crew off from here! If the bastard comes any closer, we'll move along the back of the wall and stalk the fucker! When he breaks through the wall, we'll use the bombs on him! Okay?"

The three other soldiers shouted their acknowledgement above the noise and then, following their corporal's example, two of them pushed themselves back up into a fire position and began engaging the enemy once more.

"You two try and pick off the crew! I'll keep those infantry in the hedgerow busy!" Dawes called out, then immediately fired a couple of bursts into the foliage across the field.

There were plenty of bullets coming back at him now and he heard them crack past him, just inches away. He vaguely registered a grunt to his left and glanced that way between bursts. One of his men was collapsed, face down on the parapet. The back of the man's head was a sickening mess of blood, bone and flesh. Dawes looked away quickly and began firing at the enemy across the field once more, shrinking as low as he could against the parapet whilst still being able to use his weapon.

"Jesus..." He cursed softly to himself as he engaged his target with short, controlled bursts. "We could do with a bloody Bren Gun here...And a PIAT for that matter..."

"He's laying onto us, Jack!"

The voice to the left of Dawes was full alarm, and the corporal glanced left once more, ignoring the dead man next to him and concentrating on the other rifleman.

"What?"

"That fucking tank is laying onto us!"

Dawes switched his eyes to the still looming enemy assault gun across the field. Sure enough, the vehicle was manoeuvring itself so that it was aligned onto the trench that Dawes and his men were occupying. The vehicle's crew were cowering behind their armoured gun-shield and it was obvious that the barrel of the gun itself was being depressed towards them. Surely they wouldn't be able to depress the gun far enough? Not at such close range? The corporal, oblivious now to the bullets that were thudding into the grass in front of his position and slapping into the stone wall on either side of it, watched with horrid fascination as the assault gun's barrel slowly drooped to a point where he felt he was looking straight up it. He made a decision.

"Get out!"

With a speed born of desperation, Dawes threw himself sideways and up over the edge of the trench, rolling behind the stone wall.

"Get out!" He screamed as he went. "Get out of the fucking trench!"

Neither Hulme nor the other surviving rifleman needed prompting and the pair of them were already rolling over the parapet and behind the wall with Dawes.

"Get away from it..." Dawes gasped, scrabbling on all fours to get more distance between himself and the hastily vacated trench. Hulme and the other man were with him, the former clasping a Gammon Bomb in one hand, his rifle in the other.

Crack-boom!

The high explosive shell smashed straight into the trench behind them, causing the ground to lurch with sickening force. The shockwave sent all three men sprawling flat on their faces among half-ripened apples.

For long seconds, Dawes just laid there, gathering his breath. Eventually, he looked over his shoulder to see Hulme and the other man staring back at him with wide eyes.

"Fuck me!" Hulme breathed.

Dawes didn't answer, but simply pushed himself up against the back of the orchard wall. Despite the noise and shock of the near miss, the corporal's mind was working overtime, trying to figure out the next step.

"We'll fight from behind the wall..." He said at last, looking at his companions. "Keep low and spread out. Keeping moving around behind the wall so they can't get a fix on us. If that tank comes close enough we'll fucking do it with that Gammon Bomb..."

Even as he was uttering the words, Dawes became aware of the strange new noise that cut through the cacophony of battle like a knife through butter. It sounded a bit like incoming artillery fire, but of a kind that he'd never experienced before. The ominous sound of the shell descending from the culminating point of its trajectory was of a volume that defied belief. Then he remembered the strange looking aircraft that had passed over just minutes before and, as he realised what was about to happen, the first of the fifteen inch naval shells slammed into the field beyond the wall against which he was sitting.

Dawes felt himself being lifted up and then dumped sideways onto the floor, and a moment later, a lump of stone dropped onto his shoulder, making it throb. He cried out loud at the pain in his ears as that first shell erupted with a ferocity that was unimaginable. Above him, the branches of the apple trees swayed as if caught by a high wind and loose apples dropped down around the corporal and his two comrades, followed a moment later by a hail of earth and grass.

None of the three paratroopers made comment, nor attempted to, for the second big shell was already screaming down to slam into the hedgerow across the field, where its devastating blast hurled the German assault gun through the air and onto its side like a child's toy. The Germans were desperate to evict the British paratroopers from the high ground east of the River Orne. The British 6th Airborne Division were desperate to hold onto it; and the Royal Navy were determined that the latter would do so.

TACTICAL HEADQUARTERS 125TH PANZER GRENADIERS – 1 MILE SOUTH OF RANVILLE
TUESDAY 6TH JUNE 1944 – 1555 HOURS

"Stay down! Keep sending that message!"

Von Luck gave the order to the radio operator of his tactical headquarters as some of the massive shells from the enemy naval guns overshot his forward units and slammed into the field beyond the small farm with a spine chilling shriek and an ear shattering detonation.

Further across the farmyard, Beck, von Luck's driver, was peering out from the barn, into which he had reversed the staff car so that it would remain out of sight to enemy spotter planes. The half track, from which his radio operator was struggling to get communications with the forward units, was parked between the farmhouse and a brick out-building with a camouflage net thrown across it. As von Luck was starting to appreciate, the Tommy air power was absolute, and the massive guns of their invasion fleet could reach well inland, bringing down fire at short notice and with devastating results. Although there was often a pause of several minutes between salvoes, each one of those salvoes contained anywhere between six and twelve huge shells that could obliterate almost half a square kilometre in one go.

Now, he and his men were paying for the vacillation of the high command. He'd had a chance to launch an immediate attack during the hours of darkness when the enemy shells would not have been a problem; when the Tommy paratroopers would have been thinly spread out, ill prepared and disorientated. But thanks to the overly restrictive orders he and his men had been under, the opportunity to strike a decisive blow had been lost. The enemy airborne troops, who von Luck knew would be among the very toughest soldiers that the Tommies had available, had now managed to concentrate themselves in a defensive perimeter, effectively dominating the higher ground and shielding the captured bridges over the Orne River and Caen Canal. That position had been well sited and was now being equally well supported by the enemy's naval and air forces.

As for the Luftwaffe? Well, there had been no sign of them at all so far, and von Luck grimly suspected that there was little chance of that changing in the near future. Even if the Luftwaffe did get into the air over Normandy, he seriously doubted if they would get past the vast swarms of fighter aircraft that circled high up beyond the broken clouds, keeping watch over the equally numerous squadrons of heavy bombers and Jabos.

Even worse than that, the division had been split in two, with the bulk of the armour being sent to the west of the Orne. Thus, von Luck had been left to launch an attack with his own regiment, the reconnaissance battalion, and the improvised assault gun battalion. In theory, it was a powerful force, but it was a force unsuited to current operations. His command was largely mechanised, and trying to use them effectively in the close country of Normandy was difficult to say the least. The Tommies were concealed behind the thick hedgerows and copses that covered the terrain for kilometres around, and his vehicle-borne troops were finding themselves driving into one small ambush after another. It was a wasteful way to do business, he reflected, and found himself longing for the wide open deserts of North Africa or the sweeping plains south of Lille, where armoured troops could properly influence a battle.

"They've got the message, Sir."

The radio operator's voice cut into von Luck's thoughts.

"They're already pulling back anyway; they said the enemy shell-fire is too heavy..."

The commander of the 125th Panzer Grenadiers grunted in acknowledgement.

"Okay..."

Von Luck mulled over the problem. How was he supposed to make an impact on the battle under such circumstances? His mind thought through the various options. Had this been an experienced, well-drilled division, like the old 7th Panzer used to be, or even the original 21st Panzer that had fought in the desert, he could have tried some more sophisticated methods; but his regiment was largely filled with new, inexperienced men... or tired ones. He needed to keep things relatively simple.

As he turned the various issues over in his mind, von Luck became aware of the sound of engines. The major jumped to his feet and jogged across to the gateway of the farm where it met the narrow road to Ranville. Stepping across the dung-mired threshold of the farm, he looked up the lane and spotted the column of vehicles heading towards him. The first vehicle was one of the assault guns that had been improvised by mounting an anti-tank gun onto the old chassis of half completed French tanks, captured back in 1940. The ungainly looking beast was followed by a procession of half-tracks, armoured cars, at least one motorcycle combination, and another assault gun.

As the lead vehicle got to within fifty metres, von Luck stepped out into the middle of the road and began pointing into the large wood at the other side of the narrow way. Gawping over the bullet-shield of the assault gun, the vehicle's commander spotted von Luck's indication and shouted down an order to the driver. Moments later, the big armoured vehicle swung off the road and into the wood, using a section of ripped up hedgerow as its access point.

The remaining vehicles in the convoy did likewise, following von Luck's hand signals. As he stood there, waving the survivors of the last attack into the cover of the wood, von Luck felt the first drops of rain start to slap against his face. He looked up, grimacing into the steady drizzle, and studied the gathering cloud. Now that would do nicely, he thought.

Looking back along the road, von Luck saw a command variant armoured car approaching him. Instead of pulling off into the wood, the vehicle came straight towards him and pulled over onto the verge just metres away. Looking up, the major instantly recognised the reconnaissance battalion commander standing upright in the turret. As the armoured car ground to a halt, the lieutenant who commanded the unit pushed up his goggles and stared down at the regimental commander with a grim expression.

"It's fucking murder up there, Major!" The officer commented sourly.

Von Luck nodded empathetically.

"How bad?"

The battalion commander wiped his grimy face with the sleeve of his camouflaged smock.

"We lost two assault guns; and three half-tracks at least; maybe about twenty men in all…"

The lieutenant hawked and spat over the side of his armoured car into the long grass of the verge.

"These hedgerows and narrow lanes are a nightmare, Major. The Tommies have got small groups of men around every bend; and they know when we're coming. We almost managed to break into their position at one stage, but then those bloody naval guns came down us... God it was fucking awful..."

Von Luck said nothing. He was imagining what it must be like to be struck by half a dozen of those huge shells in rapid succession. There was no wonder his men looked stunned.

"They've got spotter planes overhead most of the time..." The lieutenant continued. "We shot one down, but they just sent another one over... And they've got balloons up over the ships. They're probably using them as observation platforms too. Every time we get in a position to break through, we just get hammered by their big guns. And if it's not the ships it's the fucking Jabos..."

The shattered officer gave a deep sigh.

"Anyway... there's no point complaining... I'll go and get the men sorted out. We'll have another crack at them in a while Major, if you don't mind? I thought we might go in dismounted this time; try and infiltrate their positions one by one."

Von Luck smiled.

"Well done, lieutenant. It's difficult, I know; but we must keep the pressure on them. Besides, look at the weather..."

The major held his hands out to the sides, palms upper-most, and grinned up at the sky.

"More fucking rain!" The lieutenant observed tiredly. "Still, that cloud is starting to thicken up again. At least it should keep the Jabos and the spotter planes away for a while..."

Von Luck beamed at the other officer, trying to encourage him.

"Exactly, lieutenant; it's perfect. You know what they call this kind of weather?"

The lieutenant offered a tired smile.

"Crap, shitty, garlic-tainted, French, fucking weather, Sir?" He hazarded a guess.

Von Luck laughed at the young man's cynical humour.

"No lieutenant... They call it *'attack weather'*!"

TACTICAL HEADQUARTERS, 1ST BATTALION THE HAMBLEDON AND MOORLANDERS – 600 YARDS NORTH OF POINT 113
TUESDAY 6TH JUNE 1944 – 1555 HOURS

"Right chaps; it looks as though we might be able to put a lid on this little show just up ahead on the left, so I don't want to hang around waiting for it to finish. It looks as though Dickie should be able to deal with Point 113 on his own, along with those two Shermans he's got up there with him. 'C' Company are providing him with fire support, so my intention is to drop both them and Dickie's company into reserve once they've got the whole business sewn up."

Lieutenant Colonel Blair, commanding the 1st Battalion of the Hambledon and Moorlanders, was laying against the bank of the drainage ditch a couple of hundred yards short of the crossroads below Point 113, surrounded by his tactical headquarters staff and the commanders of 'B' and 'D' Companies.

"Now listen; George? Your company is to move through immediately and then go firm in the vicinity of the crossroads. I want you to hold on there and wait to see if Dickie is able to break into that enemy position and deal with it on his own. If for any reason he runs into bother, you are to pass through him and finish off the enemy up in that wood; understand?"

Major George Carswell, commanding 'D' Company, nodded his understanding of the colonel's plan.

"As for you Will…" Blair switched his gaze to Major William Stone who commanded 'B' Company. "I want you and your chaps to wait for George's boys to get settled in behind Dickie, and then I want you to pass through the lot of them at the double and get clear of this little scrap. Once you've got past them, you are to continue the advance towards Caen, via Periers, as per the original plan. I reckon the village should be less than a mile or so beyond Point 113. To the best of our knowledge, it isn't occupied by any substantial German force; although having said that, Point 113 was supposed to be unoccupied too…"

Stone pulled a thoughtful face as he studied his map and glanced up towards the now smoke shrouded wooded ridge of Point 113.

"Anyway…" Blair went on. "You are to advance as far as the village and secure it. I then want you to remain there until I've confirmed that we've cleared out this little rats' nest. Once I'm happy we've finally got this wrapped up. I'll send the next company after you and give you the nod to continue on towards Caen again. As Dickie's boys are almost on top of the enemy now, I'll let you take the FOO along with you. Dickie can keep the

Mortar Officer until he's finished his business, and then I'll send him on to join you; hopefully with those two tanks hard on his heels. Now does all that make sense to you?"

Stone confirmed that he understood the colonel's wishes and checked his watch.

"It's nearly four now, Colonel; we're going to have to step it out to make Caen tonight."

Blair sucked his teeth in mild frustration.

"You're not wrong there Will; I know we're a good bit behind schedule but we can still do it if we get a wiggle on. That's why I want to get things moving again. I don't want us bogged down here all day. It does mean that you and your lads will be on your own as far as Periers, but don't worry about that; we're right behind you and we'll be following up just as soon as we finish this business here."

Stone nodded again and began stuffing his map into his trouser pocket.

"No problems, Sir. George; I'll let you get your boys moving and as soon as you give me a shout on the radio, we'll come straight on through..."

"Colonel Blair, Sir?"

The conversation was interrupted by one of the battalion's signallers who was looking across at his commanding officer with a worried expression. Blair turned towards the corporal who had called out to him.

"Urgent message from Brigade HQ, Sir. They say that the Shropshires on our left have bumped into a large force of Jerry armour. Apparently they're having a right old ding-dong with 'em. Brigade say that the Shropshires believe the enemy tanks are being pushed over towards us. They've told us to prepare to receive an armoured counter-attack..."

The words hit Blair like a physical blow. Tanks? And all he had was a couple of Shermans to receive them with. There was a long, heavy silence amongst the group. After a few seconds of thought however, Blair suddenly rapped out a string of quick instructions.

"Right, cancel what I just said... George? Get your company moving *now!* Take them forward at the double and plonk yourself down right behind Dickie's company, about a hundred and fifty yards beyond the crossroads. Shake out into a hasty defensive position and get your PIATs deployed. Will, start shaking out your chaps back here at the rear of the crossroads so we've got some depth. George, I'll send the anti-tank platoon up to join you. Get them deployed across your frontage as quickly as you can. Prepare to receive tanks imminently."

"Right, Sir!"

Carswell was already on his feet and turning back towards where his company were laid, waiting patiently in the afternoon drizzle.

"And George?"

"Yes Sir?" The harassed looking major checked himself, glancing back down at the colonel.

"Don't let anything past you, George. Nothing. You've got to hold them…"

Carswell gave a firm nod.

"Yes, Sir." He replied, his voice full of gravity. Then he was gone.

As the company commander from 'B' Company also sped off to brief his men, Blair called out for the man who he knew could get things moving quickly.

"RSM? RSM?"

"Here, Sir."

The battalion's senior warrant officer appeared out of nowhere to kneel beside the colonel.

"Did you hear all that?"

"I did, Sir; Jerry tanks inbound."

"Exactly." Blair confirmed. "Now do me a favour if you would, please? Get back there to where the anti-tank platoon is parked up. Tell the platoon commander to get moving immediately. I want him a hundred a fifty yards plus of that crossroads with his six pounders deployed in a screen covering due south."

"Got it, Sir."

"Oh, and RSM, tell him he'd better be ready to earn his money…"

THE CRUCIBLE – POINT 113
TUESDAY 6TH JUNE 1944 – 1555 HOURS

"Fucking hell! This is chaos! I can't see a fucking thing!"

Gritz was cursing like there was no tomorrow as he stumbled along the communication trench, heading from the forward left position of The Crucible, back towards his rear left positions that overlooked the old ruined forge and the track that led up to it from the main Periers-Hermanville road.

The last ten minutes had been devastating. Even to a veteran like Gritz, the sudden deluge of concentrated artillery and mortar fire had been all consuming, simultaneously battering at his consciousness and ability to think straight, whilst physically dragging the oxygen from his lungs and throwing him around on the floor of the machine-gun pit.

As the maelstrom of explosive death had continued, tree after tree had come crashing down within the confines of the small wood, adding to the terrifying din of the bombardment, and bringing the possibility of being crushed to death as close as that of being decapitated by red hot shrapnel. At the same time, the entire position had filled with a dense smoke that had started as the fleeting wisps of burnt explosive, then developed into a deliberately targeted smoke screen. The high explosive shelling appeared to have ceased now, but the smoke rounds continued to drop through what remained of the tree canopy, adding to the choking grey fug that made observation beyond a few metres impossible.

"Come on!" The sergeant major roared at the stunned and terrified soldiers he had dragged with him from Gunther's platoon.

Of the sergeant himself, there was no sign. He had crawled off to round up additional men from the forward right platoon and collect as many panzerfausts as he could muster. Gritz wondered if Gunther had even managed to make it that far, or whether he had been caught by the tremendous, overwhelming barrage that had come down on them just a few minutes earlier.

"Come on!" He roared once more, grabbing a coughing, stumbling soldier by the sleeve and pulling him along.

"Agh! Fuck!"

Out of the smoke, a tree appeared, its not inconsiderable trunk laid across the top of the trench and its thick branches and foliage completely blocking the trench itself. Gritz ploughed headlong into the thing before he even realised it was there, suffering a painful jab in the face from a shattered branch in the process.

"We can't get past…" The stunned young soldier beside Gritz blurted.

"Out of the trench! Go round it; come on! Move it!"

Gritz was in no mood for compromise. He was performing like some kind of automaton now; just as he had during those three cruel winters on the Eastern Front.

"Out of the trench and around it; come on you fuckers!"

He turned round and swore at the half dozen men from Gunther's platoon who'd followed him along the communication trench. They stared back at him with dirty faces and wide, dumfounded eyes; almost completely at their wits end following the murderous artillery barrage.

The sergeant major pulled the man whom he still held by the sleeve and threw him against the side of the trench.

"Get your hands together; give me a leg up…"

With dumb obedience, the soldier obliged, clasping his fingers together to form a stirrup which he placed on his knee. Gritz hesitated only long enough to remember to use his right leg and not his weak left leg. In an instant, his hobnailed boot was pushing down onto the soldier's hand whilst he scrabbled with his one free hand to grab a vertical revetment post. Having got some purchase, the grimy veteran emitted a grunt of effort and then pulled himself up and over the head of the soldier, and then over the lip of the trench itself. As he did so, the sound of bullets cracking through the inside of the wood reminded Gritz that the enemy had brought up more machine guns too, and these had now taken over where the artillery and mortars had left off.

"Next one!" Gritz snapped, rolling onto his side and looking back down into the trench. "Follow me and keep low..."

Surprisingly, the remaining soldiers surged forward and fought to be the first one to follow on after their commander. It was not through bravery and Gritz knew it. He'd seen the same thing before. The looks on their faces said it all. These men were terrified; their senses overwhelmed by what was happening to them. When that happened, men tended to behave like sheep and would follow the natural leader of the pack. It wasn't done through conscious thought or valour; men just needed to be around the person who seemed most likely to get them through whatever danger they were threatened by. But that was enough, Gritz thought. He didn't care how scared they were; as long as they followed. And follow they did; every last man.

In a long, field grey snake, the file of German infantrymen followed Gritz as he negotiated the fallen tree. It was surprising, Gritz noted, how much bigger trees looked when they had fallen over. After long moments of thrashing through undergrowth and tree foliage, the NCO finally located the bottom end of the trunk where it had been severed from its roots and, keeping low still, he slid over it, followed faithfully by his men. With the thickness of the tree trunk behind him to absorb the impact of enemy bullets that came snapping through the trees, Gritz moved faster, wincing every time he stumbled over an exposed root or rock and felt a painful twinge shoot through his damaged knee.

Within another minute of blundering through the smoke filled wood, he found the line of the communication trench again. Or rather, it found him. One moment he was wading through knee high undergrowth; the next he was toppling sideways into the trench which had suddenly appeared beneath his feet as if from nowhere. He bounced painfully off a loose revetment post and then hit the bottom of the trench with a painful thud. The sergeant major screamed in agony as his injured left knee twisted in its socket, despite the support of his knee brace. At the same time he tasted blood where he'd bitten into his own tongue during the fall.

"Aghhh! Fuck! Fucking fuck!"

Gritz lay there in the bottom of the trench, writhing in agony as one of his men slid carefully down beside him. Virtually every man in the company was like Gritz, carrying a variety of lower limb injuries that made them completely unsuited to the robust nature of infantry fighting.

"Are you alright, Sir?" The soldier was asking, staring down at Gritz with concern.

"Yes, yes, I'm fine!" Gritz snarled as he dragged himself up, enraged by how his leg kept betraying him at the most inopportune times. "Keep fucking moving; follow me!"

And with that, he hobbled off along the trench towards the rear positions once more. Behind him, his men clambered awkwardly down into the trench and hurried after him.

Fortunately, the company position was not especially big, and so it was just moments later when Gritz reached the fire trenches that constituted the depth fighting positions of the forward left platoon. Even as the sergeant major turned into the first fire trench, he heard the machine gun burst into life. Gritz stopped dead and stared in disbelief at the scene before him. Gunther was there, along with the MG34 from the forward right platoon and another half dozen men, all of them carrying panzerfausts. There was a cloud of smoke rising from the machine gun as the gunner and his No.2 engaged some unseen target beyond the edge of the wood. Gunther himself turned as he noticed Gritz standing by the opening to the fighting position.

"Gunther! You're here!" Gritz said, astounded.

For the life of him, he couldn't understand how the sergeant had managed to traverse the entire position and round up the resources needed, and then make it back here before Gritz and his men, who'd come directly down the communication trench. Gunther blew out his cheeks and raised one eyebrow.

"Only by the grace of God, Sergeant Major. That bombardment was something else…"

"And you've got the panzerfausts. Perfect… well done…" Gritz enthused, walking further into the trench as his own contingent began filtering through the gap behind him.

Gunther threw a glance at the riflemen who were already in the trench and preparing their simple yet effective anti-tank rockets.

"Yes… I've got every one we could lay our hands on…"

He looked back round at Gritz.

"But I don't think you need to worry about going tank hunting anymore…"

The sergeant major frowned at the comment.

"Why? What do you mean?"

The sergeant jerked his thumb over his shoulder towards the smoke shrouded slope beyond the wood-line.

"Those tanks that we thought were going right past us for Caen… Well, they've just turned off the main drag onto the track… They're coming right for us."

DICKIE SMITHSON'S FLANK ATTACK – THE CRUCIBLE TUESDAY 6TH JUNE 1944 – 1555 HOURS

"Ruddy hell fire!"

Smithson cursed out loud and ducked automatically as the two lines of orange tracer streaked out from the two separate pieces of high ground, curled towards him and converged on the track just a few yards to his front. The two bursts of automatic fire were melded into one as the deafening crack of passing bullets filled the air. Several orange blobs bounced off the hull of the leading Sherman and then flashed away with sickening whines, whilst the track just a few yards ahead suddenly erupted in a flurry of muddy spurts. Just in front of the leading tank, one of the riflemen from the nearest platoon suddenly collapsed sideways into the middle of the track and lay still. There was no scream, no theatrical dance of death, just a fully grown man dropping to the floor like a sack of potatoes; his life force already a memory before his body hit the floor.

Despite understanding that stark truth, Smithson nevertheless called out in horror as he saw that the body of the fallen soldier had landed right in the path of the advancing tank.

"No!" The company commander cried, stricken at what he knew was about to happen.

Nobody heard him above the din of battle of course, and even if they had of heard him, there was no way anyone could have done anything about it. Even as the cry of despair was leaving his mouth, the tracks of the 33 ton metal beast were beginning to churn the dead body into a bloody mass of unrecognisable flesh and bone.

Smithson averted his eyes; not wanting to witness the abhorrence. He took his mind away from the horror by yelling out orders to the men around him.

"Get in behind the tanks! Use them as cover! Get in behind them!"

He was already stumbling along behind the first Sherman with his signaller in tow, and now the men of his two assault platoons began dropping in behind it too. The battle-school instructors would have kittens to see so many men bunching together in such a small space, but confronted by the reality of having two German machine guns raking you with fire at an unbelievable rate, this was by far the best option. Rather take your chances behind the armoured hull of tank than out in the open.

As the tank rolled forward, the remains of the fallen soldier emerged from beneath the right hand track, his upper body and legs completely detached from each other and the intervening space just a welter of bloody tissue and bone. With a start, Smithson almost danced a jig to avoid stepping in the remains of the dead man, then leapt over him gingerly. As he did so, he heard Corporal Haines retch behind him, followed a moment later by the sound of watery vomit hitting the ground.

"Come on Corporal Haines, keep up!" Smithson encouraged the poor man, hoping to distract his attention from the scene of horror beneath their feet.

With an effort, Smithson began to wrestle with the problem of how best to launch his assault. They were almost halfway up the track now, and had just turned the final bend. Now Smithson was able to see more clearly the objective that was proving to be full of surprises. The wood on Point 113 seemed to be much deeper than he had at first thought, and the hill itself was more like two knolls separated by a narrow saddle of land. They were now approaching the position up the track which led directly into the saddle between the two wooded knolls, from both of which machine guns were chattering away at them.

The barrage that had just been laid down had been devastating. Even though Smithson and his men had been several hundred yards away, they had heard the hiss of the shrapnel passing over their heads as they advanced, and the infantry major had assumed, or *hoped* to be more precise, that the enemy would be completely overwhelmed by it, leaving him and his men to just walk onto the position and mop it up. It seemed he had been overly optimistic.

Now that the deluge of high explosive had finished and been replaced by smoke rounds, the enemy had come alive once more. Their machine guns were already in action, firing blindly yet accurately it seemed, and the random snap of rifle fire was beginning to join the unholy din of small arms fire. With a sudden, terrible jolt, Smithson realised that he was being channelled. He had walked into yet another killing area. Did he really expect the enemy to just sit there and let him outflank them? He now saw that his men were concentrated in a single column of packed men and armour, advancing up an ever narrowing defile, with a piece of high ground dominating either side of it. Shit. Smithson whispered a silent prayer that the enemy didn't have any anti-tank guns on this side of the wood. As he did so, his mind began to race once more; attempting to work out how he was going to deploy effectively from such a narrow frontage in order to capture two elevated strongpoints simultaneously. The scenarios in training were never this complex he reflected, bitterly.

"Sir! Major Smithson, Sir!"

The urgent appeal from Corporal Haines snapped the officer out of his grim thoughts.

"Yes?" Smithson paused and looked back at Haines. In addition to the radio operator there must have been another twenty men following on behind the Sherman. Further down the track, another forty yards or so, the second tank was also advancing steadily in their wake.

"What is it?"

Haines was holding onto one ear piece, his face creased with concentration as he struggled to hear the message coming through it above the hellish row of gunfire.

"Urgent message from Battalion, Sir!" The corporal replied. "They say we should prepare to receive tanks!"

Smithson's heart lightened for a moment.

"Thank God for that! We could do with some more..."

Haines was already shaking his head.

"No, Sir... Not ours. Enemy tanks. There's enemy tanks approaching from the south apparently. The CO wants us to watch our flank. He's sending the anti-tank platoon up behind us with 'D' Company."

Smithson stumbled to a halt and gaped at the radio operator with a dumbfounded expression.

"Enemy tanks?" He managed to blurt.

He could hardly grasp this latest twist. Smithson knew that the Gods of War were fickle, but now it seemed they were rolling their dice yet again.

"How many?"

Haines regarded his company commander with a worried expression.

"Apparently they've just come right past the Shropshires, Sir. Battalion says there are dozens of the buggers..."

WEIMER'S PLATOON – THE 21ST PANZER DIVISION'S COUNTER-ATTACK TUESDAY 6TH JUNE 1944 – 1600 HOURS

"Left Weiss; go left. Head towards the left hand side of that prominent wood where you can see all the smoke and artillery fire."

Weimer passed the order down to his driver as he saw the tanks of the flanking company pushing towards his own company's formation.

"There should be another road that passes Point 113 to the left. We'll try and pick that up. I just hope it's not already clogged up with the 192nd."

The big tank gave a powerful roar as Weiss, the driver, turned the vehicle half left and accelerated hard towards one of the ubiquitous thick hedgerows that bordered the fields here in Normandy.

"Hartmann? You keep your eyes peeled on these hedgerows; just in case there are any Tommies hiding behind them waiting for us…"

From the co-driver's seat where he manned the bow machine gun, Hartmann replied to his commander.

"Will do, Staff Sergeant. But do you really think the Tommies have got this far forward yet?"

Weimer considered the question for a moment.

"They must have. That's why we're being pushed left. The Second Battalion have run into strong Tommy forces over towards the right, so now the whole regiment is being pushed left; we're going to by-pass their main position and get in behind them. Just like we did with them in 1940 and just like we did with the Ruski's."

There was no reply from below, suggesting that Hartmann was mulling the answer over.

"Besides…" Weimer continued, "That smoke on Point 113 says it all. At the very least, the Tommies know we've got troops up there. If I know the Tommies, they'll sit back and hammer the place for a while before they attack. They won't be far away, let me tell you…"

"Village ahead!" Weiss interrupted Weimer mid-flow.

The panzer platoon commander glanced up over the lip of his cupola and saw the first squat, tidy, stone buildings of Periers village sticking up above the line of the hedgerow to their front. With a surge of power, the heavy tank reared up the bank on which the hedgerow was planted, reached tipping point and then crashed through the heavy foliage; snapping the small tress and interwoven shrubs as it crashed its way through. With a stomach heaving lurch, the Panzer IV dropped over the bank and onto a cobbled road that led into the village.

"Hard right, driver; onto the road and straight through the village."

As Weiss swung the huge tank round onto the roadway, Weimer got onto the radio to inform the company commander that he had reached Periers village and was moving through it. Instantly, the lieutenant who commanded the company replied that he too was in the village and would lead the company in column out of the built up area and down the Hermanville road, aiming to pass to the left of '*The Crucible*'.

"The Crucible?" Wesser, sitting next to Weimer in his gunner's seat pulled a face. "What the fuck is that?"

Weimer humoured the dour gunner.

"It's the new code-name for Point 113. We got it issued at the orders group this morning, just before we deployed."

Wesser had no time to reply, for at that moment, another column of Panzer IVs appeared from a side street to their front.

"There's the company commander's group…" Hartmann alerted them.

Weimer saw the identification numbers on the side of the turret and recognised the serial number that confirmed the tank as being that of Lieutenant Jung.

"Okay, let his group get on the road and then follow them on." Weimer ordered. "And keep your eyes peeled on the houses as we go through; just in case."

On they rumbled, the eleven tanks of Weimer's company forming up in column as they assembled in the village of Periers following their cross-country detour having being pushed left off their original axis of advance. Behind Weimer's company came the Second Company of their battalion with a further ten Panzer IVs. Somewhere else, possibly even further left beyond the village, was the battalion commander with the other two companies. Slowly, steadily, maintaining wide spacing between each vehicle, the heavy tanks trundled through the village which appeared, at first glance, completely deserted. Weimer wasn't fooled. He knew that behind the locked doors and shuttered windows, terrified civilians would be cowering in their cellars; praying that the horror of war would pass them by unmolested. From his long and bitter experience in Russia, Weimer also knew that those prayers would almost certainly be in vain.

They emerged from the village into open country again, where the little green pastures were bordered by the barrier-like hedgerows. They were going ever so slightly uphill, ascending the long low ridge that ran across the front of the village they had just left. Somewhere up on the plateau of that low ridge was the tiny pinnacle of Point 113, or '*The Crucible*' as it was now dubbed. The rising plumes of smoke denoted where that high point lay, just a few hundred yards ahead beyond the crest of the ridge, on which Weimer could see a small farm sitting hard by the roadside.

As the tanks ground steadily up the slope in line astern, Weimer fancied that he could hear the crackle of small arms fire in the distance.

"Stand-by fellahs…" He warned his crew. "I think there might be trouble up ahead."

Barely had he spoken the words when the Company Commander's voice crackled over the radio, issuing a collective call warning.

"All callsigns, baton down and extend into assault formation. There are Tommies all over The Crucible. Seven Platoon right, Eight Platoon left, extend now!"

Weimer dropped down into his seat, pulling the cupola hatch closed behind him as he went.

"Okay boys; this is it! We've been waiting long enough so let's make every shot count."

He settled himself in his seat and pressed his eyes to the forward periscope.

"Go half-right, driver; turn into that farmyard ahead and we'll shake the platoon out in the field beyond… Top speed… Advance."

LEGG'S TANK – HARD BY THE CRUCIBLE
TUESDAY 6TH JUNE 1944 – 1600 HOURS

"Jesus Christ! The Sarge just ran over one of our own boys!"

The cry of disgust from the co-driver was merely an echo of Legg's own thoughts. He'd seen what had happened but realised that there was nothing to be done on such a narrow track. What else could you do but keep advancing? The corporal tried to forget what he'd just seen and concentrate on the job in hand. He took his eyes away from the side periscope and jammed them back against the commander's sight. He found himself looking at a smoke shrouded wood-line, from which regular streams of tracer emerged.

"Keep on trying to suppress that bloody machine gun!" He encouraged Wells, his gunner. "The bastard's in there somewhere! Aim as low as you can because he'll be in a trench or laying flat on his belly…"

"Peggy? There's some footslogger waving at us up here!"

The call from the driver had Legg throwing himself sideways again to look through the side periscope. He hated being locked down in the turret; it was so disorientating. Peering through the viewfinder, the corporal saw Sergeant Saddler's tank rumbling on up the track some forty or fifty yards ahead. Behind that tank, pushing his way through the gaggle of infantrymen who were cowering behind the Sherman's armoured hull, he could see what looked like an officer, waving towards them.

"I think he wants to get on and speak to us..." Holloway, the driver, suggested.

"Bloody hell, he'll get his turnip shot off!" Remarked the co-driver as another burst of fire pinged off the side of the turret.

"Slow right down." Legg ordered. "I'll open up and wave him on board."

"Keep your ruddy head down then mate..." Wells murmured from beside him, without taking his eyes away from the gun sight.

Legg fumbled for the locking lever on the turret and slid it open, then pushed the double hatch doors open.

"He's climbing up the front deck!" Holloway informed Legg, as the tank commander gingerly popped his eyes above the lip of the cupola.

Despite the acrid, cloying smell of burnt explosive and smoke generators, the sudden rush of relatively fresh air was a welcome relief after being shut up in the fetid confines of the fighting compartment for so long. As Legg drank in a good lungful of air, a voice came to him from somewhere out on the hull of the vehicle.

"Commander? Tank commander? Hello in there?"

Legg cautiously scanned all around the top of the tank and spotted a khaki figure laying as flat as he could manage on the side deck of the hull.

"Yes? Here... What is it?" Legg shouted down to him, whilst keeping as low as possible.

The infantryman's voice was well spoken; upper-class.

"We've been told there are enemy tanks approaching from the south... so off to the right of your tank; the side I'm on."

"Jerry tanks? Are you sure?" Legg demanded, his heart rate increasing markedly.

"That's what we've just heard on the radio. Lots of them apparently; coming from the south. Can you keep an eye out in that direction for us? Once we get into the wood, you and the other chap can hold on at the edge of the trees and keep your eyes peeled in case they appear..."

Legg's mind began whirring with the complications and dangers that this latest piece of news presented.

"Okay." He shouted back at the infantry officer. "I'll radio the other vehicle and tell him..."

Legg's full sentence remained incomplete because at exactly that point, several bursts of tracer laden automatic fire came streaking in from the right hand side. One burst cut straight through the group of infantry behind

Saddler's tank, dropping three men instantly, whilst at least one other burst rattled off the front of the hull on Legg's tank, making him duck back inside the cupola in alarm.

"Bloody hell! They're here!"

Legg heard the terrified warning from the man outside on his tank's side deck, just a split second before the air was split by a huge, ear shattering crack, followed immediately by an explosion of obvious proximity judging by the way his tank shook.

"Shit the fucking bed!" Legg heard Wells cry out in shock from inside the turret. "Where the fuck did that come from!"

"Bollocks, but that was fucking close!" Holloway was shouting.

"Enemy south!" The upper class officer outside on the hull was shouting. "Panzers to the south!"

That one word, *panzers*, was enough to make Legg's blood run cold. He'd spent many sleepless nights mulling over the mind-numbing terror of a tank on tank battle, and wondering how he would react. Now he was about to find out. There was no doubt what was happening outside, because the terrified cries coming up from the infantrymen who surrounded the Sherman were plain enough to hear; even above the cacophony of gunfire.

"Panzers!" The word was taken up like a chorus as the word spread amongst the infantry. "Panzers!"

DICKIE SMITHSON'S FLANK ATTACK – THE CRUCIBLE TUESDAY 6TH JUNE 1944 – 1600 HOURS

The conversation with the tank commander was over. If the burst of machine gun fire bouncing off the hull just a foot away from Smithson hadn't been enough to convince him, the impact from the high velocity tank shell that slammed into the ground just a yard to the forward right of the Sherman had certainly confirmed that it was time to get off the tank.

Getting off the tank was proving more difficult than Smithson expected however. The deflated amphibious skirt that surrounded the DD tank had provided a useful purchase point when mounting the tank's front decks, but now, when attempting to roll off the side of the vehicle without sticking one's head up into the hail of incoming fire, the folded canvas screen was proving to be something of a hindrance.

The tank driver sorted the problem for Smithson unintentionally however, by suddenly jerking the vehicle forwards and then jamming the brakes on just as quickly. The company commander was catapulted unceremoniously over the side and onto the muddy track below. He hit the ground with a breathtaking thud and, remembering the fate of the man who had fallen in front of the leading Sherman just minutes before, rolled away onto the grass verge immediately.

Smithson lay there for just a couple of seconds then pushed himself up onto his knees. The air was filled with the crack of passing bullets and the sound of panic stricken voices. He looked up the track and saw the men from his company throwing themselves in against the verge and the hedgerow, pressing themselves as flat as they could get. Next to Smithson, the Sherman gave another deep growl and spewed out exhaust fumes, before lurching forwards several more yards. As the big, drab-green tank rolled forward, he saw the turret swing round, the fat little gun suddenly traversing over the right hand deck, and he let out a groan of apprehension.

Once more, Smithson threw himself flat on the grass and this time he clamped his hands firmly over his ears. Just a moment later, the Sherman fired its main gun. The blast that came sideways from the gun's muzzle slapped at his prone figure like a giant's hand and, once again, he cried out involuntarily at the shock of being so close to the gun's report. As the vibrations passed through him, Smithson realised that he needed to get away from the Sherman and start gripping his own men. He was useless laid here, cowering away from the muzzle blast of the 75mm tank gun.

Breathing heavily and forcing himself to stay calm, the major pushed himself to his feet and began doubling up the track, ducking low and sprinting under the overhanging muzzle of the Sherman's main armament; dreading the shockwave of another report. Fortunately, he cleared the blast area of the tank's gun without incident and ran onwards, towards where a large group of his men were piled up against the hedgerow, looking completely at a loss.

"Spread out!" He roared at the group as he approached them, ignoring the bullets that tore through the hedge to his right, missing him by inches. "Spread out and get ready to repel a counter-attack! Come-on; NCOs get a grip! Where's the PIAT team for this platoon?"

As he reached the centre of the khaki mass, Smithson felt the desperation rise inside him and he began lashing out at the men who seemed to be moving with infinite slowness.

"Come on!" He yelled, reaching down and grabbing a Bren Gunner by his webbing straps. "Get that bloody gun into action! Get into a fire position!"

He was hoarse with exhausted anger yet Smithson's fear-induced rage drove him on, kicking the listless men into position.

"Come on you idle bastards! Get lined out and start firing back! Where the bloody hell is that PIAT?"

A figure appeared beside him.

"Sir! We've got Jerry tanks pushing across the fields from that farm down the slope!"

Smithson whirled round and recognised the face of his Company Sergeant Major.

"Yes, I know! Find me the bloody PIAT teams from these two platoons and get them into position! As soon as those tanks come close I want them fucking well knocked out!"

For a second, the Company Sergeant Major blinked in surprise, for he wasn't used to hearing his company commander using such foul language. He recovered quickly however and nodded his head in understanding, shouting his acknowledgement above the din of battle.

"Will do, Sir! By the way, the anti-tank platoon are at the bottom of the track; they're going into action now!"

Smithson accepted the information without comment.

"Find me the Mortar Officer too! He's round here somewhere. Send him to me; straight away!"

"Right, Sir!"

The warrant officer gave his commander a thumbs-up signal then sped off at a low crouch.

Whoomph!

Behind Smithson, up the track, the other Sherman, the one with the longer gun, rocked on its tracks as it let loose with its main armament towards an unseen target.

Smithson knelt there blinking for a moment or two, breathing raggedly as he tried to compose himself. Blobs of rain dripped from the rim of his helmet, as he stared out from beneath it at the chaos around him.

Whoomph!

The second Sherman with the shorter gun fired again, sending a shell off towards the enemy tanks that were coming across the fields to the south. He needed to get a grip, Smithson knew. This was just like his experience four years ago, and his shoulder was aching like hell, just to remind him. The battle was turning on its head every few minutes; first giving advantage to one side, then to the other. Smithson needed to regain that advantage and keep it. The question was, *how* the hell was he supposed to do it?

Sucking in a deep breath, the major struggled to his feet once more and began doubling back along the track.

"Mr Normanton! Mr Normanton; where are you?"

"Dickie!"

The voice came from behind him. Smithson slid to a halt on the muddy track, turned round and saw the platoon commander waving his hands madly at him from back up the track towards the leading Sherman. Immediately, Smithson retraced his steps and ran back up the slope towards Normanton. As he ran, another burst of enemy machine gun fire arced over the hedge to his left and slammed into the track and undergrowth that bordered it, just yards ahead of him. He stopped dead as the mud spurted up before him and vaguely registered somebody grunting and keeling over on the verge to his right.

As the ruthless crack of the burst finally subsided, Smithson leapt forward again, veering towards where Normanton was crouching in the hedge bottom. The major was vaguely aware of the chugging sound of a Bren Gun in action and the dull thump of rifles being fired. That meant his men were returning fire at something or somebody. It was a start.

"Charlie!" Smithson gasped as he slid down beside Normanton in the wet, trampled grass of the verge. "Listen... We're in the middle of a real turd sandwich here! We've got enemy tanks coming in from the south, and we're right under the noses of the Jerries in this wood."

The platoon commander was looking worried and nodded his understanding.

"Yes..." The young officer replied. "I think we'd better pull back Dickie... We've bitten off a bit more than we can chew here..."

"No!" Smithson snapped at the lieutenant with unusual vehemence.

"We're not going anywhere! We're staying here and we're going to beat those bloody tanks, and then we're going to go up that hill and capture that bloody wood! Do you understand?"

Normanton blinked in surprise, stunned by the look of rage that had suddenly appeared on his company commander's face. He knelt there in stunned silence for a moment, gawping at the mud-spattered, sodden, dirty spectacle of his immediate superior and saw that the calm, cultured, scholarly mask of the man had dropped completely, revealing a grim, angry and exceptionally determined warrior who was literally foaming at the mouth. For a split second, Normanton's mind recalled the stories of the Viking Berserkers from the Dark Ages; men who had succumbed to a wild blood-lust in the midst of battle.

"Do you understand, Mr Normanton?"

Normanton jumped physically as Smithson demanded an answer.

"Yes, Sir..." The platoon commander blurted, suddenly more terrified of his company commander than of the presence of enemy armour.

"Good." Smithson barked. "Now listen carefully. Get your entire platoon to split its fire between those two bits of high ground in the wood. Keep that wood-line suppressed. Ignore the tanks for now and just keep those Jerries heads down on the high ground. Keep your PIAT team facing this way though; nobody else, just the PIAT. If any German tanks cross that field, blow the bastards sky high! Have you got all that?"

Normanton was nodding rapidly now.

"Yes, Sir... Got it."

Smithson seemed to calm slightly, but the grim, uncompromising look remained set on his features.

"Right, get to it. I'm going to sort out No.3 Platoon. There's no going back Charlie; not this time. We started this battle, and we're bloody well going to finish it!"

MAX WEIMER'S PLATOON – IN THE VICINITY OF THE CRUCIBLE
TUESDAY 6TH JUNE 1944 – 1600 HOURS

"Fucking hell, Wesser! How the fuck did you miss that!"

Weimer swore at the gunner as he saw their first shell miss the tank by a whisker.

"The fucker rolled back as I fired!" Protested the gunner as he opened the breech to allow the loader to feed in a new round.

"Re-lay onto him and fire again!" Weimer ordered.

The gunner was already adjusting the sights, but even as he did so, Weimer saw through his own sight that the Tommy tank was moving again.

"Sit still you island-monkey fucker!" A frustrated Wesser growled as he attempted to track the moving tank. At four hundred yards, the enemy vehicle should have been a sitting duck, but the thick hedgerows that ran across the fields to the front meant that only the turret of the enemy tank was visible.

"He's stopped! Lay onto him quickly!" Weimer ordered as he saw the tank's turret cease its forward motion.

"He's traversing onto us!" Wesser yelled.

Weimer had already seen it. The enemy vehicle's turret was spinning round to face them and, with a sick feeling that had become familiar after several years in Russia, the veteran NCO realised that the enemy gunner was going to beat them to the shot.

"Shit!" Weimer hissed. Then, shouting into the intercom... "Driver – reverse! Hard left!"

The big tank's engine roared and, with a powerful jerk, manoeuvred rearwards and to the left just as the Tommy tank's armour piercing shell came slicing through the air towards them.

The round missed the Panzer IV by just a few feet and even inside the confines of the armoured turret, Weimer and his crew heard the distinctive sound of the shell thumping past, displacing the air as it went.

"Driver – stop! Forward and left!"

Weimer decided to go straight back into their original position to reduce laying time in an attempt to catch the enemy vehicle with an opportunist shot.

Responding instantly to his commander's instructions, Weiss slammed on the brakes and threw the vehicle back into forward motion again, tossing the turret crew around the fighting compartment interior like rag dolls. Both Weimer and Wesser clung onto the turret equipment grimly until they felt the vehicle buck forward on its front drive wheels and then rock back down. As soon as the tank was settled, Wesser and Weimer had their eyes to the sights.

"There he is..." Weimer prompted, but the gun-sight was already shifting as Wesser laid their main armament onto the turret of the enemy vehicle.

"Up slightly..." Weimer advised. "Go for smack bang centre..."

The sight picture moved accordingly and a moment later Wesser signalled his readiness.

"On!"

"On – fire!" Weimer acknowledged.

"Firing now!"

Whoomph!

The tank shook as the big 75mm gun spat out another armour piercing shell straight towards the Tommy vehicle. Even as it did so however; Weimer spotted the movement of the target in his viewfinder.

"Bastard!" Wesser was screaming even as the tank was still shaking under the gun's recoil.

"Bastard, bastard, bastard!" The agitated gunner slammed his clenched fist against the breech block of the main gun. "The fucker moved again!"

Weimer grimaced.

"That Tommy knows his business..." He commented grudgingly. "Looks like they've learned some new tricks these last few years."

"Reload!" Wesser barked out in a sour tone, and flicked open the breech.

As the loader slid yet another armour-piercing round into the gun's smoking breech, Weimer made a decision.

"Bollocks to this…" He said to the crew across the intercom. "Let's just do this the old fashioned way shall we and see how big their balls really are?"

The tank platoon commander flicked his pressel switch to send on the radio net.

"All one-seven callsigns, advance straight for them. I say again, advance straight for them. Run them back into the sea… Go, go, go!"

Wesser looked sideways at Weimer as he heard the orders go out to the other tanks in their platoon.

"Sounds good to me." He grunted.

"Let's do it then." Weimer growled. "Driver – forwards. Go straight for them. Advance…"

The Panzer IV gave another growl of its powerful engine then began pushing forward through the hedgerow…

GRITZ AND COMPANY – THE CRUCIBLE
TUESDAY 6TH JUNE 1944 – 1605 HOURS

"What the hell is going on now?"

Gritz shouted out the rhetorical question as he stared in bewilderment at the confused scene below. One moment the enemy had been pushing directly up the track towards them, all guns blazing; now they had stopped dead and seemed to be turning their attention away to the south.

"What are they shooting at?"

Beside him, Gunther shook his head.

"Not sure, Sir; looks like they're being engaged from across those fields…"

The sergeant looked as puzzled as Gritz felt.

"By who? We haven't got anyone across there. That's where the farm is…"

The sergeant major's words tailed off as he raised his binoculars. Carefully he scanned the smoke distorted scene downslope of his position towards the track. He could see the turrets of the two enemy tanks, peeking above the hedgerow that bordered the lane. Now however, those tank turrets were clearly pointing away from his position and facing south. As he focussed on the lead enemy tank, he saw its main gun spit flame as it fired at some unseen target off to the south.

Carefully, trying to keep his hands steady, Gritz swung his binoculars slowly to the left, away from the enemy vehicle, and traced a route

324   Crucible of Fate

southwards across the open fields that sat alongside the road to Periers village and to Caen beyond. At first he saw nothing but a wide expanse of lush grass, on which, numerous cows were galloping around madly as they were caught in the middle of a vicious fire-fight. He noted more of the unfortunate animals lying still on the ground, obvious victims of the battle that was currently raging in the vicinity. He paid them no heed and continued to scan left.

A hedgerow came into view. This one cutting up from the road itself and coming across the field, partially obscuring the farm beyond. At first he saw nothing unusual, but then he saw a flash of orange flame; a mere dart of light, over by the road itself. He focussed on the Periers road and caught his breath. There were tanks there. They were some four hundred metres away at least, just in front of the farm, trundling steadily up the road in the direction of the crossroads. He'd seen enough of these types of tank to recognise the outline instantly; even through the fleeting smoke. They were Panzer IVs.

Hardly daring to believe his eyes, Gritz began scanning left again, back across the frontage of the farm. There. He saw it. The sight made his heart leap. Another Panzer IV, pushing through the foliage like some primeval beast emerging from its lair. A surge of joy ran through the harassed commander's mind. He had no idea which formation these panzers belonged to, only that they were definitely German and they were definitely attacking the Tommies.

"They're ours!" He cried out jubilantly.

"What?" Gunther was still squinting through the battlefield smoke, trying to fathom what was happening.

Gritz snatched the binoculars away from his eyes.

"They're ours!" He grinned madly at Gunther. "There are friendly tanks coming up from the village! Fuck knows who they are but they're German and that's all that matters; a whole bunch of Panzer IVs!"

Gunther stared at his commander in astonishment, hardly daring to believe that their salvation had arrived.

"Now the Tommies will get a lesson in tactics." Gritz thumped his fist on the sandbagged parapet of the fire-trench in delight.

Over to one side, the two men crewing the MG34 released another long burst through the haze, and bright tracer streaked downslope towards where the enemy had apparently gone static by the bend in the track. As Gritz watched the tracer slice into the dull linear silhouette of the hedgerow, a thought came to him.

"Right let's give those tank boys a hand shall we?"

"Pardon?" Gunther blinked in surprise.

"Those Tommies are caught like rats in a trap!" Gritz enthused. "They're busy dealing with our panzers coming from the south, so while they're distracted, lets go and give them a kick up the arse shall we? We've got plenty of Panzerfausts so let's get down there and pick off that lead enemy tank; show those Tommies that they've picked on the wrong Germans!"

"Sergeant Major..." Gunther started to speak but stopped mid sentence, not sure how to express his concern. "Surely it would be..."

Gritz wasn't listening; he was caught up in the moment. He knew it was happening to him but wasn't remotely concerned. He had experienced this feeling many times before in the frozen wastes of Russia. The feeling had always come upon him when the situation had seemed hopeless and the outcome was almost a foregone conclusion. It was a feeling of release; of invincibility almost. If he was going to die then why not die like a warrior of ancient legend, surrounded by the corpses of his enemies? It was that mindset that had taken hold of him on the day he had won his Knight's Cross, defending a relatively worthless piece of woodland, not that different from his current position.

Suddenly sensing that all was not lost and that this could be another day of glory, Gritz felt the sense of helplessness slip away. The disorientation was gone, as was any thought about the instability of his injured left leg and the mind-numbing shock of the recent bombardments. The enemy were stranded right in front of him, their attention diverted; and here he was looking down on them ready to strike. The 'red-mist' as he often referred to it had descended on him. Gritz wanted a fight.

"We'll go by the ruins and straight down the track at them. They won't be expecting a frontal counter-attack..."

Gunther was staring, open-mouthed, at his commander, but the sergeant major was oblivious to the NCO's obvious reservations.

"Gunther, stay here with the gun team and keep those Tommy bastards occupied." Gritz ordered him. "You, you, and you..." He pointed to three riflemen in rapid succession. "Grab a Panzerfaust each and follow me..."

The sergeant major slung his machine pistol over his shoulder and grabbed hold of one of the man-portable anti-tank rockets that had been deposited on the floor of the trench. He grasped it in both hands and flashed a devilish smile at the men around him, his eyes gleaming with wicked anticipation.

"Let's go kill us a Tommy tank!"

1650 SQUADRON, ROYAL AIR FORCE – OVER NORMANDY TUESDAY 6TH JUNE 1944 – 1610 HOURS

Windy Whittaker scanned the ground below like a hawk searching for prey as he and his squadron roared across the Normandy coast for the second time on that momentous day. They had enjoyed no more than six hours break whilst their aircraft were refuelled and rearmed before being launched across the Channel once more in support of the huge operation. Rumours had abounded back at base during their time on the ground, but the consensus of opinion was that the initial landings had been successful and that the Army was now fighting to extend its toe-hold in France. It was hard to believe Whittaker thought, for only a day before, a successful invasion of mainland Europe still seemed to be far away. Now however, it seemed that the combined Allied armies had done it and broken through Hitler's much vaunted Atlantic Wall.

This second sortie was a much more flexible business than their earlier escapade that day of course. There was no fixed target. Rather, 1650 Squadron had been tasked to join the 'taxi-rank' over Sword Beach, the eastern-most landing area, and be prepared to conduct interdiction against enemy reinforcements should they attempt to move up to the coast. Now it seemed, they would be released to do exactly that. Called off station just minutes earlier, Whittaker's squadron had been ordered to fly a wide circuit over Caen to try and spot enemy armour, fragmented reports of which were beginning to come in to the forward air controllers attached to the landing force.

Thus, Whittaker and his men were now roaring above the green fertile countryside of Normandy at a mere four thousand feet, just below the cloud base that was threatening more rain, heading towards the western edge of Caen. Below them, much of the countryside was punctuated by small clouds of artificial smoke of various colours and hues, marking where numerous small units were fighting their own particular actions. And it was as the squadron passed by one of the more substantial palls of battlefield smoke that the extreme left section leader came onto the RT in a state of some excitement.

"Tanks, Red Leader! Nine O'Clock! Loads of the buggers!"

Whittaker responded instantly.

"Who's tanks, Yellow Leader?"

"Jerries I think… If not, then our boys are driving the wrong way…"

Whittaker felt the hairs prick up on the back of his neck. It sounded too good to be true.

"Peel off into spin-wheel then hold there whilst I take a look; line-astern, follow me..."

With practiced ease, Whittaker pulled his aircraft up out of formation and banked gently to port. One by one, the remaining rocket armed Typhoons peeled off and formed a single line behind him which gradually curled into a large circular formation. Once assembled, Whittaker gave his men one more reminder.

"Hold your formation up here chaps until I've had a look... and keep your eyes peeled for Jerry fighters."

A moment later, Whittaker dropped out of formation and headed south, losing height as he went. He searched for the large smoke cloud he had noted when the original sighting was made and thought he could see it hard over his left shoulder. He brought his aircraft around in a tight turn to port once more and then dropped his nose, diving down to just a thousand feet as he ploughed north, back towards the coast.

As he flew, he kept his aircraft weaving gently from side to side, partly from the habit of self-preservation, and partly to enhance his view of the terrain below. At first it just looked like a patchwork of different greens and browns, punctuated by smoke. However, just as he lined himself up on the large patch of dirty grey smoke, Whittaker caught something out of his eye corner. He looked down sharply and caught his breath.

"You buggers!" He gasped to himself. "There you are!"

Initially he had spotted just the line of vehicles trundling up the narrow road towards the coast, partially hidden as they were by the thick hedgerows on either side. Then however, as he'd executed a sharp turn to starboard, Whittaker had seen the other vehicles strung out across the adjoining fields. More than a dozen tanks at least he reckoned, and big buggers at that; precisely the kind of targets the Typhoon had been developed for. If he'd needed any confirmation as to the nationality of the vehicles, it came just a heartbeat later as a stream of tracer came snaking up from the ground towards him.

Whittaker flung his plane into another sharp turn then brought his nose up, searching for his squadron in the flat grey sky above. He spotted them and flogged the heavy aircraft upwards towards the deadly looking collection of fighter-bombers as they circled like vultures above the battlefield.

"Red Leader to all sections; they're Jerries alright. Well spotted Yellow Leader. We'll go in with sections in echelon, from the south. Stand-by to peel off. All sections acknowledge..."

One by one, the other three section leaders in the squadron acknowledged Whittaker's warning order.

The squadron leader brought his aircraft up, straight through the centre of the formation so that everyone could take station on his aircraft with its distinctive Star and Garter badge on the nose; the emblem being Whittaker's small tribute to the Army regiment that had saved his bacon during the Dunkirk campaign. At the same time, he reached down and touched the brass Coldstream Guards capstar that he'd been given by a sergeant of that regiment as a lucky charm.

"Okay 1650, there are plenty of targets so make your rockets count. Sections astern, follow me…"

DICKIE SMITHSON'S POSITION – HARD BY THE CRUCIBLE
TUESDAY 6TH JUNE 1944 – 1610 HOURS

Whoomph! Whoomph!

The sound of the 6 Pounder anti-tank guns barking out defiantly from the area where the track met the main road was hugely reassuring to Smithson; as was the sight of the leading enemy tank on the road burning fiercely and belching thick black smoke. Every few seconds, small secondary explosions would rip through the burning hulk as the unused ammunition inside the vehicle detonated with the heat.

Despite the sudden intervention of his battalion's own anti-tank platoon, Smithson was still far from returning to his usual state of professional calmness. The enemy tanks were advancing on a broad front and he could see at least three of them advancing straight towards him across the fields by Point 113, all of them seemingly decided on charging straight through his little force.

It was a terrifying yet crazy sight, Smithson thought. The three big German tanks were ploughing through the last hedgerow as they roared headlong towards the British defenders, blazing away wildly with their machine guns demonstrating a surprising degree of inaccuracy. The major could see the lines of enemy tracer arcing high over the heads of his men and realised that firing on the move must be exceptionally difficult for the enemy tanks crews. It wasn't just the enemy who were experiencing problems in the heat of the close contact engagement however, for the two Shermans attached to his force had problems of their own. Despite the close range of the enemy, trying to engage a moving target was proving something of a trial for the British tank gunners, as their armour piercing rounds sliced through the damp air, only to slash past their fleeting targets harmlessly.

There was no other way this could end, Smithson realised. The enemy were almost upon them and he was about to experience once again the terror and mayhem of a full-on gutter fight between a confused mix of infantry and armour on a battlefield partially obscured by smoke. The last time it had happened to Smithson, he had been on the losing side, completely overwhelmed by the ferocity of the enemy assault. This time, he told himself, it must be different. His determination was reinforced as the Sherman with the longer barrel spat out another armour piercing shell, following which, one of the enemy tanks pushing through the hedgerow suddenly reared up on its rear idlers and disappeared inside a cloud of flame and smoke. They could stop them, Smithson told himself as he ran along the smoke shrouded, body strewn track. They *must* stop them. Smithson was so absorbed with these thoughts that he never even noticed the roar of the aircraft engine, nor the shadow of the plane that raced above his head at just a few hundred feet.

He spotted the PIAT team from No.3 Platoon, accompanied by their platoon sergeant, crouching in the hedgerow at the ready, their faces dripping with sweat and etched with fear. Their look of fear was unsurprising really, Smithson thought, because in order to stand a chance of hitting the enemy tanks with the rudimentary missile projector, the crew would have to hold their nerve and allow the vehicle to get within one hundred yards. Panting heavily, the major slid in beside the three men.

"Here they come..." He patted the man holding the projector, on his shoulder. "Leave it to the last moment then put it right up his snout!"

The private soldier glanced briefly and nodded at his company commander, his face pale and serious.

Smithson looked through the opening in the hedgerow and saw that the two remaining enemy tanks were in the middle of the field and grinding inexorably upslope towards them.

"Here they come... take the bastard nearest to us..." Smithson spoke calmly to the man behind the PIAT, despite experiencing a thrill of private fear that he fought desperately to control.

He must stay calm for the sake of his men. They must know that they could win here. Even as he was telling himself this, a movement further back across the field caught his eye. Smithson squinted through the shrubbery towards the far side of the field and he clamped his mouth shut in an attempt to prevent himself from crying out in despair. Pushing through the hedge behind the two advancing German tanks, and advancing through the smoke of the burning panzer, came a further four enemy tanks.

"For fucks sake!" The sergeant swore. "How many of the bastards are there?"

Smithson was thinking exactly the same thing.

Whoomph!

He heard the sound of the 6 Pounders firing again and watched with fascination as one of the panzers in the follow-up wave suddenly swerved to one side as something bright flashed against it. Even before the tank rocked forward to a standstill it was throwing out dirty grey-black smoke, and flames were beginning to lick from beneath the broad armoured skirts that almost fully covered the vehicle's running gear.

If the company commander hoped that things were turning his way, then his hopes were dashed just a moment later when a sudden, deafening blast erupted somewhere to his left. Smithson, the sergeant, and the two crewmen on the PIAT instinctively ducked lower, pressing themselves as far into the bank and hedgerow of the narrow lane as they could, just as huge bits of metal and rubber came flying above their heads at unimaginable speeds, slashing into the bushes around them. The major looked to his left sharply and felt his heart sink as he saw smoke and flame pouring from the nearest Sherman, the one with the stubby gun. He had no idea where the tank had been hit but it was brewing up rapidly, with huge great flames leaping up from its rear decks.

"Stand-by…"

The PIAT gunner's voice cut through Smithson's thoughts and he tore his eyes away from the burning Sherman, just as he saw the turret hatch being pushed open. The nearest enemy tank was almost upon them; so close in fact that Smithson could hear the squealing and grinding of the tank's running gear as it clawed its way across the sloping field towards them. At just a hundred yards distance, the panzer looked huge, its long main gun protruding over its front decks like the deadly snout of a giant ant-eater.

"Make sure you…"

"Firing now!"

The PIAT gunner ignored Smithson's unfinished sentence and fired his projector. There was a sharp bang, a loud plopping noise, and then an ungainly looking bomb that resembled an oversized gnat was arcing clumsily through the air towards the oncoming vehicle. The fat little bomb seemed to hang in the air in front of the tank for a second before suddenly dropping like a stone onto it.

Crump!"

The PIAT's bomb thumped into the front of the tank's hull with a resounding explosion, a bright flash, and a great cloud of smoke.

"Target!" The PIAT gunner shouted triumphantly, then, "Reload!"

With frenzied actions, the No.2 fumbled with a second bomb and began inserting it into the front of the PIAT. The gunner meanwhile was cocking the weapon, ready for another shot.

Smithson allowed the men to go through their drill without interruption for he was too busy staring at the enemy tank that had just been hit. The smoke was gradually thinning and from behind the dissipating skeins, the big armoured beast jerked forward; awkwardly at first, but then with more purpose.

"Shit!" The sergeant exclaimed, once more echoing Smithson's own thoughts. "The bastard's still coming!"

"Fire again!" Smithson blurted out. "Hurry up! Put another one right into him!"

The major dropped his head against the bank at precisely that point because the enemy tank, having presumably spotted the danger, fired a lengthy burst right towards them. Several rounds cracked above the heads of the four men crouching in the hedgerow, just inches away, whilst others thumped into the front of the earth bank against which they were laid.

Smithson twisted his head sideways and yelled at the PIAT gunner.

"Come on! Hurry up and kill that bloody tank!"

"What's that noise?" The platoon sergeant was asking of nobody in particular, laying on his back against the bank and frowning up into the grey sky.

Smithson wrinkled his brow and stared across at the NCO.

"What bloody noise?" He asked in irritation, wondering how the sergeant could mistake the sounds of gunfire and tank engines for anything else but what they were.

Almost as soon as he'd spoken however, Smithson checked himself. He could hear it too.

Rolling onto his back, the major stared up into the sky like the sergeant, trying to spot the source of the new and somewhat ominous sound that had intruded on the already chaotic symphony of battle. Aircraft. It was definitely an aircraft; or several. Not only that, the aircraft was obviously close by and its pilot was putting the machine through its paces judging by the screaming of the powerful aero engine.

"Fucking hell! Get down!"

The PIAT gunner's cry of alarm could only just be heard above the sudden, all-consuming, shrill sound of straining aircraft engines. Smithson rolled back onto his side and threw a quick glance through the hedgerow back towards the advancing enemy tank... and caught his breath.

Descending from the grey, leaden skies, like avenging Harpies from Greek legend, a swarm of deadly looking single-seater aircraft came sweeping down across the hedgerows and fields to the south of Point 113, just a few hundred feet above ground level, coming in behind the waves of German tanks. For a second, Smithson caught an image of slightly angled wings and wondered if the Germans had somehow managed to whistle up a squadron of the legendary Stukas to aid them in their counter-attack. But then, from underneath the wings of the leading aircraft, there was a flurry of smoke and sparks as eight armour piercing rockets were released towards the German armour.

Smithson watched, mesmerised, as the first aircraft began pulling up from its attack run whilst its rockets began curling down onto target. He spotted the distinctive black and white bars that had been painted onto the plane's wings as identification markings and his fears were momentarily dismissed as he understood that he wasn't seeing a squadron of Stukas in action, but a squadron of the Royal Air Force's deadly rocket-firing Typhoon fighter bombers coming to his rescue. And then, just as quickly, the fear returned, for Smithson had already recognised the fact that he was engaged in a close-quarter battle with the enemy armour, and that in turn meant one thing. He was just as much in the target area as the Germans were.

"Everybody down!" Smithson screamed out at the top of his voice. "Get bloody down!"

The infantry major pushed his face into the grass and dirt, trying to burrow his way even further into the bank as the first eight rockets slammed into the ground surrounding the German armour that was now less than a hundred yards from his position. And then the following aircraft began releasing their own deadly cargoes, and turned the entire hillside into a living, explosive filled hell...

GRITZ'S TANK STALKING PARTY – THE CRUCIBLE, POINT 113
TUESDAY 6TH JUNE 1944 – 1610 HOURS

"Come on; quickly!"

Gritz crouched behind the ruins of what was once the main building of the derelict forge and beckoned urgently to the three other men who had followed him down from the trenches of his main defensive position. The trio of soldiers, all of them men carrying leg injuries like himself, peered out from behind the tumbled down barn at the other side of the muddy yard with worried expressions.

"Come on!" He mouthed the words and beckoned again.

He could have shouted at them of course, for the background noise of battle was overwhelming and nobody beyond his small group would have heard the words, but the habit of secrecy was deeply ingrained in the seasoned campaigner and the thrill of the hunt was upon him.

He placed his spread fingers on the crown of his helmet and mouthed the words again, his eyes bulging in frustration, then held his clenched fist out to the side and pumped it up and down rapidly several times to emphasise the urgency of his order.

"Come on you fuckers!" The sergeant major snarled under his breath.

Much to Gritz's relief, the soldiers crouching behind the barn seemed to find their courage and came doubling out of cover, limping towards him as fast as their feet could carry them. He noted with wry amusement how low they were crouching as they ran. Any lower and they would be on all fours.

As a veteran of several campaigns, Gritz knew how to read a battle. There was lots of noise filling the air, from small arms fire to the main armament of tanks; yet as a man of experience, Gritz could see that little, if any of it, was coming in their direction. The Tommies it seemed had turned virtually all of their attention to the new and pressing threat of the panzers on their southern flank. Besides that, Gunther, who had remained on the main position, was co-ordinating as much fire as he could onto the thick hedgerows that demarcated the lane, thus giving Gritz and his small group a substantial amount of fire support. And that was all Gritz needed; just a few minutes to get close enough to launch one, if not two Panzerfausts at the leading Tommy tank, before withdrawing rapidly, leaving the Tommies to wonder where the sudden strike had come from.

He'd done this many times before on the Eastern Front; even playing dead on one occasion whilst a T-34 had rolled over his position, after which he and several others had 'come alive' and put several rockets up the Ruski's arse. Gritz could feel the adrenalin surging through his body now; not the disconcerting adrenalin rush of sudden fear, but the exhilarating adrenalin surge that heralded the *'battle-lust'*; that feeling of sheer joy at the prospect of aggressive action. It was a terrible feeling of rage combined with exultation that left one feeling as if they were walking amongst the Gods. And that feeling had now taken full possession of Gritz.

As the three other soldiers squeezed in behind the ruins of the forge, Gritz flashed a wicked, toothy smile at them.

"Right then, lads, it's time to give the Tommies the shock of their lives!"

He held his machine-pistol out to one of the men.

"Here. Sling your rifle and get hold of this. You stay hard by me and get ready to spray the hedgerows if you see any Tommy infantry pop their heads up."

Handing his weapon over to the soldier, Gritz drew his own automatic pistol and pushed it half inside his tunic, before gripping his Panzerfaust with both hands.

"You two…" He looked at the remaining soldiers in turn. "One of you on either hedgerow, just behind us two, rifle s up at the ready. Same detail. If you see any Tommies, then plug the bastards as soon as they stick their stupid heads up. And be prepared to use your own rockets if we don't take care of the tank with this first one…"

He gestured at the Panzerfaust rockets that the two men had thrust awkwardly through their equipment braces.

"Understand?"

They nodded that indeed they did.

"Good. Let's get to it then." Gritz bared his teeth in another devilish grin. "It's time to book our place in hell!"

The look on the faces of his men suggested that they were happy for their commander to make that a single booking, rather than a group affair. Nevertheless, when Gritz struggled to his feet and shook off his aching left leg, they all rose with him and followed on behind as he emerged from the ruined stone building and stepped onto the narrow lane, on which a full company of Tommy infantry and their two Sherman tanks awaited them.

They moved quickly, despite their shambolic gait. A distant observer could easily have laughed at them as they limped and hobbled down the track towards a significantly more powerful foe, looking for all the world like four old men who had been pressed into unexpected service. Looks are often deceptive though and Gritz, despite being hampered by his weak left knee, was a warrior of experience and his mind was set. He advanced down the track at a low crouch, the Panzerfaust held ready at his side. To his right, the private carrying his machine-pistol limped along beside him, keeping pace, his nervous eyes flicking from one hedgerow and grass verge to the other. Just a little behind them, on either side, the other two men tip-toed forward, their rifles up in the aim, their nervous eyes scanning feverishly just above the battle-sights of their weapons.

Down the track, the leading enemy tank was coming head onto them around the bend, continuing its repeated jockeying drill of moving backwards and forwards between releasing shots, in order to make itself a difficult target to the German armour.

"Here he comes!" Gritz called out in anticipation. "He's driving right into us, God bless him!"

The veteran broke into a clumsy jog as he encouraged his men.

"Come on; faster! Let's close the range before he realises the danger!"

Together, the group broke into a laughable attempt to rush the vehicle.

The big green Tommy tank came rolling around the corner in a spray of mud and advanced maybe ten metres towards them before suddenly coming to an abrupt halt, the entire vehicle rocking forward on its suspension as it did so. Even as the tank was settling back down on its running gear, the long gun was moving, adjusting its aim onto some unseen target somewhere to the south, beyond the hedgerow. The vehicle was less than fifty metres away now; perhaps forty at the most.

"Come on!" Gritz yelled. "Another ten metres and we've got him!"

The four soldiers increased their speed, limping and hopping as fast as they could through the water filled potholes in the muddy track.

From out of nowhere, a small cloud of gunsmoke erupted from the hedgerow on the right, making all four men jump. No bullets came their way however and, searching the long grass and bushes, Gritz spotted three strange looking helmeted heads sticking up. The faces beneath those helmets were completely focussed on the wooded knoll that was The Crucible. Gritz spotted the tell tale shape of a curved, upright magazine, just as the Tommy Bren Gun rattled into life again with its unusually slow rate of fire, spitting its large .303 inch rounds up towards where Gunther and his men still manned the trenches.

Without saying anything, Grits removed one hand from his Panzerfaust, grabbed his pistol and yanked it from inside his tunic, then began firing into the group of three enemy soldiers at the rapid rate. Beside him, the soldier with the machine-pistol followed Gritz's lead and sprayed the group with a long, noisy burst. The Tommies didn't cry out, or make any exaggerated movements, they simply slumped forwards, face down in the grass, and their funny looking machine gun fell silent.

"Okay… leave 'em. They're dead…" Gritz snapped and turned back to the face the tank.

As he fixed his eyes on the target, he noted another figure come around the bend; a lone figure dressed in the dreary brown battle-dress of the British Army, and like Gritz, armed with nothing more than a pistol it seemed. All of this Gritz registered in his peripheral vision as he stuffed his pistol back in his smock and took proper hold of the Panzerfaust again.

"Kill him!" Gritz snapped peremptorily as he dropped to his knee and prepared to launch his rocket.

The sound of the MP40 machine-pistol filled the air again, backed by the angry, singular bark of a rifle. The khaki figure toppled into the hedgerow. Gritz ignored it all. He was staring straight towards the observation slits of the enemy tank. The driver must be able to see them, Gritz thought. He didn't have long.

Whoomph!

With an ear splitting roar, the long gun on the Tommy tank spat a heavy calibre shell towards the attacking German armour and the whole vehicle rocked. Gritz raised the rocket and aimed it as accurately as he could, aiming straight towards the spot where the turret met the hull.

There was a sudden flash of bright light from the front of the tank's hull and the sound of machine gun bullets cracking past his head made Gritz wince again. He kept calm however and levelled the rocket. He heard a grunt, a thud, and the clatter of something metallic hitting the floor behind him. Gritz ensured that the rear of the Panzerfaust was clear of his clothing and equipment and called out a warning to the men behind him, assuming they were still alive of course.

"Stand-by… watch the back-blast!"

He took hold of the trigger and steadied his breathing, just as the enemy tank revved its engines and began rolling rearwards once more. Gritz squeezed the trigger. There was a moment's pause and then the rocket leapt in his hands, a wave of heat suddenly erupting from both front and rear of the tube.

Gritz held on tightly and squinted through the choking smoke and searing heat as the warhead of the anti-tank rocket streaked forwards towards the retreating enemy vehicle. A heartbeat later, a large bright flash momentarily obscured the front of the tank, turning instantly into a cloud of dirty grey smoke, and Gritz whooped with joy as he tossed the warm, expended tube to the floor.

"Go on you fucker!"

He looked round for his men, intent on firing a second rocket to make sure of the vehicle and saw the man with the machine pistol laying on his back in a puddle, his arms flung wide and the machine pistol laid in the mud beside him. Of the other two men there was no sign.

Gritz frowned, unsure of where they had disappeared to, but as he scanned the grass verges and hedgerows behind him, the veteran became aware of the unusual noise that seemed to be drowning out everything else. He whipped his head back to look down the track, trying to identify the source of the strange throaty-screaming sound that filled the air. Gritz saw that the enemy tank had come to a halt and that flames were licking the front of its hull but he had no time to reflect on the success of his shot, for just at that moment, a great dark shadow passed overhead with an almighty growl.

The sergeant major glanced up and caught sight of an aircraft with huge wings that were decorated with a strange black and white striped design. His mind worked quickly, taking in all the new information that his eyes were sending to his brain, and it was just as he realised that the Tommy air force had brought in its deadly Jabos to join the battle that the first bank of rockets came screaming down from the heavens to land amongst the advancing German tanks that were now less than a hundred metres from the track on which Gritz was kneeling. Instinctively, Gritz threw himself flat on his face in the puddle to his front and covered his head with his arms; just as the world around him erupted into a maelstrom of fire, smoke and death.

1650 SQUADRON – ATTACK RUN OVER THE CRUCIBLE
TUESDAY 6TH JUNE 1944 – 1610 HOURS

"Here we go Red Section… keep it nice and tidy…"

Whittaker murmured the advice over the RT to the other two aircraft in his section as he tilted the flying column and took his aircraft into a steep dive down onto the target. With a dramatic growl and strain of its engine, the Typhoon dipped sharply and dropped like a bird of prey towards the patchwork of fields, trees and woods below.

Whittaker had noted the landmarks well and led his section straight towards the small wood that crowned the prominent knoll on the ridge. To his right, his first wingman was aligning himself slightly to the right of the wooded knoll whilst over to his left, the second wingman was tracking the line of the road that passed to the left of the feature. All three aircraft were diving together, but with Whittaker slightly ahead of the other two, guiding the trio of fighter-bombers onto their axis.

The descent time from just a few thousand feet was a matter of seconds, but even so the negative G force being pulled by the diving aircraft was resulting in what the crews had come to know as 'greying'. As his heavily laden Typhoon dropped furiously towards the yellow-brown, metallic, box-like targets below, Whittaker sensed that his peripheral vision was becoming increasingly blurred and he felt an uncomfortable build up of pressure in his temples. Fortunately there was little time to worry over the unpleasant sensation as the ant-like targets loomed bigger in his weapon sights. The squadron leader picked a group of five tanks that appeared to be advancing in two separate waves to the right of the road and just short of the wooded feature, and aligned his sights onto the rear centre vehicle, knowing that some of his rockets would over-shoot.

He couldn't faff about with the aiming procedure. Against small, moving targets, the opportunity to release one's rockets would be fleeting and so he focussed all his concentration on the sight picture as he began to prepare for his pull-up. And then, a second later, it was all there; exactly as it needed to be, the sight markings falling momentarily onto the chosen vehicle. Whittaker pressed the fire button and instantly felt the release of the rockets from beneath both wings. Ensuring that all the rockets were away cleanly, Whittaker hauled on his flying column and brought the nose of the Typhoon up.

The engine roared and strained and protested and the veteran pilot held onto the flying column with all his strength, urging the machine upwards and out of its dive as its deadly cargo streaked towards the target. For long moments, man and machine fought gravity, and then suddenly the sound of the engine eased slightly and the downward pressure seemed to disappear as the nose of the aircraft lifted toward the flat grey cloud base that was beginning to re-establish itself. Instantly, Whittaker felt the pressure ease in his temples.

He brought his aircraft up to the patrol ceiling again and began to execute a wide, sweeping bank to port, meaning to swing back onto the attack line. As he began to level out, Whittaker glanced left and right and saw his two wingmen coming onto station on either side of him. He swung the section around so that they were peeling back in behind Green Section, which as yet remained uncommitted, waiting for those in the first three waves to clear the target before following up with their own attack run. Far below, Whittaker saw Blue Section pulling out of their own attack, whilst Yellow Section were already in the process of releasing their own barrage of deadly armour-piercing missiles. Beneath the waves of camouflaged aircraft, the green patchwork of fields, and the numerous armoured vehicles advancing across it, had disappeared completely in a shroud of explosive induced smoke and dust. Somewhere beneath that canopy of obscuration, chaos reined.

"Green Leader, this is Red Leader. Hold on for a moment and maintain your current station. We'll let the others get clear and then see what we've got left. I don't want to waste any rockets firing blindly into smoke."

Whittaker transmitted the message to the leader of Green Section before the three aircraft committed themselves to an attack run.

"Roger, Red Leader." Came the acknowledgement, and Whittaker watched the three aircraft in Green Section wheel to starboard and conduct a short figure of eight circuit as they awaited orders to engage.

Whittaker cruised across the target area at maximum possible height, tilting his aircraft from side to side so that he could view the scene below. He could see little but smoke on his first pass so conducted a second manoeuvre over target whilst the remainder of his squadron waited patiently, maintaining station and keeping their eyes peeled for enemy aircraft.

As the squadron leader made his second observation pass over target, he spotted movement to the edge of the dust cloud and smoke below him and banked sharply round to take a closer look. There. He could see them. Two tanks veering away from beneath the shroud of smoke and heading for the wooded area. The buggers were running for cover. Whittaker didn't hesitate.

"Green Leader, this is Red Leader. Looks like the survivors are running into that wood on the ridge. Take your chaps down and clobber those trees. The Jerries are in there somewhere so just hit the whole thing. Give them everything you've got."

"Roger Skipper." Replied the leader of Green Section brightly and, a moment later, the trio of waiting aircraft peeled off and dropped out of the sky in line astern onto their attack run.

Today, the Allied air forces ruled the skies over France, and for the Germans, there was nowhere to hide…

WEIMER'S TANK – JUST SHORT OF THE CRUCIBLE
TUESDAY 6TH JUNE 1944 – 1610 HOURS

"Got the bastard! At last!"

Wesser thumped the breech block of his gun exultantly as he saw the Tommy tank disappear in a cloud of black smoke following the impact of the armour piercing shell he'd just fired into it at virtually point blank range. They were pushing through the last hedgerow now and accelerating towards the meandering hedge-lined farm track on which the enemy tanks and infantry were ensconced. Below the fighting compartment of the Panzer IV, the bow-gunner was blazing away with his machine gun.

"Don't get too excited!" Weimer warned the main gunner. "There's infantry all over the place by the looks… Keep your eyes peeled. Now swing onto that other Tommy tank over to the right…"

Wesser was already traversing the turret towards where the track ran into the small saddle between the two wooded knolls on the ridge line. The second enemy vehicle was up there somewhere and still in action. As the gunner searched for the new target, Weimer pulled away from the commander's sight and pressed his eyes to the far-side periscope, leaning over the stooping Wesser in the progress. The problem with being locked-down in the turret was that it was easy to get disorientated, so the veteran tank commander used the small view-finders around the turret rim to scan the surrounding area.

As he pushed his eyes against the periscope, his eyes lighted upon a scene of utter confusion. He could see some other tanks from his company; some over on the main road, others by the hedgerow his own tank had just crashed through. At least one of their company's tanks was on fire and thick smoke drifted across the lush green meadow partially obscuring the limited view. Just as Weimer was about to pull his eyes away from the periscope, the entire panorama that he was currently viewing suddenly exploded with a series of bright flashes, and these were followed by what seemed like an immense wave of grey-brown smoke rolling towards him like a giant wave. A second later, the terrifying sound of an unbelievably loud bombardment flooded the fighting compartment.

"Jesus fucking Christ!" Wesser screamed out loud. "What the fuck is that?"

A roar of engines, only just audible above the din of exploding ordnance came to Weimer as he stared dumbfounded at the scene of hell that was unfolding outside his tank.

"Shit!" He breathed.

"What's happening?" Demanded Wesser, pulling back from the gun-sight as his view became obliterated by a blanket of dust and smoke.

Weimer dropped heavily back into his seat, his eyes wide with fear.

"Jabos!" He blurted to the gunner in shock.

"Jabos?" Wesser gawped back at his commander. "Oh, for fucks sake!"

Weimer yelled into the intercom in a voice tinged with panic.

"Driver – hard right! Get us into those trees now! Move, move, move…"

The driver needed no urging and, with a powerful growl, the heavy tank veered to the right.

"I can't see a fucking thing!" The driver was shouting up to Weimer.

"Neither can I; just go straight ahead until you hit the trees!"

Responding to Weimer's orders, the driver forced the vehicle on, churning up the great clods of earth as it ploughed blindly across the sloping meadow in the general direction of the now invisible wood.

Nobody spoke now in the tank. Every man simply sat there in terrified silence as the world outside erupted in flame and smoke. Even with the usual juddering of the speeding armoured vehicle, the impact of the aerial onslaught could be felt inside the crew compartment of the Panzer IV as one bank of rockets after another slammed home amongst the German formation.

Some of those rockets bit deep into the armoured hulls of the German tanks, others simply smashed into the earth between the moving vehicles and added to the general chaos.

As Weimer's tank ground on through the smoke and flame of the air delivered bombardment, it began to climb a steeper part of the slope and just off to the left, the gunner spotted a fleeting glimpse of ruined buildings.

"There's some old building to our left... I think we're near the wood..." Wesser shouted above the racket.

"I can see trees..." The driver added. "Shall I go for them?"

"Yes; straight forward!" Weimer yelled. "Get us into cover, quickly!"

The tank roared again as the driver gave the big lumbering beast all the engine had to offer as it fought its way up the slope into the tree line between the two knolls that constituted Point 113.

Weimer was pouring with sweat now and he exchanged a fearful glance with Wesser, who's face was also dripping with perspiration; partly as a result of being closed down inside the turret and partly due to the absolute terror that was gripping the whole crew as they waited for one of the lethal armour piercing Jabo rockets to burst through their armour any second and turn them all into red mist in the blink of an eye.

Suddenly the tank lurched violently and the three men in the turret grabbed onto any piece of equipment they could for purchase as the huge steel monster reared and fell alarmingly.

"What's that?" Weimer shouted over the intercom.

"Hang on!" The driver shouted back. "We're into the trees! There's obstacles and shit everywhere! We're going through a pile of smashed up trees..."

Weimer accepted the information willingly enough and continued to hold onto the turret fittings for all he was worth. For what seemed like an eternity the tank rose and fell, dropped and bucked like a wild horse in an American rodeo as it crunched and ground its way through the saddle of land in the centre of the shattered wood, whilst all the time the lethal rockets from the Allied aircraft followed them; tearing through the trees and adding to the carnage and chaos of the close terrain.

"I can see the edge of the trees again!" The driver suddenly shouted. "There's a field beyond, sloping away from us. What shall I do?"

Weimer thought on the point for a second or two before replying.

"Stay here. Don't go out into the open. We'll just sit tight until the Jabos fuck off. If they want to get us in here they'll have to guess where we are..."

"Good plan..." Wesser commented, his face still showing the fear that had taken hold of them all.

The tank engine settled down to a steady throb as it idled contentedly after its desperate struggle to penetrate the thick woodland. The explosions outside seemed to be dying away slightly and a strange kind of hush descended on the tank crew. After a few moments, Weimer heard the driver let out a long sigh.

"Fuck me…" The driver murmured, his voice tinged with exhaustion; both physical and emotional.

"No thanks…" Wesser grunted into the intercom. "You're even uglier than your mother and that takes some doing…"

There was a moment of silence and then a ripple of relieved, nervous laughter carried through the vehicle as the five crewmen released the pent up terror they had just endured over the last few minutes.

As the laughter settled, Weimer spoke into the intercom again.

"Alright, lads… let's get a grip shall we? Sounds like the Jabos have fucked off, but there are still Tommy tanks and infantry about the place. Let's see if we can pick up the rest of the company again then get stuck back in. We're meant to be heading for the coast, remember?"

Having addressed his own crew, Weimer switched to the radio frequency for the remainder of the company and sent a call to the other tanks in his platoon. Nothing came back on the net and so the staff sergeant tried again. Still nothing. Weimer, Wesser and the loader-operator exchanged grim looks.

The tank commander decided to try company headquarters. At first there was no answer, but after a second call, a feint, badly broken up message buzzed in Weimer's ear-phones.

"… no chance… of time…go round… coast… grenadiers…"

Again the turret crew exchanged a knowing look.

"That doesn't sound too encouraging…" Wesser ventured.

Weimer didn't reply. Instead he spoke into the intercom, his face set with a dark look.

"Okay driver – forwards. Break out of the trees and then go hard right. Follow the tree line round and we'll see if we can pick up the rest of the company again.

"Got it." The driver acknowledged and immediately revved the tank's engines before ramming it forward over the fallen limbs of broken trees.

"Okay gunners; eyes to your sights and keep them peeled for Tommies. Let's get back into the battle…"

The big tank crashed through the last trees that marked the edge of the wooded high ground and emerged into a wide open meadow that was littered with dead cows. The poor animals presented an absurd sight, laid on their backs with their legs poking in the air. Far beyond the sloping meadow, the ground rose gently again to another low ridge about a mile off, that was also covered in smoke that lit up every few seconds as fresh explosions erupted within the thick haze. Weimer was feeling a little disorientated so decided to open up the hatches for a short while. He clicked over the locking lever and pushed the hatch upwards as the driver swung the tank to the right and began tracking the edge of the wood.

Pushing himself up into a standing position, Weimer drank in the air that came rushing into the turret. To call it fresh air was an overstatement for it was heavy with damp and the acrid smell of explosives. He wiped his grimy, sweat drenched face with a sleeve of his black tank overalls and scanned the area quickly. The sound of gunfire and explosions could still be heard, yet it seemed a little way off. Of the Tommy aircraft that had pounced on them out of nowhere, there was no sign. He watched as the trees went past to the right of his vehicle, forming a thick covering over the small but prominent knoll on which they stood.

Suddenly, the trees were gone, veering away to the right, following the line of the knoll, and Weimer found himself looking back across the fields over which he and his company had advanced just a few minutes before. He could see the farmhouse sitting against the side of the road a few hundred metres downslope, and the big intervening hedges complete with the great gaps ripped in them by advancing tanks. And dotted across those fields, and down on the road itself, were the burning remnants of his company.

"Driver – stop."

He uttered the words sharply and the tank slewed to a sharp halt on the downward slope.

Weimer stared bleakly at the scene of devastation that now presented itself to the veteran tank commander. To his rear right, the shattered trees of the wooded heights of Point 113 loomed out of a bank of smoke. Across the field to his front he scanned the fiercely burning wrecks of what had once been Panzer IV heavy battle tanks. Most of them were whole but enveloped by flames. One vehicle however, was missing its turret, which lay upside down on the grass some fifty metres from the burning hull on which it had once sat. Bits of tanks were strewn across the lush grass of the hillside; wheels, brackets, cages, bits of track…

"Oh, my God…"

Wesser was still down in the turret, looking through the gun sight.

"Shit…" The driver gasped. "They're… they're all dead…"

"What the fuck do we do now?" Wesser queried, his voice devoid of any real passion.

Weimer couldn't answer for a moment. He was too stunned by the level of destruction he was witnessing. Eventually he managed to find his voice.

"Let's go..." He grunted. "There's nothing we can do here. Driver – go left. Hard left and left again. Towards the coast..."

"The coast?" Wesser asked sharply over the intercom.

"Yes." Weimer snapped irritably. "Towards the coast. We have our orders. We're wasting our time blundering around here. Let's go find some Tommies and kill the fuckers. Come on, driver – get me away from this place..."

Obediently, the driver revved the Panzer IV once more, disengaged the left track and then spun the vehicle around in a neutral turn.

"To the coast it is then, Staff Sergeant..." The driver grunted, reengaging the left track.

The tank lurched forwards, back along the eastern extremity of Point 113 and towards the village of Hermanville. The driver was still talking to himself over the intercom, trying to suppress the shredded nerves that were so evident from his shaky voice.

"To the coast it is... I could do with a swim..."

THE TRACK – HARD BY THE CRUCIBLE
TUESDAY 6TH JUNE 1944 – 1620 HOURS

Smithson wasn't sure how long it had been since the aerial bombardment had finished. He felt as if he'd been lying there in the grass by the hedgerow for hours rather than minutes. His ears were buzzing with a strange noise, as if he was listening to a wireless that hadn't been correctly tuned. Despite that, there was little in the way of additional noise beyond that strange rushing sensation in his ears and after the racket of battle that he had endured these last few hours, the perceived silence was extremely surreal. The major was reluctant to move or speak. He felt that if he did, he would somehow be the person responsible for breaking the sudden peaceful spell that seemed to have been cast over Point 113 in the wake of the air strike.

He gave his arms and legs an experimental shake and was relieved to find that he could feel all four limbs and that they seemed to be attached and in working order. Then, as he blinked grass and dirt out of his eyes, he heard a voice.

"Jesus Christ... my bloody hands!"

He looked sideways and was surprised to see several men laid beside him. They were all dressed in khaki battledress but wore no web equipment or helmets, though the nearest man, who wore a full corporal's chevrons on his sleeve, had a black beret stuffed under one epaulette.

The corporal pushed himself up into a sitting position with his elbows and held up his hands, examining them with horrified fascination. Smithson too blinked in surprise as he studied the man's hands. They were bright red, blistered and covered with what looked like dried candle wax. With a jolt, Smithson realised that the corporal was one of crewmen from the Sherman that had been hit just before the air-strike, and that his hands had been burnt terribly.

"Aaagh, shit… my fucking hands… they're burning…"

The corporal began to sob; a terrible, child-like, pain wracked sob.

"Oh shit, my hands! They're hurting!"

The two other men who were laid beside him suddenly jumped up and grabbed hold of the sobbing corporal. Smithson noted that one of them appeared to have lost his eyebrows and caught the unpleasant smell of singed hair.

"It's alright, Peggy…" The man without eyebrows reassured the corporal, grabbing the NCO by his shoulders and hugging him carefully from the side. "We'll sort you out mate; don't worry…"

Around about this small vignette, other characters seemed to be coming to life; heads appearing from out of the bushes and grass, staring about in apparent shock.

"Fuck me! Look at that!"

The sound of the platoon sergeant from No.3 Platoon, cursing expertly, dragged Smithson's attention back to his other side, where he found the NCO still laid beside the two PIAT crewmen. All three of them were staring open mouthed through the small gap in the hedge, out towards the field. Smithson suddenly remembered the threat of the advancing German armour and pushed his head up above the small bank, his heart suddenly lurching with dread as his mind finally caught up with where it had left off prior to the air-strike.

Staring out across the meadows to the south, the infantry major caught his breath. Even during his last battle in 1940, he had never seen such devastation. He made a quick count and reached a figure of seven. Seven German tanks, or at least the remains of them, sat burning away at various points across the landscape, the detritus of battle scattered all around. Down to his forward right, Smithson could vaguely make out the line of the road, bordered by its tall hedges. Whatever was on that road was also burning fiercely. He could see at least three plumes of thick black smoke pouring from behind the thick foliage of the roadside borders.

346   *Crucible of Fate*

"Bloody hell!" The PIAT gunner breathed. "Those fly-boys took them fucking Jerries to pieces!"

Smithson could only lay there and gawp at the scene before him as his eyes took in the truth of the young private's comment. Of the German armoured counter-attack that just minutes before had threatened to overwhelm Smithson and his men, there was nothing left but twisted heaps of broken, burning metal. The enemy tank force had been obliterated.

"Major Smithson? Major Smithson?"

The familiar voice broke in on the company commander's thoughts. He twisted round to search for the owner of the voice. As he turned, he saw that the corporal with the burnt hands was soaking them in a puddle of filthy water whilst his two comrades patted him on the shoulders and unwrapped bandages that they had produced from their trouser pockets.

A lithe figure in full battle order appeared on the track and Smithson linked the voice of a few seconds earlier to the business-like figure. It was his company sergeant major.

"Sergeant Major! Over here!"

The warrant officer stopped in his tracks, turned his head towards Smithson, appeared to scan the grass verge and hedgerow for a moment, before finally settling his gaze on the officer.

"Ah! Sir! There you are! 'D' Company are down at the bottom of the track. Their Company Commander wants to know if we need a hand taking the wood?"

Smithson blinked at his company sergeant major for a moment, struggling to take in the announcement and make sense of it. Then, with a sudden rush of memory, Smithson caught up again.

"The wood!" He yelped as if he'd been stung. "Shit! Fucking hell! Shit!"

The major pushed himself up.

"Tell them to follow us up! We'll go in first; tell them to follow on!"

Smithson forced himself to his feet and shook his head as if trying to clear his thoughts, before looking back at his company sergeant major.

"And get our company moving! Get them on their feet!"

The infantry major swung round abruptly, facing up the track past the burning Sherman tank.

"On your feet 'A' Company!" He yelled, hoarsely. "Come on! 'A' Company! Get on your feet. Into the wood! Everyone; get moving! Take that wood while the Jerries are still in their dugouts!"

He stumbled into a run and began kicking at the khaki clad infantrymen who were strung out along the borders of the muddy track.

"Come on 'A' Company, on your feet! Get up this fucking track! Rush the bastards and take this fucking wood, now! Come on 'A' Company!"

All along the track, his men were springing up now. Just a minute ago, Smithson had feared that he might be the only man left alive on that burning, blasted hillside, but now an increasing number of his soldiers were surfacing from the undergrowth and stumbling after him as he fought his way through the mud and puddles of the meandering track. He was approaching the leading Sherman now, which he noted was also on fire. There were more men jumping up in front of him and he waved his pistol in the air as he neared them.

"Follow me 'A' Company! Come on! Up the hill!"

He didn't look behind him but he knew his men were with him. He could hear the thud of booted feet on the ground, the rattle of equipment and weaponry, the laboured breathing of heavily laden men, and now the additional snarling of non-commissioned officers as they took their officer's lead and began driving their men up the track towards the ridge, crowned by its shattered wood. Smithson veered past the second Sherman, turning his face away from the flames that licked up the side of the vehicle and coughed on the choking smoke that it emitted. And then he was past it, staring straight up the track towards several derelict buildings and a smoke shrouded double knoll that was covered by shredded trees and undergrowth.

There were bodies on the track in front of him and as he pounded up the muddy lane, one of those bodies moved. He noted, almost absently, that the moving figure was wearing an unusual grey-green uniform, and as the figure rolled over onto its back, Smithson realised that he was looking at a German soldier. He noted the array of curious badges on the man's jacket, and the small metal cross that decorated the top button of the jacket, close to his throat. He noted the dirty, lined face of a man that was old in war and used to hardship and watched with disappointment as the man reached an arm towards his jacket and curled a hand around what looked like the handle of a pistol.

In a simple, fluid movement that seemed ridiculously easy to Smithson, the infantry major lifted his own right arm and, almost without looking, fired a single shot at the German on the floor as he ran past him. The company commander didn't even stop to make sure of his victim. He raced on up the track as he heard the German emit and grunt and flop back into the mud. A sudden sense of elation flooded through Smithson as he realised that he was finally going to do it. There were no more complications. The tanks were gone, the planes were gone, and it was now just he and his men against whatever was left alive on the hill. Point 113 was his for the taking and, by God, he was going to make sure of it.

The major flung a quick look back over his shoulder and felt his heart leap with joy as he saw more than a score of men lumbering after him, brandishing bayonet tipped rifles, Brens and Sten Guns.

"Come on then, 'A' Company!" Smithson roared. "Chaaaaarge!"

THE TRACK – HARD BY THE CRUCIBLE
TUESDAY 6TH JUNE 1944 – 1620 HOURS

Gritz lay there motionless for long moments; keeping his head covered until he was sure that no more rockets were going to slam into the ground around him and that all of the debris and bits of destroyed vehicle had stopped falling to the ground. As the last echoes of explosions died away and the sound of the powerful aircraft engines faded into the distance, a strange kind of silence descended on the immediate area.

The veteran infantry soldier laid there motionless, holding his breath, terrified lest the sound of his breathing should draw yet another pounding from the Allied air forces, mortars or artillery. He had only once before been on the receiving end of such intense bombing and shelling, and that had been on that awful morning earlier in the year when the Ruski's had unleashed their terrible multi-barrelled rocket launchers against his defensive position somewhere in the frozen wastes of Russia.

On that occasion, the relentless, overwhelming barrage had left Gritz and his men completely stunned and incapable of thinking straight for some considerable time afterwards, and that was when the Ruskis had launched the vast waves of tanks and infantry at the German front lines. That had been the day he had won the Knight's Cross, although in truth, he could barely remember winning it. The entire battle had gone by like a fleeting dream and Gritz remembered only that he had fought like an automaton, driven by some slightly distant, almost mechanical instinct to survive. And that was how he felt now. Somewhere deep in his mind, the experienced soldier told him that the sudden silence meant danger; even more danger than the explosive orgy of death and destruction that had just visited itself upon this seemingly insignificant point on the map.

As if to verify Gritz's subconscious conviction, the deafening silence was suddenly broken by the sound of voices. He could hear them, several voices screaming and shouting in an unusual language; one that he couldn't understand yet one which he knew to be English. It was the sound of officers and NCOs yelling urgent orders and chivvying their men, desperate to get them moving. The sound of such things was the same in every army, regardless of the language its soldier spoke. Then, finally jerking Gritz into action, he heard the sound of the boots; heavy, studded boots clumping along a muddy, pot-holed track and splashing noisily through the puddles of filthy water. Then, even more alarmingly, he heard the sound of breathing; the ragged, laboured breathing of exhausted men making a desperate rush forward.

Gritz began to roll. He rolled over onto his left arm, noting with a certain amount of curiosity that he seemed to be moving with unusual slowness. He glanced up as he rolled and noted the billowing black smoke that belched out from the front of the Tommy tank.

"I did that..." He mumbled in a thick, awkward voice that made him sound like he was drunk.

Then he caught sight of the figures emerging from the bank of smoke. Tall, bulky, dark looking figures with helmets covered in foliage, their faces shadowed and haunted looking.

He registered the khaki uniforms and large ammunition pouches that were worn high up on the body in that unusual British way, and he noted the variety of weapons that were being carried by what had become a surge of men. Some of the men within that khaki crowd were carrying rifles across the front of their bodies and Gritz spotted the small, thin, deadly looking pig-sticker bayonets that were fixed to the end of those rifles. Of course... The Tommies loved their bayonets. Every other army he knew of used their artillery and tanks and machine guns to hammer the enemy into submission, but the British, and only the British, believed that all the paraphernalia of modern war was just a means to an end; an end that must ultimately consist of getting in close to their enemy at the point of the bayonet.

"Fucking stupid Tommies..." Gritz blurted, still half stunned by the earlier rocket attack.

He noted that the man leading the group of Tommies seemed to be less heavily burdened than the rest, and appeared to be armed solely with a pistol, whilst a small pair of binoculars bounced off the man's chest as he clattered up the track towards Gritz.

"Commander..." Gritz realised out loud.

Then he remembered his own pistol. With that same, surreal slowness, Gritz reached his right hand towards the Walther pistol that was half-stuffed inside his tunic. He grasped the handle of the weapon and began to withdraw it. It seemed like it was stuck in thick mud, Gritz thought, as he tried to drag the weapon free. Eventually he felt the resistance disappear and he was drawing the weapon across the front of his body. He glanced up, searching for his target and saw that the Tommy commander was almost on top of him, his thin, drawn face staring beyond Gritz and up the track. As Gritz raised his own pistol, he saw the Tommy officer glance down at him fleetingly, give a small flick of his right wrist, and then Gritz was staring down the barrel of the man's revolver.

Then it all happened so quickly. He saw a bright flash, heard the deafening bang, and felt the huge punch to his upper chest, between his right shoulder and collar bone. He vaguely registered the impact as he was thrown onto his back, hitting the ground with a harsh thud, and gasped out loud as he suddenly felt the tremendous burning sensation in his upper body that spread across his chest, throat, shoulder and then upper back. Gritz watched as the crowd of khaki-clad enemy came rushing by him; nothing more than brown blurs as they stomped past. Then he remembered the bayonets on the end of the Tommy rifles.

"Not with a bayonet..." Gritz rasped breathlessly as the enemy leapt over his supine form. "Not with a bayonet... please..."

GUNTHER'S PLATOON – THE CRUCIBLE
TUESDAY 6TH JUNE 1944 – 1620 HOURS

Like every other person on Point 113, Gunther felt like somebody had just been playing football with his head for an hour. As he pushed himself up from the bottom of the trench, his ears were ringing like cathedral bells. His sense of balance was somewhat askew and he found that he had to grab hold of the revetments to steady himself. Before he got himself fully upright, his head disappeared inside thick foliage.

"What the fuck..."

He dropped down to his knees again, gathered himself, then looked up and scanned down the fire-trench.

A tree, or a large portion of one, had collapsed across the top of the position, essentially sealing him into it as effectively as a roof. He could see that further along the trench the light of late afternoon could still penetrate and so he began crawling on all fours in that direction. He came across a body after just a couple of metres and at first assumed that it was of the dead variety. When he began crawling over it however, he saw that the body was shaking violently, and then a moment later he registered the subdued, child-like sobbing coming from beneath it.

With a start, Gunther realised that the man was still alive.

"Who's that?" He demanded, shaking the prone figure by the shoulder. There was no response.

"Who the fuck's that?" He growled, yanking the man over onto his side. The soldier had his hands over his face. He was crying uncontrollably and Gunther suddenly felt a surge of anger. He reached down with his free hand and prized the man's fingers away from his face.

"Who the fuck is it?" The sergeant snapped. "Stop fucking crying!"

The sergeant managed to free one of the soldier's hands from his face and instantly recognised the face of the MG34 gunner. The man's eyes were bloodshot and staring, tears streaming down his dirty face, and he shook his head feebly from side to side, not wanting to look at the sergeant.

"No…" The man sobbed weakly. "No… no…"

Gunther let go of the man's hand and snarled at him.

"Fucking spineless bastard!"

He left the sobbing gunner and scrabbled over him, heading for the clear stretch of trench beyond. He immediately came across the No.2 for the MG34 who was, undoubtedly, dead; given that he had a huge, jagged spike of splintered tree protruding from his throat and that the front of the man's uniform was entirely soaked in sticky, dark blood. The iron tinged stench of the blood made Gunther gag and he clamped his mouth shut, holding his breath as he struggled on past.

In the part of the trench that was open to the air, Gunther found a stunned looking soldier with a rifle crouching in the corner.

"Get up!" Gunther snapped. "It's over. Come on; get up!"

He grabbed the young soldier by the sleeve and dragged him upright so that both of them could look over the parapet of the trench. Any view they would have had of the ground beyond the wood was blocked by the bushy, green foliage of the fallen tree limb.

"Shit!" Gunther muttered. "Up. Come on; up out of the trench… We can't see a fucking thing from here…"

As Gunther and his lone companion struggled up onto the parapet, the sergeant heard the first voices shouting from down the slope, somewhere beyond the mass of tangled trees and undergrowth. At first he thought that it might be Gritz and his tank hunting group hurrying back up to the main position after their successful strike against the Tommy tank. Gunther had seen the vehicle erupt in flames just seconds before the Tommy aircraft had come screaming down from above to rain death and destruction upon Point 113. Any hope was dashed a second later however, when he heard a voice call out from not too far away in a language that clearly wasn't German.

Having emerged onto the parapet now, Gunther struggled into a standing position and strained to see above and beyond the mass of foliage. Much of the view beyond the tree-line was covered in smoke and, much to Gunther's surprise, there was a Panzer IV sitting right amongst the ruined buildings of the old forge down in the saddle, and it was burning fiercely; its turret sitting at an angle that didn't look quite right. Swarming around that burning vehicle and spreading out in various directions was a mass of figures. He gawped at them stupidly for a moment or two, trying to discern the details of the uniforms and equipment. Before he'd been able to identify the scurrying figures by their appearance however, their voices gave them away.

"Shit!" Gunther breathed, bringing up his MP40. "Tommies!"

He raised his MP40 into the shoulder and aimed towards the centre of the biggest group, then squeezed the trigger. The heavy metal weapon lurched in his hands and the relative post-bombardment silence in the wood was suddenly shattered by the clatter of the automatic weapon.

"Fire, man!" Gunther yelled at the private soldier beside him. "Shoot the fuckers!"

In his peripheral vision, Gunther saw the young soldier's weapon come up, and an instant later, there was a deafening report as the man fired a hastily aimed shot towards the fleeting figures amongst the smoke below.

Gunther fired again, several times, letting off lengthy bursts towards the enemy as they milled about in the saddle of land below. In a matter of seconds however, the Tommies had either gone to ground or dispersed to the flanks. In the chaos of the smashed up wood, it was difficult to see very far in any direction. As the sergeant began fumbling for a fresh magazine for his weapon, he heard the whistle sound from over to his left, just a few metres away through the trees. The high-pitched shrill of the whistle was followed by a loud, urgent voice shouting in English, and then the bullets came whipping through the undergrowth, snapping past the sergeant and his companion or thumping into the surrounding tree trunks menacingly.

"Sergeant!" The young private beside Gunther yelped in surprise. "They're here! The Tommies! They're in the wood!"

THE COMMAND POST – THE CRUCIBLE
TUESDAY 6TH JUNE 1944 – 1625 HOURS

"Hello? Regimental Headquarters…"

The sharp, tense sounding voice answered the phone at the far end of the line. Kole, sitting dutifully by the telephone in The Crucible's Command

Post, sighed with relief that at last, somebody had answered. Not only had somebody finally picked up, Kole realised as he heard the voice at the other end, it was Colonel Krug himself.

"Colonel, it's Corporal Kole here at The Crucible…"

"Where? Who?" Krug demanded, cutting Kole off in mid-sentence.

"The Crucible, Sir… Point 113…"

"Oh, yes… Gritz's company. Well, what is it?"

Kole took a deep breath, realising that he was acting without orders, but given that just about every senior NCO in the company had vanished amongst the chaos of battle, Kole had decided that he should try and do something on his own initiative. He'd been outside into the trench-line a number of times over the last couple of hours and it was clear that the enemy had almost entirely surrounded their position now. Their artillery and now their aircraft were pounding the company position relentlessly and so Kole figured that it was about time the Tommies got some of their own medicine.

"I need a fire mission, Colonel. I need mortars or artillery brought down all around our position; especially by the crossroads. We've got Tommy tanks and infantry all round us. They're coming up the road from the coast in great strength…"

Once again, Krug cut-off the corporal's words in mid-flow.

"Tell me about it!" The colonel let out a bitter laugh that sounded more like a bark. "I've got the bastards all over my position too… In fact, they're right on top of me! We're trapped down here in the bunkers…"

Kole was silent for a moment, taking in the colonel's words.

"But…" Kole began again hesitantly. "Is there any chance of getting in contact with the artillery and…"

"None." Krug interrupted him brutally. Then, his voice losing some of its tension, Krug said. "Listen Kole… I'm afraid there's nothing I can do for you. We're busy fighting for our lives here. There's nothing I can do for you. Give Sergeant Major Gritz my apologies… I wish there was something I could do…"

Kole remained silent for a second before speaking again.

"What shall I tell him, Sir? What shall I tell Sergeant Major Gritz? What do you want us to do?"

This time it was Krug who hesitated before replying.

"Tell him… Tell him that he must use his own judgement regarding how long to resist and when to withdraw. I cannot give him any more orders for now. There's nothing I can do…"

Kole took a deep breath.

"Right, Sir… I'll find him and let him know…"

"Oh, and Kole..." Krug went on hurriedly. "Tell him... Tell him... well done and good luck..."

"Yes, Sir." Kole said mechanically, staring into nothing as he realised that they were essentially being abandoned by higher command.

The phone line went dead.

Kole placed the handset down on the receiver. He didn't look at Kellerman who he knew was still sitting on his bed, gibbering like somebody who'd just seen a ghost. The poor fellow had lasted longer than Kole had expected before finally succumbing to the shaking and crying that denoted a complete nervous breakdown. It had been the terrifying impact of the aircraft rockets just a few minutes before that had finally sent the man over the edge.

"They can't help us..." He murmured, almost to himself. "We're on our own."

The corporal sat there with a deep frown etched on his face. What was he to do now? And where the hell was Gritz? He'd heard nothing since the last runner had come in from Gunther's platoon, with a message for the checkpoint. Kole took a deep breath, then stood up and reached down for his rifle and helmet. Clapping his helmet in place he limped across to the groundsheets that covered the doorway to the command post. Reaching the door, the corporal grabbed the edge of the groundsheet and pulled it aside. The tree covered hillside on which the command post and reserve trenches were situated was thick with smoke and huge, foliage laden branches had come down all over the place, creating an unexpected abatis-like barrier beyond the lip of the trench. Outside, somewhere beyond the mass of vegetation in the smoke shrouded saddle between the command post and the forward platoons, the sound of English voices echoed through the shattered woodland.

The corporal jumped involuntarily as one of the new boys suddenly came skidding along the trench from his left.

"Corporal! The Tommies are in the wood! They're everywhere!"

Kole felt his heart lurch.

"Tommies in the wood?"

That wasn't good. It wasn't good at all.

Bang!

The sound of the gunshot from within the command post sent Kole diving to one side out of sheer instinct. He lay there for a moment, wondering what on earth was going on, until the new-boy outside took a tentative step towards him.

"Corporal! Are you alright?"

Kole levered himself up, feeling slightly embarrassed, and grunted at the young man.

"I'm fine..."

He looked back into the dark interior of the command post, squinting to pick out detail. His eyes picked out the telephone and the ammunition box cum seat that was beside it. From there he tracked his eyes along the back wall of the bunker until his eyes fell upon Kellerman. Well, he supposed it must be Kellerman.

The shattered private had shot himself. Judging by the position of his body and what was left of his head, Kellerman had placed his rifle barrel in his mouth and pulled the trigger. Now his lifeless body lay slumped back against his bedding and equipment; what was left of his head hanging to one side like a pile of minced meat and bone. One eye, bizarrely sitting atop the mess, seemed to stare at Kole in frozen terror. The corporal felt the bile rise in his throat but gulped it back down, averting his eyes from the awful sight.

For want of nothing better to do, Kole scanned the remainder of the command post, his mind numbed by the constant sequence of minor crises, one upon the other. As his eyes flitted across the oddments and general bric-a-brac that was stowed in various corners of the subterranean room, he came across the medical box. Wordlessly, keeping his eyes fixed on the small wooden box, the corporal walked over to it and flipped up the lid. He bent down, rummaged around briefly, then pulled out a large, rolled up bandage; of the kind used for immobilising injured limbs. With his rifle in one hand and a bandage in the other, Kole walked quickly back to the doorway, swept the curtain aside, then stepped out into the trench.

The young soldier who had been outside was still standing there, his face betraying complete and utter terror as he stared into the smoke filled woodland and listened to the sound of sporadic gun-fire and the angry, vengeful shouting from men with English voices. When Kole reappeared, he jumped in surprise and turned on the corporal, wide-eyed.

"Corporal Kole? What do we do? I can't see where the Tommies are but I can hear them? What do we do?"

Kole shook out the broad-fold bandage and began tying one end of it around the muzzle of his rifle.

"Put your rifle down, lad..." Kole said quietly but firmly to the private who couldn't have been much beyond eighteen years old. "Then go along the trench and tell everyone else to do the same..."

COMMAND TANK, 100TH PANZER REGIMENT – NEAR PERIERS, NORMANDY
TUESDAY 6TH JUNE 1944 – 1640 HOURS

Colonel Hermann von Oppeln-Bronikowski scanned the map that sat flapping in the breeze on the top of his Panzer IV's turret, his brow creased in a deep frown. His radio headset was still clamped firmly to his ears as he studied the detail of the map, making small strokes with his pencil as he plotted the information he was being fed, intermittently, by his battalion commanders.

Things weren't going well. In fact, things were going decidedly badly. His second battalion had driven straight into a firestorm between the villages of Bieville and Periers as they had approached the crest of the low ridge. It seemed they had advanced straight into the teeth of the British spearhead coming south from the coast, and that spearhead had bitten deep into the panzer battalion's ranks. Initial reports suggested that the unit had lost almost a dozen Panzer IVs to well concealed anti-tank guns, tanks and heavy artillery, before being forced to swing left in an attempt to outflank them.

Now, the badly depleted battalion was coming straight up behind his small headquarters group, which in turn was sitting behind his first battalion. And that battalion had suffered just as badly. Having driven through Periers village, the battalion had arrived by Point 113, only to find the friendly German garrison to be under attack from a substantial combined force of enemy infantry, tanks and guns. Initially, good progress had been made, until the intervention of the Tommy Jabos had brought the advance to an abrupt halt.

Once again, details were sketchy, but the few that he'd received suggested that the leading company of that battalion had been obliterated by the devastating air strike. Von Oppeln-Bronikowski had actually witnessed that air-strike himself from a relatively safe distance, with his tank tucked in between two cottages for cover. The sight of those big Tommy fighter-bombers screaming down from the grey skies, unleashing their deadly banks of armour-piercing rockets, had turned the colonel's blood cold. Where the hell was the Luftwaffe, he wondered?

A lone drop of rain landed on his map, causing the colonel commanding the 100th Panzer Regiment to glance up at the sky. His frown only deepened. The weather, though far from seasonal, was not as bad as it had been twenty four hours earlier. If the Tommies had come yesterday then their superiority in the air would have counted for nothing. But of course, that was exactly why they hadn't come yesterday. They'd come today instead, knowing that even though there might be intermittent rain showers and brisk winds, the cloud would be largely broken up; leaving the skies clear enough for their air force to operate.

"The one time I pray for shit weather..." The colonel mumbled to himself.

"Sorry, Colonel?"

Von Oppeln-Bronikowski dragged his eyes away from the grey, but relatively clear sky and glanced at his battle-adjutant who sat perched on the rear-cage of the tank's turret.

"That weather could kill us." The colonel elaborated. "It doesn't look like the Luftwaffe is playing today, so the Tommies have got the skies to themselves. If only that storm had kept on going for another couple of days..."

The adjutant gave a sympathetic nod but maintained a non-committal silence.

Von Oppeln-Bronikowski released a huge sigh and removed his headset, rubbing his ears and hairline irritably.

"Right..." He snapped, looking back down at the map and jabbing his finger at the area just to the west of Periers. "We're not going to get anywhere attacking on a broad frontage, especially with the Tommies already established on the ridgeline to the east in strength. We need to swing left. We'll bring both Panzer battalions over to the left and tag them onto the First Battalion from the 192nd Panzer Grenadiers. At the moment they're the only ones who seem to be making any progress, so we'll stack up alongside them and barge our way through to the coast here, near Douvres and Luc-sur-Mer."

He looked up at his adjutant again.

"Make sense?"

The lieutenant nodded curtly.

"It does indeed, Colonel. It's the old fashioned way isn't it? Massive force at one concentrated point... *schwerpunkt*."

The regimental commander nodded grimly.

"Yes... it is, isn't it..."

He stared down at the map again for long moments before slapping his hand down on top of the document, snatching it up and becoming suddenly animated.

"Come on then... Let's give the Tommies a good old fashioned kick in the bollocks, shall we? Pass the order to all battalion commanders. The main effort is now with the 192nd and is centred on Luc-sur-Mer. All units are to converge onto the new axis and support the Panzer Grenadiers with immediate effect. There is to be no stopping or dispersal of effort. Every tank, every half-track and every man we have is to switch onto this single axis..."

He fixed his adjutant with a determined look.

"And drive like hell for the coast..."

TACTICAL HEADQUARTERS, BRITISH 3RD INFANTRY DIVISION – NEAR HERMANVILLE
TUESDAY 6TH JUNE 1944 – 1700 HOURS

Colonel von Oppeln-Bronikowski was not the only man studying his map with grim interest that evening. On the north side of Hermanville, leaning over the bonnet of his jeep, Major General Thomas Rennie, DSO, MBE, used the stub of his pencil to sketch small marks on his map. The document was a mass of detail. Arrows of various kinds ran in all directions, whilst little bubbles and ellipses adorned the terrain features that were printed upon it. The commander of the British 3rd Infantry Division, the formation that had stormed ashore on Sword Beach at daybreak and smashed its way inland, was glaring with knitted eyebrows at the series of large, heavily shaded arrows that had been drawn on the map in the vicinity of Periers village, just a couple of miles down the road from his current location.

Also leaning over the bonnet of the jeep were two of Rennie's staff officers, both of them young captains.

"So, it seems that Jerry has finally stirred himself..." He murmured, thinking out loud. "We've been that busy trying to get past this series of strongpoints, he's had time to bring some of his heavy stuff up..."

One of the captains reached out a finger and pointed at several areas of the map in turn.

"It seems that his main strength is now on our side of the Orne River, Sir. Earlier on it looked as if 6th Airborne were going to take the brunt of it, but they've held on magnificently and they've now got 1st Special Service Brigade over there to bolster their position. I think that for the time being they're fairly well ensconced, but it's this sudden appearance of armour over here that's worrying..."

Rennie considered the captain's words for a while and nodded his agreement.

"Yes, I think you're right. And of course the reserve brigade of 6th Airborne should be flying in very shortly too, so they'll be pretty well off with fresh bodies and anti-tank guns by nightfall, won't they..."

Again, the general traced his finger around the Periers area on his map.
"Whereas, over here, we've got battalions all over the place. The Suffolks have only just put Strongpoint Hillman to bed, haven't they? And the Hambledons are still finishing off the unexpected strongpoint at Point 113..."

The general stood up straight and rubbed his chin thoughtfully.

"I'm beginning to think that pushing on as far as Caen by nightfall is becoming increasingly unlikely. I know that our leading units have rebuffed that Jerry armour that has made an appearance, but we've also got reports of it working its way around our flank, towards Juno beach. I'm of the mind to call it a day regarding the advance and start consolidating our gains by reforming the brigades and establishing a solid perimeter around the beach-head..."

The other captain added his own thoughts.

"I think you're absolutely right, Sir. We can't afford to plough on blindly until we know the true size and extent of this German armoured push. The last thing we need is the buggers getting in behind us."

The first captain chimed in.

"And at the end of the day, Sir, Caen was always a very big ask. The fact that we've got ashore and pushed this far in against all the odds is a feat in itself. The brigades must be pretty whacked by now. I think a chance to reorganise and gather themselves will do them the world of good. By tomorrow morning we'll have even more armour and men ashore, and then we can launch an all out push for Caen at first light."

Rennie stared at the map for a long while, taking in the myriad details. He had fought many desperate actions in his time. He'd suffered the ignominy of defeat at the hands of the German panzers in 1940 and been taken prisoner. Unprepared to spend the war in a prisoner of war camp, he'd escaped from his captors after just a few days and made his way back to England. Following that, he'd commanded troops across North Africa, finally learning the secret of how to defeat the Germans in open battle. This was now his biggest opportunity yet, to deliver a hammer blow to the German war-machine. He'd trained his division and its supporting elements rigorously in preparation for the invasion, and his men had done a sterling job thus far. They were back on the continent now, and taking the fight to the Germans. There was no way he wanted to get thrown back into the sea now. He would not throw away the impressive gains already achieved at so much cost.

"Alright then..." He spoke again, a decisive tone to his voice. "Let's not waste any time. We've done well today and I don't intend to yield a single yard of what we've already taken. Start preparing orders for the three infantry brigades. I want all brigades reformed and reconstituted and placed into all-round defence. I don't want any gaps anywhere. If the Jerries *are* still roaming around in their tanks, and if they come near us, I want them torn to bloody pieces. Let's get this beach-head secured properly. Once that's done, we'll start making plans for the morning. Tomorrow we're going to finish the job and capture Caen."

WEIMER'S TANK – SOMEWHERE BETWEEN THE CRUCIBLE AND HERMANVILLE TUESDAY 6TH JUNE 1944 – 1715 HOURS

"Have they fucked off, do you think?"

Wesser, his face dripping with sweat, looked across at his equally sweaty commander. Weimer shook his head ever so slightly, staring through the side periscope of the tank turret.

"Not sure... They might be looking for us... Or they might not think we're big enough to worry about, so maybe they've moved on?"

The last hour had been sheer madness. Having driven away from the killing fields around Point 113, and headed north for the coast as per their original orders, it had become more and more apparent that Weimer and his crew were on their own. Of the rest of their company, battalion and regiment there was no sign. Only the occasional bit of heavily broken up radio traffic hinted that any of their comrades were still in one piece.

The crew had debated more than once the merits of turning back and heading towards their original start position, reasoning that what was left of their unit had probably withdrawn in the face of heavy enemy resistance. Weimer however, was a man accustomed to victory. He'd been in so many desperate situations in his time, yet always won through by applying aggressive, high-tempo professionalism. To that end, he'd insisted that they press on for the coast.

"One tank can make all the difference..." He'd told his reluctant crew. "Now let's go and make our presence felt."

They had done exactly that. Just ten minutes after emerging from the smouldering, shattered woodland on Point 113, Weimer's tank had run right into a company of enemy infantry strung out on the march. Weimer had ploughed through the mass of heavily laden foot soldiers, with Wesser and the co-driver spraying the enemy relentlessly with both the co-axial and bow-mounted machine guns. Only a minute or two later, they had happened upon a gun-line of self-propelled howitzers. A cracking shot at point blank range had destroyed one of the gun-platforms outright, before the others had taken to their heels and disappeared. But then, a column of four enemy tanks had appeared on the scene, and for the last forty minutes or so, Weimer and his crew had been playing cat and mouse with the Tommy armour amongst the orchards and heavily hedged-in back roads of Normandy.

Weimer unlocked the turret hatch lever and then pushed the hatch upwards.

"I'm going up to take a look around." He told the rest of the crew. "Be prepared to move fast if I say so…"

With that, the staff sergeant clambered into a standing position and poked his head out of the cupola. He scanned full circle with the naked eye before lifting his binoculars and training them on the terrain to the north. He moved the field glasses slowly, taking in every bit of detail as he tried to pin-point his exact position. As he did so, the options ran through his mind for the hundredth time.

He was following orders, heading for the coast, doing his best to cause havoc amongst the Tommies as he went. The problem was that the Tommies were obviously ashore in strength, and their damn Jabos were everywhere. The tank commander shivered involuntarily as he remembered the all consuming aerial assault of just an hour earlier. How the hell was he supposed to fight Jabos? That was meant to be the Luftwaffe's job, but of them there was no sign. And as for the remainder of his regiment, well, only the Gods knew what had happened to them.

He froze as a line of grey roof tiles came into view beyond the hedgerows and trees. After a moment or two, Weimer began scanning again, assessing the size of the built-up area that had loomed up within the field of view of his binoculars. Then he froze again. Far beyond the roofs of the buildings that must be only half a mile away at most, Weimer could see balloons; the kind of balloons that were flown above important military targets to ward off low flying aircraft, or the kind that could be used as observation platforms; the kind of balloons that would be flown above an invasion fleet.

With trembling hands and a rising sense of excitement, Weimer lowered his binoculars and fumbled for his map from inside the turret. Pulling it up onto the cupola, the staff sergeant quickly traced the route of his advance until he reached Point 113, then assessed where his most recent manoeuvres had brought him to. Even though he had been closed down inside the turret for much of the time, it was obvious that his routed had taken him inexorably northwards, which meant that the village that was visible just up ahead must be… Hermanville. Weimer jabbed his finger at the small village on the map and took a deep breath.

If that was Hermanville, then it meant that he was less than two and a half kilometres from the coast. He felt the blood begin to rush in his ears. This was it. This is what they had been ordered to do; reach the coast and wreak havoc amongst the Tommies as they attempted to move off the beach and establish a firm foothold. He might be on his own, but he had nearly a full load of ammunition and plenty of fuel. Besides, this is what the German Army did best; infiltration of the enemy's front line and destruction of his command and logistics hubs. And if *he* could do it, then surely the surviving tanks from his regiment could do it. One more attack; one more thrust; one more sacrifice and they might finally end this forever. If they could throw the Tommies back into the sea then surely those stubborn island-monkeys would have to sue for peace after all these years, and realise that they could never defeat Germany on the field of battle.

An intoxicating mix of fear and excitement welled up inside Weimer. This was just like 1940 again; a journey into the great unknown, but with the possibility of eternal glory and fame up for grabs. It just needed a few bold men; a few believers who were prepared to give everything to tip the battle in Germany's favour...

Weimer made up his mind. He dropped back into the turret and spoke into the intercom.

"Alright lads, this is it. We're almost at the coast, which means we're past the frontline of enemy troops. Any moment now we're going to run into their rear echelons and their headquarters; and then we'll start tearing this invasion of theirs to pieces..."

Wesser gave his commander a sceptical look.

"What about their tanks?"

Weimer was in no mood for pessimism.

"Tommy tanks are shit. We'll blow them to fucking pieces. Just another couple of hours and we'll leave this invasion dead in the water. The rest of the regiment will be doing the same. We just need to make one more push."

The veteran tank commander stuffed his map onto the side shelf and snapped an order into the microphone.

"Driver – forwards..."

PART SIX
AFTERMATH

THE CRUCIBLE – POINT 113
TUESDAY 6TH JUNE 1944 – 1720 HOURS

"**D**ickie... Well done old boy! Well done indeed! That was one hell of a punch up, eh? You and your boys were absolutely first class; well done!"

Colonel Blair was thumping Smithson enthusiastically on the back, as the remainder of the battalion tactical headquarters flooded into the trench. Smithson, who was still desperately trying to co-ordinate the securing of the position with 'D' Company's commander, mumbled an embarrassed and exhausted reply.

"Thank you, Sir. Sorry about the time... I wasn't expecting to bump into so many Jerries to be honest; never mind all those tanks. Thank God the RAF was on the ball today..."

"Yes, well, not to worry... I think we were all a bit surprised to find the Jerries dug-in up here in such strength. And then that bloody counter-attack with their armour! Thank God we had our own anti-tank platoon and the self-propelled guns from the artillery up front, too. I'm afraid it's rather put the brigade's timetable out somewhat. There's no chance of us making it to Caen by last-light now."

Smithson looked up at his commanding officer in surprise.

"Don't you think so, Sir? There's got to be a good four hours of light left, surely? If we get a shift on then..."

Blair was already shaking his head.

"I'm afraid there's not a chance of it, Dickie. I mean, don't get me wrong, it's only a few miles up the road and we could forced-march it in just a couple of hours, but the problem is that the brigade is spread out all over the place and there are still Jerry tanks all over the shop. Besides, it's going to take a while longer to clear this place up properly and I don't want to send half the battalion off into the unknown without proper support. You saw what nearly happened here. If we hadn't had everything up front ready to go then

365

that Jerry armour would have torn right through us, despite the timely assistance from our RAF colleagues."

Smithson's shoulders slumped at his commanding officers words.

"So we've failed?"

Blair became even more animated, patting the major reassuringly on the shoulder again.

"Of course we haven't, Dickie! Nothing of the sort! This entire operation was always going to be difficult and the tasks that were allocated were deliberately ambitious. If truth be told, half of those in the high command fully expected this invasion to be a complete and utter disaster, just like that show at Dieppe a couple of years back. The fact is that we've fought our way ashore and broken into German occupied France. We've got more tanks and planes and ships and men than the Jerries could possibly throw at us, so now that we're here there's no going back. It's not a matter of *if* we win any more, it's simply a case of *when* we beat the buggers..."

Smithson nodded dutifully at his commanding officer's words, but in truth he felt as if he had let his battalion down by not clearing up Point 113 more rapidly and pushing on for Caen. Blair saw the look in the young major's eyes and went on, soothingly.

"Anyway, Dickie... whether we want to go on or not, we've been given orders from above. Brigade HQ have been on the radio and ordered us to go firm and dig-in. They want us to consolidate our gains for the night now while all the reserves and heavy stuff are brought ashore and sent up to us. They also want to make sure that if there are any Jerry tanks left in the area we can be ready for them and finish them off for good next time. It's not just us you see? The whole brigade, indeed the whole division is in the same boat."

Smithson perked up at the words slightly, feeling better to know that the decision had been forced on them from higher formation. In truth, no matter how desperate he was to fulfil their original mission, he knew that his own company at least was in no fit state to make further progress that day. They had been through their baptism of fire and come out of it victorious; but it had been at a cost. He didn't know for sure how many men he had lost today but he knew that his company would be much lighter in manpower come nightfall than it had started out that morning. He needed to find his company sergeant major, he decided, and start the business of getting things reorganised. The firing seemed to have stopped at the far side of the wood, which indicated that 'D' Company, who'd been hard on the heels of Smithson's company during the mad scramble to take the position by storm in the wake of the air strike, had finally cleared the last enemy positions.

"Well, Sir..." Smithson began. "If that's the case, then when we kick off again tomorrow, I'd like to take the point with my company again please?"

Blair gave Smithson a fatherly smile.

"That's very generous of you Dickie, but the other companies in this battalion also need to earn their keep. We'll let your boys take it easy in reserve tomorrow, but I promise you that when we get to Caen, I'll let your boys lead us down the high street."

Smithson simply nodded, feeling the strain and fatigue of the last thirty six hours catching up on him. The lack of food or proper sleep; the boat journey with its wretched sea-sickness and constant odour of vomit; the foul weather, the abhorrent lack of concern for human life he had witnessed on the beach, and of course the unbelievably fierce, and completely unexpected fight here at Point 113. In truth, he was physically and mentally shattered. Although he would never admit it publicly, the prospect of a full night of sleep in pre-dug trenches, followed by a day of traipsing along behind the rest of the battalion, seemed entirely agreeable to him.

"That's very kind of you, Sir. We'd be honoured." Smithson managed a tired smile for his colonel.

"That's the spirit, old boy!" Blair slapped him on the back again. "It's the least we can do. You did a cracking job today; make sure your lads know that. I'm exceptionally proud of you all."

The colonel gestured vaguely around the battle-scarred remains of Point 113 which was still clogged in a thick veil of smoke that hung on the damp, summer air.

"Get yourself a good nights sleep, Dickie. You've got plenty of trenches and dug-outs here to make use of. I'll put 'D' Company down in the open ground to the east and 'B' Company down on the main road and crossroads. 'C' Company can hang back in reserve. I'll also send the anti-tank platoon up here so they've got good coverage across the entire ridgeline. And tomorrow... Well, tomorrow we shall push on and finally clap our eyes on the ancient city of Caen..."

DOWNEY'S PLATOON, 2ND BATTALION THE EAST YORKSHIRE REGIMENT – JUST OUTSIDE HERMANVILLE TUESDAY 6TH JUNE 1944 – 1730 HOURS

Downey watched as his men began dropping their packs and equipment onto the wet grass at the edge of the meadow and started pulling their digging tools free, ready to break the ground in the lee of the thick hedgerows on the edge of Hermanville. Downey was exhausted and bleary eyed; his mind now fuddled from the combination of lack of sleep, extreme physical activity, and the shock of battle. He was going about his duties now like a man in a trance; the orders and instructions coming out automatically, the product of years of training and discipline. His men were in a similar state, for it had been a long day for all of them.

Their landing against the strongly held enemy coastal positions seemed as if it had taken place days ago, rather than just a few hours. Following the storming of the beach and the bloody clearance of Objective Cod, their battalion had moved swiftly on to secure their secondary objectives, those being Objective Sole and Objective Daimler. That sequence of fresh assaults had taken the men of the East Yorkshires on a three mile advance against stiff opposition in a south-easterly direction, via the suburbs of Ouistreham until they had finished their day at St Aubin-de-Arenquey.

The sense of achievement had been enormous. Downey, having experienced battle before, had seriously doubted if he and his men would survive the assault against the beach defences, let alone see the entire day through to secure every one of their D-Day objectives. To have achieved every mission and overcome every hardship and still be in one piece had given rise to a sense of near-elation amongst the usually phlegmatic country boys from East Yorkshire. As the pressure of battle had eased however, and the adrenalin had finally stopped pumping, the physical and emotional exhaustion had crept in on their consciousness. So too had the realisation that only two thirds of the platoon were still together. As a battalion, the East Yorkshires were missing more than a quarter of their strength. Downey's platoon commander was still missing, believed killed, as were half a dozen others. Another half dozen or so were definitely dead or wounded, for the sergeant had witnessed their fates with his own eyes.

Therefore, it had been with some relief that the East Yorkshires had been relieved by a Scottish battalion from one of the reserve brigades, just an hour or so before, and instructed to return to Hermanville and dig-in, as part of the depth protection for the fledgling beach-head. The battalion would dig-in around the village and remain here overnight, it seemed; to recover its strength and replenish its ammunition, prior to being launched into the next operation which would, undoubtedly be a rapid advance to break-out from the beach-head into open country.

Downey glanced to the north, towards the main part of the village and the flat meadows that lay beyond it, running down to the thin strip of houses on the beach front. The entire landscape beyond the village was a mass of men and vehicles. He could see columns of small vehicles forming up in the open fields, lines of men traversing the landscape, laden with equipment, whilst in the village itself, where the main road ran through it, piles of stores and ammunition were stacking up; dumped there by the advancing infantry who had manhandled it ashore in the follow-up waves. The invasion was already building up a head of steam. More and more men and tanks and equipment would pour ashore during the evening, the night and on into the new day. They had done it, Downey realised with exhausted pride. They had broken into fortress Europe.

A sudden grim thought crept in upon that realisation however. If he had lost a third of his men on just the first day, then how many of them would be left by the time this business was finally at an end? He shook the thought away, not wanting to dwell on it.

"Sarge? Sarge?"

The call from one of his men caught Downey's attention.

"Yes, Jakey?" He turned and answered Corporal Jacobs, the man who had hailed him.

"There's a tank across the fields there, Sarge... It looks a bit dodgy if you ask me..."

Downey pulled a face that showed a lack of concern.

"There are tanks all over the place, mate..."

Jacobs wrinkled his brow in concern.

"No... I know that Sarge, but... well... it just looks a bit dodgy. For a start off it doesn't look like one of ours, and besides that... well, it looks like it's hiding..."

Downey's brow creased now, in bemusement.

"Hiding? What d'you mean, Jakey? Are you sure you're not just being a bit jumpy?"

The corporal shook his head.

"No Sarge, I'm telling you... it just doesn't look right. The fucker keeps speeding from one bit of cover to the next, and he's coming our way too. Surely he should be going the other way?"

"Where is he? Show me."

Downey stepped up next to Jacobs and together they peered through the thick hedgerow. One of the privates nearby laid down his shovel and came over to join the two NCOs, pointing southwards across the next field.

"He's just behind that clump of trees over there Sarge, just off to the left of the main road as you look across at it..."

Downey squinted through the bushes of the hedge and stared towards the small copse. At first he could see nothing, but then, from over to his right, a small convoy of Bren Carriers emerged from Hermanville and began rattling down the road, heading inland, their small squat shapes only fleetingly visible from behind the fences and hedges that lined their route.

He watched them as they drove rapidly along the road, getting ever nearer to the copse where the mystery tank had apparently been seen last. Downey was just at the point of declaring the whole thing to be a false alarm when suddenly, like a bolt of lightning, there was a dazzlingly bright flash from amongst the undergrowth in the copse, followed a second later by a sickening 'crump' as the leading carrier literally erupted in a ball of flame, and shattered into a thousand pieces of twisted metal before Downey's very eyes.

"Fuck me!" Jacobs cried out in shock.

"Jesus!" Downey breathed.

A heartbeat later, a plume of dirty grey exhaust fumes belched out from within the copse, and the sound of a powerful engine revving up drifted across the field on the evening air. Then, like a lion breaking cover to pounce on its prey, a massive, deadly-looking, yellow, brown and green mottled German tank, burst forth from the copse, bright flashes from both its turret and hull showing where its machine-guns were chattering away in a symphony of death. The tank's engine seemed to roar like a wild beast as it accelerated towards the main road, bearing down on the now stalled convoy of lightly armoured carriers. Downey and his men could only stand there agape as the tank systematically began to massacre the vehicles and their occupants, right there in front of their very eyes.

With a sudden rush of fury, Downey came alive. He and his men had busted their guts all day to make sure that this invasion succeeded. Now he was determined that no German was going to take that away from them. He whirled round to fix Jacobs with an implacable look.

"Get me the fucking PIAT, Jakey; sharpish!"

WEIMER'S TANK – JUST OUTSIDE HERMANVILLE TUESDAY 6TH JUNE 1944 – 1735 HOURS

Weimer watched the little convoy of curious looking armoured vehicles clattering up the road through his commander's sight and marvelled that the British were still using the things. He'd come across these vehicles before during the 1940 drive to the sea and knew that they had nothing in the way of proper armour. Even so, the Tommies seemed to love the strange little machines. Whatever, they would soon be short of another half-dozen.

"Stand-by…" He warned his gunner.

"You do realise..." Wesser murmured. "That as soon as we open fire and break cover, every Tommy for miles around is going to know we're here?"

Weimer fought down his irritation and gave a small grunt of a laugh instead.

"Perfect. Once they know there are enemy tanks in their rear area they'll panic and run like hell for their boats. Remember, I've fought them before. The Tommies don't like complications. If their carefully laid plans get derailed, they just fall to pieces."

Wesser glanced at the staff sergeant briefly, not entirely convinced that his commander was giving their adversaries enough credit.

"Stand-by!" Weimer said more sharply, the excitement rising in his voice suddenly.

Wesser jammed his eyes back to the gun sight and watched as the leading enemy vehicle came rolling into his sight picture.

"Whenever you're ready..." Weimer said.

Wesser watched the curious looking vehicle clattering up the cobbled road, several heads sticking up from inside the olive green hull of the little armoured cars that sported a white star on their sides. Just a heartbeat later, the nose of the first vehicle seemed to touch the graticule on his gun-sight. He didn't hesitate. With an urgent jerk of his leg, Wesser stamped down on the foot firing pedal.

"Firing now!"

Whoomph!

The big Panzer IV rocked back on its suspension as the powerful 75mm gun spat its deadly shell directly towards the enemy carrier at less than two hundred yards range. Wesser didn't even have time to register the fall of shot, because before his very eyes, the enemy armoured vehicle seemed to disintegrate into a million pieces.

"Target!" Weimer cried out aloud from beside him, then... "Driver – forward!"

Even as Wesser was sliding open the breech so that the loader could feed in another round, the big tank was lurching forward with a growl of its 12 cylinder engine.

"Use the machine guns!" Weimer was shouting. "Spray the bastards! Driver – go straight down the side of them!"

Their tank surged forward, breaking down small saplings and bushes within the copse as it emerged into the open field beyond. Wesser had managed to focus his eyes once more through the gun-sight, even though the sight picture bounced and jolted correspondingly with the vehicles movement across the field. He was vaguely aware of a smoking pile of debris on the road way but focussed all of his attention on the now stationary line of vehicles behind it and the alarmed faces of the men who were peering out of them in terror at the sudden appearance of the German tank. They were that close to each other that Wesser could plainly see the looks of dread and fear etched on those pale faces beneath their foliage draped helmets. He tried not to think of them as people and concentrated on dropping the elevation off his guns instead.

He watched as the graticules fell some small amount; level with the line of Tommy vehicles. The forward movement of their own tank brought the graticule onto target just a second later. Having already switched to secondary armament, Wesser reacted through instinct and opened fire. The turret was filled with the noisy clatter of machine gun fire as the co-axial gun began raking the line of enemy vehicles. From below, the sound of the bow-machine gun joined in the cacophony.

The tank rolled forward at speed, all attempts at remaining hidden now dispensed with. It was time to fight, and Wesser, despite his reservations, was a gunner of experience. He tweaked the elevation gear of the guns as they advanced, ensuring that his constant stream of high velocity rounds continued to tear into the helpless armoured vehicles. The gunner absently noted khaki clad bodies slumping over the sides of the tiny little carriers, or throwing themselves over the sides and into the hedgerows as the Panzer IV ripped into them with unrelenting automatic fire.

Just as quickly as it had started, it was suddenly over, with the tank rumbling past the last of the stranded vehicles, leaving the dead and dying crews to bleed out inside their peppered vehicles.

"Driver – left! Onto the road; then on into the village!" Weimer snapped, his voice edged with a mixture of vengeful desire and nervous energy.

The driver obediently swung the vehicle onto the road, crashing through the low hedge and then swinging right again, straightening up and accelerating along the cobbles towards the village itself.

"Here we go lads!" Weimer was shouting excitedly, an almost school-boy like exultation seizing hold of him. "There'll be loads more of the bastards in the village! We're going to tear them to fucking pieces! Shoot everything you see! Driver; anything we don't shoot – you drive over it!"

The crew shouted their understanding over the intercom, less Wesser, who was already swinging the turret from left to right and back again, scanning for new targets.

"What the fuck are those?" He demanded suddenly, spotting the large piles of boxes and containers by the side of the road.

"Stores dump!" The co-driver confirmed.

"Crush them all!" Weimer shouted at the driver.

The driver began swinging the big tank to the left, ready to mount the grass verge when they entered the village, which was less than a hundred metres away now. Further into the village, Wesser could see large groups of men sitting around or standing beside vehicles. They were looking towards the oncoming tank now, and several men had begun darting across the road in obvious panic.

"We've caught the fuckers with their pants down!" Weimer enthused. "Shoot the fuckers, Wesser! Open fire!"

Boom!

The unexpected, deafening explosion, took them all by surprise, and the tank suddenly veered sharply to the left, smashing into a telegraph pole and then jolting to a sudden halt. The abrupt stop sent the turret crew flying around their fighting compartment and Wesser felt his teeth shatter as his face smashed into the breech of the co-axial machine-gun.

"Aagh!"

The loader cried out as his head smashed into the bottom of the main gun, opening a huge gash in his skull which immediately began pouring with blood.

Weimer made no sound, because his head smashed straight into the side of the turret, knocking him unconscious immediately.

"Fucking hell!" Wesser groaned through a mouth full of blood and broken teeth. "What the fuck…"

"We're hit!" The co-driver's voice began screaming hysterically from below. "We're hit! Willi's dead!"

Wesser, still half-stunned, tried to register what was happening. While he was still trying to come to his senses, the tank shook violently once more as a deafening explosion erupted against the rear of the vehicle.

"Uurgh!" Wesser grunted a he was thrown against the turret ring once more.

A moment later, despite his dulled senses, the gunner's mind suddenly came alive. The smell was unmistakable, and seconds later, the dark, noxious black smoke that began filling the compartment confirmed the gunner's worst fears.

"Get out!" He began yelling through his shattered mouth, yanking off the radio headset as he did so and groping for the release levers for the side escape hatch. "We're on fire! Get out!"

DOWNEY'S POSITION – HERMANVILLE
TUESDAY 6TH JUNE 1944 – 1735 HOURS

"Fucking Jerry bastards!" Downey snarled, staring in horror at the tragedy being played out before him.

He turned briefly to snap an order to one of the nearby private soldiers, just one of many who were standing behind the hedgerow, shovels and picks in hands, watching with utter shock as the lone German tank progressed across the field, meting out death and destruction to the platoon of carriers that were now stranded on the road.

"Atkinson! Get around the Company position and raise the alarm! Tell everyone to stand-to!"

The soldier looked at his sergeant dumbly for a moment.

"Fucking move, lad!"

The young soldier was startled into action and leapt away towards where the company's headquarters were setting up. Meanwhile, Downey roared out at the men around him.

"Stand-to! Come-on! Don't just stand there gawping! Get your weapons and stand-by to take on this tank! Get your grenades out!"

He was pushing and shoving his men into action, stunned as they were by this sudden development, just at the point where they had thought their bloody work was done for the day.

"Where's that fucking PIAT?"

Downey whirled around looking for the weapon.

"Here, Sarge!"

The sergeant looked towards the voice and saw Jacobs running back towards him, accompanied by two soldiers; one carrying the large, unwieldy projector, the other hefting a container of bombs.

"Get over here! Give me the bloody thing!" Downey raged.

He snatched the weapon off the soldier who was carrying it and dropped down against the low bank on which the hedgerow had been planted.

"Get me a bomb out, quickly!"

Beside him, the second soldier was fumbling for one of the fat, ungainly looking bombs with its protruding nose-tip.

"Come on man!"

As the private dragged a bomb clear of the olive-green container, Downey began aligning the PIAT onto the enemy vehicle which was almost at the end of the line of carriers, tearing into them with its machine gun at point blank range. He judged the distance. Still over a hundred yards perhaps? A bit too far for an accurate shot, but what other choice was there? Men were dying at the hands of the big, German tank.

The private with the bomb began feeding it into the front cradle of the projector.

"Make sure he's pushed home..." Downey instructed, knowing that he wouldn't get more than one chance at hitting the vehicle before it moved on.

Just as the soldier rammed the bomb fully home and ensured it was snugly positioned however, the German tank suddenly swung to one side and crashed through the hedgerow and onto the road behind the line of carriers. Downey watched with increasing horror as the tank swung sharply right again onto the cobbled road and accelerated straight towards the village.

"Shit!" Downey swore. "He's going through the village!"

The sergeant pushed himself upright, growling with rage as he hauled the heavy anti-tank weapon up with him.

"Come on!"

Without looking to see who was following him, Downey began racing along the hedgerow, straight towards where it met the road into the village, determined to head the vehicle off. He could hear the roar of the tank's powerful engines above the thump of his own footfalls on the wet turf and the rushing of blood in his ears. He was tired and bruised and battered from a full day of fighting, yet every ounce of energy that remained in the sergeant's body was now being expended in this last, desperate venture of the day.

Downey reached the gateway of the field and glanced left. With a lurch of fear he saw that the enemy tank was only fifty yards away and accelerating fast towards him, its left hand tracks on the grass verge as it rattled noisily towards the entrance to Hermanville. He had just a matter of seconds to act.

Throwing himself down behind a water trough that sat by the gatepost of the field's access point, the sergeant slapped the whole projector down onto the rim of the metal box. He reached out and made one final check that the bomb was correctly fitted then ducked his head behind the weapon, pulling the butt back into his shoulder and gripping hold of the weapon tightly. Downey felt a thrill of fear run through him as he stared straight up the barrel of the tank's main gun, wondering absently if the crew had spotted him. The tank was only thirty yards away now and the clatter of its tracks and roar of its engines filled Downey's ears, drowning out all other sounds, as he aligned the PIAT onto target.

Thonk!

Downey pulled the trigger on the PIAT and the weapon thumped back in his shoulder and spat out its chubby looking bomb towards the oncoming armoured vehicle. At a range of just twenty yards, there was no more than a second of delay before the pointed nose of the PIAT bomb punched into the front of the tank, right in front of the driver's observation slit.

The bomb exploded with a hollow thump, a bright flash, and belch of black smoke. A heartbeat later, the German tank suddenly swerved hard left and ploughed through the opposite hedgerow, taking out a telegraph pole en route, before slamming to an abrupt stop.

"Reload!" Downey was yelling, even as the tank veered away from him, not even aware if his comrades had caught up with him yet.

They had.

A hand appeared over Downey's left shoulder and slid another bomb into the weapon as the sergeant hauled back on the cocking lever. A second later and the bomb was rammed home.

"Out of the way!" Downey snarled, realigning the PIAT onto the rear end of the stationary tank.

Thonk!

The weapon lurched for a second time and once more the bomb arced through the air and slapped against its target, the shock-wave of the detonation slapping Downey hard in the face and causing him to screw his eyes shut and drop down behind the water trough.

He lay there on one elbow for a moment, the heavy projector falling onto him from atop the trough. Glancing round he saw that the man carrying the bombs was still beside him, a third bomb in his hands should it be needed. Behind the private, Jacobs lay flat on the floor, peering across at the enemy vehicle with a look of disbelief etched on his face, his Sten Gun cradled across his arms.

The sergeant pushed himself upright and stared across the road. Thick black smoke filled the roadway, and deep within that smoke, hungry orange flames licked up at the rear decks of the tank.

"I think you've got his engine, Sarge..." The private with the spare bomb shouted above the crackle of flames.

Downey stared at the vehicle some more, assessing if a third round would be needed. Judging by the rapid spread of flames across the tank's rear deck, he doubted that it would.

"Jakey?" Downey growled over his shoulder. "Get that Sten Gun ready. Go see if any of the bastards inside are still alive..."

PRISONER COLLECTION POINT – THE CRUCIBLE
TUESDAY 6TH JUNE 1944 – 1800 HOURS

When Gritz open his eyes, he felt calm, relaxed, if a little confused. He was laid on his back, staring up at scattered, grey clouds that partially obscured an equally grey sky. A cold breeze ran over his body and he shivered involuntarily.

"Brrrr…"

Almost instantly, a face appeared over him. The sergeant major stared up at the face, recognising it as a familiar one but struggling to put a name to it.

"Sergeant Major? Lay still, I'll get something to cover you with…"

The face disappeared again and Gritz wrinkled his brow. Why was that person talking to him like he was a poorly child? Who was it again? He was sure he knew the face…

The face reappeared and Gritz felt something like a blanket being draped over him.

"There you go, Sir. That should keep you warm for a bit until they put us under cover."

Gritz's confusion grew.

"Under cover?" He managed to say, his voice coming out as a surprisingly weak groan. "Who?"

The face regarded Gritz earnestly.

"The Tommies, Sir. The Tommies are going to put us under cover somewhere I think. We're prisoners now…"

In a confusing rush, Gritz's memory came flooding back. He remembered who he was, where he was, and most of what had happened. He blinked in shock as the memories poured back into his mind.

"Corporal Kole?" He uttered the name in surprise as he finally recognised the identity of the face that was staring down at him.

"Yes, Sir; it's me…" Kole confirmed in a quiet voice.

"Shit!" Gritz spluttered and made to sit up.

The sergeant major got his shoulders about a centimetre off the floor, but then felt a terrible pain shoot through his upper body. He felt as if a tremendous weight was on his chest, pushing him back down, and he exploded into a fit of painful coughing that sent unbearable ripples of discomfort through his entire body.

"Lay still, Sir!" Kole reached down and pressed him gently back against the floor. "It's best if you lay still…"

"Fucking hell!" Gritz gasped between coughs. "My fucking shoulder! My chest!"

Kole regarded his commander with a sympathetic look.

"You've been shot, Sir; through your upper chest. We think it's gone up into your shoulder and splintered your collar bone. The Tommy medics seem to think it's missed your lungs though, thankfully. There's no blood when you cough..."

As the coughing fit subsided, Gritz, feeling terribly weak and vulnerable of a sudden, managed to speak again.

"Shot? How?" His mind worked feverishly, trying to remember the details of the last few hours. "I blew up the Tommy tank... Our panzers were attacking... How are we prisoners?"

It didn't make sense. Gritz remembered little snapshots of everything but he couldn't piece them together somehow.

Kole's look had a tinge of sadness in it.

"The Tommies won, Sir. They beat us. Those of us who were left had no choice but to surrender..."

The corporal's eyes betrayed a hint of shame at the admission.

"What?" Gritz furrowed his brow. "We lost? How did we lose?"

Kole pulled a wry face.

"The Jabos, Sergeant Major. You remember what you said about the Jabos? You were right. They did for us in the end. They tore our panzers to pieces then tore our position to pieces afterwards. There was nothing we could do..."

Gritz just stared up at the corporal, remembering slowly that terrible moment when the enemy fighter bombers had pounced; just at the point where Gritz had sensed a glorious victory against all the odds.

"Sergeant Gunther is dead." Kole stated quietly. "He went down fighting on his position when the Tommies charged us.

Gritz took in the news, remembering Gunther's face as he struggled to come to terms with the terrible realisation that not only had he lost his battle, he was now a prisoner. Other faces came into his mind and the sergeant major began putting names to them.

"Kellerman?" He said out loud. "Where's Kellerman?"

"Dead." Kole replied quietly. "Poor bastard couldn't stand it any longer. He shot himself."

Gritz frowned at the news. After a moment of thought, he spoke.

"Doesn't surprise me... Should never have been here. He'd lost it. It was Russia that, you know... Fucked him up completely..."

Kole nodded his agreement.

"Yes... well, I reckon Russia fucked us *all* up..."

Gritz considered the comment silently. After a while however, he spoke again.

"What are the Tommies doing now?"

Kole threw a quick glance over his shoulder.

"They're digging-in by the looks. Bringing up all kinds of heavy stuff. Anti-tanks guns, heavy machine guns, armoured cars, mortars... I even saw some self-propelled artillery moving up..."

Gritz nodded weakly.

"They won't give this place up now. We've lost Kole... the whole war... we've lost it."

Kole stared into space for a while then looked back down at his wounded commander.

"Well, we won't be around to watch it. It's a prison camp for us, Sir. We're being moved back towards the coast shortly. The Tommies told us. One of the new boys speaks good English. The Tommies told him to make sure we're ready to go when they tell us."

Gritz managed a grim smile.

"A day at the beach... nice!"

The corporal emitted a mirthless chuckle.

"Well, suits me fine... This place stinks of death... They can take us all the way to England for all I care..."

There was a small commotion somewhere nearby and Kole looked around sharply. Gritz heard a German voice that he didn't recognise, calling out instructions.

"Okay, they want us to line up on the track. They're moving us towards the coast. We've got to carry all the wounded with us..."

"What's that?" Gritz demanded, unable to see the person who had shouted out the orders and not recognising the voice.

Kole looked back down to him.

"That's the new boy, Sir. He says we've got to get ready to move. The Tommies are taking us down to the beach. You're coming with us. I've got a stretcher party organised."

Gritz nodded his understanding and, suddenly, Kole's dour face broke into a tired smile.

"I hope you've got your bucket and spade with you, Sergeant Major?"

DICKIE SMITHSON – THE CRUCIBLE
TUESDAY 6TH JUNE 1944 – 1805 HOURS

Smithson watched the battered, ragged line of German prisoners as they hobbled and staggered down the muddy, body-strewn track, carrying their stretcher cases with them as they were escorted to the rear by a party of men from the battalion's defence platoon. They looked a sight; beaten, battered, pathetic.

"Hard to believe that a bunch of odds and sods like that could have put up such a fight, eh?"

Smithson turned at the sound of the voice and found that he had been joined on the edge of the wood-line by Lieutenant Edward Stockdale, the battalion's intelligence officer.

The infantry company commander gave a tired smile.

"Yes… quite. You have to give it to them; the buggers gave us a good run for our money. I just wish they'd realise that they can't possibly win any more; save a whole load of lives on both sides."

Stockdale nodded in silent agreement. After a moment, he nodded towards the shambling column of enemy prisoners.

"Their stubbornness is even more admirable when you consider that there's barely a fit man amongst them."

Smithson looked quizzically at Stockdale.

"How do you mean?"

The lieutenant took a deep breath.

"I had a good chat with one of the prisoners; a young lad, only arrived here yesterday morning. He spoke fairly good English so I managed to get quite a bit out of him. It seems that this position isn't very old; barely a couple of weeks in fact, which explains why we didn't know anything about it. Most of the garrison here were scraped together from the waifs and strays of other units; men who'd suffered lower limb injuries and who couldn't run about very much. The Jerry I spoke to says that they were known as 'The Cripples' by their own high command."

Smithson stared incredulously at the junior officer.

"What? You mean we've been held up here all afternoon by the enemy's sick and wounded?"

Stockdale nodded uncomfortably.

"Er… sort of… But, what you have to remember is that most of these chaps got their injuries fighting on the Russian front, so in effect you were fighting against a position full of veterans. Bad legs or not, this lot knew their business. Apparently the commander was a non commissioned officer who was a bit of a hero; a holder of the Knight's Cross. To be honest Dickie, you and your boys should be proud of the fact that you managed to take this position at all; after all, three quarters of our battalion are just like me... green as hell; fresh out of school. There are only a handful of old 1940 boys amongst us. On the other hand, the Jerry garrison here was full of old soldiers."

Smithson relaxed slightly, reassured that he'd done a good job after all, given what Stockdale was telling him about the enemy garrison that had resisted his own company's efforts for the best part of three hours. He glanced off to one side and noticed a small group of men sitting on the trunk of a fallen tree; the surviving crew from one of the knocked out Shermans.

"I think I might walk round the position quickly." Smithson said quietly, changing the subject. "See how everyone is getting on..."

He nodded his goodbye to Stockdale and wandered across to where the tank crew sat, gathered around a corporal with heavily bandaged hands. One of the privates amongst the crew was holding an enamel cup up to the injured corporal's lips.

"Hello chaps..." Smithson said as he drew near to them.

The tankers sat upright suddenly, hearing Smithson's well-bred accent and spotting his major's crowns on his epaulettes. They looked as if they were about to spring to their feet and adopt the position of attention, but Smithson waved them down.

"No... please, stay seated; don't get up. You deserve a rest. I just wanted to say thank you for helping us out this afternoon. I'm sorry about your friends in the other vehicles. You all did a marvellous job. We wouldn't have managed it without you..."

The tank crew smiled up at him appreciatively, and Smithson addressed his next comments directly to the corporal with bandaged hands.

"How are you doing? Are you in much pain?"

The corporal grinned up at Smithson, but there was more pain than pleasure in the smile, which in actual fact was just an exceptionally broad grimace.

"Not too bad, Sir, thank you..." The tank commander lied. "Could have been worse. Your medical orderlies have sorted me out nicely, but I don't think I'll be playing the piano for a while though."

Smithson laughed at the brave attempt at humour.

"No, perhaps not... Listen, I don't think there's any point in you wandering around the lanes tonight looking for the rest of your regiment. Why don't you stay here and get a good night's sleep in one of these Jerry dug-outs? Our QM is on his way forward with some food apparently so you're more than welcome to stay and help yourselves. We'll probably be moving on early tomorrow and then you can have a steady walk back towards the coast to try and pick up your own chaps."

"Thank you, Sir..." The corporal replied tiredly. "That's very kind of you."

Smithson smiled back.

"We're just in the process of getting the position sorted out. My Company Sergeant Major will get a party of men to bury your dead from the other two tanks..."

The tankers didn't reply for a moment or two, but after a slight hesitation, one of the privates answered for the corporal.

"We'll do it, Sir. If you can lend us some shovels..."

The major nodded confirmation.

"Yes... I'm sure we'll be able to do that."

He excused himself and began to walk around the south-western edge of the wood-line, where it looked down onto the old ruins, stopping to give a word of encouragement and praise here and there as he caught up with his men. As he toured the company position, he gradually caught up with the news on which individuals had 'copped it', 'got a Blighty' or escaped from the afternoon's battle unscathed. His men were tired, some of them a little shocked, but on the whole rather proud and positive that they had prevailed in their first proper test of battle.

Among those he came across was Jeremy Willis, whose platoon had taken the brunt of the initial contact with the enemy. His platoon had lost over a third of its strength, including several experienced NCOs, and the young second lieutenant was clearly still shaken by the whole experience. Smithson sought to reassure the young officer and clapped him on the shoulder like a proud father.

"Well done today Jeremy. It was a tough one I'm afraid, your first battle, but it was always going to be the case. I've just been talking with Eddie Stockdale. He says that the Jerries up on this hill were all veterans of the Russian front, so you and your boys did a great job considering what you were up against..."

The ensign gave a half hearted smile.

"Thank you, Sir... But... is it true about Charlie Normanton?"

Smithson winced, the recent bad news still raw in his mind.

"Yes, Jeremy... I'm afraid it is. He got hit during the final assault as we charged up the track."

Willis' face seemed to drop.

"Charlie was ever so good to me when I joined the battalion. He was such a good officer. So confident, and organised and..." Willis paused, almost choking on his words. "I... I don't know how I shall manage to get by if Charlie got hit on the first day..."

"Enough, Jeremy." Smithson squeezed the young man's shoulder firmly. "Don't think like that. It was just bad luck, that's all. And today's fighting was especially heavy. Once we've got our full tank strength ashore, we'll just blast our way through the German defences. You'll see, Jeremy... everything will be fine from here on."

He gave the ensign a hard look.

"Now then... enough talk of poor old Charlie; you've got some work to do."

Willis glanced up and met his commander's eye, intrigued.

"You speak French, don't you?"

"Yes, Sir." The junior officer confirmed, puzzled.

"Good..." Smithson grinned. "You see that farm down there to our front? Beyond the brewed up Jerry tanks?"

Willis strained his eyes to see, and nodded his acknowledgement a moment later.

"Well..." Smithson continued. "We're not going to push any further forward today, but I want to know if that farmhouse is clear, and we don't want the enemy to make use of it in the meantime. I want you to send a small standing patrol down there to have a look round and then keep an eye on the place overnight. You go down with them initially and have a look for yourself; see if you can find any locals to speak to; find out if they know what the Jerries are up to."

Willis nodded, his face brightening again somewhat.

"Yes, Sir; no problem. I'll get on with sorting that out straight away."

Smithson left the platoon commander to his duties and continued on down the hill to where he could see a lone figure digging a small shell-scrape by the track. The individual seemed to be working on a solitary position in the small gap between Smithson's company and the flanking company. As the major neared the man, he noted with increasing curiosity that the individual was devoid of any web equipment or weapon. Finally, when he was just a few yards away, Smithson realised he had come across Michael Heydock, the battalion's padre.

"Michael? What are you up to digging a shell-scrape here? You can come and bunk down in one of the Jerry dug-outs with us..."

The big, middle-aged padre glanced round in surprise at the sound of Smithson's voice.

"Oh, Dickie... Hello old boy..."

The padre straightened up, stretching his back and rubbing his hips as he did so, leaving the shovel sticking upright in the half dug hole. "That's very kind of you; but I'm not digging a trench. It's for poor old Charlie..."

He gestured over at the hedgerow and Smithson followed his indication. There at the side of the hedgerow lay a groundsheet, and sticking out from beneath the groundsheet was a pair of boots. Suddenly, Smithson understood.

"God! Yes, of course... Poor Charlie." He whispered.

Heydock let out a long, sad breath of air.

"I know his parents, you know? A lovely couple. They live in Malton; got a nice little farm up there..."

He glanced across at where Normanton's body lay hidden beneath the olive green cover.

"I thought it only right that I made sure he got buried properly. It might help his parents to come to terms with it when they... when they get the news..."

Smithson didn't reply at first. He just stared at Normanton's shrouded body for long moments before stepping up beside Heydock and reaching down for the shovel.

"Here... let me give you a hand..."

THE COAST OF NORMANDY – BETWEEN SWORD AND JUNO BEACHES
TUESDAY 6TH JUNE 1944 – 1900 HOURS

Nobody said anything. None of the tank crew could find words. Judging by the silence on the radio net, the same was true for the other tanks that had managed to reach the coast of Normandy. Of those tanks that had rolled across the start-line some ten kilometres to the south, just three hours ago, there were a little over half left. Most of the half-tracks, armour cars and trucks of the 192nd Panzer Grenadiers had made it here in one piece, for it was they who had been lucky enough to find the gap between two of the main landing areas being used by the Tommies and their allies. Both of the tank battalions however had been cut up badly en route, and pushed, very roughly, westwards so that they had arrived at the coast as a tangled mass alongside their infantry comrades.

Now, the commander of those two tank battalions could only stare in wonder at the sight that met his eyes. Colonel Hermann von Oppeln-

Bronikowski, the dashing, dark-haired, forty five year old commander of the 100th Panzer Regiment, holder of the Knight's Cross, gawped openly at the endless mass of ships, boats and landing craft of all shapes and sizes, barely able to comprehend the sheer scale of what he was seeing. Above those ships, dozens of large barrage balloons floated brazenly, daring any enemy aircraft to come and have a crack at them. In both directions, east and west, and as far as the eye could see, the vast armada filled the ocean.

There was no wonder that his tanks had not been able to penetrate the advance line of enemy units, for a fleet as big as this must have brought an army of unimaginable size and strength with it. There was no doubting what was happening here, the colonel realised. The Tommies and their American friends meant business this time. This was no raid, and certainly no diversion. This was the real thing. And the veteran colonel, who was far from being easily frightened, felt a distinct sense of unease as he surveyed the coastal waters of Normandy.

"Fuck me, Colonel! The Tommy bastards must have brought every ship in the world with them! Have you ever seen anything like it? How many men must they have sitting out there?"

The awe-stricken voice of the sergeant who acted as von Oppeln-Bronikowski's gunner snapped the regimental commander out of his trance.

"And I thought the Ruski's were the experts at doing things '*big*'!" The colonel commented, unconcerned about revealing his astonishment to his men. "This is taking the piss! How are we supposed to deal with all that?"

He never had the chance to hear his gunner's reply, for just at that moment, the radio operator, who was monitoring both the divisional and regimental nets, interjected.

"Colonel? I've got the commander of the 192nd's First Battalion on the net. He says he's just arrived at the radar station near Douvres. It's still being held by our lads, as are some of the sea-front positions on the coast itself, but he says there is already lots of Tommy pressure coming from his north and west, from the St Aubin-sur-Mer area. He wants to know what the plan is."

Von Oppeln-Bronikowski leaned back in his cupola, staring silently at the huge fleet of ships out on the grey ocean for several moments as his mind worked feverishly. What was he supposed to do? He had a battalion of panzer grenadiers, and what was left of his own First Battalion, along with some waifs and strays of his Second Battalion. Against that, he had two large Tommy forces on either side, both of which he knew were well equipped with tanks, artillery and anti-tank guns. And of course, he was under the nose of this mighty enemy fleet; and under its massive guns too. Was this how it was going to be? Was he expected to save Germany and throw the enemy back into the sea with just his tiny battle-group?

"Colonel?" The radio operator prompted, not sure if his commander had heard him.

The commanding officer of the 100th Panzer Regiment stirred himself.

"Tell him to hold Douvres and the radar station at all costs. Tell him I'm bringing the tanks across to him and we'll discuss our next move once we get there."

The colonel picked his map up and studied it with a grimace.

"Okay driver..." He spoke over the intercom. "Forward and left... Let's get over to Douvres, sharpish. I don't want to sit here sticking out like a boil on a baby's arse all day..."

APPROACHING FARMOUSE PELLETIER – NEAR POINT 113 TUESDAY 6TH JUNE 1944 – 1915 HOURS

Willis had been stunned earlier in the day when he had been subjected to the withering, deadly fire of the German machine guns; learning the hard way just how obstinate and resourceful the enemy could be in defence. Now however, the young second lieutenant was beginning to realise just how awesome was the destructive power of the Allied air forces.

His standing patrol, consisting of the five surviving men from one of his sections, was trailing behind him in single file across what had once been a lush green meadow, but what had now become a charnel house. Leading the small group, and carrying a Sten Gun at the ready, he swung his astounded gaze left and right at the still burning and smoking remains of the German tanks. As he passed each successive, smoke-blackened, smouldering hulk, he experienced fresh amazement and horror at how such large, heavily armoured vehicles could have been ripped open as if they were no more than tins of bully beef.

Those once seemingly-solid hulls were rent with huge gouges and holes, from which flame licked and smoke poured. Road-wheels, sprockets and bits of track lay scattered about the churned up turf; the triumphant products of quality German engineering now cast about the field contemptuously. The big, heavy turrets with their deadly looking 75mm guns, sat askew and harmless atop their ruined hulls, whilst one of the turrets lay upside down in the thick grass, more than twenty yards from the hull that had once owned it. Along with the acrid smell of burning metal, rubber, and long since detonated explosive, came another, peculiar smell that Willis would come to know only too well in the coming weeks. It was a smell that was distinctive in its ability to turn ones stomach. It was the smell of roasting human flesh and hair.

Even worse than the graveyard of enemy tanks through which the officer and his patrol passed cautiously, were the numerous, almost comical looking corpses of dead cattle. The poor animals, caught up in the middle of a human altercation that they had no part in, lay on their backs mostly, their rigid legs, seeming ludicrously thin, stuck upwards into the air like pins protruding from an overfilled black and white cushion. It was an absurd sight, and a surreal one too; so much so that Willis thought that perhaps this was just an unusually vivid dream from which he would wake soon enough.

But he didn't awake. He just kept on walking. Walking until he found himself just twenty yards short of the low hedgerow that marked the boundary of the small, humble looking farm. As he approached a gap in the hedge; one that appeared to have been torn open by a passing armoured vehicle, Willis suddenly came to a sudden halt as three figures appeared in the opening. The adrenalin in his body, which had begun to dissipate after the final assault on Point 113, suddenly returned in an instant and he brought his Sten Gun up, ready in case he found himself at the forefront of battle once more.

The little squeak of fear from the middle-aged woman who stood between the hefty looking man, also of middle age, and the strong-looking, but terribly young teenage boy, was enough to persuade Willis that his alarm wasn't warranted on this particular occasion. With something of a start, he realised that he was pointing his sub machine gun straight at the little trio of civilians and he hastily dropped the muzzle away.

Rather oddly, he felt himself reddening in embarrassment as the three French locals stared back at him in what appeared to be abject terror. Lowering his weapon now so that the muzzle was pointing directly at the floor, he took several more cautious steps towards the three civilians, forcing his mind to settle down and produce the necessary French words that he needed at this precise point in time. Fortunately, after a moment or two, the words came flooding back to him.

"Good evening…" He began with formal politeness in his best school-boy French. "We are the English… We bring the liberation…"

It wasn't his best attempt at French, but he thought it was clear enough to be understood. For their part, the three French civilians just stared back at him, wide-eyed. Willis tried again.

"Long live liberty… Long live France…"

FARMHOUSE PELLETIER
TUESDAY 6TH JUNE 1944 – 1915 HOURS

"Emile, please don't go upstairs... It could be dangerous..."

Madam Pelletier pleaded tearfully with her husband as he stood, listening carefully, on the stairs of the cellar. He turned back to look down at his weeping wife, who stood with her son, the latter with his arm around her shoulder for comfort.

Monsieur Pelletier, never known for his gentleness, replied in soothing tones to his distraught wife.

"Hush now, my love. Everything will be fine. The bombing and shooting has stopped. It has been quiet now for an hour. Mademoiselle Lisseur said to stay in the cellar until it all stopped, did she not?"

Maurice, his son, nodded silently in affirmation.

"Good." The burly farmer murmured. "Then I will go up and see what has happened. It will be safe now."

His wife responded immediately.

"If it is safe then we will all go up together. I cannot spend another moment down here Emile..."

Monsieur Pelletier stared down at his wife and, through her tears, he saw the stubbornness and resilience in her eyes that had first attracted him to her more than twenty five years before.

"Very well then..." He said with a feint smile. "Together then... Come..."

Madam Pelletier stepped up towards her husband, taking his hand, whilst their son followed on immediately behind. Then, slowly, together, the three of them ascended the remaining stairs, and carefully pushed open the door into the kitchen.

Surprisingly, the kitchen looked almost exactly as they had remembered it, other than that every pane of glass in the small window was broken, and the door had been blown inwards, as if by a tremendous wind; the heavy wood hanging precariously by just one hinge. Other than those obvious signs of violence, everything else seemed to be as it should... until they emerged into the farmyard.

It was the smell that hit them first. Usually, when you took a lungful of air in the yard of Farmhouse Pelletier, the first odour that came to you was that of cow dung. Often it was enriched by the smell of sweet, fresh, damp grass from the nearby meadow, or sometimes in Spring by the smell of apple blossom from the orchard. Occasionally, when the wind was blowing in the right direction, you got a blast of the sea too; a mixture of salt and sand. Now however, the odours that permeated the air around Farmhouse Pelletier were entirely alien.

The smell of acrid smoke; the result of something unnatural being burnt at high temperature, was the all pervading smell that filled each lungful of air, causing Madam Pelletier to cough several times as the noxious smoke got to the back of her throat. Another smell, quite nauseating, was melded into that harsh cocktail of chemically produced smoke. None of them could quite identify it, but it seemed strikingly similar to roasting meat; although the odour was so sickly sweet that instead of making the mouth water, it made one want to gag.

The source of the terrible smell became immediately evident as the three civilians crept cautiously across the centre of their farmyard. Out on the road, strung out over a distance of some hundred and fifty metres, were no less than three vehicles, all of which burned fiercely, belching out thick black smoke as the flames crackled hungrily away. Monsieur Pelletier was the first one to note the large gap that had been torn in the hedge, obviously by something heavy, judging by the unusual track marks in the mud of the yard that led up to, and through, the gap.

Pulling his wife and son along with him, the weathered farmer approached the gap warily. As he did so, he first caught sight of the burning tanks in the middle of the large meadow, belching smoke like their companions on the road. Next he noted the upturned, lifeless forms of his treasured dairy herd.

"My God..." He managed to whisper, his heart lurching with despair at the loss of his lifetime's work and his chief livelihood.

There were many in the local community who viewed Monsieur Pelletier as a 'hard man', yet, to see his prized cattle laying butchered in the great meadow, which was now littered with the debris of war, the big countryman felt as if his entire body would collapse beneath him any second.

A sudden movement from beside the nearest burning German tank caused all three members of the Pelletier family to jump in alarm, especially when a man with a grim expression, clad entirely in brown garb and a helmet covered in strips of green and brown hessian cloth, and brandishing a gun of some kind, suddenly emerged into the open grassland directly in front of them. The three civilians stared directly at the man for a moment, their eyes bulging with fear as they stared down the barrel of his gun. Then they noted the other men, also armed, who followed on behind him. Monsieur Pelletier heard his wife emit a small gasp and her hand suddenly squeezed his own much tighter.

"Oh! Emile!" She whimpered.

The farmer squeezed it back, reassuringly, never for a moment taking his eyes off the man with gun.

They all stood there for long moments, just looking at each other. Then, as if on some unseen signal, the soldier in brown clothes dropped his weapon's muzzle so that it was pointing towards the ground, and his face seemed to soften somewhat.

"Good evening..." The man stuttered in reasonable formal French, but with a heavy accent. "We are English... We bring the liberation..."

Again, Madam Pelletier gasped and placed her free hand over her mouth.

"My God..." Monsieur Pelletier whispered under his breath.

"Long live liberty..." The Englishman said again, seeming to grow in confidence with his French vocabulary. "Long live France..."

The three French civilians stood staring at the man for a while longer. After a moment or two, he heard his wife begin to sniff away tears once more. Monsieur Pelletier had been married a long time however. He knew when his wife was shedding tears of grief and when she was shedding tears of relief. These tears, he knew without looking, were of the latter variety.

"We're free Father..." Maurice whispered from the other side Madam Pelletier. "The English have come to free us..."

His son's words struck Monsieur Pelletier like a slap in the face. He was an old fashioned kind of man; concerned only with his farm and his family. He had never really cared for politics, nor for travel, but his son's words seemed to awaken a deep, profound, and long buried sense of patriotism and identity that the bluff farmer would never have thought he possessed. Much to his own surprise, Monsieur Pelletier felt a lump appear in his throat, and tears pricked at the corners of his eyes. He decided to say something... anything, in order to stave off the unfamiliar emotion.

"Long live the English..." He blurted.

And then the tears began to pour.

TACTICAL HEADQUARTERS 125TH PANZER GRENADIER REGIMENT – 1 MILE SOUTH OF RANVILLE TUESDAY 6TH JUNE 1944 – 1945 HOURS

Von Luck took a welcome drink of the coffee that Liebeskind had brought up in a flask, the latter having arrived at the regimental rendezvous in a staff car just moments earlier. As the veteran major swilled the luke-warm, bitter liquid around his mouth, he gazed out, with red-rimmed, tired eyes at the collection of men and vehicles that were spread amongst the trees of the expansive orchard.

His regiment, and in particular the Second Battalion, had been in constant action since the early hours of the morning and they were pretty much blown out now. They needed rest and a chance to reorganise. They had been fighting all day against an initially illusive enemy. Even when that enemy had finally established himself in an extensive defensive position centred on Ranville, trying to make progress against him had been difficult.

That enemy consisted of the best the Tommies had to offer; their elite parachute units. The lightly armed, yet superbly trained British paratroopers and glider troops had hung on tenaciously all day, backed up by overwhelming firepower from the massive fleet of warships that was anchored off the coast, and regular, low altitude sweeps by the dreaded 'Jabos', that pounced on any German vehicle unlucky enough to get caught out in the open.

Added to that, it had become obvious by the level of resistance being met on the ground that the parachute and glider troops had been substantially reinforced. Either that or they had finally managed to concentrate their full strength after the initial confusion of their night drop. Whatever the reason, von Luck's ad hoc collection of units was finding it difficult to make any further progress. In the back of his mind, the experienced panzer officer was beginning to realise that the German forces had missed their window of opportunity. The Tommies could only get stronger now. Hour by hour, day by day, the enemy would begin to land more and more of the huge reserves von Luck knew them to have.

As he swallowed a mouthful of the coffee gratefully, Liebeskind, his adjutant, held out a piece of paper.

"This just came in from Divisional Headquarters, Sir."

The major smacked his lips together.

"Read it out please? I'm too tired to bother…"

Liebeskind obediently withdrew the note and lowered it. He didn't need to refer to it, for he'd already studied the content of the new orders several times over.

"Our orders are to consolidate our current positions and keep the enemy sealed off until first light tomorrow…" The lieutenant began. "We are being placed under tactical command of a new formation from first light tomorrow until further notice."

Von Luck, greedily swilling down more of the harsh-tasting coffee, looked up sharply at his adjutant with one raised eye-brow.

"Really? Who?"

Liebeskind went on.

"We're being absorbed into 1st SS Panzer Corps. The Hitlerjugend are on their way as we speak and will arrive to the west of Caen during the night. The Panzer Lehr are on their way too."

Von Luck's long, horse-like face brightened slightly.

"That's good. The Panzer Lehr is a good division. The Hitlerjugend are a bunch of pups but they're as fanatical as hell and their officers and NCOs are all from the Bodyguard, so they'll fight well."

He creased his brow slightly.

"So... who's commanding this new formation?"

Liebeskind answered immediately.

"I believe that Obergruppenfuhrer Dietrich is to command, Sir."

Now von Luck smiled.

"Sepp Dietrich? That's even better news! He's a tough bastard if ever there was one. He won't stand for any messing."

The regimental commander drained the last of the coffee from the mug.

"We need to do a check on the regiment, Liebeskind. I want every available man and vehicle brought forward. Every round of ammunition and every spare part we can get hold of; I need it brought forward immediately. We have to make sure we keep the Tommies bottled up until the rest of our divisions can come up."

Liebeskind nodded his understanding.

"I'll see to it at once, Sir."

The lieutenant looked as if he was going to say something else but appeared to think better of it. Von Luck caught the lieutenant's hesitancy and smiled at his adjutant indulgently.

"Go on, Liebeskind... What is it you were going to say?"

The lieutenant cleared his throat and lowered his voice slightly, not wanting to be overheard by any other members of the regimental staff.

"Do you... Do you think we can still win, Sir?" He asked tentatively.

The weather-beaten major stared at the young officer for a moment before replying, as honestly as he dared.

"No Liebeskind. We cannot beat the Tommies and win this war any more..."

He saw the young man's face drop slightly, and he forced another smile.

"But perhaps we can hold them to a draw, eh?"

THE SERGEANTS' MESS KITCHEN – RAF DOWNHAM MARKET
TUESDAY 6TH JUNE 1944 – 2100 HOURS

Corporal Janice Wilkinson, wearing her kitchen whites, spied the furtive looking figure at the end of the hot-plate as she used her spatula to tidy the arrangement of the bacon rashers in the tray. She glanced over at the man dressed in the blue battle dress who was clutching a bundled up greatcoat, and her look darkened instantly. The bulk of the aircrew allocated to ops that evening had already passed through and the hot-plate was due to close in a matter of moments; and here, for the third night on the trot, was Flight Sergeant McWilliams. Tonight, unusually, he was very smartly dressed. He'd even made a point of combing his hair, she noticed.

"Flight Sergeant McWilliams?" Wilkinson greeted him suspiciously in her high-pitched Geordie accent. "A third night on ops is it? Someone has really got it in for you! Hadn't you better get changed if you're flying tonight?"

Her thinly disguised sarcasm seemed to cut through the rear-gunner like a knife, for he visibly winced and reddened instantly, looking down at his feet in embarrassment. Wilkinson felt a pang of satisfaction at that, and she realised, with a little surprise, that she was wielding the spatula as if it were a cosh.

McWilliams, obviously suffering some discomfort, allowed a nervous grin to break across his thin features.

"Er... no, I'm not flying tonight. They decided I should have a night off... being the big hero that I am and all that..."

Despite herself, Wilkinson felt a smile starting to spread across her face at the flight sergeant's less than modest reply.

"Did you hear that I was the first one to see the invasion fleet?" He asked lightly.

Wilkinson shook her head.

"No... I didn't hear that. Good news though..."

She paused for a moment, not sure where the conversation was going.

"I bet it was a pretty impressive sight?" She said in the end.

The flight sergeant shrugged his shoulders.

"Yeah... I suppose so. You see so much though in my line of work..."

He hesitated for a second or two, but then went on quickly.

"You've put the hours in recently too, I noticed. You got a day off any time soon?"

The question took Wilkinson unawares.

"Oh, err... yes. It's my day of tomorrow actually."

McWilliams smiled again nervously. He was actually quite handsome when he smiled, Wilkinson thought, especially when he'd had a wash and brush up.

"Ah... That's handy. You see... I was going to pop up to Cambridge for the day. The Skipper's lending me his car. Thought I'd get off the camp for a few hours and visit a nice little tea room they've got up there. Don't suppose you fancy coming along for a brew and a slice of cake? I thought we could maybe celebrate the invasion together..."

McWilliams tailed off, his attempt at subtlety reaching its limits. Now, it was Wilkinson who went red. Of all the questions she had expected to face over the hot-plate that evening, it hadn't been that one.

"Erm... Yes... I suppose so. Why not?" She found herself saying.

"Great... yeah... spot-on..." McWilliams blurted, trying to maintain the pretence of casual interest. "I'll meet you at the Guardroom about ten o'clock, then?"

Wilkinson blinked in surprise. How had this happened so quickly?

"Yes, that's fine... Look forward to it." She found herself saying.

"Right, good... See you tomorrow then." McWilliams mumbled shyly, and made to leave the kitchen area.

"Oh..." He stopped suddenly and turned back, placing his folded greatcoat onto the serving area and lifting one end of it surreptitiously. "I almost forgot..."

He produced a small bunch of flowers, camouflaged in a thick roll of wrapping paper.

"I noticed they were trying to get rid of these at the shop in the village. Shame to let them get chucked out. I thought you might like them..."

Wilkinson flushed an even deeper red now. In all her days, she had never expected to have such an encounter over the hot-plate in the Sergeants' Mess.

"Oh... they're lovely... thank you..."

McWilliams smiled sheepishly and folded his greatcoat over one arm, leaving the flowers on top of the serving counter. Looking around quickly to make sure he hadn't been seen handing over the flowers, the flight sergeant nodded briefly, smiled again, then turned to leave.

Wilkinson, on a whim, shouted after him.

"Flight Sergeant!"

He stopped abruptly again and looked back towards the auburn haired WAAF.

"Talking of not wasting things... We're just about to close the hot-plate and there's still a bit left over. Don't suppose you fancy a bacon sandwich do you?"

THE RADAR STATION, DOUVRES – BETWEEN JUNO AND SWORD BEACHES
TUESDAY 6TH JUNE 1944 – 2105 HOURS

Another salvo of big shells from an Allied ship came screaming through the late evening air and slammed into the large field between the station and the village of Douvres, causing the ground to tremble ominously in the wake of the thunderclap explosions. Von Oppeln-Bronikowski winced slightly at the racket and raised an eyebrow at the captain who commanded the battalion of panzer grenadiers.

"If we stay here, there's going to be even more of that." The colonel observed to the junior officer. "What's the Tommy pressure like over on the north-western side?"

The captain grimaced.

"Rough, Sir. My left hand company got cut up a little as we came in. Got hit by a small force of tanks and armoured cars, backed up by infantry. We've managed to hold them off and I've got three of my four companies covering that flank with the remaining infantry defending this place. They've started pasting us with artillery now though, and that shelling from the ships is only going to make life even more uncomfortable. I can't help feeling like I've got my balls dangling between a pair of wire cutters!"

Von Oppeln-Bronikowski smiled tiredly at the captain's dry humour.

"I know what you mean. I'm beginning to think that higher formation haven't quite realised the scale of the Tommy landings. How on earth we're meant to do anything here worthwhile I'll never fathom. If the Tommies launch an all out attack, they'll eat us for supper. And we don't have the strength to attack in both directions. As you say, we certainly seem to have put our nuts firmly in the fryer."

The two men fell silent for a moment, mulling over their predicament.

"I'll get in touch with Divisional Headquarters..." The colonel announced at last. "Or try to. Let the general know what the situation is. I'm going to recommend we pull back to a..."

The commander of the 100th Panzer Regiment fell silent in mid-sentence. His attention had been grabbed by the sudden low murmur of aircraft engines; dozens of them. Both the colonel and the commander of the panzer grenadiers looked upwards into the fading light of the evening sky as a wave of aircraft appeared overhead, coming in from the coast and heading inland. The two German officers stared open mouthed at the breath-taking site above them. Wave after wave of planes passed over them, large four engined bombers towing smaller, strange looking aircraft.

"Gliders…" The captain of the grenadiers stated bleakly.

The two men, and all of their soldiers in the immediate vicinity, were lost for any further comment. For what seemed like an age, they simply gawped up at the heavens as the vast aerial armada rumbled inexorably over their heads. After some time, the captain spoke again.

"How many troops do you reckon, Colonel?" He asked.

Von Oppeln-Bronikowski didn't take his eyes from the passing waves of transport aircraft. Instead he just shook his head vacantly.

"Two thousand men perhaps? Two and a half maybe?"

The colonel turned and watched the mass of aircraft as they droned onwards, heading south towards Caen. Even as he watched them, he saw the leading aircraft cast off and saw the first gliders begin to bank left out of formation.

"Bollocks." He stated simply.

The captain followed his gaze, watching the awesome display of formation flying.

"They're going to cut us off, aren't they?" He said bleakly.

Once more, Von Oppeln-Bronikowski remained focussed on the site above them in the grey skies. Eventually however, he lowered his gaze and glanced towards the captain of grenadiers with a look of resignation.

"Cancel my last regarding getting hold of Divisional Headquarters. There's nothing to discuss now; that much is obvious."

The colonel heaved a deep sigh.

"Get your men mounted up, Captain. We're pulling back to Caen."

SWORD BEACH
TUESDAY 6TH JUNE 1944 – 2110 HOURS

The four men sat there in the middle of the wide lawn, encircled by barbed wire, staring up at the sky in stunned silence. They weren't on their own. They were surrounded by their countrymen; although in fairness many of them weren't *actually* German, but Eastern European *'volunteers'*. Along with the motley collection of infantry soldiers, artillerymen and headquarters personnel, many of them swathed in bandages, the four panzer crewmen, distinctive in their black overalls, gawped up into the fading light as the final waves of aircraft passed overhead.

As the last of the gliders and bombers disappeared southwards, the large assembly of German prisoners lowered their eyes to stare at the endless stream of armoured vehicles, tanks and wheeled transport that was flowing endlessly through Lane 8; one of the main exits from Sword Beach. That convoy of vehicles was flanked by long files of heavily laden Tommy infantry who tramped steadily past the improvised prisoner of war compound, casting curious looks at the collection of enemy soldiers sitting exhausted and disorientated behind the wire.

Beyond those vehicles and infantrymen, sitting out on the dark ocean, was that huge, omnipotent fleet of warships and landing craft; blocking the horizon in an impenetrable wall of steel. The smell of burnt explosive, petrol and diesel fumes filled the evening air, which was heavy with damp; threatening another downpour.

Hartmann, the co-driver of their now immobilised panzer, was the only man amongst the four inclined to speech.

"How the fuck we were ever supposed to throw this lot back into the sea I'll never know. There's fucking thousands of them..."

The remaining three of the surviving four crewmen just stared blankly at the passing columns of men and machines. Wesser, the gunner, didn't want to talk because it caused him enormous pain in his smashed up mouth, which he now covered with a blood soaked field dressing. The loader-operator was just feeling sorry for himself; his head heavily bandaged and padded to protect the hasty stitches sewn into his split scalp by a Tommy medic. Weimer, with his freshly broken nose, simply gawped wide-eyed at the endless comings and goings of the enemy, still struggling as he was to catch up with events, having being knocked unconscious inside the turret of their stricken tank.

Hartmann of course, was happy to talk; anything in fact that stopped him thinking of the shredded face and upper body of their driver who had been killed by the impact of the first Tommy anti-tank round. Realising he wasn't going to get an answer from his crewmates, the co-driver gabbled on.

"There's not a Luftwaffe plane in the sky, look..." He waved a hand vaguely at the sky above that was beginning to cloud over again. "No wonder those Tommy planes were able to jump us back at Point 113. How we managed to get as far as we did is a mystery to me. Nobody can blame us for not making it..."

He tailed off, running out of things to say.

"Stupid plan anyway, aaagh…" Wesser suddenly spluttered from behind his field dressing, ending with a gasp of pain.

Hartmann glanced to his right, delighted to have elicited a response from one of his comrades at last.

"We did our best though, eh, Staff Sergeant?" Hartmann tried to sound upbeat.

For a moment, Weimer didn't respond. After a while however, he managed to speak, giving his head a little shake as he did so.

"I can't believe it's come to this. Five years of victory… and now this…"

Again, Hartmann tried to put a positive spin on things.

"Look on the bright side though, Staff Sergeant… At least we reached the sea in the end…"

The veteran tank commander allowed a bitter laugh to escape from his mouth.

"Yes, Hartmann… At least we reached the sea…"

HMS FAULKNOR – PORTSMOUTH HARBOUR, ENGLAND
TUESDAY 6TH JUNE 1944 – 2145 HOURS

Haldane was standing outside Montgomery's cabin on the small destroyer at precisely a quarter to ten; as instructed by the Army Group Commander. Montgomery had a strict routine that he rarely broke, and tonight would be no exception. The general would be in bed tonight at ten o'clock sharp, and would remain there until 0600 hours in the morning. He believed that a tired general was of no use to his troops and thus ensured that he abided by a strict routine that allowed him to remain fresh enough to use his brain.

That meant that Haldane would have no more than fifteen minutes to brief Montgomery on the final situation reports from Normandy, before the general took a final cup of tea or glass of milk and retired for the night. Whilst the general slept, the remainder of his small tactical headquarters would embark on the destroyer which itself had just returned from its first trip to Normandy to replenish its stocks of ammunition. Once loaded up, the ship would slip anchor once more and take the general and his staff across the Channel so that they could control the great battle from the very front.

Having rehearsed his lines, Haldane gathered himself and knocked on the cabin door.

"Yes."

The single word, spoken from inside the tiny sleeping quarter, was a command rather than an enquiry. Accordingly, Haldane opened the door and stepped inside. Montgomery was sitting on the single bunk, already dressed in pyjamas. The thin, shrewd looking general was his usual calm self, and appeared to have no problem at all holding court whilst dressed for bed. Standing in the corner of the cabin was Freddie de Guingand, the Chief of Staff for the Army Group, and one of Monty's old desert boys. He of course, was fully dressed.

"Jamie, good evening." Montgomery quipped happily. "You have the evening situation report?"

"Yes, Sir." The young staff officer confirmed.

"Good. Let's have it then." Monty said, never one to waste time on pre-amble.

Haldane cleared his throat and began.

"Well, Sir, the divisions landing on Sword, Juno and Gold have secured their beaches and pushed inland, in some cases as much as five miles. At the moment there is no word on Caen, but the last reports suggest that the Third Division have been forced to stop and dig-in after they were counter-attacked by enemy armour. The good news is that the enemy armour appears to have been stopped dead, and suffered heavy losses for their efforts."

The staff officer paused to let Montgomery take in the news. Surprisingly, the general seemed unfazed by the news that Caen had not been captured yet, which had been part of the plan for the first day of the invasion.

"Good. Well done the Third Division. If the enemy wishes to throw away his tanks in piecemeal attacks then I shan't be in a hurry to dissuade him. As for Caen, well, it was always an ambitious target; just to give the divisions a spur to their own efforts. It will be ours in due course. What of the British airborne landings?"

Haldane continued.

"The Sixth Airborne is now consolidating its hold east of the Orne, Sir. The reserve brigade is landing as we speak and the 1st Special Service Brigade is already across the Orne and supporting them. General Dempsey seems confident that the flank will hold nicely. His main concern is whether the enemy can produce any more armour in front of Caen come tomorrow morning."

Montgomery made no comment on that particular point. He simply nodded, then quipped.

"And the American sector?"

Haldane, with some relief, confirmed to his commander that the Americans were making good progress off Utah beach and had already linked up with some of their airborne forces. He also explained that even on Omaha, where the battle just to get off the beach had raged until after midday, the Americans had finally managed to secure the beach and establish a toe-hold on the high ground beyond. Montgomery nodded curtly at this information.

"They've done well. I knew they would. The American fighting man is a good quality soldier. A shame about some of their commanders' planning abilities; but not to worry... Their soldiers will always make up for any deficiencies there. Yes... well done to those chaps indeed."

The general was never one to reserve judgement, Haldane reflected silently.

Montgomery asked several questions of Haldane concerning minor detail before nodding emphatically to signal that he had heard enough. The general looked happy, Haldane thought; almost like a school boy excited at the prospect of beginning his summer holidays.

"Well, gentlemen, that is all very good, thank you. A highly satisfactory day all round I feel, given the obvious frustrations that will always occur with an operation of such scale. I think we can look forward to starting the day with confidence tomorrow."

The commander of the 21st Army Group looked from Haldane to de Guingand then back.

"Thank you, gentlemen. That will do nicely for now. I'll be woken at 0600 hours as planned and hear any reports that have come in during the night. And then, gentlemen, we can get about the business of knocking Germany out of the war for good. This is the end, gentlemen, make no mistake. We are ashore now. There is no going back. We are going to win this war, regardless of any minor setbacks or hiccups that will invariably occur."

He looked up at the two officers with his fox-like, sparkling eyes.

"The Germans have lost the war, gentlemen. They just don't know it yet..."

THE LIBRARY, SOUTHWICK HOUSE, NEAR PORTSMOUTH
TUESDAY 6TH JUNE 1944 – 2230 HOURS

Eisenhower dropped gratefully into the deep leather armchair and stretched out his long legs, cigarette in one hand, a glass of scotch in the other. He sat there for long, long moments in utter silence, enjoying the solitude. The long-case clock in the corner ticked steadily away, never missing a beat; chugging along in the same dependable manner it had always done for goodness knows how many years. For some reason, the rhythmic ticking of the clock reminded him of Montgomery, and as the image of the British general's pinched, lupine face appeared in his mind's eye, Eisenhower couldn't resist a tired smile.

Montgomery; that fussy, clipped, shrill-voiced, vainglorious little pipsqueak of an Englishman. Montgomery; that confident, competent, efficient, annoyingly calm and decisive leader of men. A man who could irritate you like an infected horsefly bite, yet also a man who you could depend on, whatever the circumstances, to get a result. And what a result!

The Supreme Allied Commander in Europe let his head fall back against the backrest of the armchair and closed his eyes, releasing a lengthy sigh of utter relief as he did so. It was done. Almost ten Allied divisions were ashore on the continent of Europe. Five invasion beaches had been stormed; beachheads secured, bridges captured. And now Montgomery, that insufferable yet indispensible Englishman who commanded the Allied 21st Army Group, would be on his way across the Channel to join his men and do what he did best; lead from the front. They had done it. Against all the odds, in the face of all the pessimism and hiccups, the fears and doubts, they had finally done it. D-Day, the final act of the vast Operation code-named *Overlord*, had finally come to fruition and, unbelievably, it had been completely successful; better than Eisenhower could have hoped for in his wildest dreams.

The clock chimed once to mark the half-hour, making Eisenhower jump. He opened his eyes and sat up a little straighter. He crushed out the cigarette in the nearby ashtray then took a sip of the scotch. It had been a long, worrying forty eight hours. Eternal ignominy or eternal glory had been the two possibilities just twenty four hours before. Now the American general knew that whatever happened, it was the latter that would forever attach itself to his name. He suddenly remembered something and placed down the glass of scotch on the nearby console table.

Fidgeting in his seat, Eisenhower delved into his pocket and pulled out his wallet. Opening the leather pouch, he removed a small slip of folded notepaper. He opened out the note and scanned the words that he had jotted down on it just last night, before the start of the invasion; a short, regretful passage that would, in the event of disaster, have been released to the world's media. He read the words several times over, remembering the fear and anguish that had wracked his soul these last two days.

'Our landings in the Cherbourg-Havre area have failed to gain a satisfactory foothold and I have withdrawn the troops. My decision to attack at this time and place was based on the best information available. The

troops, the air force and the Navy did all that bravery and devotion to duty could do. If any fault or blame attaches to the attempt it is mine alone.'

After reading through the note for a couple of minutes, Eisenhower slowly screwed the piece of paper up into a tight little ball and then dropped it onto the table next to his glass of scotch, before reclining in the chair and closing his eyes once more. The Supreme Allied Commander Europe took a deep, satisfied breath.

"We won't be needing that anymore..." He murmured.

EPILOGUE
30 YEARS ON

THE RUINED FORGE, POINT 113 – NORMANDY
THURSDAY 6TH JUNE 1974 – 1700 HOURS

"**G**entlemen, thank you for your time and patience. I hope you have enjoyed your little tour over the course of today. If anybody has any further questions then I will be around in the hotel bar from about ten this evening; please feel free to grill me as much as you like."

A ripple of polite laughter ran through the crowd of senior term officer cadets from the Royal Military Academy Sandhurst, but Smithson could see from the young faces that this group of potential officers had heard enough about war and tactics for one day. The only thing on their minds right now was getting back to the hotel for dinner and drinks.

It had been a long day for everyone, walking the seemingly endless beaches, viewing old pillboxes and fortifications, stomping through fields, not to mention tours of no less than three museums. There would be more museums tomorrow, and more walking and analysis of maps and diagrams. Smithson realised that these young officers were ready for some down time.

"I'll see you all later then. Enjoy dinner and thank you once again for your enthusiasm and attention over a very long and very hot day."

With a collective murmur of thanks, the group of cadets broke up into twos and threes and began wandering back down the lane towards where the coach waited on the main road.

As the crowd ambled casually down the sun-baked track, dressed in their Sandhurst issue blue blazers, moleskin trousers and formal shoes, Smithson imagined the track as it had been thirty years before. Almost identical, other than that it had been muddy and slippery underfoot; partly from the rain and mud resulting from the previous day's storms, and partly from the blood and leaking vehicle oils that had soaked the ground on that breezy, grey June day long ago.

Smithson was snapped out of his private thoughts as a lone figure from amongst the group detached itself and approached the fifty-five year old retired officer. This individual was different to the remainder of the group. For a start he was much taller, and his face somewhat older; around thirty perhaps. He also wore a thick, yet well-trimmed moustache on his upper-lip, very much in the fashion of the British Army's other ranks these days. The immaculately polished shoes, razor sharp creases in the grey slacks, and the blue-red-blue banded tie that he wore beneath his well-cut blazer marked this man out as one of the colour sergeant instructors from the military academy, and a member of the Guards Division too.

As the NCO approached Smithson, the veteran of the Second World War recognised the hard, professional look of a man who had made soldiering his life. No doubt this particular individual had learned some harsh lessons of late during tours of duty in Northern Ireland, where the terrorist situation was deteriorating rapidly. A very dirty kind of war, that was, Smithson thought. The man came to a halt in front of Smithson, fixing the retired officer with a serious look.

"Colour Sergeant Travis, Sir; Grenadier Guards..." The big man introduced himself with a West Country twang. "I'd just like to say a huge thank you for today, Sir. It's been absolutely fascinating, and a real inspiration..."

The big colour sergeant offered his hand out to Smithson as he spoke. Taken aback slightly, the retired officer accepted the hand and shook firmly.

"It's my pleasure, Colour Sergeant... The least I could do..."

"Are you sure you won't join us for dinner, Sir?" The NCO pressed him, his eyes taking on a sort of pleading look which touched Smithson somewhat.

"That's very kind of you, but I'm meeting a couple of old friends this evening for a little get together. I should be back at the hotel by ten so I'll catch up with everyone there."

That wasn't a polite lie; it was the absolute truth. Arthur Haines, Smithson's faithful signaller who had followed him across the battlefields of Europe from D-Day to VE Day, would be meeting his former company commander at the little crossroads in about half an hour. Haines would motor to the RV in his own car. In the passenger seat would be Jeremy Willis; another one of the handful of D-Day veterans from Smithson's company who had survived the war, despite being deficient an arm courtesy of a German mortar bomb, fired during another battle somewhere in Holland.

As they had done twice before, on the tenth and twentieth anniversaries of D-Day, the three of them would meet at the crossroads and then walk the ground over which they had fought so desperately thirty years earlier. They would each describe the battle from their own perspectives, sharing their memories. It didn't matter that they'd heard each others versions of the battle before. They needed to hear it all again, regardless. It was therapy.

"No problem, Sir. Thank you again for today; it's been a real eye-opener. I'll see you back at the hotel later."

The Colour Sergeant's voice brought Smithson back to the present.

Smithson watched the man stalk confidently down the track after his cadets before turning around and scanning the view beyond the pile of ruined buildings. Up on the high ground on either side of the tumbledown old forge, the trees of the wood loomed up, huge and green and full of life. A small movement to his right caught his eye, and Smithson snapped his head over in that direction. He immediately spotted the other man standing by the smallest of the ruined buildings.

He presented an interesting figure, Smithson thought. Of average height, but obviously broad-chested and well built, the lone individual was of similar age to Smithson, with thinning, light-brown hair that was already running heavily to grey. He wore a very plain brown suit and orange-gold tie that gave him a very European look, Smithson thought. And he was watching Smithson with a hawk-like gaze. For a moment, the two old gentlemen stood perfectly still, staring straight at each other, but then the man in the brown suit smiled suddenly, almost shyly, and moved forward into the small courtyard of the ruined buildings.

As he came forward, Smithson noted that the man limped heavily, favouring his right leg. The man's face was strong and healthy however; that of a man who carried himself with confidence and who had spent a lifetime working hard in the outdoors. The man in brown stopped just a couple of paces from Smithson, and his half-smile broke into a full and friendly grin.

"A most interesting talk that you gave to those young people…" The man in brown said in good English that was tinged with a strong, unusual accent. "The bit about small groups of determined men altering the course of history was most fascinating…"

Smithson smiled at the compliment.

"Thank you." He murmured his appreciation.

"I assume that you must once have fought at this place?" The man in brown asked lightly.

"Yes… I did indeed…" Smithson replied hesitantly, trying to fathom the man's accent.

Suddenly, Smithson remembered his manners, and held out his hand.
"Dickie Smithson, formerly of the Hambeldon and Moorlanders, but retired now. My company captured this hill back in 1944... On D-Day. Thirty years ago today."

The man in brown regarded Smithson with a strange look; one that contained a bit of sadness, a bit of pride perhaps; maybe even a bit of respect.

"Ah..." The man in brown said, reaching out and gripping Smithson's hand and shaking it warmly. "Then perhaps you and I have met once before?"

Smithson cocked his head to one side quizzically, his interest aroused. The man in brown beamed back at him as he shook Smithson's hand vigorously.

"My name is Gritz..." The man in brown said. "Sergeant Major Roland Gritz... Commanding Officer of 'The Cripples'."

Smithson experienced a sudden surge of memory. He remembered that name from thirty years ago, *'The Cripples'*. The battalion's intelligence officer had told him that the German garrison here had been dubbed that by their own commanders. He looked at the man in brown with more interest now, suddenly recognising something familiar about the man.

Roland Gritz was still pumping his hand enthusiastically however.

"Welcome back!" He was chuckling out loud to Smithson. "Welcome back to the *Crucible of Fate*..."

Historical Note

A s already mentioned in the foreword, the D-Day operation was so vast that I have no intention of trying to write a potted history of the whole thing here. Rather, I will comment on just a few of the key points, as I see them, from the novel.

Firstly, just about every ship and unit I have mentioned in this novel was real, as were some of the well known historical characters, like Eisenhower, Montgomery, Hans von Luck, Hermann von Oppeln-Bronikowski and Erich Marks. All of the minor characters are fictional, although I hope that they reflect in some way the diversity of troops on both sides. By this stage of the war, both the British and German ranks were a mix of war-weary veterans, other veterans who had been cheated of victory in 1940 who were desperate to 'get their own back', wounded second or third line troops, reluctant conscripts and fresh faced idealists. Amongst that mix of soldiery were cowards, heroes and villains aplenty, as well as just thousands of 'average blokes'.

The only fictional units that I have created for this story are the Hambledon and Moorlanders (literary veterans of *Seelowe Nord* and *Thunder in May*) and 'The Cripples' who defended The Crucible on Point 113. Although 'The Cripples' are one of my own creations, they are typical of how the Germans began organising their troops into 'Static Divisions' along the Atlantic Wall. With manpower in short supply and the Eastern Front consuming men and equipment at a startling rate, the Germans had no real equivalent of a 'Blighty wound'. General Marcks himself was missing a leg after being wounded in Russia but still took to the field in 1944. Those with injuries and illnesses would often be brigaded into units composed of those suffering with similar complaints, in order to make the dietary and medical arrangements for those troops somewhat easier. Classic examples of this initiative were the 'Stomach Battalions'. A similar principal was used with 'Eastern European Volunteers', and several battalions of these were deployed in Normandy.

Point 113 and 'The Crucible' did not exist. I squeezed this imaginary topographical feature in just to the west of Objective Hillman or, as the Germans called it, WN17. Colonel Krug was indeed the regimental commander based at that position and he surrendered his command early on the morning of 7th June 1944 having been essentially trapped underground by the British attackers. In reality, Point 113 would have sat somewhere on the low, yet obvious Periers Ridge, about halfway between Hermanville and Periers. Although 'The Crucible' is a fictional position, there were plenty of other similar strongpoints that were all too real and which cost the Allies heavily on D-Day.

Although the Hambledon and Moorlanders are fictional, I hope that their protracted battle at Point 113 reflects the difficult and dangerous work undertaken that day by many fine, yet sadly now disbanded regiments; for D-Day was the victory of the Line Infantry and Line Cavalry, and of course their supporting arms and services. For all the bagpipe-playing dash of the Commandos and the lightning fast coup-de-main at what has become known as Pegasus Bridge, the bulk of the fighting that day, on both British beaches (the other being Gold Beach) was done by the British Army's 'County Regiments'. The Guards would not set foot in Normandy for a while yet, this time organised as a complete armoured division, and even amongst the 6th Airborne Division, many of the battalions were simply County Regiment battalions converted to role as air-landing troops.

The advance on Caen was led by the battalions of 185th Infantry Brigade, in particular the Norfolks, the Warwickshires and the King's Shropshire Light Infantry, supported by the Staffordshire Yeomanry. In order to give the fictional Corporal Legg and his crew a continuous story line, I have 'borrowed' a couple of tanks from the 13/18th Hussars for the purpose of this novel. I hope the surviving members of that distinguished regiment will forgive me for allocating them one extra, and completely imaginary battle.

Two main types of Sherman battle tank were used on D-Day, those being the 'Wading Tanks' and the 'Swimming Tanks', the latter also known as Duplex Drive (DD) Tanks. The DD Tanks are remembered with mixed feelings by their crews. Some remember being seriously wary of their fragile swimming equipment whilst others had every confidence in the adapted vehicles. On D-Day, these amphibious tanks had mixed fortunes. In the western sectors, many of the US tanks went into the water at the pre-planned distance from the shore and were promptly swamped by the heavy swell of the sea, which had been whipped up by the storms of the preceding days. The majority of the tanks went to the bottom along with many of their crews. In the British sector, many of the tanks ran in closer to the shore on their landing craft before entering the water, and thus the majority of them made the beach where they were able to add their firepower and support to the assaulting infantry and engineers.

The specialist tanks, such as the Sherman Crab Flail Tank were British designs and proved their worth on the British and Commonwealth beaches. Unfortunately for the Americans, British industry just could not produce enough in time to equip the US assault divisions and thus they were forced to rely solely on their armoured bulldozers and dismounted engineer teams. The employment of specialist tanks on 'Bloody Omaha' beach for instance, *may* have helped the infantry to clear the beaches and overcome the strongpoints a little faster and therefore reduce their casualties, although this is purely speculation and is something we can never know for sure.

The poor weather conditions caused many difficulties on D-Day for the Allies, apart from giving the DD Tanks a fraught time of it during their 'swim' ashore. One of the problems experienced on many of the beaches was the fact that the tide rose at a much faster rate than predicted, and thus many of the follow-up troops and armoured units found themselves being thrown out onto extremely narrow beaches that were jam packed with men and vehicles. Many of those who were wounded in the assault were drowned before they could be rescued and treated, and the engineer clearance teams had great difficulty in clearing obstacles. Many of those deadly contraptions were submerged under the incoming tide, where they subsequently wrought havoc among the approaching craft. One of the other major problems caused by the weather was the fact that many of the paratroopers from all three Allied airborne divisions became widely dispersed during their drop.

Objective Cod, on Sword Beach, was very real indeed, and both the East Yorkshires and South Lancashires suffered heavily during that deadly and terrifying initial assault. Some later commentators, quite unfairly, would comment that the initial assault battalions took too long to deal with the beach defences but, quite frankly, this is utter nonsense. Landing onto a flat, wide open beach, in the face of fixed defences that were reinforced with mines, wire and obstacles of various natures, just after dawn, following a sickening sea voyage, the assault troops from both Yorkshire and Lancashire performed a minor miracle. I have stood on Sword Beach (and all four of the other beaches for that matter) up to my knees in the surf, staring inland, and wondered to myself how anybody ever managed to get off the beach at all. I was, for twenty four years, an infantryman by profession, and I am under no illusion whatsoever about the scale of achievement that should be ascribed to those two particular battalions.

Further to that, it should be pointed out that the 2nd East Yorkshires, having subdued Cod and smashed their way off the beach, then proceeded to attack and capture two further strongpoints, Sole and Daimler, before moving to Hermanville to establish a depth defensive position for the night, thus becoming one of the few Allied units to achieve *all* of its D-Day objectives.

Equal credit goes to the other units engaged in the D-Day landings, regardless of nationality or which beach they landed on. The entire operation was a huge undertaking and the sheer physical and mental resilience needed to storm such a heavily defended coastline was phenomenal. Each of the five beaches, even the 'walk-over' beach of Utah, presented its own unique difficulties and dangers. It was over in the east however, in the Sword Beach sector, where the potential for disaster truly lay.

If you stand on Sword Beach and look inland, you can still see the imposing, ominous silhouettes of the beach-front villas; indeed, several of the originals are still there. Look hard over your left shoulder and you will see distant Le Havre and the Seine Estuary, from where a flotilla of German S-Boats (E-Boats to us English) appeared on D-Day to attack and sink the Norwegian Destroyer *Svenner*.

Swing your gaze over to half-left and you can see the rolling green fields of the high ground, east of the River Orne, where the infamous Merville Battery was located. This high ground was key terrain on D-Day. Whoever controlled it would control the Orne River, Sword Beach and its hinterland.

As for Caen, that glittering prize? The British never reached it on D-Day. In fact, it would take over a month of bitter fighting before it finally fell; nothing more than a smouldering ruin. The planned 'dash for Caen' came to an abrupt halt in the late afternoon when the German 21st Panzer Division made its first concentrated counter-attack. That said, the 21st Panzer were themselves brought to a sharp halt by the ferocity of British anti-tank fire. Thus it was that the tanks of the 100th Panzer Regiment (shortly afterwards renamed the 22nd Panzer Regiment) were either stopped dead in their tracks, losing almost half of their fighting strength, or pushed westwards to fall in with the 192nd Panzer Grenadier Regiment who did, finally, reach the coast.

This was not of course, any kind of victory for German manoeuvrist tactics. Rather than defeating their enemy, or by-passing them, the Germans were 'pushed' and 'shaped' as they moved around the battlefield, until they found themselves caught between a rock and a hard place, with a Canadian Division squeezing them from the west in the area of Juno Beach, a British Division ready to tear into them for a second time from the east, whilst to their north they were staring down the gun barrels of dozens of Allied warships. The straw that broke the camel's back was the appearance of the glider borne reserves for British 6th Airborne Division passing overhead. The troops of 21st Panzer knew that their game was up and, fearing that they would be cut off, subsequently withdrew to form a defensive position in front of Caen.

Hans von Luck, the highly decorated and experienced commander of the 125th Panzer Grenadiers, recounts in great detail the frustration of that long night of 5th/6th June in his memoirs as he fought to gain permission for an immediate, concentrated attack towards the coast. The German take on D-Day is fascinating, although sadly, several key figures like Rommel and Marcks did not survive the war to give us their own opinions. Those accounts we are left with show a command structure that was unfit for purpose, hampered by personal rivalries and inherently inflexible. This led to confusion and delay on the night of 5th/6th June and consequently gave the Allies the breathing space they needed to get themselves firmly established. Poor old General Marcks was killed just a few days after D-Day and thus one of the key German accounts of that momentous day will never be heard. The German story of D-Day gives us, perhaps, the biggest collection of 'what ifs' in military history.

But there are no 'what ifs' in the real world. It happened. The Atlantic Wall was breached by the biggest amphibious and airborne invasion force ever deployed and the final chapter of the war in Europe began. It was really only a case of how the Germans chose to close that particular chapter. In the end, for better or for worse, they chose a very Wagnerian ending; not too far removed from the concept of Gotterdammerung itself.

Normandy today is a beautiful place, still remarkably quiet and unspoilt, even during the pilgrimage month of June. The local populace have integrated their history with the need to return the landscape to its natural, productive state, in a way that is quite sublime. There is little obvious sign of the Atlantic Wall at first, until you realise that the museum or memorial you are looking at is not a 'cutting edge modernist' piece of architecture, but a former German strongpoint or bunker. You will note too that many of the road names are those of the Allied commanders whose units liberated that particular piece of France.

If there really was a road that led directly from Hermanville to Periers, passing by a small wooded knoll with a ruined forge in its shadow, then I imagine the locals would have named it *'Le Avenue Major Smithson'*.

Lest we forget…

ALSO BY ANDY JOHNSON

THUNDER IN MAY

'Unputdownable' isn't in the Oxford English dictionary, but if it was it'd surely mention 'Thunder in May' as an example. Andy Johnson has perfected the ability to write an historical novel using character that zips along with pace, unfolding events informatively without boring the reader. Both sides of the conflict are dealt equal time to explain perspectives and experiences with such vividness, at the end I fully expected to find dirt under my fingernails... A brilliant adventure.

M Ogden, Manchester (from a 5 Star review on www.amazon.co.uk)

Andy Johnson once more produces a Corking War Novel. There is a lot of good War Fiction out there at the moment but recently retired WO1 (RSM) Andy Johnson of the Coldstream Guards is in my opinion knocking them all for six.

P Brooks, Manchester (from a 5 Star review on www.amazon.co.uk)

Andy Johnson has produced a genuinely excellent read in Thunder in May... he's a very talented story teller.

TM Wilson, UK – (from a 5 star review on www.amazon.co.uk)

SEELÖWE NORD: THE GERMANS ARE COMING

"I've just finished the book... absolutely brilliant! I was completely engrossed and really taken in by the realism of it all.

Serving Officer – British Army Staff College

"A thrilling, detailed and very cinematic novel from new author Andy Johnson. The novel sizzles with very cinematic action sequences that are character-driven, from both the British and German forces' points of view... Seelöwe Nord is chockfull of gripping and all-too-human characters, ranging from Winston Churchill to the British and German soldiers fighting it out on the ground. Seelöwe Nord bristles with knockout battle action, from close quarters fighting on land to breakneck sea engagements."

Lee Davis - www.inthenews.co.uk